PHILLIP WRIGHT

NOT WITHOUT MERCY

THE PASSAGE HOME
A HISTORICAL FICTION NOVEL
BOOK TWO

THIS IS BOOK TWO IN THE SERIES, NOT WITHOUT MERCY

Book One is Not Without Mercy The Black Death

This is a work of fiction based on historical events. Some of the characters and events described herein are imaginary and do not refer to specific places or living persons—other characters, such as Pope Clement VI and King Edward II, are real and did exist. The opinions expressed in this manuscript are solely the author's opinions and do not represent the opinions or thoughts of the publisher. The author has represented and warranted full ownership and/or legal right to publish all the materials in this book.

Not Without Mercy
The Passage Home

All Rights Reserved.

Second Edition Copyright © 2022, Phillip C. Wright

ISBN-13: 9781542451192
ISBN-10: 1542451191

P&Q Publishing and the P&Q logo are trademarks belonging to P&Q Publishing

PRINTED IN THE UNITED STATES OF AMERICA

Not Without Mercy
The Passage Home

About the Author

Phillip C. Wright has been married to Shaun (McKinney) Wright since 1982. They are the parents of seven children and fourteen grandchildren. Phill has worked professionally as a writer, director, and producer of documentaries, TV and Radio commercials, and infomercials. He is the recipient of Telly Awards for video productions— including a Silver Telly Award for the infomercial production he wrote and produced for Sterling International, the "Yellow Jacket Trap"; He also won five Silver Microphone awards for radio commercials. Phill served ten years as the president of a local community theater. He has written and directed numerous plays, including a full-length musical re-creation called "First Light" with Brett Raymond (who wrote the original musical score), with an original cast of over 200 people. Phill is an avid history buff, especially with religious history and archeological discoveries. He is a gifted public motivational speaker with quick wit, timing, and a keen sense of humor.

Other books by Phillip C. Wright

Not Without Mercy The Black Death

Man Against Messiah The Sanhedrin Plot Against Jesus

Return From Rysa

This book and others by Phillip C. Wright can also be found at www.TheStoryTellerCollection.com and www.ReturnFromRysa.com.

"I highly recommend Phill's book, Not Without Mercy. First, it is a story of faith and family during one of the world's darkest chapters – the Black Death. Many of the challenges the Beorn family faced in this book will parallel the challenges our own families will endure in the coming days of trial. Secondly, Phill's story is unique because it is based on numerous dreams and visitations wherein the book's characters appeared at his bedside and told them their stories firsthand. Phill later learned that these characters were his family members who lived during the mid-1300s in Bristol, England. The story, they said, is timely for our day and the desolating pestilence that has been foretold.

Furthermore, this story demonstrates that the veil is thin and that the hearts of the fathers have turned towards the children. I believe in the administration of angels. Who would have a more vested interest in administering to us than our own family? Not Without Mercy is a beautiful testament that family bonds do not end in the grave."

Michael B. Rush, *author of, A Remnant Shall Return, Daniel 11, Revelation, The Vision of John The Devine and Delight in Plainness*

CONTENT

Prolog

It has been a remarkable experience writing the Not Without Mercy series. This second book completes the story that I began four years earlier. In the prolog of book one, The Black Death, I explain that I dreamt of one short scene in the story several years ago. It took me a few years later to start writing the story. The process of writing the story opened a new world for me. As the story began formulating in my mind, I was drawn into it. I could hardly wait each day to write more. I assume that you have already read book one; if not, put this book down and get a copy of book one, and read it first! There are too many characters and storylines to pick everything up in book two. I truly enjoyed seeing William and Michael grow with their many experiences and difficulties. Somehow, William kept his unwavering faith, even during the most complex and challenging trials life could give. Yet, Michael, being thrust into adulthood by taking on the responsibility of his family in the absence of William, reacted much differently. Although his challenges differed from William's, his faith wavered and nearly crumbled under tremendous pressure as things worsened. But something remarkable happens to Michael in book two. And William and Jillian, kindred spirits, have such a strong spiritual connection that time and space cannot keep them apart. The Passage Home completes the journey of this remarkable family, as it reminds them that there is nothing more important than family. Life was fragile for William, Jillian, Michael, and many others of the day; time was short, and death surrounded them on every side. Yet even in the most terrifying moments, they knew God had left them Not Without Mercy.

Phillip C. Wright

< i >

To my wife, Shaun, who embodies faith, family, love, courage, and hope.

< ii >

< iii >

Chapter One

All is not Lost

"...and he hath spoken to you in a still small voice, but you were past feeling, that ye could not feel his words." I Nephi 17:45

AS HE HEAPED the last shovel of dirt upon her grave, he felt a sense of conquest. He knew she would no longer have control over him; she would no longer reign over helpless servants, shouting orders and commands. He knew that her piercing blue eyes would never again stare at him digging their way into his soul. He knew that he was free of the woman who never indeed was his grandmother. She was a Chattingworth, and he was a Beorn. Looking at the freshly covered grave, he glanced at the marker next to it. The name read Alexander H. Chattingworth. *"Who was this man?"* He thought. He thought about Jillian and her gentleness, ardent love, and compassion for everyone. He knew Jillian was nothing like her mother, so he reasoned that she must have taken after her father. He hesitated for a moment and then realized that he needed to begin his next task, the retrieval of the remains of Margaret and Sarah and a proper burial. He took one last look at the grave and the grave of the Grandfather he never knew. He looked to the sky and said, "If she's with you now, God, you deserve   her!"   He   turned   and   walked   away.

The fog was weightily accompanied by the dampness and coldness of the day. As he walked toward the cottage's charred remains of the cottage, he looked toward the large

< 1 >

estate and thought how empty it looked except for the two last people, Monson and Jillian. Jillian had not spoken a word since her mother's tragic fall and death. Monson helped her to her room as Michael took the body to the family plot for burial. Michael wondered if the end of Sarah and the unexpected death of Miriam had been the final blow to Jillian's sanity. He stood at the remains of the cottage. Smoke continued to discharge from different sections that had not entirely burned. He took a stick and began to push through the burnt debris making his way toward what used to be the room where Margaret slept. He turned over a few pieces of wood and then discovered several fragments of a bone, a partial skull, and other human remains. He knew it was the remains of Margaret. He picked up a small wooden box and began to scrape the bones into the box. It did not seem real that he had looked through her window two hours earlier, discovering her fateful condition racked with the pain of the Black Plague. He reminded himself that burning the cottage and extinguishing both Margaret and Sarah was the right thing to do and the only way to protect the others. It did not take long before he could gather all of her remains. As he dropped the last bone into the box, it occurred to him that, unlike his experience burying the bodies of Thebes and his two sons, he could handle this without a sick feeling in his stomach; he was past feeling.

He put the small wooden crate down next to a tree. As he picked up the other box, he hesitated, waiting to experience that familiar feeling of a rapid heartbeat, but it never came. Feeling somewhat calm, he took a deep breath and maintained the composure he had just used while gathering the bones of Margaret. He began to walk toward the other room but stopped as something moving in the debris startled him. He bent over, picked up a rock, and threw it in the direction of the movement. A small white bird flew from the precise spot and headed directly toward his face. He leaned his head to the side as the creature quickly flew past him. It made no sound as it

< 2 >

flew toward the tree and perched on a limb as if to watch the scene. The anticipated feeling came as his heart began to race, but this was not a feeling of apprehension; it was a feeling of anger and complete hatred, hatred for a small white bird. He looked back at the ruins and then to the limb, but the bird was gone. Michael quickly looked from side to side and searched each limb of the tree but saw no bird. He looked toward the sky and the surrounding landscape but saw nothing. For a moment, he wondered if there had ever been a bird. The feeling of anger began dissipating as he walked to the sight of Sarah's room. He reached out with the stick and moved the debris back and forth, noticing several hot spots and embers. He remembered seeing Sarah's beautiful little face staring out the window, yelling and begging him to save her. His head began to pound as the memories started flashing in and out of his mind. He felt the heat of the burnt wood and thatch as he wrestled to regain control of his mind. Finally, he broke through as he shook his head and shouted: "Stop!"

The scenes ended, and he slowly continued to pick through the rubble. He then realized that he had not yet found any remnants of the body of Sarah. He began to shuffle the stick faster, shoving, scooping, and scraping, but there was no sign of human remains. His breathing became rapid. He began to choke as he breathed in some lingering smoke he had churned with his stick. He stepped into the hot embers and felt the heat coming through the bottom of his shoes. He began kicking debris; he leaned over and grabbed onto hot pieces of wood, throwing pieces to either side, not paying any attention to the smoke coming from his burning shoes or the pain or smell of burnt flesh from his fingers and palms. Sweat was running down his face and cheeks and making loud sizzling sounds as it dripped from his chin and nose onto the red-hot embers at his feet. He could not find her. *"Where was she?"* He thought. Suddenly he realized that no trace of her body was found anywhere in what was left of the room where he knew

< 3 >

she spent the last moments of her life, at least where he thought she spent the final few moments of her life. He felt his head pounding, his heart beating, and the excruciating pain in his feet that traveled up his legs, his thighs, his lower back, his arms, his hands, and the tips of his fingers. In agonizing frustration, he lifted the stick above his head, looked up toward the heavens, and shouted, "Sarah!"

< 4 >

Chapter One Notes

During the plague of 1348, it was common for people to burn the homes of those who acquired the disease. Afterward, they would gather the bones and bury them either in a mass grave or a family grave of a loved one.

Over the centuries, scientists have tried to determine the cause of the Black Plague. Although most medical professionals agree that the plague came in two basic types: type A, through the bloodstream causing visible black decay from skin rotting from the inside out and visible pustules usually in the groin, underarms, neck, and face or type B, the bronchial type that lodged in the lungs and caused massive internal bleeding from ruptured blood vessels. This type was the most contagious because an infected person could pass on the disease simply by breathing on another person. The other point of scientific contention was the mode of transportation that brought the plague from one place to another. As I have studied the historical information about the plague, I am convinced that the actual culprit was, in fact, the flea and that the plague itself mutated from type A to type B.

< 5 >

Chapter Two
Like Father like Son

"It is a wise father that knows his own child."

William Shakespeare

(March 15, 1350. The streets of London)

William pulled Lucas close to his chest and held him tightly. There was something familiar, but although he tried, his mind would not open and reveal any memories; his mind was locked, and he did not know where to find the key. Was it the young boy he held in his arms whose sobs created a mixed emotion of compassion and love, or would something else trigger his memory? He did not know, but he did know that this little boy loved him, and for what it was worth, he felt some emotional connection to him too. William began to loosen his arms, and Lucas held him tighter and cried louder.

"Oh, Father, I thought you were dead. We all thought you were dead. Where have you been?" Lucas asked between choked-up coughs and tears.

William did not know what to say. He could see that this boy loved him and believed that he was his father, and he did not want to alarm the child further by denying his relationship with the boy. He thought for a moment and replied,

"My son." He hesitated and then spoke again. "I do not…I mean…I am not sure…what to tell you."

The words seemed as jumbled as his memories. He slowly pulled the little boy away from him, held his arms, and looked into his watery eyes.

"Please do not be alarmed when I tell you that…." He hesitated, looking for the right words. He knew this child but did not know his relationship with the boy. "I do not know you."

< 6 >

Lucas flinched and shivered as he tried to hold back his emotions.

William looked into the watery eyes of Lucas and softly spoke, "I believe you. I believe that I am your father. It is just that, for some reason, I do not know who I am. Can you understand me?"

Lucas looked at William, wrinkled his eyebrows, and said,

"You are my father, William Beorn."

As William heard the words *William Beorn,* he felt a strange connection to the name. Somehow, he knew that the boy spoke the truth but did not feel any internal awakening or confirmation of the name. Lucas then added,

"And I am your son, Lucas" Do not you remember me, father? Do not you remember me?"

He began to cry. Tears rolled down his face as his large brown eyes pierced William's soul. At that moment, it did not matter to William if he knew this child or his own name; what mattered to him was that a small boy was alone, terrified, and desperately trying to communicate to the man he thought was his father. He did not want the boy to suffer anymore. He pulled him tightly against his chest, closed his eyes, and in his mind pleaded,

"Oh, dear God in Heaven, please help me to remember. Help me to remember this child."

Suddenly William heard voices and opened his eyes. The other Monks had arrived. They stood in a semi-circle around him. One of them asked,

Brother John, what is it? Are you alright?"

William looked up at the Monks and replied,

"My friends…" he stopped and closed his eyes as a peculiar feeling overcame him. He could see something in his mind. A blurry vision opened up to him. He saw himself lying under a tree on a beautiful spring afternoon. He saw a little curly-haired boy running toward him, yelling, "Father, Father!"

< 7 >

It was Lucas, the little boy he was now holding in his arms. In the vision, he looked up and into the most beautiful green eyes he had ever seen. It was the face of an angel, he thought. She smiled at him. Her powder-white skin glistened as sparks of sunlight flickered through her long luminous, auburn hair. The brightness of the sun made it difficult to focus on her face. She smiled at him and mouthed the word "William."

The vision was immediately cut short as William felt the arm of one of the monks on his shoulder.

"Brother John, are you alright?"

William opened his eyes, looked at the monks, and exclaimed,

"My name is William, and this is my son Lucas!"

Lucas began to cry again; he held William tighter. The Monks looked confused for a moment and then realized that their friend and brother, John, had been blessed with his memory.

"Brother John, I mean, Brother William, this is wonderful. God has been merciful to you. But you and your son must come with us before those men you fought return with the authorities."

The monks reached down and helped William and Lucas to their feet. William looked down at Lucas and said,

"I remember you, my son, but I do not remember everything. I remember my name is William, but the rest is too foggy. I will need your help to remember more."

"Yes, father, I will help you."

Lucas could not contain his emotions. William leaned over, picked him up, carried him, and followed the monks back to the monastery.

< 8 >

Chapter Two Notes

William likely suffered from **Transient** *global* **amnesia,** *a condition triggered by sudden immersion in cold or hot water, physical exertion, emotional or psychologic stress, pain, or medical procedures.* **Transient global amnesia (TGA)** *is a neurological disorder whose key defining characteristic is a temporary but often total disruption of short-term memory with a range of problems accessing older memories. A person in a state of TGA exhibits no other signs of impaired cognitive functioning but recalls only the last few moments of consciousness, as well as deeply encoded facts of the individual's past, such as their own name*

< 9 >

Chapter Three
This, I recall

" This, I recall to my mind, therefore have I hope.."
Lamentations 3:21

(March 16, 1350. The monastery just outside of London)

William woke early the following day and quietly rose from his bed as the darkness began to disperse, making way for a new day of hope and thankfulness. He knelt on the floor and leaned over the bed. As he looked at the sleeping, small, precious child God had brought to him, his eyes began to fill with tears of gratefulness. He closed his eyes and silently began his prayer.

"Oh, dear Father above, I thank thee with every fiber of my being for bringing my child back into my life. I thank thee for thy kindness and mercy for giving me a glimpse into my past and hope for my future. I thank thee for the safety thou hast bestowed upon my son and me. I thank thee for leading me to these Monks, my friends who have loved and buoyed me in my time of confusion. I thank thee for protecting me while I was in prison and putting good, kind people in my path. May thy grace, love, and hand of protection be upon those I love and those who have loved me. Oh, dear Father above, I ask that my eyes be opened, and my mind be filled with the memories of my family and those I have long associated with. Thank thee, dear God and faithful friend. Amen!"

William opened his eyes and quietly surveyed the room, noticing the other sleeping Monks. His heart was whole, and he could not stop the flow of tears that rushed down his cheeks. As he brushed his eyes, he caught a glimpse of the book he had been writing in, lying on a desk on the far side of the room. He

< 10 >

quickly clothed himself in the dark robes of the priesthood and quietly walked to the desk. He sat in the chair, looked at the large Vulgate still open, and placed to the left of the book he had been writing. He gently passed his left hand over the Vulgate as an immense feeling of reverence and thankfulness for the sacred words of God filled his heart. He then looked at the other book. Although it would be another copy of God's scripture, it was unfinished. He had carefully copied word for word in the Latin tongue from left to right. He looked at the feather quill he had gently placed to the right of the new book the day before. He noticed the half-full bottle of ink next to it. He looked at the page where his writing stopped. He had written up to the third chapter of Lamentations. He began to read, starting with verse seventeen.

"And thou hast removed my soul far off from peace: I forgat prosperity.

And I said, my strength and my hope is perished from the Lord:

Remembering mine affliction and my misery, the wormwood and the gall.

My soul hath them still in remembrance and is humbled in me.

This I recall to my mind, therefore have I hope.

It is of the Lord's mercies that we are not consumed, because his compassions fail not.

They are new every morning: great is thy faithfulness."

The copied text ended. William looked back to the Vulgate and began to read where his text ended. He started quietly reading aloud with verse twenty-four.

"The Lord is my portion, saith my soul, therefore will I hope in him.

The Lord is good unto them that wait for him, to the soul that seeketh him.

< 11 >

It is good that a man should both hope and quietly wait for the salvation of the Lord."

He stopped reading. He looked up and closed his eyes as a powerful sensation overcame him. Suddenly, his mind was filled with a vision of a life past. He was sitting at a table with his father, Lance Beorn. The waiter leaned over the table and began pouring from a large water pitcher. As William looked at the pitcher, the wavy image of a beautiful young woman sitting across the room glistened through it. The waiter lifted the pitcher, turned, and walked to another table. Suddenly the face of the woman made contact with his. Her bright green eyes connected with his. She smiled, and the whiteness of her teeth shone with a luminance matched only by her wavy auburn hair. William looked deeper into the vision, and it changed. He saw himself holding her hand while walking down a path of red rose petals. A long line of people had formed on either side of them, smiling, clapping, and speaking words of endearment. He saw a familiar woman, a servant he felt close to, shedding tears of joy. He looked at her; their eyes connected, and the vision changed. He was sitting under a large tree, looking up into the eyes of the red-haired woman. He knew he loved her. She leaned over and kissed him. He breathed in her essence; he knew her name: Jillian—his wife. The vision changed. He was standing in front of a tall man, the town Sherriff. He could smell the salt air. He looked upward where he saw a harbor—it was familiar. It was Bristol; it was his home. The Sheriff moved aside, revealing a young boy. The boy had thick shoulder-length wavy black hair and deep blue eyes. *"It was Michael!"* William thought. The boy smiled at him. The smile began to change as the boy's eyebrows raised on the outside edges and dipped near the bridge of the nose. William felt a chill, and the vision changed. He was kneeling at the edge of his

< 12 >

bed. He lifted a baby, his son. It was Lucas. He saw Jillian mouth the words, *"Our son is born!"* The vision changed. Again, he found himself kneeling on the bed of Jillian. He smiled as she turned down the edge of the small blanket, revealing another baby's tiny little head. He knew the child; it was Sarah. The scene changed, and many new scenes began to dodge in and out of his mind like the stormy waves of a rough sea. He saw men clutching their hearts and falling to the streets. He saw death all around, dead people lifting from their deathbeds and reaching out to him. The intensity of the vision became terrifying. He felt his breathing become heavy and stuttered. The vision changed. He was standing behind a carriage, watching it pull away from him as it rolled down a country road. He saw two small children peeking out the sides and waving at him. Their hands disappeared into the carriage. He then saw the beautiful and graceful hand of Jillian. She turned her head toward him, touched her fingers to her lips, kissed them, and then tossed the kiss toward him as she mouthed, *"I love you!"* William tightly closed his eyes to freeze the vision at that moment. His love for Jillian, Lucas, Sarah, and Michael overwhelmed him. The vision went black, and then a shock of lightning streaked through his mind. He saw himself closing the window shutters in the lighthouse as a storm began to brew. He saw himself running down the winding stairway and stepping into a pool of water at the bottom. He watched as he saw himself run out of the lighthouse and toward the house. William felt his heart race as he watched the vision in his mind. He slipped further into the vision and became the participant, not the viewer. He looked up at another strike of lightning. He heard the loud, explosive sound of lightning hitting a large tree. The earth shook with the deep rumbling sound of destruction. He looked up and saw a large tree limb flying toward him. He knew it was too

< 13 >

late to move from its path. He felt the sting of its impact as it collided with his head. Everything was black again. William hesitated to move. The vision ended. He opened his eyes and caught the first rays of the early morning sun coming over the horizon. He breathed deeply, filling his lungs with air, life, and profound gratitude.

"Thank you, dear God! Thank you!" He said as he realized that all had returned.

He knew who he was and from where he had come. He turned and looked at the sleeping boy. Tremendous gratitude filled his soul to know that his son was alive, was with him, and he had hope that the rest of his family was healthy.

He stood up, walked to the window, and looked out into the countryside. Off in the distance, he could see the tops of buildings peering over the trees; it was the city of London. He remembered being there on other occasions. He knew that he had friends there or at least a friend that came to his mind. His head began to ache as all the new memories took their place in his cognizance. As he shuffled through the memories of Jillian and his children, he discovered holes in his life storyline. Although he was grateful that God had seen fit to return his memory to him, he knew that it would take some time for his brain to process everything, and some memories simply had to wait.

He felt a hand on his left shoulder and tilted his head to the left; it was Dom Friedman.

"William, my son. It is good to call you by your name." He smiled and continued while William kept looking out the window.

"What will you do now that God has given back your son and your identity?"

William turned and embraced the Monk. He released him and said, "Oh, my dear friend Dom Friedman, you have

< 14 >

been so kind to me, and I cannot begin to return your charity."

"William, there is nothing to return. You have helped me and the others. Your writing is truly a gift from God, and you have imparted that gift in a form that will benefit the lives of many who have the blessing of reading from the holy books you have transcribed. But now, God has another journey for you, a journey home. Have you learned anymore? Do you know from whence you came?" The Monk asked.

William smiled and said, "Yes, Dom, I know more. My mind is beginning to open up hidden treasures to me. I have seen so much more. I have a wife, Jillian; she is beautiful, tender, and compassionate. I have a small daughter, Sarah, and an older son named Michael. They are all out there somewhere, and none of them knows that I am alive. I can only imagine the grief my sweet Jillian must be feeling, not knowing the whereabouts of her small son Lucas. My heart pains for her."

William paused and began to search for any other clues in his mind, but nothing was making it to the surface. He knew that he had to be patient; he knew that he had to wait on the Lord and that doing so would bring him greater happiness.

"Dom, as God has returned me pieces of my life, I feel a much greater closeness and love for him. It is as if my relationship with him has grown." He hesitated and continued, "No, it is as if I had remembered my relationship with him before my mind became clouded. I cannot express the overwhelming happiness I feel knowing my family, but the greatest happiness is knowing that my God had never left me. What mercy he has shown to me, allowing me to retain a memory of him, a memory that has strengthened me through much heartache, confusion, and sadness.

< 15 >

Although I lost the memories of my consciousness through sickness and fever, I never lost the feelings of my heart. As he has returned some of them to me, each of them has gently returned to the place of my soul where I cherished them most. But God has always been there with me. I now know that he has guided me here. It is almost too much to comprehend and think that amid such death, destruction, and total pandemonium, he has somehow seen fit to preserve my life and, for all I know, my son's life. But I feel deep in my being that my wife and other children are also alive, and I know that I must find them, I must find them before this plague finds them."

William took a breath, closed his eyes, and opened them with a new determination. He knew that God had spared his life so that he could gather his family and loved ones. He knew that God had not led him to his current situation in life, only to take it away from him. He had faith that God would allow him to find those he loved.

The monk smiled at him and said, "William, I knew you were a man of God when I laid eyes on you. You may have thought it odd that I would have allowed you to join our Abby without knowing anything about you. But the truth is, God spoke to me that day. He whispered his wishes into my heart. The still, small voice of his spirit told me that I was to take you in. It was a decision I shall never regret. I knew that it would only be temporary, and I share in your joy that God has preserved your life and hopefully the lives of your loved ones."

He stopped, thought for a moment, and then continued.

"But what will you do now? Where will you go? Do you plan to travel back to your home in Bristol?" The Monk asked, extremely concerned.

< 16 >

William started to respond, but the Monk began speaking again, visualizing the daunting task ahead of William.

"Unfortunately, we do not have the money you would need to make such a trip, or we would gladly give it. The key to your success will begin with the funds for your travel."

William stopped him and asked, "What did you say?"

The monk looked confused and tried to remember everything he had just said.

"I…I am not sure which part you are referring to. Shall I start over?"

"No, of course not, I was listening to all that you said, and I appreciate all of your kind words, but it was something about a key."

The monk ran through the words in his mind. "The key to your success?" He asked.

"That's it!" William stated. "The key!" He pulled back his collar, carefully lifted the chain around his neck, and slid it through his fingers until he saw the key.

"This key!" He said. "This key will unlock a box of mine located at 555 Copper Street in London. I remember the box, and it is in a shop, down a long stairway, well beneath the street level." William held the key several inches from his face and looked at it as he continued speaking. He then looked at the key and off into the distance.

"I see a door, a large door. I see the keyhole, and this key will fit."

The monk smiled and said, "Wonderful, William, but you are forgetting that there are those in London looking for you. If you return, your life will be in danger. You cannot simply gallop into town, break into the shop of who knows who, run down the stairs, unlock a door, retrieve a box of treasure and then retrace your journey back here."

< 17 >

William smiled at the Monk and said,

"Yes, you are wise, and I have no intention of simply returning to London according to your scenario. However, I know that there is something of mine in that shop, and I also know that it is a large sum of treasures. How wonderful it will be to find and impart much of it to you for the Abby."

The monk leaned his head back and shook it as he began to speak.

"William, there is no need to give the Abby any of your money. You have surely covered your room and board with the services you have already rendered, and you are not in debt to the Abby."

"That may be, but I am in debt to God, and I shall eagerly give what I can to the Abby as a small token of my appreciation, a tithing if you will. I could never repay God for all he has done for me, and I could give him all of my earthly treasures, which would not be enough. The only thing I have to give God is *my* will, and it is the only gift he asks of me?"

The monk smiled. "I am sure God will receive that as a token of your faithfulness. But you need a plan. If you go back to the city, you cannot go dressed as a monk, and unfortunately, none of us can travel with you either since we all look alike in dress and mannerisms; we would be quite the target. In fact, I believe that it will be quite some time before it is safe for any of us to return. Remember, a renegade monk burst from the group, overtaking two large men, beating them to a pulp while rescuing a small boy." The monk winked.

"Dom, I am sorry for my behavior. It had not occurred to me that it would make each of you an object for retaliation."

< 18 >

"Nonsense! You did what God wanted you to do, even if the rest of us were not listening as he spoke. You heard his words and harkened; you did!"

William and the monk began to chuckle as they remembered the scene. They were careful to not wake the others with their laughter. The monk shook his head and said,

"Oh brother, William, I shall miss you so."

William added, "And I you, but I know that our paths will cross again."

The monk smiled and said, "Yes, but for our safety, we shall be wearing camouflage robes, perhaps something more lively with flowers and grass, maybe lilies. I do like lilies." They laughed again. "Come, let us fetch milk and eggs before the others wake."

As the sun began to rise a short while later, so did the other monks. They each made their beds and quietly cleaned and organized their personal areas.   William and Dom Friedman made the breakfast. Each of the monks gathered in the kitchen to eat. One of them asked,

"Shall I go and wake the boy?"

"No, let him sleep," William responded.

The monks agreed, cleaned the breakfast dishes, and continued their daily activities. William checked in on Lucas after about an hour. He was amazed that Lucas was still sleeping. As he watched Lucas's chest fill with air and then depress over and over, he was so thankful that his young son had somehow found him. As he thought about the possibility of such a reunion, it amazed him that somehow his young son had the fortitude and determination to survive, especially during the plague. He marveled that Lucas had escaped the plague, but he still did not know how Lucas ended up in London when he was sent with his mother, brother, and sister to Cardiff, Wales. He gently

< 19 >

kissed Lucas on the forehead and quietly left the room, knowing there would be time for questions later.

Several hours passed, and it was time for the afternoon meal. One of the monks asked,

"Brother William, shall I go and wake the boy? He has nearly slept the entire day."

"No, my friend, let him sleep. I would guess that he has not had such a good sleep in a long time. He will wake when his body is ready."

The monk smiled and agreed to the request. As the day continued on, William thought about his plans. He knew he needed to figure out how to retrieve his box of treasures, but up to that point, nothing seemed like the right strategy.

Each monk took his place at a desk and resumed creating new copies of books. From time to time, one of the monks would chime in,

"I could create a distraction and get the authorities to chase after me while you retrieved your belongings."

Another monk said,

"Right, and what type of distraction could you create?"

"I do not know yet; I am still working on it." He thought for a moment and then added, "Perhaps I could sing loudly."

The other monk raised his eyebrows.

"Sing loudly? Surely that would not be a distraction."

Another monk asked, "But have you heard him sing? He screeches like a wounded animal."

Another monk added, "More like a tone-deaf mute."

"Precisely, and that may create a distraction."

The first monk concluded, "While you two are having fun at my expense, I am trying to come up with an idea to help Brother William accomplish his goal."

< 20 >

The other monk said, "How about if you juggled apples while you sang? Surely that would do it!"

The other two laughed. Another added, "Yes, juggling apples, singing, and skipping like a loony would surely distract the authorities."

The laughter continued as each of the monks added additional ideas. William smiled and pretended not to hear the conversation. He then heard a noise, looked up, and saw Lucas standing in the doorway.

Each monk looked up at Lucas, and one said, "Brethren, the resurrection has occurred."

Another added, "Yes, and we somehow missed it."

Another added while looking at the head of the first monk and said, "Yes, and so did the top of your bald head the missing hair must have gone elsewhere." Light laughter erupted.

Dom Friedman calmed the monks, "Brothers, settle down; too much levity excuses the spirit."

William stood, and Lucas ran towards him.

"Oh, father, as I slept, I thought it was all a dream, but now I know it is real. I am so happy to be with you again. I could never have imagined such an occasion, for I thought you were dead." He then looked at the monks and asked, "Resurrection?"

The first monk said, "Oh, no, son. We were silly and inappropriate, and no resurrection has occurred yet."

Another monk clarified, "Except for the resurrection of Christ our Lord." Each of the monks bowed their heads and performed the sign of the cross on their chests.

William sat Lucas on a chair, and he pulled a chair next to him and sat.

"My son, did you sleep well?"

"Yes, father. It was wonderful, but I am still confused about seeing you before me. What has happened to you?"

< 21 >

William smiled and said, "God has kept me safe just as he has kept you. Please tell me how you ended up here in London when you should be with your mother and family in Cardiff."

Lucas began to cry. "Father, it was awful. I was in the barn with Elizabeth when three men entered." William cut him off.

"Wait, who is Elizabeth?" William asked.

"She is Michael's wife, and she is with child." Lucas matter-of-factly stated.

"His wife?" William questioned. "Michael has married?"

"Oh, yes, father, and she is lovely and very kind. I know that you will love her. And I am proud to announce that you are probably an uncle by now." Lucas smiled.

William was confused.

"An uncle? Do you mean that you are an uncle, Lucas?"

Lucas thought for a moment and said, "Yes, that is what I mean, for I am not an aunt." He confidently stated.

One of the monks bit his lower lip to keep from laughing. William thought about what Lucas had said.

"So, you are telling me that Michael married, and he and his new wife, Elizabeth, now have a child?"

"Yes, that is exactly what I am telling you. So, what does that make you, father?"

"It makes me a grandfather, Lucas, a thrilled grandfather. Was it a boy or a girl?"

"I do not know, father. I was taken before the baby came."

"What do you mean taken?"

"The men who came into the barn. One of them held me, and another attacked Elizabeth."

< 22 >

"Is she OK, Lucas?"   William asked with much concern.

"Yes, father. Elizabeth is a fighter. When one of the men was on top of her tearing at her clothing, she slung a horseshoe into his head and killed him!"

William was surprised at the account. He asked,

"What happened with the other men?"

"One held me, and the other ran to his brother. He was very mad that Elizabeth had killed his brother. He slapped her to the ground, pulled a knife from his boot, and raised it to her neck. But before he could do his deed, a nasty arrow pierced his throat, and he fell to the ground too."

"What arrow? Where did it come from?" William asked, still confused.

"It came from my brother, Michael! He stood in the doorway and fired his crossbow, sticking the neck of the evil man with an arrow."

"Then what happened?" William asked.

"The man who was holding me had covered my mouth. He took me to the back of the barn, stole one of our horses, and carried me away with him."

"Oh, my dear child. I am so sorry that you had to experience such a thing, and I am so sorry that I was not there to protect you." William pulled Lucas to his chest and held him tightly.

"It is well, father. Michael protected us and has been a good protector since we left our home in Bristol."

"So, your mother and the others do not know where you are?" William asked.

"No, they do not. And I am sure they are worried. For months, I have lived alone on the streets of London." He hesitated and restated, "But not really alone, just God and

< 23 >

me. He has protected me and shown me where to find food and shelter daily. And now he has brought my father to me."

William spent the next few hours questioning Lucas. Lucas told him of everything that had happened since they left for Cardiff. Lucas rehearsed all that had happened to him since being kidnapped from the barn in Cardiff.

William shed a tear as he heard of all of the danger his family experienced from time to time. He felt guilty for not accompanying them to Cardiff. He thought that somehow if he had done so, none of the other bad experiences would have happened. He sobbed with Lucas as Lucas described the reaction of Jillian when Michael returned without William. It was a bitter-sweet moment to listen to his son tell of the heartache and joy they all had experienced after leaving home. He was excited to see all of them again. He was thrilled at the thought of Michael being married and a father. He was overjoyed to meet Elizabeth and his first grandchild. He was more anxious to be reunited with Jillian; thoughts of her amplified his rekindled love for her. It was a reunion he longed for.

When Lucas finished telling William all that he could remember, William thought about the accident during the storm at the estate. He remembered dragging himself through the house's front door, wrapping himself in a blanket, and lying on the floor of his study, but nothing else. He understood from Lucas's account of the events Michael returned for him, but he had no memory of seeing Michael; his last memory was passing out on the study floor. He asked another question.

"Lucas, can you tell me what Michael told each of you when he returned to the estate and found me there?"

Lucas began to cry. "He said you were dead, father. He said you were dead. It was awful, especially for mother, who cried for days."

< 24 >

William asked, "Did Michael say what he did when he thought I was dead?"

"Yes, he said he took your body to the docks and placed you in one of the death carts." Lucas thought for a moment and asked, "But father, if you were not really dead, why did Michael put you in a death cart?"

William looked into the distance as if trying to find the right words. He looked back at Lucas and said,

"Lucas, I was very ill, and I am sure Michael thought I was dead. Surely, that is why he placed me there."

William thought about it for a moment longer. He wondered how Michael could have assumed such a thing. He brushed off any thoughts of malice, and then it occurred to him how he ended up on the ship. He remembered telling Sheriff Reginald weeks earlier that placing the death carts close to the vegetable carts, waiting to be loaded onto the ships, was inappropriate. The sheriff agreed and pledged to make sure the practice ended.

William continued to put the pieces together until he concluded that Michael had inadvertently placed his body onto a vegetable cart instead. He and the cart's contents were dumped into one of the shipping crates and loaded onto the ship. The actions that led to the events of his life over the last year now all made sense. He realized that a mistake saved his life, for if Michael had placed his body on a death cart with other bodies, the odds were that William would have become infected with the plague and indeed have died. *"What a blessing from God. And Michael listened to the spirit,"* He thought. He felt great gratitude toward Michael, while at the same time, he sensed an odd feeling, a stupor of thought. He knew that something was not right but did not know what.

As the fog in his mind lifted, he felt great liberation and tremendous guilt. It seemed like so much would have

< 25 >

been so different if he had not stayed behind but had journeyed with his family when they left Bristol. He remembered that staying behind was only to secure the estate, affirm arrangements with Big John, and secure the various hidden treasure locations on the estate. He wondered how those he had left behind in the southern part of the estate had faired. He wondered if he would see them again. He wondered if the estate had survived vandals or squatters looking for food, shelter, or riches to trade with. He hoped all was well, but primarily for his friends he had left behind. The more he thought about the things Lucas had told, the more intense his feelings of longing and separation from his family, especially Jillian. He fell to his knees and began to pray.

"Oh, dear God and friend. I thank thee with every fiber of my being for my life and family. I thank thee for this safe journey that has brought me here and kept me safe from this terrible plague. I thank thee, oh God, for preserving the life of my dear child Lucas. Please, God, forgive me for making mistakes that put my family in difficult and tumultuous circumstances. Please continue to bless and protect them. And please, Lord, help me find each of them, and when I do, please let them be alive and well. Please bless my precious little Lucas. Please help him heal the wounds of loneliness and the hardship of separation from his family at such a young age. He is a good boy, and I am so thankful that he found me. Thank you, God, for always being there for my family and me. Thank you for these Monks, my friends. Thank you for inspiring them to open their arms and hearts to me. Please, God, if it is, thy will let each of them live and survive long past this trying time. I trust thee, God. I know that thy will be done. All I ask is that I may be reunited with those I love one last time. My heart and will I give to thee, oh gracious Father. Amen.

< 26 >

He finished his prayer, looked up, and realized that he must soon leave for Cardiff.

< 27 >

Chapter Three Notes

The Vulgate was not divided into verses until 1445 by Mordecai Nathan, a Jew, and a scholar named Athias: *Although our modern-day Bible(s) are divided into chapters and verses, the original texts were not but the Latin Vulgate was in the 14th Century. However, sometime in the mid-thirteenth century, the Catholic Cardinal Hugo divided the Bible into sections, which the Church in William's day used, eventually becoming the chapters we are familiar with today.* ***I took the liberty in this chapter to refer to the book of Lamentations by chapter and verse so that the reader of my novel could relate to the message William understood as he worked on the copied text of his day.***

The ***Book of Lamentations*** *(Hebrew:* אֵיכָה, *Eikhah, 'ēkhā(h)) is a poetic book of the Hebrew Bible composed by the Jewish prophet Jeremiah. It mourns the destruction of Jerusalem and the Holy Temple in the 6th century BC. It would have been a very timely book for William to read as he mourned the death of many during the devastation of the Black Plague of his day.*

The version of the Bible used by the Roman Catholic Church for over a millennium and a half, the Vulgate, is a Latin translation of the original Bible texts, created mainly by St. Jerome during the end of the third and start of the fourth centuries CE. Vulgate derives from the phrase versio vulgata, which translates into English as "common translation." http://en.wikipedia.org/wiki/Books_of_the_Latin_Vulgate

< 28 >

Chapter Four
The Journey Home

"The journey of a thousand leagues begins from

beneath your feet."

Lao-Tzu

(April 16, 1350. The monastery just outside of London)

Shortly after breakfast, William asked Dom Freidman if they could speak privately. They went into the office of the Priest.

"What is it, William?" The Priest asked.

"I believe that I must go to Cardiff and find my family."

"You do realize the danger in such a journey?"

"Of course, but I cannot stay here indefinitely."

Dom Freidman smiled and said, "William, you and your son are welcome to stay here as long as you like."

William smiled. He thought about the offer; it brought a level of peace and comfort. But something much stronger was tugging on his heart, something much more profound.

"I appreciate your offer, but I have family out there, and I know they need me."

"William, I do not mean to sound like a pessimist, but how do you know they are still alive?"

"I feel it in my soul. I know they are alive, all of them, and I must go to them."

"But, what of the boy?" Dom Freidman asked. "

William looked at the monk and said, "I was hoping I could leave him here in your care, just for a short while, until I return."

< 29 >

The monk smiled and replied, "Of course, he can stay here, but you must take extreme precaution that you may be protected from the plague and those out there who carry it."

"I understand," said William. "I realize the danger of such a journey, but I feel compelled to make the trip. I believe that God will keep me well."

The monk smiled at William, knowing full well that God seemed to have taken a particular interest in him. Even Dom Friedman had lost friends and fellow clergy members to the plague, including those who appeared far removed from society. The bacterium attacked an entire monastery more than five leagues from London, and all twenty-two members died within one week. He thought about the danger of the plague, how it spread and how defenseless people were to it. He looked at William, shook his head, and said,

"William, it is nothing less than miraculous that you and your son Lucas, in all your travels and interaction with people from all walks of life, never contracted the ailment. I must admit, having you around seems like a shield against this plague. God has made it clear that, for some reason, he needs you here on this earth. Although I will support you in this journey, and we will gladly look after Lucas while you are gone, my apprehension is not as much for your safety as ours."

William smiled and said, "Dom, one thing I have learned from all of this is that God is still in charge, and if it is his desire to take one of his children home to him or leave them here to toil, His will, will be done regardless of ours. Besides, if I am, as you call it, a "shield" against this disease, based on what you consider God's miraculous intercession for my life and safety, you forget that Lucas, too, has been spared. His safety is no less miraculous than mine. Perhaps he will be your protection and shield while I am gone."

Dom Freidman smiled and said, "I guess you are right. I did not think of it that way. And you are right that God's will, will be done, no matter what."

< 30 >

William added. "Of course, it doesn't mean that we can throw all caution to the wind, like a man who believes he is invincible as he stands in the path of raging wild beasts and assumes that God will swoop down and deliver him from his arrogance or stupidity. We must use as much caution as possible and do all we can to protect ourselves from this sickness. Do you still wear the garlic in your clothing and shoes as I have instructed?"

The monk began to laugh. "If you have to ask that question, I will assume that your nasal passage can no longer smell better than mine since I have become a walking garden of bitter herbs. Yes, William, I and all of my brethren keep as many cloves of garlic on our bodies as is inhumanly possible!"

William smiled and said. "I realize that the aroma is not as attractive as flower petals and that you probably detract more than you attract, but I am convinced that this plague is spread by the flea, and the creature is most definitely repelled by the smell of garlic."

"As are most humans," the monk added.

"That may be true, but it is also beneficial to avoid most humans, especially since the odds are that they are the unwitting hosts to these vile death-carrying pests."

"The truth is, William, that before you join our order, we have cooked and even medicated with fresh garlic. We have discovered the healing benefits of the smelly plant. I do not mind eating it; it is a wonderful ingredient in most cooked foods, but smelling or eating it is tolerable; wearing it, on the other hand, crosses the line." He changed the subject and asked, "When will you leave?"

"I would like to leave within the hour. How long do you think I would take to make it to Cardiff on foot?"

"That is easily a four-day journey by foot. Surely you are not planning on walking the distance?" Asked the monk.

"I have no horse, so there is no other option."

< 31 >

"Nonsense!" stated the monk. "We have two horses. They aren't fast, they are only used for pulling wagons, but I insist you take one of them. They are both female, mother and daughter, actually. The mother is stronger, but I believe the daughter is faster and has been ridden more than her mother."

"But how will you fair without the horse? Should I take it?" William asked.

"We will do just fine without her."

William looked at the monk and said, "You do not think I will come back, do you?"

"It is not that I think you do not intend to come back, William. It is that I am afraid that you may fail on this journey."

"If you believe that, why would you give me your horse?"

"William, I would give you my robe if you need it; why would I not offer my horse to allow you to make the journey in three rather than four days?"

"It is my plan after arriving in Cardiff and finding all well that I will journey back here with Michael to retrieve Lucas. Several horses are on the estate in Cardiff, including two of my own. We will ride my horses back with your horse." William paused and then continued. "Dom Friedman, I know that my journey will be a success. I feel compelled to make it, and I know I will return here. Have faith, my friend." He smiled.

The monk nodded in agreement.

Suddenly William experienced a strange feeling. He closed his eyes and began to slowly sway from side to side. The monk grabbed his arm to steady him.

"Are you alright, William?" The monk asked.

William opened his eyes and regained his stability.

"Yes, I just had an odd experience." He hesitated and then spoke again. "I know the old woman."

"What old woman?" The monk asked.

< 32 >

"The old woman from my visions. Her name is Martha, and she has been with me since I was a child. She is a good woman; she is my friend."

The monk smiled and said, "How wonderful that God continues to bring things to your remembrance."

"It is more than that, Dom. He is causing me to remember the most important things and events in my life. I remember when Martha contracted the plague." The monk cut him off.

"William, I am so sorry that you lost your friend."

William turned and looked into the eyes of the monk and said, "But Dom, I did not lose her." The monk leaned back in disbelief.

"Then surely, she did not have the plague." He stated in less than confident belief.

"Yes, she did have the plague. She had just witnessed the death of two others, also dear friends of mine, Beatrice and Terrance Edwards, who had died within a short time of each another, just hours before the plague attacked Martha."

"How is it possible that your friend could have survived the plague when no one survives once infected?" The monk asked in disbelief.

"Dom, you of all people know that anything is possible with God; if it is his will, death cannot extinguish life."

Dom Freidman took a breath and asked, "What happened? How did she survive?"

William thought a moment, and then the scene came to him.

"We were in a barn. It was cold and raining, and there was an odd stench of burnt wood in the air. Martha was lying on a pile of hay. She was shivering, not so much from the cold but from the fever. I held her in my arms. Michael called out to me to leave her. He said she had the plague, and there was nothing I could do. I did not know what to do, but I pleaded that God would not take her at that moment. As I felt the life leaving her

< 33 >

body, I remembered the garlic. I caused her to drink the garlic oil. She had tried to get Beatrice to drink it, but it was too late. I told Martha to drink, and she complied with my insistence. Michael again screamed at me. He said he was wet and cold and that we needed to leave her and save ourselves. I told him that he could dry his hands by the fire of my faith. At that moment, I knew that I had done all I could to save Martha and that it was now up to the Lord to hear my prayer, to answer my pleading. Somehow, I knew that faith alone was not enough to heal Martha. I knew I had to act and do all I could before expecting the Lord to compensate for my weakness and shortfall. I closed my eyes and asked him to heal her, and at that very moment, I felt a power rush through me and into her body. I felt the will of God course into her veins, annihilating anything foreign to her body. I witnessed his perfect healing power overcome the feeble weakness of filth and decay, which was no match for his purity and perfection. I opened my eyes and looked into the bright blue, tear-filled eyes of this great woman who also recognized God's miracle and power at that moment. I kissed her on the cheek, and we embraced and thanked God for his love and mercy."

The monk stood still. He had been listening intently and hung on every word. "William, you are a testimony to me that faith can heal our hearts, our minds, and our wounds."

"Yes, but it takes more than mere faith, Dom. God has given us the agency to choose for ourselves. And with that free will, he expects us to choose righteously and wisely. Dom expects us to listen to and learn from the words of his holy scripture and to take counsel from his ordained ministers, and with that knowledge and testimony, he wants us to act before we ask. He is not a lazy parent who does everything for the selfish child. He is the loving father who teaches his children to act by what he has taught them. He expects them to do all they can before they ask him to do the rest. God did not heal Martha without any work on my part. He told me how to heal her, and

< 34 >

that process started with me giving her a healing herb. The question is not whether the herb had the power to heal; the question is, was I willing to do all I could before I asked God to do the rest. Was I going to be like the ignorant man who stood in the path of raging wild beasts, maintaining a selfish and slothful belief that through my faith, God would save me? Or was I going to be the man to exercise my agency to do all that I could for my friend before calling upon the Lord and exercising my faith that he would finish the process, that he would sustain and sanctify my works with his miracle? Dom, I know that this plague is deadly. I know that those who contract it will likely die and that many good people have died. But I also know that if it is God's will for us to survive, and if we do all we can to keep ourselves out of that proverbial path of wild beasts, we will be protected. Wearing or ingesting garlic may seem pointless to the educated or the spiritual elite. Still, I am convinced that doing so shows my willingness to God that I will do all I know to protect my safety and the safety of those I love, with faith that he will do the rest. "

The monk smiled and put his arm around William's shoulders.

"William, you are truly a man of God, and I am honored to be your friend. Rest assured that I will see to it that all of my associates and your son are well clothed in the garlic cloves of the priesthood while you are gone."

William smiled. "Dom, I do not know what my future will bring, but I pray that you will always be a part of it."

"I, too, share your prayer, my friend. Come, let us find the others and tell them of your plan." William agreed, and the two men sought out the other monks and Lucas to give them the news.

William and Dom Freidman found Lucas and the other monks standing around a large table in the dining hall. No one noticed as they entered the room. They quietly walked toward the group. When they reached the table, both men were

< 35 >

surprised to see the monks huddled around Lucas as he entertained them with a shell game. William leaned in between two of the monks for a better look. As his right shoulder pressed between the two, followed by his head, he was surprised to see exactly what Lucas was doing. At first, William was irritated to discover that Lucas, a boy of only seven, was versed in a gambling game. William knew this game was commonly used by cheats to swindle money from unsuspecting sailors. His first reaction was to tell Lucas to stop, but something strange happened. As he watched the boy, his mind was caught up in a distant memory. He saw himself standing on a cobblestone street in a familiar place. It was Bristol, and he knew it. He noticed a small crowd of sailors who had just anchored a ship in the harbor. They were standing around a small table, around a ten- or twelve-year-old boy. The boy quickly moved the three shells around the table while taking bets from the sailors who eagerly tossed their coins on the table for a chance to guess which nut covered the prize. William was standing at the corner of a storefront building several yards from the event. He began to move closer to the table to get a better look at the boy. He realized as he walked that he was not physically there but only a spectator looking in on a vision of the event. He stopped when he was within a few feet of the boy. He heard the boy calling out the bets, "Which shell hides the pea? Make a bet, and you shall see." The boy's voice sounded familiar. William moved closer. He was standing behind the boy. He could see the child's dark, wavy, shoulder-length, unkempt hair. He began to move to the left to see the face of the boy. As he moved, the jawline and profile appeared out of the messy hair. The scene started to fade in and out. At one point, he saw the face of Lucas, and then it changed to the original boy. He was having trouble focusing on keeping the vision from changing. Men began to walk and crowd in front of him, blocking his view of the boy's face. Two of the men were obviously intoxicated.

< 36 >

They were getting louder and causing the crowd to become more disorderly. Suddenly one of the men yelled.

"Cheat! You miserable, cheat! Sheriff! Where is the Sheriff?"

He reached in, grabbed the boy's collar, and continued screaming. William made out the boy's face as the crowd moved away from the table. He leaned in, and his eyes connected with the deep, dark eyes of the boy who was being lifted from his chair by the giant arm of the angry man. William knew the face of the boy. He was overcome by a moment of shock that almost took him out of the vision. He looked again at the boy who looked at William with terror in his eyes as he exclaimed,

"Father!"

The vision ended, and William was again in the present. He saw the face of Lucas blending in and out with the face of the other boy. He closed his eyes, shook his head, opened his eyes, and yelled,

"Lucas! This is not appropriate! Stop immediately!"

The monks quickly pulled away from Lucas; no one said a word. William reached across the table, and swept the shells off and onto the floor. He was breathing heavily. Lucas was shocked. He looked at William, his face wrinkled, his deep dark eyes attempting to penetrate William's. Lucas hesitated for a moment and then blurted out.

"Father?"

William did not say a word. He seemed to be caught between the past and the present. Lucas spoke again.

"Father, what is wrong?"

The entire room was silent, everyone waiting for a response from William. Suddenly, William was back in the room with Lucas and the monks.

"I am sorry, Lucas. I do not know what came over me."

< 37 >

He looked at the monks, who hesitated, slowly looked at one another, and then back at William.

"I just had another memory come to me. I did not mean to be rude, and I just wasn't prepared for the moment."

Dom Freidman spoke. "No worry, William. No harm was done."

He motioned for one of the monks to pick up the shells. Two of the monks bent over and gathered the shells.

"Now, I believe each of you has duties to attend to. Am I right?"

The monks nodded in agreement and began to file out of the room. William smiled at the monks, acknowledging a couple of them as their eyes met. He hung his head in embarrassment, knowing that no harm had been done and that they had only gathered around Lucas to see what he was showing them. William looked back at Lucas and asked.

"How did you learn that game, and for what purpose?"

Lucas seemed emboldened as he replied,

"Father, I lived on the streets of London for nearly one year. I learned the game by watching other boys do it. From time to time, I could earn a few coins that sometimes helped put food in my stomach."

"Lucas, it is a game of chance, gambling, and gambling is of the devil."

Lucas thought for a moment and replied,

"It may be of the devil, but at least when I had coins, I could buy food instead of stealing it from the merchants. I always thought that God taught me to do it. I do not understand why the devil would want to fill my stomach and God would not. Oh, father, I did not want to displease God and only wanted to eat. Do you think he will forgive me?" Tears began to well up in his eyes.

< 38 >

William realized that he had misspoken. He knelt in front of Lucas and reached for him. Lucas quickly embraced him.

"My dear son. I am the one who needs forgiveness, not you, a boy still six months from his eighth birthday. Please forgive me, my son."

William held Lucas tightly.

"Of father, I promise I will not gamble again if you promise never to leave me again."

William felt tremendous guilt that he had not been there for his sweet little boy, and he felt genuine sorrow that this precious little child of God had to fend for himself on the dirty streets of London. He held Lucas tighter, savoring the moment of holding his first-born son in his arms and knowing his child. It occurred to him that the memory of Lucas' birth had returned to him; it was October 10, 1342. He knew that his son was seven years and six months old. He slowly released Lucas and held both of his arms as he placed Lucas in front of him.

"My sweet boy, I promise I will never leave you again."

Just then, William heard the voice of Dom, who cleared his throat to get his attention. William looked up at Dom, who shifted his eyes in an upward motion as he mouthed the words, "your journey and your plans." William realized what the monk was telling him. He remembered that he and Dom Freidman had entered the room to find Lucas and tell him about William's plan to find his friend Saxton Bentley.

"Lucas, there is something that I need to do, and it could be perilous for a small boy."

Lucas lowered his eyebrows and wrinkled his brow.

"What are you talking about, father?"

"I need to return to Cardiff and find your mother, sister, and brother, and I am afraid the journey is too dangerous for you to go with me."

Lucas shook his head and said, "Father, do you not remember where I have been the last several months of my life?

< 39 >

If God protected me while I was stolen from my family, why would he not protect me on a journey to return to them? Besides, does it not seem obvious to you that God brought us together so that we may go and reunite our family?"

William smiled. Dom Freidman looked at William and raised an eyebrow.

"My son, I know God protected you, and he brought us together. But I fear that taking you along with me on this journey will be testing the Lord, and that is something I do not want to do."

"But father, at this moment, you are all that I have." He looked at Dom Friedman and the other monks and said, "And although these men are your friends, and they have been very kind to you, they are not your family; I am. And I am all that you have. Why separate what God has brought together? It seems that to test God would be to leave me again and see if he would bring us together again."

William knelt in front of Lucas and placed his hands on each of his shoulders.

"Oh, my son, I love you and never want to be separated from you again. If it was God's will that you and I would find one another in the largest city in the land, then it must be his will that we are together and stay together."

Lucas reached his arms around William and hugged him tightly.

"Thank you, Father, thank you!" he cried.

William pulled Lucas away and looked into his eyes.

"Lucas, I know that this journey will be dangerous. If I followed my own will, I would leave you behind. However, I believe you are right, and we should stay together." He pulled Lucas to him and held him tightly. "I need to go to my room and pack some things. You stay here, and I will be down in a few minutes. "

Dom Friedman spoke. "Fine, then. Your father has plans to make."

< 40 >

He motioned for William to stand and leave the room. William kissed Lucas on the forehead and then stood. Dom Freidman tilted his head and shook it to the side, directing William toward the door. As William began to walk, the monk opened his hand and dropped the shells onto the table. Lucas stood.

The monk asked, "Why do you not show me how this game works?"

Lucas looked toward William for approval. William smiled and gently nodded.

"But what about the devil?" Lucas asked.

"Do not you worry about him. Besides, he would not want to play with me because I always win, and he doesn't like losing, even though he is the master of losing."

Lucas smiled, hopped onto a chair, and began explaining the game's workings. Dom Freidman looked at William, who was standing in the doorway. William smiled and shook his head as he left the room.

William went to his room and began to pack a few things for his journey. He found the clothes he had worn at the prison; they had been carefully rolled and placed in a basket under his bed. As he unrolled the clothes, he remembered the day three months earlier when he escaped the prison. He remembered the dark cloud that formed above the prison and the loud thunder and harsh lighting that scared the king's marksmen away long enough for him to make his escape. He remembered crossing the bridge and seeing the group of monks walking almost single file. He recalled seeing the face of Dom Freidman, who was leading the group, as he stopped the procession, looked at William, and nodded for him to join in line with them. How odd he thought it was that this monk did not hesitate to allow him to join them, even though he was not really one of them. *What a blessing it has been to be among these good men, what a blessing."* He thought to himself. He opened the dark tunic and laid it on his bed. He slipped his

< 41 >

hand into the neck hole and gently removed the map. One last memory entered his mind; it was the warden handing him the map to his cabin, where he had sent Saxton Bentley to take his wife and unborn child to safety. William looked at the map for a few moments and surmised that it would take him a least a day and a half to make the journey. He carefully folded the map and gently placed it into the pocket of his robe. Suddenly he heard a loud scream that came from the kitchen. He raced out of the room and down the single flight of stairs. He rushed into the kitchen in time to see the cook attempting to fight off a large animal that had locked its jaws around a big mutton chop, pulling in one direction as the cook feverishly holding to the meat was pulling in the other. As William entered the room, the cook yelled that the creature was trying to steal their food; he yelled for William to help! William ran to the scene, grabbed a large pot from a rack of pots hanging above the counter, and slammed it onto the animal's head. The first blow dazed it, but the second ended its life. It fell to the side and rolled off the counter while its jaws were still locked onto the mutton chop. The Cook released the meat and jumped back. He grabbed his apron and, while wiping his hands, exclaimed,

"I have never seen anything like it before! It is the size of a cat and has lion's teeth. What is it, William?"

William took a large knife lying on the counter and walked closer to the animal. He bent down, placed his shoe on its back, and used the knife to pry open its mouth. After a few attempts, he succeeded.   The dead animal rolled over, revealing its long sharp claws and enormous fangs. William, too was surprised as he looked back at the cook and said,

"This is no cat! I am afraid things are about to get much worse than we are prepared for."

Dom Friedman. Lucas and several other monks rushed into the kitchen to see the commotion. One of the monks looking at the dead animal, shouted, "Dear God in Heaven, what is that?"

< 42 >

"I believe it is a rat." Answered William.

"A rat? Are you sure? I have never seen a rat that size?" Exclaimed the monk.

"It is a roof rat." Answered Dom Friedman. "They tend to be larger than the average rat, but I have never seen one engage a human. They are typically spooked easily and avoid humans."

"Well, this one was not spooked. It grabbed onto my mutton chop and would not let it go!" Said the cook. "If William had not clanked its head with that pot, I suppose the two of us would still be fighting."

The monks began to laugh. William looked closer at the animal and noticed that its mouth was covered in foam. He looked back at the cook.

"I think it is best if you did not cook that meat. This animal is sick and diseased."

The monk threw his hands into the air and down again. "I will close the shutters so that none of his friends or family try to join him for dinner."

Dom Friedman looked at one of the monks and said, "Go find a shovel and get this thing and the mutton chop out of here. Dig a hole and bury both deep."

The monks left the kitchen. Dom asked the cook, "Please fill a bag with bread and onion. William and Lucas will leave soon and need it on their journey."

"Thank you, Dom Friedman." Said, William.

"William, do you know that path you will take to Cardiff? There are several routes to take, and the fastest is probably to follow the river."

"Yes. I have a friend named Saxton Bentley who lives in a cabin in the woods about a day's journey from here. I have a map." William pulled the map from his cloak and rolled it onto the table.

Dom Gordon looked at the map. "I know this area, and there is not much there." He ran his finger along with the map

< 43 >

and stopped at one point. "This is a small shire called Havens Stop. It is deep into the woods; maybe thirty to forty people live there. You realize that if you go this route, it will take you, several leagues, off the most direct path to Cardiff?"

"Yes, but I believe Saxton will be able to provide us shelter for the first night of our trip. And it will be good to see him again."

"I understand. Do you have your things packed?"

"Yes, I believe that we are ready."

"Then let us go to the main room and ask that God protects you on your journey." He motioned for the group to follow him. They all knelt in a circle as Dom Friedman offered the prayer. After the prayer, William and Lucas began to hug each monk. Dom Friedman was the last. As he and William embraced, Dom Friedman whispered into William's ear,

"My dear brother, I do have faith that God will protect you and that you will return. But please, remember that no matter what you find in Cardiff, God has not and will not abandon you."

William smiled and said, "Thank you, my friend, thank you for everything."

William and Lucas rode Daisy, the younger horse, off into the forest a few moments later. As they entered the forest, William looked back toward the monastery on a hill off in the distance. He saw four small figures, Dom Friedman and three of the priests. He looked ahead at the tall tree-laden forest, took a deep breath, and directed the horse in. He felt Lucas tighten the grip around his waist. For a moment, he felt peace, and then suddenly, the foggy image of a man spun around in his head. Seconds later, the spinning stopped, and the face turned until it looked directly at William.

The fog dissipated slowly, revealing a terrified pale face surrounded by thick black hair. A flash of yellow flames momentarily blinded William. The flames encircled the face,

< 44 >

and thick black smoke covered the image.   William leaned forward into the vision just as the face burst through the smoke and stopped eye to eye with him.   A quick flash of perfect clarity revealed the face. It was Michael. The vision ended as abruptly as it began. William knew that their journey would not be without struggle. He remembered the words of Dom Friedman, "No matter what you find in Cardiff, God has not and will not abandon you." He clung to hope and prayed for faith, knowing God was with them. He hoped God had also been with Saxton and his little family.

< 45 >

Chapter Four Notes

Julian and Gregorian calendars. When quoting dates along with the day of the week, I have used the Julian calendar, not the Gregorian. By 1000 AD, most European countries had adopted the Julian calendar of 365 days in a year and 366 days every fourth year. This calendar was used over the next 500 years until astronomers discovered that astronomical events were not coinciding with the calendar as they should have. They determined that the calendar had lost one day every hundred years. In 1582 the Pope issued a decree that dropped ten days, September 4 was followed by September 15. It took the next 350 years before all Western countries adopted the new calendar. This means that the dates of historical events will differ depending on which country's calendar was used at the time.

< 46 >

Chapter Five
The Orphan Boy

"The Lord watches over the foreigner and sustains the fatherless and the widow, but he frustrates the ways of the wicked." Psalms 146:9

July 1349

The barn at the estate in Cardiff

Lucas tried to scream, but the large hand covered his mouth. He tried to run, but the man was much larger and more robust. He swept Lucas under his arm and held him tightly against his side as he ran. Lucas knew that he had no way to escape the shocked and terrified assailant. He knew that his little boy's body was nothing more than a rag doll to the man who seized him as he fled the barn. Three horses were tied to a post behind the barn. As the man jumped onto one of the horses, he flung Lucas on the saddle in front of him. He loosed the other two horses and swatted the reigns at each of them, causing them to run off in another direction through the dense forest. The man leaned over Lucas squashing his small body tightly against the neck of the horse. The horse ran at full speed for more than three leagues.

Although Lucas only had a partial view of the direction ahead, he had no idea if anyone had seen them leave the barn. He did not know if Michael knew the direction to follow. The horse struggled to run as the man forced it off the dirt road and directly into the forest. As it ran, it was pummeled by tree branches and thick brush, making it difficult for the two to stay atop the horse. Lucas felt the throbbing heartbeat and heard the

< 47 >

loud breathing of his captor, whose body was tightly forced against him in a challenging effort to keep both of them on the running horse. It had been over an hour before the man allowed the animal to slow down and finally rest. When they came to an opening in the forest, the man stopped the horse, leaned back, and tossed Lucas onto the ground. He landed face down, forcing all of the air from his lungs. He rolled to his back and attempted to breathe. The man jumped from the horse and walked over to Lucas. Finally, after several attempts, the air began to fill his lungs. He breathed deeply. The man stood above him and looked down at him. His eyes were bloodshot, and his nose was running. It was evident to Lucas that the man had been crying. Lucas started to speak when suddenly the man kicked him in the side, just below his rib cage. The blow rolled him back onto his stomach, but the man kicked him again before he could react. He began to yell as Lucas attempted to rise to his knees. The pain was intense, but Lucas knew he had to be strong; he believed that Michael was somewhere nearby, ready to rescue him, just as he had done for Elizabeth.

"Your horrid sister killed my brothers, and now you will die too! You worthless little rat! You are going to die! Did you hear me?" He kicked Lucas again.

"But first, I am going to have some fun with you. Too bad you're not a lass; it would be much more enjoyable that way."

He began to loosen his belt around his tunic. Lucas did not know the man's intentions, but he knew they were not good. The man took another step toward Lucas, then raised his left arm and wiped his nose, momentarily burying his face into his sleeve. Lucas scooped up a handful of dirt and pebbles and waited for the man to lower his arm from his face. Lucas flung the rubble directly into the man's eyes when his face was in view. The man yelled, stumbled backward, tripped, and fell on his back. He began screaming vulgarities at Lucas while attempting to remove the debris from his eyes.

< 48 >

Lucas struggled to stand; the pain in his side was intense, but something deeper inside caused him to run. He ran a few yards alongside a small stream that turned back and forth and began to wind into the forest. The trees became too thick to navigate quickly. He stopped, looked ahead, and behind as best he could. It appeared as though he had lost the man somewhere in the woods. His heart was racing as he breathed quickly, with short, thin breaths. Suddenly he heard a noise behind him. He stood still and listened. Something was moving slowly in his direction. He lifted his head, and the sound stopped. He then heard another sound still behind him. At first, he thought the man had found him, but then he realized that he was being stocked by something deadlier than a bitter, angry man. He remained still, knowing that he had become the target, the anticipated dinner for a pack of wolves. He slowly turned until his body faced three salivating wolves just a few yards behind him. He knew that the animals could outrun him. He knew they could reach him before climbing high enough in a tree. It seemed he had no options but then heard the man's voice calling after him from behind the wolves. The animals turned and began to act unsure. Lucas yelled out to the man.

"I am over here, you skinny bag of bones! I am over here!"

His voice startled the wolves; they looked at each other, and two more appeared from the woods. The man yelled again. He was only yards behind, and Lucas could distinguish the man's body through the thick brush. He had removed his shirt and was holding a long shiny knife in his hands as he ran. He yelled at Lucas again.

"I will find you, my little rag doll. I am not finished with you yet!"

The wolves looked at Lucas; they looked behind and slowly dispersed in different directions into the brush. Each animal hid a few feet from Lucas's trail through the brush. Lucas realized that they had not retreated but had hidden

< 49 >

instead. He knew they now had two targets to choose from, Lucas or the flesh, revealed the white-skinned man. Lucas began slowly walking backward, feeling his way through tree limbs and brush. He gave no thought about the possibility of other wild animals that he could be backing into. He hoped the wolves would choose a more substantial, meatier meal than him. Suddenly, the man's body appeared through the brush. Lucas stopped only a few yards from the man. He began to laugh as he saw Lucas. He yelled at him.

"Come, child, this will not hurt too bad, I promise! It'll be quick, and the pain will be over before you know it!" He laughed again.

The man stopped, not realizing that he was within just feet of five hungry wolves hidden on two sides of him. Lucas could see three of the wolves crouched in the brush. He began to breathe erratically. He knew the wolves would likely choose the human closest to them, and he knew it was not him. He began to shake; he felt himself losing control. He mumbled the words, *"Please, God, help me."* He then heard a voice in his head. A familiar voice he had heard before. The voice yelled, *"Run, Lucas! Run!"* Without hesitation, he turned and began running away from the man. His movement startled the wolves, and they jumped out in the open. The man screamed and turned in the opposite direction. He tried to run when one of the wolves leaped into the air and onto his back, knocking him to the ground. When he hit the ground, the other wolves attacked. Lucas heard the man screaming as the frenzied beasts began attacking him. Lucas continued to run, scraping and scratching his body through the thick forest. He had run for nearly twenty minutes before his body gave out, and he fell to the ground. He lay on the ground for several more minutes until he could catch his breath and regain his strength. He stood, looked back, and could not see any sign of the wolves. He turned ahead and noticed the stream that he had followed earlier. He walked to the stream. He looked around and, seeing no animals, bent

< 50 >

down and began to scoop the fresh water into his mouth. After a few minutes, he stood and began to walk alongside the stream. He did not know where he was, but he knew that if he followed the creek, chances were that it would lead him to a town, a farm, or some sign of community. It began to rain. He had walked well over a league, wet, cold, and tired when his strength gave out. He looked for a place to rest and noticed a large dirt, tree-covered mound ahead. When he reached the ridge, he saw a large boulder like a cow protruding from the side of the hill. It created a slight cave-like indentation underneath it, just deep enough and far enough for his tiny body to be hidden from the elements. He climbed into the crevice, curled into a ball, laid his head on his arms, and slept.

The rain continued through the remainder of the day and into the night. Lucas woke to the startling sound of nothingness shortly after midnight. The rain had stopped, the clouds had dissipated, and the skies were clear. Lucas looked up toward the sky from his dry and safe shelter. The stars shined brilliantly in the dark black sky. He looked all over the sky but could not find the moon. He closed his eyes and remembered a moment with his father. He remembered sitting at William's. He could not remember how old he was, but he knew he was much younger at the time. He pictured himself looking up at his father and touching a mark just behind his left ear with his eyes closed. Lucas cleared his mind and allowed the memories to take over.

"Father, what is that mark behind your ear?"

"What mark?"

Lucas touched the mark again.

"Right there, that mark!"

"Oh, that mark. Yes. I will tell you what it is, but you must keep it a secret. Alright?"

"A secret? Why cannot anyone else know about it?"

"Because right now, I am the only one who knows about it."

"Even mother does not know?"

< 51 >

"That is right; even mother does not know!"

"Even mother does not know. Tell me, father, tell me!" He pleaded.

William placed his finger on his lips and motioned for Lucas to be quiet.

"If I tell you can you keep it a secret just between you and me?"

"Yes, father. I think I can."

"You think you can?" William asked, pretending not to believe that Lucas could keep the secret.

"I mean, I know I can."

"That's better." William took a deep breath and stood to his feet with Lucas in his arms. He walked over to the window, opened the shutter, and leaned toward the open window.

"Do you see all the stars in the sky, Lucas?"

Lucas held his right arm tightly to William's left shoulder and began to shiver as the sharp, cold breeze began to flow into the room. Lucas looked up into the night sky.

"Yes, father, I see the stars in the sky."

"Do you see anything else, my son?"

Lucas surveyed the sky for a moment and then looked back to William.

"No, father, I do not see anything else."

"Are you sure?"

Lucas looked again, then back at William, and shook his head.

"Do you know what is missing from the sky tonight?"

"No. What is it?"

"The moon! The moon is missing from the sky!"

"Father, where is the moon?" Lucas asked with some anxiety in his voice.

William smiled at Lucas and, while pointing to the birthmark behind his ear, said, "It is right here, my son. Anytime it hides, you will find it right here."

< 52 >

He touched it and asked, "Really, father? Is that really the moon on your neck?"

"Does it look like the moon to you, son?"

Lucas pulled William's hair back and looked closer. He softly touched it as his finger outlined the curve of the mark.

"It looks like the moon to me, father."

"Well then, I think we both know where to look when we cannot find the moon in the sky!"

"Will it always hide there, father?"

"Lucas, as long as I am here, the moon will be there."

As the memory ended, Lucas wiped a tear from his eye. He looked out into the dark star-glittered sky and said,

"Oh, father, how I wish you were here. I miss you dearly, father. And I miss the moon too."

Tears began to escape as he closed his eyes and slept till morning.

He was awakened by the sound of chirping birds and the warmth of the morning sun. He slowly crawled out of the indentation, dusted himself off, looked about his surroundings, and walked to the stream. He knelt, cupped his hands, and began to lap the water to his mouth. After his fill of water, he followed the stream's path. The forest was dense, and it was impossible to see beyond it. Although he did not know where he was or how far from home, something told him to follow the stream. He believed that doing so would lead him to a town. He walked alongside the creek for about two hours when fatigue and hunger set in. He stopped and sat under a large tree. The stream had provided him with much-needed water, but his stomach needed food. As he sat under the tree, he looked around at the forest. Everything looked the same, he thought. He hoped that there would soon be an opening in the woods, something that opened up into a valley. The trees seemed so crowded and thick that he felt out of place with the elements. He continued to survey his surroundings, hoping to see

< 53 >

something edible. After a few moments, something caught his eye. Off in the distance, just a few yards to the North, he noticed color that stood out from the monotonous shades of green. He stood up to get a better look. He began walking toward the paint.

As he walked and pulled his way through the forest, the color became more apparent. It was berries, and he knew that he could eat berries. His heart began to race, and his breathing intensified as he started to run toward the berries. After a few moments, he reached them. It was a large and thick Pyracantha bush filled with bright red berries. The shrub seemed out of place in the forest since it was the only one of its kind as far as he could see. He quickly plucked a few of the berries from the bush and shoved them into his mouth. He was unprepared for the bitter taste and quickly spat the chewed berries onto the ground. He thought for a moment and then decided to try another berry. He slowly plucked another and put it into his mouth. Again, the bitter flavor overcame his ability to keep it in his mouth, spitting it onto the ground. His stomach began to growl, and he looked around for something more palatable but only saw the forest trees. He knew that he needed to eat and that the only food was in front of him. He closed his eyes, took a breath, and picked another berry. As he placed it on his tongue, he pretended it was candy, one of his favorite candies that his father used to bring home after returning from a long trip. The memories of his father handing him a small bag of candy made him smile. He began to chew the berry, the bitter flavor started to take him out of the memory, but he forced it back, chewed, and quickly swallowed it. He had never known hunger before. Food was always a treat, and he never thought much about taste, type, or flavor. He loved that his mother and Martha always cooked enjoyable food. But now, he had to eat to live, not just to fill his stomach enough until the next meal. He picked several more berries and put them into his mouth. Again, he thought of eating candy from his father, and the

< 54 >

memory made the bitter taste bearable. He ate until he felt full, and then he headed back toward the stream to return to his journey. As he walked, he began to feel pain in his stomach. He thought that perhaps he ate too many berries. He stopped for a moment, and the pain went away. He looked up at the sky. The trees were so thick and tall that it made it difficult to see the blueness of the sky.

"Thank you, God, for helping me to find food. And thank you for helping me escape from that evil man. I know that I am just a lad, but please let me find some nice people who can help me get home."

He finished his prayer and attempted to make the sign of the cross. He touched his forehead, left shoulder, and then his forehead again. He knew that he did not complete the gesture appropriately. He attempted it again but could not remember the process. He looked up at the sky and said,

"I am sorry, God, I cannot remember the sign of the cross, but I know that you know it. So please, can you do it for me?"

In his mind, he waited for a moment to allow God to make the sign.

"Thank you, God. You are a good friend."

He continued walking alongside the stream. He walked for another two hours and rested again. After his strength had returned, he continued his journey, stopping every so often to rest. After another two-hour walk, he found a resting place on a large rock protracted from the ground in an open, sandy area a few feet from the stream. The area created a small beachfront cove that stretched about twenty feet alongside the stream with a distance as far as ten feet across. Although the sun was still hidden by the trees, Lucas could tell that it had nearly completed its daytime journey and was not far from setting. His stomach began to growl. The berries he had eaten earlier in the day were long gone, and he needed more nourishment. As he sat on the rock, a thin memory entered his mind. He was

< 55 >

playing on a beach near the ocean. He saw Sarah running toward him. He laughed that she was so small, a toddler learning to walk. He then heard a voice coming from behind him. It was his mother. She told him to watch his baby sister and keep her away from the water. He enjoyed the moment but was quickly startled out of the memory at the sound of breaking branches a few feet from him. He looked into the forest but could not distinguish anything distinct other than the trees and brush he had traveled through all day. Suddenly he saw a large bird flying down from a high perch above him. The bird began to squawk. It flew back toward the tree and around what appeared to be its nest. It continued to squawk and dive at the nest. Lucas stood on the rock to get a better look until he finally saw what had caused the commotion. A snake had made its way up the tree and to the nest. The bird was attempting to save its eggs. Lucas watched for several more moments as the bird flew toward the serpent. He marveled that the mother bird was so determined to save her young that the snake continued toward the nest regardless of her dives. The bird seemed to dive closer and closer to the snake. Lucas saw the snake jump toward the bird. It was wrapped around one of the small branches where the nest was sitting. Although the snake seemed irritated at the bird, it did not take its eyes off the nest. Suddenly as the bird flew at the snake, the snake lurched forward with its jaws opened wide and latched onto the neck of the bird. The bird struggled to get away as the snake hung onto it, releasing its venom into the neck of the bird. The bird continued to fight, slapping its wings and claws at the snake. Small red feathers began to float down toward Lucas. Finally, the snake released the bird. The bird tried to fly but lost its strength and began to flap its wings sporadically as it fell from branch to branch until it hit the ground a few feet from Lucas. His heart ached for the unfortunate creature that appeared to be dead, leaving its young alone and defenseless. He looked at the nest and saw that the snake had reached its destination. He could not see its head, but

< 56 >

he knew it had reached the eggs. He watched for a few more minutes as the snake rustled around the nest. Unexpectedly, one of the eggs fell from the nest. As it fell, it rolled upon small limbs and leaves that seemed to gently catch it as it rolled from one to the other. It appeared like the egg would somehow make it to the ground without breaking. The last leafy limbs gently tossed it to the ground on top of a soft, thick green patch of moss. The egg stopped. Lucas climbed down from the rock and walked toward the egg. He noticed the dead mother bird not far from where the egg landed. When he reached the egg, he was startled that it began to move. He knelt down next to it and discovered that the bird was alive inside the egg, and it had begun pecking away at the shell. Part of the shell had peeled off during the fall, and one of the birds' little feet had poked through the hole. Lucas reached for the egg to help the creature but remembered his father telling him that a human should never interfere with nature as a bird came into the world; doing so could kill the animal. He watched for a few moments and marveled that the bird could come out of its shell. After it was completely exposed, Lucas could see its tiny heart beating from its chest. The bird looked at Lucas; it breathed erratically, made a few short squawks, and then laid its head down on the moss. Lucas knew that the bird could not survive on its own without a mother to protect it or feed it. He felt a tear begin to roll down his cheek. He had witnessed a miracle during his own fear and loneliness. The bird made a few more sounds, breathed in, and then out for the last time. Lucas cupped his hand and dug a small grave in the dirt. He gently placed the small bird into the grave and carefully covered the grave. He then looked up at the sky and said,

"God, thank you for letting this little bird live long enough to appreciate its life. Please do not let the snake find its grave. And please, God, lead me to more berries. But this time, can they at least taste good?"

< 57 >

He stood again and began to walk next to the stream. After a few moments, he noticed something a few feet ahead. He stopped and carefully looked through the brush. It was a small rabbit eating from a plant. He slowly walked toward the rabbit and noticed that the plant had berries. He began to run toward the plant, surprising the rabbit, which ran off into the woods. When he reached the plant, he began to look for berries. He became frustrated as he discovered that the rabbit appeared to have eaten all of the berries. Just as he was about to give up, he noticed one plump blue-colored berry that hadn't been eaten. He plucked the berry and tossed it into his mouth. He anticipated a bitter taste but was pleasantly surprised that the taste was sweet and very desirable. He continued to rustle through the plant in search of more berries but could not find any. He was frustrated that God had led him to the berries but only left one for him after the rabbit had eaten the rest. Lucas sat on the ground next to the plant. His head began to pound, and he felt dizzy. He tried to shake it off but could not. He leaned back and slumped to the ground. As he looked up at the sky, he noticed an opening ahead; he could see the forest opening up to a valley. He smiled and said,

"Thank you, God."

He felt weak and tried to close his eyes, but they would not close completely. He knew that something was wrong. He could no longer feel his hands or feet, and his body seemed weightless. He did not realize that he had eaten a poisonous berry from the Atropa belladonna plant, more commonly known as the Deadly Nightshade plant. Everything became black, and he felt himself slip away into nothingness.

He opened his eyes to deep blackness, as wide as possible, but saw nothing. He seemed to be floating but could not feel a physical sense. He tried to move his head but felt nothing, yet he had conscious thought. "Where am I?" He kept asking himself. "What is this?" he thought. "Am I dead?' He wondered. Several moments passed, and suddenly a tear in the

< 58 >

blackness appeared. He watched as the tear ripped from the bottom upward. As it tore, streaks of blinding brightness raced toward him. The light was so quick and illuminating that the blackness fled in fear as the light became everything. He closed his eyes, but the light pierced deep into his being. He opened his eyes and was as blinded as he was in the immense darkness. He felt himself breathe; the first hint of physical existence returned to him. He felt weight and form and flesh. He stretched out his arms, brought his hands to his face, and fought with his eyes to comprehend the form of his fingers amidst the intensity of light. He continued to contract and expand his fingers until, finally, something reflected a beam of light and refracted it in another direction. And then another, and another, and another, until he understood the form of fingers and hands. He traced his vision on his right hand down to his wrists, forearm, and elbow. He noticed a shining white robe with a brilliant green front, and a silky white sash tied around it was draped about his body. He turned his head, looked at his left hand, and repeated the task. He lifted his arms above his head and looked down at his chest, stomach, legs, and feet. He was whole, he thought, he was physical, and he was alive! He was filled with a moment of joy and then suddenly shaken as another burst of light flashed in front of him. The intensity slowly decreased until he could comprehend another being in the place with him. He felt himself standing upright yet floating above the ground. The being gently took him by the left hand and slowly pulled him. He hesitated and then stepped forward. Although he felt his feet firmly on a surface, he could see that he was several feet in the air. As the presentation continued to pull him, he repeatedly stepped until he gained enough confidence to walk without fear. The presence stopped. It reached out its right arm and slowly waved it toward the left, stopping inches from Lucas's right shoulder, and then slowly continued the sweeping motion back toward the right, opening what appeared to be a large curtain that separated the place of

< 59 >

whiteness from the physical world. Although adorned with color and form, the dullness of the world caused Lucas to wince with pain and discomfort. He turned toward the personage that had opened the curtain. He strained his eyes to understand the form of the being. Bright light radiated the entire body from head to foot, making it impossible to comprehend specific detail or structure. Lucas could tell that it was a tall, brawny man. His hair was whiter than clouds on a sunny day, thick and blowing gently in various directions upon the beams of light racing through it. Lucas could not decipher his face but did notice the being smile at him as he pointed ahead. Lucas turned his head in the direction the man had pointed. He looked and saw home! It was Bristol! He saw himself running toward his father. His father knelt down, threw his arms open, caught him, and tightly wrapped his arms around him. He saw Sarah run up behind him. He watched as he saw himself pull Sarah into the hug. His father released them and kissed them several times on the cheek, neck, and forehead. He watched as his little body ran toward a carriage. He saw Michael place him into the carriage and then reach down and place Sarah after him. The scene changed, and Lucas was no longer watching the scene; he was in the scene. He held his head out the window, waved at his father, and watched him shrink in the distance. Suddenly the scene changed. He found himself in a field. He heard Michael yell at him, *"RUN, LUCAS! RUN!"* He began running and then felt the arms of someone grabbing him from behind and lifting him into the air. The scene changed; he was back in the carriage. The scene changed; he was on a ship shaking hands with a man named Philip. The scene changed, and everything began to move quickly and faster as his young life began to race in front of his eyes. He saw glimpses of happy moments, tears, fear, pain, heartache, and confusion. The scenes moved so quickly in front of him that he could no longer distinguish one from the other; it had all become one massive life experience warped and twisted together. He felt his head pounding and his

< 60 >

heart beating rapidly. His fingers and toes began to tingle and burn. His body felt heavy, hot, and extremely uncomfortable. The massive event abruptly stopped. Everything was quiet. He felt the weight of his body while lying on his back. His eyes were closed. He felt the warmth of the sun on his face. He slowly opened his eyes but immediately closed them like the sun's rays beamed brightly at them. He lay breathing heavily for a moment until something terrifying caught his attention. It was a familiar stench floating just above him. He heard a sound and felt heavy breathing on his face. Something appeared to block the heat and brightness of the sun just enough for him to open his eyes again. He slowly opened his eyes and was overcome by the horror of the man whose body claimed the vile stink. The man lowered his face inches above him. His face was covered in large bloody claw marks, his left eye patched with a torn strip of fabric. He opened his mouth, releasing a revolting odor as he spoke.

"You little fool. Did you really think you would get away from me?"

As he spoke, a drop of blood oozed from the patch and landed on Lucas's cheek. Lucas turned his head as the man lifted his right hand, revealing a sizeable shiny knife. He continued to speak.

"Even a pack of wolves cannot stop me from killing you! They got one of my eyes, so I will start by slicing one of yours!"

The man leaned over and grabbed Lucas's left arm.

"Get up, you little waste of flesh!" The man lifted Lucas into the air and then dropped him onto his feet, still holding Lucas's arm. He reared back his right arm in a striking motion with the knife in hand. Just as he was about to strike, Lucas tightened his left hand into a fist and thrust his entire body forward, slamming the total weight of his body behind his fist, deep into the man's groin. The unexpected blow knocked the man to the ground in agonizing pain. He dropped

< 61 >

the knife, grabbed his groin with both hands, and began rolling on the dirt from side to side. Lucas tried to get the knife, but the man, still suffering from his pain, was able to knock it away from him. Lucas turned, yelled, and began to run away. The man held his breath and rolled toward the direction Lucas was running. He noticed a broken, thick branch about a foot in length just within his reach. He grabbed the branch and flung it at Lucas. Lucas pleaded with God to send him the angel again. He saw a small house in the distance. His heart filled with optimism, and for a moment, he felt saved until a dull pain struck the back of his head, and everything again became black.

< 62 >

Chapter Five Notes

*Pyracanthas are valuable ornamental plants grown in gardens for their decorative flowers and fruit, often very densely borne. Their dense thorny structure makes them particularly valued in situations where an impenetrable barrier is required. The aesthetic characteristics of pyracanthas plants, in conjunction with their home security qualities, make them a considerable alternative to artificial fences and walls. They are also a good shrub for a wildlife garden, providing dense cover for roosting and nesting birds, summer flowers for bees, and an abundance of berries as a food source. Pyracantha berries are not poisonous as commonly thought; although they are very bitter, they are edible when cooked and are often made into jelly. In the UK and Ireland, Pyracantha and the related genusCotoneaster are valuable sources of nectar when often the bees have little other forage during the June Gap. **Pyracantha** is a genus of thorny evergreen large shrubs in the family Rosaceae, with common names **Firethorn** or **Pyracantha**. They are native to an area extending from Southeast Europe east to Southeast Asia, resembling and related to Cotoneaster, but have serrated leaf margins and numerous thorns (Cotoneaster is thornless). The plants reach up to six meters tall. The seven species have white flowers and red, orange, or yellow berries (more correctly poses). The flowers are produced during late spring and early summer; the pomes develop from late summer and mature in late autumn.*

*   **Atropa belladonna** or **Atropa belladonna**, commonly known as **Belladonna** or **Deadly Nightshade**, is a perennial herbaceous plant in the family Solanaceae, native to Europe, North Africa, and Western Asia. The foliage and berries are highly toxic, containing tropane alkaloids. These toxins include scopolamine and hyoscyamine, which cause bizarre delirium and hallucinations and are also used as pharmaceutical anticholinergics. The drug atropine is derived from the plant.*

*   It has a long history of use as a medicine, cosmetic, and poison. Before the Middle Ages, it was used as an anesthetic for surgery; the ancient Romans used it as a poison (the wife of Emperor Augustus and the wife of Claudius both were rumored to have used it to murder contemporaries), and predating this, it was used to make poison-tipped arrows. The genus name "atropa" comes from Atropos, one of the three Fates in Greek mythology, and the name "Bella Donna" is derived from Italian and means "beautiful woman" because the herb was used in eye-drops by women to dilate the pupils of the eyes to make them appear seductive. Atropa belladonna is also toxic to many domestic animals, causing narcosis and paralysis. However, cattle and rabbits eat the plant seemingly without suffering harmful effects. In humans, its anticholinergic properties will cause the disruption of cognitive capacities, such as memory and learning.* http://www.lealansgardencentre.co.uk/gardening-advice/pyracantha-valuable-ornamental-plant-gardens/

< 63 >

Chapter Six
Hope Precedes Faith

"To one who has faith, no explanation is necessary. To one without faith, no explanation is possible."
Thomas Aquinas

July 1349
Out of the forest and into the Shire.

He woke, lying on his back, to the feeling of a cold, damp cloth across his forehead. He slowly opened his eyes and saw long strands of thick blonde hair. As he focused, he saw bright blue eyes and powder-white skin. The pain began to dig into the back of his head. He closed his eyes but did not want to lose consciousness again. He forced his eyes open. He smiled; a tear escaped from the corner of his eye. He gathered a deep breath and mouthed the word, "Elizabeth!"

He had slept for over an hour when he began to wake. As he opened his eyes, he saw a thatched roof above him. He realized that he was lying on a straw bed. Something was touching his right forearm. At first, he thought it was a fly and swatted at it. He rubbed the length of his right arm and rested his left hand on his right forearm. He felt the annoyance again, this time flittering on his left hand. He leaned his head to the right, opened his eyes, and was startled at the face of a small girl. She had pointed her index finger and was touching Lucas's hand. She cocked her head to the right and smiled at him. Her face was small, with large blue eyes and rosy cheeks. Several strands of blonde hair that had escaped the ponytail

< 64 >

hung across her forehead. Lucas tried to lift his head, but the pain kept it down. He closed, opened his eyes, and spoke to the little girl.

"Who are you?" He asked.

She continued to smile but did not respond. He asked again.

"Who are you?"

She raised her eyebrows and darted her eyes from side to side. Lucas started to ask again when suddenly she raised her hand in front of her face, lifted three fingers, and blurted out,

"I am this many!"

Lucas smiled as he remembered his little sister Sarah. He knew this was not Sarah, but her smile and countenance filled his heart. He smiled at her and asked,

"Is your mother here?"

The little girl lowered her hand and nodded her head. She continued to smile but did not speak.

"Can you go find your mother and bring her here?" Lucas asked.

The little girl nodded her head again. She turned and scampered out of the room. Lucas surveyed the room; it was small and cramped. It looked as though the bed he was lying on was just large enough for two adults to crowd into. A single chair sat across from the bed, beside a small table, directly under a window. A large pitcher and a tin mug sat on the table. Lucas heard a commotion from the other room. Although he did not know where he was, he felt safe. The little girl entered the room leading the blonde-haired woman by the hand behind her.

They stopped in front of the bed, and the little girl said, "My mommy."

The woman smiled at Lucas and asked, "Are you alright, child?"

Lucas looked at her and realized that she was not Elizabeth. However, she did have a remarkable resemblance

< 65 >

and looked similar in age. Lucas replied, "I believe that I am well, Madam." He hesitated and then asked, "Are you an angel?"

She smiled at him, gently laughed, and said, "No, of course not, but my name is Angelia."

"You look like an Angel. God sent you to save me. Thank you." He began to cry.

She smiled at him as tears welled in her eyes. She leaned over, hugged him, and said, "You are safe little one. There is no need to cry."

She caressed his face and wiped his tears with her fingers. Even her touch felt like Elizabeth's. He longed for Elizabeth; he longed for his mother. He tried to control his emotions, and Angelia kissed his forehead.

"What were you doing in the forest, and where is your mother?" She asked in a soft, concerned voice.

Lucas began to shake and cry as the memory of the last two days began to haunt him. He wondered how he survived and if Elizabeth was still alive. Thoughts of terror raced through his mind as he wondered about the fate of his family. Angelia continued to gently caress his cheek.

"I promise that all will be fine, child."

Lucas caught his breath and blurted, "My name is Lucas. You do not need to call me child."

"Lucas, it is a pleasure to know you."

She looked down and said, "And this is my daughter, Faith. Say hello to Lucas, Faith."

The little girl smiled again, raised her fingers in front of her face, and said, "I am this many."

Lucas laughed; Angelia smiled at her and laughed with Lucas.

"You see, I told you all would be fine."

Lucas tried to clear his head of sadness. Angelia handed him a cloth, and he wiped his nose. She smiled at him, walked

< 66 >

to the table, poured water into the tin cup, and offered it to Lucas.

"Would you like some water, Lucas?"

Lucas nodded. Angelia helped him sit up. She pressed the cup to his lips and held it. He raised his hands to hers. He gently clasped his hands over hers and slowly tilted the cup, causing the water to flow into his mouth. He finished drinking, and Angelia returned the cup to the table.

"He took me from my family. He tried to kill me, but God helped me escape from him. Then he found me again. I thought I was going to die, and I begged God to send me the angel again. Something struck the back of my head, and I woke up and...." He stopped, thought for a moment, and continued. "The angel was standing above me."

Angelia smiled at him. She leaned over and hugged him tightly. The thought of an evil man so close to home concerned her, but she did not want her concern to cause more fear in Lucas. She tried to brush off the thoughts of the man.

"You poor child. You will be safe here with us. And Percival will be home soon."

"Who is Percival?" Lucas asked.

"Percival is my husband, and he is kind. You will like him, I promise."

"Where is he?" Lucas asked.

"He has gone to find his mother and father. They live in a small shire a few leagues from here. We have heard rumors of a strange sickness coming from the East. His parents are getting old, and we did not want them to be alone now."

"It is not a rumor; it is called the Great Morality, and many people are dying from it," Lucas stated.

"Do you mean the Great Mortality, Lucas?"

Yes, but some just call it the Black Death."

Angelia looked at him and firmly asked.

"How do you know this?"

< 67 >

"My family lived in Bristol, and we left because too many people died from the Black Death. It is a plague."

"A plague?" She asked. Lucas nodded.

"It is terrible. People die in just a few days after it attacks them. If it gets just one person in the family, everyone will die. There is no way to stop it or to cure it,"

Angelia raised her eyebrows and touched her hand to her mouth.

"I had no idea." She thought about Percival. She was concerned about his health and safety. She knew if what this boy had told her was confirmed that it was only a matter of time before the plague reached her shire. She felt a tug on her dress and looked down at the large eyes of her little child. Suddenly her heart sank at the thought of the plague taking her child, her husband, his parents, or any of their friends in the Shire. She knelt down, looked her daughter in the eyes, and asked,

"Are you hungry, my dear?"

Faith smiled and nodded her head. Angelia swept her into her arms and held her tightly.

"Then we shall eat!" She exclaimed with a smile. "Lucas, I have a pot of stew on the fire. I am sure that you must be starving. Come, let us eat." She reached out to Lucas, he took her hand, and the three of them walked into the other room. The room was twice the size of the bedroom. It had a large rock fireplace and three cords of wood next to it. A large iron pot hanging by a rod over the fire. A small straw bed set a couple of feet down the firewall, and an oversized wooden chair sat next to a rocking chair across from the fire. A small table next to the rocking chair, with a large bowl filled with yarn and needles. A small kitchen area was just a few feet from the fireplace, a vase with freshly picked flowers sitting on a wood plank table with four wooden chairs. Behind the table and against the opposite wall was a small food preparation area, a four-foot counter with cabinets underneath, and three shelves fixed to the wall above it. Angelia gently placed Faith in a chair

< 68 >

at the table. She let go of Lucas' hand and motioned to sit in the chair next to Faith. She then opened one of the cabinets and removed three small wooden bowls. She placed the bowls on the counter, lifted one, and walked to the cooking pot. She lifted a ladle that had been placed on top of one of the cords of wood. She leaned over the pot, put the ladle in it, and began to stir the stew. As she stirred, the aroma started to fill the air. She breathed in deeply and then exhaled.

"Doesn't it smell wonderful?" She asked.

Faith smiled and nodded her head. Lucas wanted to agree, but the aroma was far from pleasant to him. However, he concluded that anything would be better than bitter berries. He mustered a smile and said, "Yes, what is it?"

Angelia breathed in the aroma and tilted her head from side to side.

"It is onion and turnip with dried pig skin. I am sure you will love it!" She concluded.

Lucas did not like onion or turnip, which sounded better than eating dried pig skin. His stomach began to growl as if telling him to be thankful and just eat it! Angelia filled the first steaming bowl and placed it on the table in front of Lucas. She turned, filled another bowl, and put it in front of Faith.

"Now, do not touch it yet, sweetheart; it is scalding. Let mommy help you with it."

She filled the last bowl and carried it to her place at the table. She looked at the counter and found a large jar filled with wooden utensils. She reached in, grabbed three spoons, and carefully placed one next to each bowl. Lucas sat in his chair with his arms folded. Angelia noticed how Lucas had waited with folded arms. It was apparent to her that he was a child of means and manners. She bowed her head and began to pray.

"Dear Lord, we are truly thankful for this food and the blessing of strength and nourishment as we eat, and please bless and protect those of our loved ones who are not here with us. Give them safety, and return them home to us swiftly, in thy

< 69 >

care." She hesitated, breathed in, and stopped herself from becoming emotional. "Amen."

Lucas added, "Amen." He lifted his spoon, placed it in the bowl, slowly looked over it, and noticed bits and pieces of onion, turnip, and what appeared to be thin strips of pig skin floating on top. He politely looked at Angelia, whose large smile seemed more extensive than the bowl. He looked back at his bowl, stirred the mixture, scooped some onto his spoon, raised it to his lips, blew on it, and slowly poured it into his mouth. As the stew touched his tongue, he was pleasantly surprised at the flavor. He chewed, then swallowed. He took another bite, smiled at Angelia, chewed again, and swallowed. It was actually good, he thought, much better than bitter berries. "Thank you, your stew is delicious."

"You are very welcome, my dear. Please eat up; there is plenty."She smiled at him while placing her hand on the back of his head and sliding it down the back of his neck and onto his shoulder. She thought about what this small child had endured, alone and afraid in the woods, running from a deranged man. She thought about his mother's turmoil, not knowing where he was or if he was alive. The thought of a small child surviving for two days alone in the forest seemed unfathomable and quite miraculous. Then her thoughts turned to Percival; she wondered if he was safe. She wondered if this plague was to the village of his parents. She felt her heart race and her emotions stir within her.

"What happened to your floor?"

The question brought her out of her thoughts. She looked at Lucas and asked, "What did you say?"

"Your floor is just dirt; where did the wood go?"

At first, his question seemed odd, but then she realized that Lucas must have lived in a home of nobility. She smiled at him and replied, "Lucas, our floor has always been dirt, never wood."

"Do you like it this way?" He asked.

< 70 >

"I have never known it any other. I guess that makes it acceptable to me."

Lucas smiled and continued eating his stew. Angelia watched him for a few moments. She realized she was sharing her meal with a lost child of nobility. She thought that nobility had never been in her home, and she and Percival had both come from peasant families, indentured servants who worked in the fields for the nobles. Somehow, she knew that finding Lucas was not a fluke but some part of God's grand plan. She and Percival had never questioned their places in society; they found love and happiness regardless of their positions. But she could not help but wonder what God had in mind for her, her family, and this small lost boy.

Lucas finished his stew and politely asked, "May I have more?"

His question tugged her back into the moment. "Of course, my dear. Eat all you want. I have made much more than usual." She thought about what she had just said. She made more stew in anticipation of having a hot meal for Percival and his parents when they returned later in the evening, but she did not anticipate feeding a small boy too. She hurried to the stew, scooped more into Lucas's bowl, and placed it on the table before him.

"Thank you again, Madam," Lucas said, looking into her eyes. She smiled at him, looked at his large, bright eyes, and thanked God for allowing her to find him and save him from whatever was out there.

"You are most welcome, Lucas."

The thought of an evil man lurking in the darkness caused a chill to run up her spine. She walked to the open window, carefully drew in the wood shutters, and placed the sizeable wooden latch over them, locking them into place. She walked to the door, lifted a wooden crossbeam, and put it on iron hooks on either side of the door. She felt a moment of peace and safety. She walked over to Faith, who was having

< 71 >

difficulty feeding herself. Angelia smiled and said, "My sweet little faith, I am sorry I left you to fend for yourself. Let mommy help you."

She took the spoon and began to feed the little girl. After a few bites, Faith began to nod. Angelia smiled at her precious little girl and wondered how she could survive without her. The thought intensified in her heart at how Lucas's mother must feel not having her baby safely home with her. She looked at Lucas and noticed that he had finished eating his second bowl of stew, and his head was lying on the table, sound asleep. She gently wiped the face of Faith and held her for a moment until she was sleeping. Angelia looked across the room at the small bed and determined it could place children in it. She carefully laid Faith on the bed. She then lifted Lucas from his chair and snuggled him tightly against Faith. She lifted a small blanket and placed it over both. A lump swelled in her throat as she looked at the sleeping children.

When Percival returned, she knew they would find a way to get Lucas back home to his family. She walked over to the fire, raised the pot, and placed another log into the fire. She sat in the rocking chair and lifted to her lap the heavy wool yarn and a half-completed sweater that had been folded in a basket under the table. As she worked on the shirt, thoughts raced through her mind. It had been hours since Percival had gone to find his parents. It seemed as though he had been gone much longer than they had anticipated. The tiny home was quiet except for the crackling sounds of the fire and the faint breathing of the children asleep on the bed at her feet. The night was tranquil. It seemed odd to Angelia that she could not hear the familiar sound of crickets chirping. Suddenly she was startled by the sound of dogs barking off in the distance. She considered the possibilities; perhaps it was a skunk, a raccoon, a giant rat, or some other creature of the night. The barking continued for a few moments and then stopped. She listened intently but could no longer hear the dogs or anything else.

< 72 >

The quiet eeriness caused goose bumps on her arms. She put her sewing away and walked over to the kitchen. After a few moments of rummaging through one of the bulky jars, her hand found what she was looking for. It was a large knife, the sharpest she had. She cautiously held the handle and walked back to her rocking chair. She sat in the chair, pulled a small blanket over her legs, and placed her arm on her lap with her fingers clenched around the knife handle. She closed her eyes and tried to rest, expecting that Percival would be home any moment and all would be well.

Within moments the hypnotic sound of cracking fire caused her to sleep. An hour passed, and a startling scream a few houses away woke her. She jumped from the chair, her hand still clutching the knife, which she instinctually raised above her head in an attacking motion. She looked around the dim, fire-lit room and saw no one but her and the children. She wondered if the scream was real or a dream. She walked toward the closed window and placed her head on it. She could hear the distant sounds of a desperate woman crying. She seemed to be lamenting the death of a child. She could also hear a man attempting to console the woman as she listened. After a few moments, she recognized the voices. Rebecca and Adam another young couple with two small children, five-year-old Tabitha and a one-year-old named Lance. Angelia wanted to unlatch the door and run to her friends, but something told her to stay put. A few moments later, she heard more voices, obviously, the voices of other community members who had gone to offer help. The commotion lasted nearly an hour, and Angelia still had no idea what had happened. She wondered if the child was attacked by the same man who had accosted Lucas. She heard two voices walking toward her house. She recognized both. She stood, still clutching the knife in one hand; she unlatched the door with the other and slowly opened it just enough to peer through and look onto the pathway in

< 73 >

front of seven tiny houses and the center of the Shire. She saw two young men walking along the path. She called out to them.

"Excuse me, Mathias, is that you?"

A voice responded, "Yes, ma'am, it is I?

"What is the matter?" Angelia asked.

"Oh, it is very sad. It is Rebecca Stoal; her baby is dead."

The words baby and dead rang in her head, and she was horrified at the thought of such a tragedy.

"Are you sure the child is dead?"

"Oh, yes, ma'am. We saw her with our own eyes, and it was awful how her mother just held her and wept. The child had hideous black pustule things on her face."

The other boy added, "We have never seen anything like it. Just about the whole shire is at the Stoal's house, trying to comfort them the best they can. It is a real tragedy, a real tragedy indeed."

The description caused Angelia to become nauseous. She quickly closed the door. When she turned around, she was startled to see Lucas standing at her feet.

"It is the plague! We are all going to die!" He stated.

"Nonsense!" Angelia responded. "Now, you need to lie back down and sleep."

Lucas stood and shook his head.

"If we do not leave now, it will find us, and we will die."

"Lucas, we cannot just leave. It is dark; where would we go?"

"It does not matter where we go; we just need to get far from here."

"Lucas, Percival will be home any minute. I cannot leave without him; he will know what to do."

Just then, another scream came from a different direction, only a few houses away. Angelia immediately recognized the voice; Amanda Swift, her dear friend she had

< 74 >

known since childhood. "Oh, my goodness, Lucas, it is Amanda. Something terrible is wrong." Angelia reached for a shawl and wrapped it around her shoulders. "You stay here with Faith, and I will return shortly, I promise."

"You cannot keep that promise," Lucas said while shaking his head.

"If you go to her, the plague will get you too. And then you will bring it here and give it to Faith and me."

Angelia closed the door, bolted it, leaned against it, and slowly slid down until she sat on the floor. She began to cry, dropping the knife and holding her face in her hands. Lucas walked over to her and placed his hand on her shoulder to comfort her.

"Angelia, we must leave. It is not safe here."

"Lucas, we cannot leave. Where would we go, and how would Percival find us when he got back?"

"Your husband is not coming back."

Angelia screamed, "Do not say that! He is coming back!" She demanded.

Lucas puckered his lips and breathed heavily, trying not to cry as he said, "I am sorry, Angelia, but I do not believe he is coming back."

Angelia began to cry. The noise woke Faith, and she began to cry. Lucas walked to Faith, picked her up, and took her to her mother. Angelia held her in her arms for a moment and then reached her arm to Lucas. He took her hand, and she pulled him next to her and the baby. Lucas began to sob.

"I do not want you to die, Angelia. I do not want Faith to die."

Angelia tried to regain her composure and remain strong. "Lucas, we are not going to die."

"Then you must believe me when I tell you we must leave and get far from here."

Angelia tried to control her emotions. The thought of leaving anywhere in the dark of night was terrifying, almost as

< 75 >

frightening as the sounds coming from the houses in the Shire. An idea came to her. There was a place they could go. She remembered the monastery of St. Jude about two leagues up into the hills. She had not been there for years but knew that monks were there who would take them in. As she considered making the journey, she struggled with the idea of simply leaving her home based on the ranting of a small boy. What if he was wrong, she thought, but what if he was right? She needed something more than the cries of two people in the night to convince her that some mysterious plague had entered her village. She pleaded for God to help her know what to do. She silently asked him to give her some kind of sign. Before she could finish the thought, another scream rang out just two houses down. She instantly knew the voice of Agatha Lot, an elderly woman of forty-five. Agatha lived with her husband of thirty years, Daniel. Agatha continued to scream his name ending with "Oh dear God, no! Please, dear Lord, no!" Angelia knew that Lucas was right, and God did indeed give her a sign. She quickly stood with the two children. She rushed to a small basket next to the door, pulled out a small wool blanket, and wrapped it around Faith's shoulders. She ran into the bedroom, returned with an oversized coat, and placed it on Lucas. It belonged to Percival, the sleeves were several inches too long, and the coat nearly dragged to the ground as Lucas wore it. Angelia felt a rush of adrenaline that allowed her to keep calm. She opened a small drawer in the kitchen and laid a cloth on the counter. She opened a cupboard, took a loaf of bread, wrapped it in the fabric, then placed it in a bag and draped it over her shoulder. She walked back to the door, picked up the knife, and carefully slipped it into the side of her skirt.

"Lucas, can you walk beside me as I carry Faith?"

"Yes, ma'am."

She opened the door, looked from side to side, and hurried Lucas around the back of the tiny house. Behind the house was an open horse stall made of thin slatted wood and a

< 76 >

thatch roof. She sat the children down and quickly saddled the horse. Afterward, she lifted Lucas onto the horse, handed Faith, and jumped on the animal. She placed Faith in front of her and Lucas behind her.

"Lucas, hold me tight and do not let go. I do not want you to fall from the horse."

Lucas wrapped his arms around Angelia. She tugged the reins and led the horse to the dirt path. Although it had been years since she had been to the monastery, she believed she knew the way. She was relieved as a full moon began to rise on the horizon, providing a measure of light. She kicked the horse on the flanks causing it to gallop. It wasn't long until the shire was quite a distance behind them. As they rode, Angelia felt a confirmation that she had made the right decision, but something still seemed out of balance. Two-thirds of the way and one hour into the trip, Angelia decided to rest the horse. She lifted the children onto the ground and sat them on a large rock next to the path. She then led the horse to a small stream on the other side of the trail. After the animal had been watered, she returned to the children who were snuggled against one another on the rock. She lifted Faith, kissed her on the cheek, and placed her on the horse. Faith leaned over into the heavy main and wrapped her arms around the neck of the horse.

"Hold on, sweetheart, while I help Lucas up."

Suddenly a sound rustled in the bushes; Angelia turned and faced the man who had taken Lucas. Before she could react, he slugged her, knocking her to the ground. The uproar startled the horse, which began to run uncontrollably down the path as Faith held on. Angelia, barely conscious, turned from her back to her side. She screamed at the horse, realizing it had run away with her three-year-old daughter. Lucas yelled, "Angelia!" As he recognized the man. The man leaned over and raised his arm to hit Angelia again. Lucas jumped on the man's back, grabbed his arm, and began kicking the man and screaming. The man

< 77 >

stood, caught Lucas with his right hand, and flung him against a tree.

The impact knocked the wind out of Lucas. As he tried to catch his breath, he saw the man turn back to Angelia. Lucas tried to scream again but suddenly felt his body numb as his eyes closed into blackness. The man straddled Angelia and began to slap her face with the front then back of his hand. She struggled to free herself, but her attempts made him angrier, and he continued to hit her harder. He started ripping her clothing. She knew his intentions, but she valued her chastity and would fight till her dying breath to protect it. The more she resisted, the harder he hit. She knocked him off her momentarily, but he quickly regained his position over her and continued ripping her clothing. Her strength was waning, and her vision was becoming impaired as swelling began to encompass her eyes. He tried to pin her arms under his knees, but she could free one of them enough to dig her fingernails deep into the side of his face. He screamed in pain as his blood dripped onto her head and neck. He yanked her upper clothing entirely from her body, but she continued to fight. Finally, he held her hands together and slammed his tight fist into her right cheek several times until her body went limp. His breathing was heavy and erratic. He opened his tunic, tore her dress, and completed his brutal assault on her flaccid body. Afterward, he walked over to Lucas, picked up his unconscious body, ripped off the oversized coat, and draped him over the back of his horse. He bound his hands and feet and secured his body to the horse.

"This is the last time you escape from me!"

One of the monks jumped from his bed and ran to the window. He signaled another monk who had also been startled awake to join him. They noticed a panting horse below as they looked out the window and down the path of four floors. Upon

< 78 >

closer inspection, one of the monks realized that a small child was hanging onto the horse's neck. The monks quickly dressed, woke the others, and ran down to the horse. One of the monks grabbed the reins to steady the horse while the other gently removed the crying child when they arrived at the horse. They looked around but did not see anyone. One monk led the horse into the stable and closed the door behind it. He then joined the other monk who took the child inside. They tried to quiz little Faith, but she only repeated "Mommy" repeatedly. It was apparent that something terrible had happened. Two more monks gathered with the first two.

"Dom Gordon, what shall we do?"

"I am not sure, Brother Richard, but it would seem that this child's mother is out somewhere alone and hurt."

"Alone and hurt? What causes you to come to that conclusion?"

"Surely a mother would not intentionally leave her daughter unattended and saddled to a running horse?" Stated Dom Gordon.

"You are quite correct, as usual. What shall we do?"

Dom Gordon thought for a moment. As the monastery's Father, he knew that it was his responsibility to keep the monks safe, but it was also his responsibility to be Christ-like in all things, and he knew that Christ would not abandon a woman in distress.

"If we wait until morning, it may be too late to rescue her mother."

"Are you suggesting we leave the child and head off into the night after her mother, whose whereabouts are unknown to us?"

"Yes, that is what I am suggesting." He motioned for the other monks.

"Go and tell the others what has happened. Take the child and see that she has warm clothes, food, water, and whatever she needs. Brother Richard and I will take two horses

< 79 >

down the road for a distance to see what we find." The other monks acknowledged him, took the girl, and headed back into the monastery. Dom Gordon had gathered all 15 monks and read them a letter from the Pope earlier that day. The letter was addressed to all spiritual leaders of the Church. It discussed the seriousness of the sickness that had begun to spread throughout the land. At the time he sent the letter, more than half of the population of France had already succumbed to the disease, and things were getting worse. The letter was hand-copied and sent to every monastery, Abbey, Church, and official Church office in Europe. He encouraged the priests to tend to the flocks but to use caution and avoid personal contact with their parishioners. He told the nuns and the monks to continue their sacred responsibilities and prevent the outside world at all costs. He said that it was essential that God's holy records be preserved to be a guide and a light unto future generations. He acknowledged that many priests, cardinals, monks, and other Church leaders had already died of the plague. Of these, he said, *"From time to time and generation to generation, God has taken his servants according to his will. Some are taken in their youth, others in their old age, but always according to the Holy Will of the Almighty."* He concluded by saying, *"God will preserve those who have been consecrated to officiate in his Holy Church, unto the manner, and number, needed to feed his sheep. We must not fear. We must be brave and a pillar to all of those in our stewardship, that their faith will not waiver, but become stronger, even unto death if by the will of God."*

Dom Gordon was very concerned by the accounts he had heard of the mysterious disease already attacking London, Bristol, and all of the port cities of England. He knew that death was making its way deep into the country land, and it was only a matter of time before it reached the monastery. The day before the letter arrived, two of his own had just returned from the small town of Elkenshire, the hometown of Percival's parents. They reported that they had barely escaped with their

< 80 >

lives, as the town officials had begun boarding shut homes of infected family members and then torching them, burning alive the sick and the well to stop the spread of the disease. One of the monks told of a man who had been boarded in his parent's home and how he screamed that he and they were well, that he had come to take them back to his shire. His screams were in vain as the tiny house burned to the ground. Dom Gordon knew the risks of leaving the monastery in the dark of night, but a strong feeling told him that the minor child's mother desperately needed their help. He and Brother Richard saddled their horses and started down the road. After fifteen minutes, Dom Gordon noticed something on the side of the road. He stopped his horse, dismounted, and cautiously walked toward the object.

"It is a woman!" He yelled. "Come, Brother Richard, I need your help. Brother Richard leaped from his horse and ran to the aid of Dom Gordon. The two knelt beside the body, lying face down with the head turned toward the left. It was evident that the woman had been severely beaten, and it was also apparent from her torn and missing clothing that she had been raped.

"Is she dead?" Brother Richard asked.

"I do not know. Help me turn her over to her back. The two men gently placed their hands on her shoulders and hips. After turning the body onto its back, Dom Gordon leaned his head over hers and placed his ear close to her lips. He held his head there for a moment, but all he could hear was the breathing of Brother Richard, who had leaned his head over Dom Gordon's. Dom Gordon lifted his head and motioned for Brother Richard to give him some room. He again placed his ear next to the lips of the woman. He prayed that she would be alive. His heart was beating rapidly with anticipation and hope. A few moments passed, and finally, he felt a faint breath. "She's alive!" He shouted in a loud but muffled whisper. "Go back to the monastery, get the cart, and bring two of the

< 81 >

brothers to help." He ordered. "I will stay here with her waiting for your return."

Brother Richard acknowledged and quickly returned to the monastery. As Dom Gordon waited, he wondered about the identity of the woman. He was sure she was the mother of the small girl, and it was apparent they had been attacked by someone, but why, other than the devilish crime of rape. He wondered what kind of man would do such a thing and how the little girl escaped. As he waited, he held the hand of the woman. He felt the slight warmth of her body; it was a reassuring sign that her health could return. He carefully draped the torn clothing over her exposed bosom, giving her a measure of dignity. He looked around and, seeing no one, offered a prayer. *"Dear merciful Father, please bless this unfortunate soul that she might recover both physically and emotionally from the ordeal she has experienced. Help me to understand this situation and what is expected of me."* He hesitated before closing his supplication and added, *"...and Father, if it is thy will, please help the perpetrator of this atrocious crime to suffer physical pain for his unrepentant sin of defiling one of thy daughters. Perhaps an abscess in his groin is a good place for his suffering to start!"* He thought for a moment and added, *"Father forgive me my anger; my heart aches for this suffering woman and her child. I know that thou art a God of mercy, love, and forgiveness."* He hesitated again. *"But if it be thy will, perhaps a little inflammation before the forgiveness."* He quickly mumbled the end of his prayer and enunciated, *"Amen!"* Almost simultaneously with his last word, he heard a soft voice.

"Where is my little Faith?"

Dom Gordon replied, "Madam, God will give you the faith you desire; you rest; help is on its way."

"My Faith, my little girl, where is she?"

Suddenly, he realized the faith she referred to was her little girl's name. He smiled at her, stroked her hair, and

< 82 >

reassuringly said, "Your little child has not been harmed. She is safe with us, and I will take you to her soon. Now please, rest."

She gently closed her eyes and slipped back into unconsciousness. Dom Gordon was relieved that the woman had woken for a moment; it gave him hope that she would recover.

Nearly half an hour passed, and Dom Gordon began to hear the sound of the wooden wheeled cart rolling toward them. He had held the hand of the woman the entire time. He prayed over her, asking God to heal her. Brother Richard and another monk walked behind the cart, pushing it by its large square handle. Two other monks walked behind them. The cart was a large rectangle-shaped flat vegetable cart with removable wooden sides. It later became known as a death cart, as communities began placing their dead on the vegetable carts to dispose of them in mass graves. All but the backsides were in place. The monks had placed hay in the cart and covered it with a blanket, making a comfortable bed. When they arrived, Dom Gordon supervised the lift and movement of the woman's body. Four of the monks gently placed her on the straw bed. After she was situated, they turned the cart and pushed it back to the monastery. Dom Gordon helped the men put her in bed on the main level of the monastery. He inquired of the small girl. Brother Simon reported that the girl was resting peacefully. Dom Gordon thought for a moment and instructed him to remove one of the drawers of the large dresser on the other side of the room. He told him to fill it with blankets and place it on the floor beside the bed. He then told him to carefully bring the girl and put her in the drawer. He excused all but Brother Richard back to their own beds for the evening.

"I will need your help, Brother Richard."

Dom Gordon was a tall, healthy-looking older man in his early fifties. He had a full head of hair, a handsome face, and a commanding jawline. He had been the Dom of the monastery for the last seven years; he was well respected and

< 83 >

loved by all monks. Before this calling, he served as a Priest for nearly thirty years in Brisbane. He was transferred to the monastery after allegations from a female parishioner who claimed he had touched her inappropriately. The truth was that the woman had made sexual advances toward him for several months, but he ignored her gestures and kept them quiet to keep from drawing embarrassing attention to her. Eventually, the woman felt scorned by the man she could not have; her revenge destroyed his reputation. Rather than defend himself and publicly tarnish her character, he asked to be transferred to an undisclosed location. The Church granted his request. Brother Richard had become a good friend. He entered the priesthood and became a monk at the age of nineteen. At age forty, he was a short, pudgy green-eyed man with a whole round face encircled with a red mutton chop beard that ended at the temples of his shiny bald head. He made up for what he lacked in handsome physical features: sweet, loving gentleness, humility, and a total lack of guile. Brother Richard nervously asked.

"What help can I render, Father?" He hoped Dom Gordon was asking for something spiritual rather than physical; somehow, he knew his hopes would not materialize.

"We must attend to her wounds, clean her, and find a clean robe to clothe her in."

Brother Richard acknowledged that statement of tending to her wounds, but the idea of cleaning and clothing a woman terrified him. Dom Gordon noticed the frightened look on Brother Richard's face and added, "Brother Richard, we must think of this as rendering aid to a person, not a man, not a woman."

Brother Richard looked at Dom Gordon and said, "I have no problem thinking not a man; it is the not a woman part that I am stressing over."

"I am sure you will overcome the stress. Just focus on the aid, not the body."

< 84 >

Brother Richard pulled a cloth from his robe and slowly wiped his sweating forehead. He carefully folded the fabric and placed it back in his robe. "I will fetch the robe while you tend her wounds and clean her parts…I mean body." He smiled and quickly left the room in search of a clean robe. Dom Gordon took a cloth from the drawer underneath a table where a large bowl of water had been placed. He dipped the material into the water and wiped the dirt, blood, and debris from the woman's face. After he had finished cleaning her face, he discovered her beauty. He offered a silent prayer that God would allow him to fulfill the task without the temptations of physical attraction to the woman. After the prayer, he cleaned her body with the cloth, dumping it from time to time in freshwater. He again felt rage toward the attacker, who left cuts, dark bruises, and marks all over her body. He gently uncovered the torn top, revealing her nakedness. He wished there were nuns nearby who could complete this uncomfortable and awkward task. He used the advice he had given Brother Richard and focused on the aid, not the body. A few minutes later, Brother Richard arrived back in the room. He had draped three robes over his arms, unsure which would fit her the best. He placed the robes on an oversized chair next to the bed. He turned and faced Dom Gordon and the sleeping woman. He was shocked to discover that all her ragged, dirty, and torn clothing had been removed. More shocking was that Dom Gordon had placed smaller-sized holy books on her breasts and private parts.

He turned away, covered his eyes, and said, Oh, Dom Gordon, I do not believe that I am up to the task of dressing this woman. Indeed there is someone else."

"Nonsense!" Stated Dom Gordon. "Focus, focus, focus, and we will have her clothed before you know it."

Roger slowly turned and looked at her body. Her breathing had returned to normal, and the books moved up and down with her breaths. He cocked his head and slowly read the title of one of the books on her breast.

< 85 >

"You covered her breasts with the Apocrypha writing of Saint Ruth, one of the most beautiful women in the Old Testament? If you were going to Old Testament writings, why did you not choose Samson after his eyes were put out? Oh dear Father above, help me NOT to see clearly now."

He made the sign of the cross, turned, picked up the largest black robe, and tossed it over the woman's body. Dom Gordon forced his lips together to suppress his laughter. The monks took about fifteen minutes to slide the robe over her body, gently covering her with a warm blanket. Both were relieved when the task was completed. Dom Gordon thanked Brother Richard and bid him good night. Dom Gordon pulled up another oversized chair and placed it beside the bed. He slumped into the chair, looked at the child, then at her mother, closed his eyes, and slept until morning.

< 86 >

Chapter Six Notes

Monks were some of the most vulnerable to wandering vandals who had either escaped the plague or not yet succumbed to it.   Monasteries were known for possessing much food, provisions, and often riches. They were targets for those who would kill regardless of the victim.

< 87 >

Chapter Seven
Salvation

"Courage is a kind of salvation."
Plato

July 1349
(Out of the forest and into the Shire.)

The blood had rushed to his head, causing pain and nausea. He felt tense and twisted. The wet, sweaty smell of horses permeated the air. It took a moment until he realized he was tied hand and foot and laid like an old blanket over the back of a horse. His chest was bruised and sore from the weight of his slumped body banging against the horse as it galloped. He moaned and tried to loosen his hands, to no avail. He tried to kick his feet lose, also without success.

"Be still back there, and I will untie ya." Shouted the voice of the man in the saddle.

Lucas heard the voice, but the horse's flanks and grassy trail below were all he could see. Suddenly the horse came to a stop. The man jumped from the horse and pulled Lucas to the ground head first. The unexpected halt and crash to the ground flung Lucas onto his stomach. The landing was not as bad as the pain of hanging over the horse. Fortunately, he landed in an expansive grassy area with soft soil. His head was still throbbing from the blood rush and knuckle punch he had received a few hours earlier.

"You have been out cold for almost three hours. I guess that it was pretty hard."

The man started laughing and taunting Lucas. He slid his foot under Lucas and turned him to his back.

< 88 >

"I would wager you wish you were big enough to fight me, little man?"

"I do not even know your name, sir. If I am going to fight someone, I should at least know their name."

The man began to laugh louder. His laughter continued for several moments.

"Kid, you make me laugh. I am at least five times your size, yet you have enough spunk to tell me you're gonna fight me." His laughter continued. Lucas turned his head away from the man.

"My name is Allard." He hesitated and then said, "And your name is Lucas." He knelt, grabbed Lucas's face with his right hand, and turned it toward him as he spoke. "I heard your pretty mother speak it many times when we were back in the barn at that big castle you live in, and I will bet she has cried many tears wondering where her little boy has gone."

"She wasn't my mother. She was the wife of my brother Michael, and he will find you and kill you, just like he killed your brother."

Allard slapped Lucas across the face, bloodying his lower lip.

"Shut up, child!" He stood to his feet, looked down at Lucas, and pointed at him. "There will be no more speak of that! Do you hear me?" Lucas turned his head away. Allard kicked him again in the ribs. Lucas tried to keep quiet, but the pain made it difficult. He began to sob quietly.

"Why have you tied my hands and feet? Are you afraid that I will hurt you?" Lucas asked.

Allard laughed again. "You could not hurt me, child."

"Then untie me unless you are afraid of me?" Allard shook his head.

"Yes, I will untie you because it will not look like you are my child if I ride into town with you tied to the back of my horse, now will it?"

< 89 >

He pulled his knife from his tunic, leaned over, and cut the ropes on his hands and feet of Lucas.

"It will never look like I am your child." Lucas matter of factually stated.

Allard smiled, revealing blackened and missing teeth. "Oh, and why is that?" He asked

"No one would believe that any woman would bear your child."

Allard laughed again. "You are quite the little entertainer, are you not? I have had many women and, most likely, many children. Surely none as weak and pale as you."

Lucas looked away as if ignoring the comments. Allard continued to speak.

"You think that you are better than me just because you lived in a big castle with a large estate. Well, you are not. You are no different from me. We are both Anglo-Saxon, with white skin and red blood. The only difference between you and me is that your father's bloodline was murdered and plundered for kings and received nobility status. However, my people were the poor and brave who fought against people like yours. I have every right to the riches and fortune that your bloodline stole from mine. God is leveling the playing field by bringing this plague, killing off the nobility. The peasants will rise and take what is rightfully theirs."

Lucas answered, "I did not live in a big castle, it was a house, and it belongs to my grandmother, and she never murdered or plundered anyone. My father was a great man, and many people loved my father, who was kind and fair to everyone, including peasants like you."

Allard spat on Lucas and yelled, "I am not a peasant. My name Allard means noble and brave!"

"A noble and brave man would never steal or kill. Your father may have named you an infant, but surely he would take your name away today if he knew what you have done with it as a man."

< 90 >

Lucas turned away and tightened his sides, anticipating another rib kick. Lucas waited a moment and breathed slowly, anticipating the pain. The kick never came. Lucas slowly turned his head and looked up at Allard, who had turned the other way.

"I have never killed anyone who did not deserve it." He said in a low voice, almost under his breath.

"What about Angelia? Did you kill her?" Lucas asked. He winced again, expecting to have hit another nerve with what appeared to be a volatile man.

"The woman is alive. That is all I know."

The statement relieved Lucas. Until that moment, he had assumed that Allard had killed her. Allard walked to the horse and tightened the saddle. He took the horse by the reins and walked to a tree close to a stream a few steps. The horse lowered its head and began to drink the water. Allard tied the reins to a tree and turned back toward Lucas. He sat on the grass a foot from Lucas. The moon was full, and its brightness illuminated the sky, appearing more day than night. Sunrise was only moments away.

"What kind of name is Lucas?" Allard asked.

Lucas thought for a moment, and then a memory flowed from his mind. He was a toddler, learning to read and write. It was a cold evening. He was lying in his bed. Someone was closing the large bedroom window and drawing the curtains. It was his father. Lucas smiled as his father turned, and their eyes met. William slowly walked back to the bed and knelt above his little son. "Father, why did you name me Lucas?" William smiled and said. "My son, you were a miracle in my life. Your mother and I never thought she could bear a child, and God put you in her womb. The day you were born was the happiest day of my life. It was as if darkness had become light. I had known your name before you were born. Lucas means..." Lucas looked at Allard and said.

"Bringer of light. My name means bringer of light."

< 91 >

Allard smiled, looked at Lucas and then toward the emerging sunrise and said, "How appropriate, let there be light."

Allard stood and pulled Lucas to his feet.

"Come bringer of light, there is a small town ahead. Surely some kindly woman will feed a poor lost father and son."

He untied the horse, climbed its back, and flung Lucas up and behind him.

"Now hold on tight, son; daddy would not want you to fall and hurt yourself, now would he?"

He laughed, kicked the horse in the flanks, and it began to run toward the small, quiet little town.

~*~*~

It took about fifteen minutes to make it to the outskirts of Brantley, a small village of approximately three hundred and fifty residents. The hillside town was about a two-hour ride from the city of Gloucester, England. Most homes were on the other side of the town, intertwined in tree-lined streets at a lower elevation, making the commerce area much higher than the residential. As they approached, the town buildings appeared on either side of the main street. The buildings were primarily narrow two-story rock structures tightly shoved together, making a cramped façade and hodgepodge of the industry. Allard slowed the horse as they drew closer to the edge of the main street. It appeared that the town was still asleep. Nothing seemed odd or out of place, especially since the sun had just begun to rise. Allard looked from side to side of the street as the horse walked along the lonely, quiet road. Lucas wanted to scream for help, but he knew doing so would only bring more pain to Allard's hands. He thought about Allard's comment about people not believing that Lucas was his son. He never asked Allard why he wanted people to believe

< 92 >

such a thing. He wondered what Allard had in mind but did not want to ask him, at least not now. The horse continued to walk past shop after shop.

Most of the window shades had been drawn. Lucas noticed an odd smell that seemed to be flowing from somewhere ahead. He did not know the aroma, but the closer they headed to the source, the more pungent it became. It smelled like a skunk, burning leather, wet hay, or... Suddenly both Lucas and Allard recognized an odor streaming in the air. It was the smell of burnt flesh. The eerie quiet now took on another feeling. Allard realized that the desolate town around them was not just asleep but something much more menacing. They continued to move along the road, still not seeing any sign of life. Allard noticed a sign in a window ahead on the right. He stopped the horse and looked at the sign. The letters seemed familiar, but he did not know how to read them. He looked over his shoulder at Lucas, who was looking at the other side of the road. He asked, "Lucas, can you read?"

"Yes," Lucas replied.

"Then look at the sign on this window. What does it say?" Allard said while turning his head toward the window. Lucas turned and looked. He felt his heart race, and the hair stood on the back of his neck.

"Well. What does it say?" Allard demanded.

"Plague. It says plague!" Lucas said as his body began to shake.

Allard sat straight in the saddle, slapped the reins, and commanded the horse to run. As their speed increased, more and more signs appeared on doors and windows of businesses on both sides of the street. Although Allard could not read, he could now recognize the word "plague," which seemed to be all around them. As the horse passed the last building, Allard felt a sense of relief. Then he realized that they would soon be coming to the neighborhoods and that the plague did not just infect the business district but that it had to have affected the

< 93 >

entire town. The burning smell became more intense. Just
ahead, the main street appeared to end abruptly, but as they
moved closer, they noticed that the road began to slope
downward. The residential area was well below the city.
Allard stopped the horse at the top of the street just before the
slope. The horse turned sideways, agitated and hesitant, as
Allard struggled to contain it. The animal finally calmed.
Allard and Lucas both looked down at the homes. Suddenly
they both knew the source of the smell as they looked upon
scores of smoldering home sites, most burned to the ground,
some chimneys still standing. Allard covered his nose as he
recognized burying bodies in the rubble.

"We cannot stay here!" Lucas said

"I know that. But we need food."

"Surely you do not want to eat anything we find here?"
Lucas said, concerned that Allard would disregard the death and
destruction for his stomach.

"Shut up, boy! I know there is nothing for us here. But
there may be something down there." He pointed toward the
burning homes. "And we'll just have to look and see." He
slapped the horse, and they continued down the road. The smell
nearly overcame them as they came upon the first smoldering
home. Lucas tried to bury his head in the back of Allard.
Allard held his tunic over his nose with his left hand and the
reins with his right. They passed burnt carcasses on either side
of the road, some were household pets, and others were the
charred bodies of men, women, and children. The further they
traveled into the village, the more intense the sight and smell
became. Allard realized, after twenty minutes, that everything
had been destroyed in the fire, and there was no chance of
finding food. He wondered how all of the homes could have
been destroyed by fire. Obviously, someone had to have started
the fires. Someone had to have barricaded people in their
homes. He realized that whoever did this must have done so to
prevent the plague from traveling further. It occurred to him that

< 94 >

they were not safe riding through the area, especially if the arsonist was somewhere watching them and assuming them carriers of the plague. He yelled at Lucas,

"Hold on tight, kid; we are leaving this town."   The horse ran until the little town was miles behind them.

Allard slowed the horse as they approached another town, but this town was familiar to him; it was his hometown, the city of Gloucester. He brought the horse to a stop.

"Why have we stopped?" Asked Lucas.

Allard waited a few moments before replying. He had a past in Gloucester that made it dangerous to return. He wanted to choose the right words before speaking.

"I know this place. It is not good?"

"How do you know it? Have you been here before? Do they have the plague?" Lucas asked somewhat excitedly.

"I lived here, and no, they do not have the plague."

"Then it must be safe to find food here. I am hungry and know that you must also be hungry."

"Be quiet, boy, while I think." He climbed off the horse, leaving Lucas still sitting behind the saddle. He reached over to a leather bag tied to the saddle. It slowly opened and peeked in, trying to cover it enough that Lucas could not see, and Lucas was able to see that it was filled with knives and shiny gold and silver pieces.

"Did you steal those things from people in this town?" Lucas asked.

Allard turned toward Lucas and slapped him off the horse, and he landed on his back and rolled to his stomach when he fell.

"You ask too many questions, boy, and one of these days, you're going to ask a question that gets you killed. Also, the answer is yes; I took those coins from people who had more than they needed anyway. I got my horse from a stupid merchant who left it untied from his cart." He laughed. "I got

< 95 >

most of my knives and a bag of coins from nobles. No more questions!" He shouted.

Lucas turned his back, dusted himself off, and propped himself on his elbows. The morning sun was beginning to get hot, and he was thirsty. He kept quiet for several minutes and watched Allard pacing back and forth, never walking more than four to five steps from the horse. Lucas knew that if the town was not overcome with the plague, there must be another reason Allard hesitated to enter. Finally, Allard tied the horse to a tree, walked toward Lucas, and sat in the grass next to him. He looked straight ahead toward the town for several minutes. Lucas noticed him breathing heavily. He watched as his lips moved, and he mumbled to himself. It looked like he was having a conversation with someone. Every now and then, he would growl, grind his teeth, and argue under his breath. The conversations stopped, and Allard looked at Lucas.

"We both need food. Here is what we will do. There is a small market just on this side of town. We will ride close to it, and I will take you off the horse. You will take this bag...." Allard pointed to an empty leather bag tied to the other side of his horse. "...and you will steal as much fruit and bread as you can stuff into the bag."

Lucas sat up and said. "But I am not a thief, and stealing is wrong. I will not do it."

Allard shoved his face inches from Lucas's face. He yelled, "You will do whatever I tell you to do!" He raised his knife and placed it against Lucas's throat. "Do you understand me, boy?"

Lucas felt his heart beating; he wanted to cry but knew he needed to be strong. "Yes," Lucas said in a shaking but controlled voice. "I will do it."

"Good! Stick to the plan, or hunger will be the least of your pain!" Allard said in a stern voice.

They slowly road toward the town. After a few minutes, they came on the market, just as Allard said. He looked over

< 96 >

his shoulder at Lucas and said, "Remember the plan. Get the food into the bag. I will be waiting behind the trees. When the bag is full, come, find me. We will quickly ride out of here. Understand?"

"Yes, I understand."

As Allard leaned to the right to untie the bag, Lucas leaned around him and saw the bag tied to the saddle's left. He slowly lifted the leather flap and slipped his hand into the bag, grabbing as much of the coin as his hands could hold. Allard finished untying the other bag and began to turn to the left. Lucas quickly pulled his hand from the pouch unnoticed. He carefully placed the coins into a pocket inside his tunic. Allard stopped the horse, hid behind a grove of trees, and took Lucas off the horse.

"Remember Lucas, I will be able to see you the entire time. If you try anything, I will kill you." Lucas acknowledged him. Lucas started to walk when Allard grabbed his left arm and pulled him up to his face. "And just to ensure you are listening, see that pretty little girl holding her mommy's hand?" Lucas looked toward the burgeoning crowd in the market. He saw the little girl and her mother. "I will slit her throat and her mother's too! Do I make myself clear, boy?"

"Yes, sir. I will do what you have asked of me." Allard released Lucas. He took his position with the horse behind a grove of trees and watched as Lucas walked toward the market. Lucas slowly made his way into the center when he reached the crowd. This made it difficult for Allard to see. At first, he became irritated, assuming that Lucas was attempting to escape, but then he saw Lucas putting a loaf of bread into the bag. Allard smiled and said. "Good boy. Just as I taught you." Lucas disappeared into the crowd again, but Allard did not worry.

Several of the merchants had gathered around Lucas. They all looked confused and concerned. One man helped him pack the items into his bag. Lucas noticed the large cart but no

< 97 >

horse. Lucas asked, "Where is the horse for your cart, sir?" The man smiled at Lucas and replied,

"He was stolen from me, it is hard to pull the cart myself, but I thank God that I still have my cart."

The man handed Lucas two large red apples. "Here you go, son, and thank you."

Lucas turned and handed the man three large gold coins. The man looked at the shiny gold pieces and said,

"Oh dear, my boy. These coins are enough to purchase everything I own and then some. Surely you have smaller than this, do not you?"

The other merchants opened their hands, revealing the gold and silver pieces Lucas had given them. Lucas smiled at the merchants and said,

"Gentleman, it has been a pleasure doing business with you. My father is a wealthy and very generous man; he taught me that everything we have belongs to God, so none of these coins is mine anyway. Now they are yours, and do something good with them."

The last merchant hugged Lucas and wiped a tear from his eye. The others waved at him as he left the crowd. As Lucas emerged from the group, he saw Allard crouched behind the trees. He slowly walked toward him. Allard was smiling with great anticipation to eat the food that he thought Lucas had stolen. When Lucas arrived, Allard took the bag and slapped Lucas on the back.

"Good work, boy! Selling you off may not be such a good idea after all. Doesn't it feel good to get what you want right under the nose of someone who will not notice it missing anyway?" He laughed and smiled as Lucas quietly replied,

"Yes, it does; it really does."

The two ate for a few minutes, then mounted the horse and rode toward the next town. Lucas could tell that Allard was much happier now that his stomach was full, and he seemed more content. They rode for another hour along a worn dirt

< 98 >

road, and it was evident that the road was well traveled between the towns. Finally, it felt safe to ask another question since Allard seemed in a better mood with a full stomach.

"Where are we going?" Lucas asked.

"We are headed to Oxford, a nice little, educated town," Allard replied sarcastically.

"What did you mean when you said that you may not sell me off?"

Allard took a deep breath, turned, and looked over his left shoulder toward Lucas. He then placed his left hand on the leather saddlebag and rubbed it. He started to answer, stopped, and then said, "It is all business, boy. It is all business. Do not worry; you will be fine." He shook the reins, and the horse began to run faster. He said nothing more during the remainder of the ride to Oxford.

Lucas knew that Allard was evil and dishonest man with bad intentions. He thought for a while and then asked a silent prayer, *"Oh dear Father above. You have been so kind to me on my unexpected journey. I have escaped from this man twice, and now I ask that you help me escape again, only this time for good. Please let me know when and where?"*

Lucas felt a Pease come over him. Although he lacked a plan, he knew that somehow God would let him know what to do and how to finally escape from the grasp of Allard.

As they came to the town of Oxford, Lucas was amazed at the size and the many significant buildings and cathedrals. He had never seen such a big town with many enormous churches and schools. Within minutes of entering the city limits, the road became hard cobblestone. The city was busy with active commerce, and the streets were filled with people, merchants, horses, and carriages. Lucas remembered leaving Bristol and seeing signs of the plague, but here everything seemed normal; it did not appear that the plague had made its way to Oxford, at least not yet. Allard turned the horse down a street, traveled three blocks, and turned right onto another road.

< 99 >

He continued to direct the horse for several minutes. It was apparent that he had been to Oxford before. Lucas thought about Allard's response when he asked what he meant by selling him off. The words *"It is all business"* continued to echo in his head. Lucas realized what Allard had in mind. He knew that Allard had planned to sell him as a slave. The thought of being sold to a stranger and never reuniting with his family was terrifying. However, the task of finding his way back to Cardiff seemed daunting and overwhelming, but he knew he would instead try to find his home than become a slave.

Allard stopped the horse in front of a blacksmith's shop. He climbed off the horse, lifted Lucas off, and gently placed him on the ground next to him for the first time. He looked down at Lucas, raised an eyebrow, and whispered.

"Do not say a word, and stay put."

Allard turned back toward the blacksmith and said,

"I need you to check the shoes on my horse and give him some food and water. I will be across the street at that pub." He pointed to the pub. The man looked at Allard and said,

"I do not work for free. Pay up first."

Allard acknowledged the comment and turned toward the horse to lift the flap of the leather pouch. As his fingers touched the leather, he heard a loud ruckus approaching from around the corner. Screams, moans, and yelling grew louder. He quickly opened the leather pouch, pulled out one of his long knives, and held it to his side, concealing it against his tunic.

"What is that?" He asked the blacksmith.

"I believe it is another one of those groups of flagellants; it is the second one this week. The last group must have had over a hundred men."

"Flagellants? What the hell are flagellants?" Allard demanded.

< 100 >

"You know religious kooks who think that if they march a pilgrimage from one town to the next and beat themselves half to death with glass-laced whips, God will remove the plague."

"The plague? Is the plague here?"

"A few have been sick, but I haven't heard of any large outbreak." He looked around and continued. "I'm…we're…" motioning to other merchants." Not afraid of some supposed sickness entering our town. Now, do you need my services or do not ya?"

Just then, the front line of marchers turned the corner and began to pass in front of them. Allard was amazed at the number of marchers. The people wore torn clothing, mostly men with their torsos completely naked. Most had long sticks with leather straps tied to the end and shiny pieces of glass woven into the leather. As they chanted, they slapped their backs and howled in pain, spurting blood into the marching crowd and the crowds that had begun to line the street. As the line progressed, he noticed many priests and monks that had joined in. One priest was dragging a large wood beam cross over his shoulder, obviously, in the similitude of the cross Christ bore to his crucifixion. Allard was not a religious man, and the sight of what appeared to be religious fanatics was appalling to him. It was challenging to take his eyes off the progression. Lucas was also fixed on the scene. Most of the blood and show was ended by the fourth row of men. As the group continued to march, the remainder included priests, men, and women. Although these were not flogging themselves, they carried whips, ropes, chains, and small leave-covered branches, making as much noise as possible. The entire group covered just over two city blocks. As Lucas watched the people coming up at the end of March, he noticed a familiar face. He looked back at Allard and saw that he was transfixed and looking at the marchers toward the front. His heart began to race again, and he knew that the moment for his escape was at hand. He

< 101 >

swallowed deeply and then heard a distinct voice in his head say the words, *"Now, Lucas, Now!"*

A crowd gathered around Allard and Lucas; he knew he could easily slip into the crowd. He slowly moved away from Allard. When he was no longer in sight of Allard, he began to run toward the marching flagellants. As he went through the spectating crowd, he again saw the familiar face; it was a priest he knew well. He ran toward the man and yelled. "Father Flanagan! Is that you?" The priest turned and looked toward the voice. The moving crowd shoved Lucas further down the street.

He yelled again, "Father Flanagan!"

The priest tried to stop but was pushed by the marchers behind him. He finally made contact with the voice and the boy, and he was shocked when he realized who it was.

"Lucas? Is that you? What are you doing here?"

He shouted. "Where is your family?"

The priest continued to look for Lucas, but the moving crowd blocked his view of Lucas from him. Lucas was being pushed along the marching route. After a few moments, he gave up and refocused on the march. Lucas became lost in the crowd. Allard had not noticed that Lucas was missing. As the end of the marchers passed, the blacksmith held out his hand and said,

"Well, I have other things to do if you are not interested in my services."

Allard replied. "Wait, I am interested; give me a moment."

He turned back to the horse, reached into the leather pouch, and fumbled through the knives, searching for the coins. He was terrified as his fingers rustled through the bag without touching a single coin. He yanked the load off the horse, turned it upside down, and dumped the three knives to the ground. He shook the bag in complete panic and shoved his fingers into it again. He looked around the horse and through the dispersing

< 102 >

crowd of parade spectators, trying to find Lucas. He looked
back at the blacksmith, who still had his hand outstretched, and
then back at the crowd. His head pounded in complete anger
and terror.

He screamed, "LUCAS!"

< 103 >

Chapter Seven Notes

The Flagellants were religious zealots of the Middle Ages in Europe who demonstrated their religious fervor and sought atonement for their sins by vigorously whipping themselves in public displays of penance. This approach to achieving redemption was most popular during times of crisis. Prolonged plague, hunger, drought, and other natural maladies would motivate thousands to resort to this extreme method of seeking relief. Despite condemnation by the Catholic Church, the movement gained strength. It reached its most significant popularity during the onslaught of the Black Death that ravaged Europe in the mid-fourteenth century. Wearing white robes, large groups of the sect (many numbering in the thousands) roamed the countryside, dragging crosses while whipping themselves into a religious frenzy.

http://www.eyewitnesstohistory.com/pfflagellants.html

"In that same year of 1349, about Michaelmas (September 29), over six hundred men came to London from Flanders, mainly of Zeeland and Holland origin. Sometimes at St Paul's and sometimes at other points in the city, they made two daily public appearances wearing clothes from the thighs to the ankles but otherwise stripped bare. Each wore a cap marked with a red cross in front and behind.

Each had in his right hand a scourge with three tails. Each tail had a knot, and sometimes sharp nails were fixed through the middle. They marched naked in a file, one behind the other, and whipped themselves with these scourges on their naked and bleeding bodies. Four would chant in their native tongue, and another four would respond like a litany. Thrice they would all cast themselves on the ground in this sort of procession, stretching out their hands like the arms of a cross. The singing would go on, and, the one who was in the rear of those thus prostrate acting first, each of them, in turn, would step over the others and give one stroke with his scourge to the man lying under him. This went on from the first to the last until they had observed the ritual to the whole tale of those on the ground. Then, each wore his customary garments, always wore their caps, and carried their whips in their hands; they retired to their lodgings. It is said that every night they performed the same penance."

References:

This eyewitness account appears in Robert of Avesbury: E.M. Thompson (ed), Robertus de Avesbury de Gestis Mirabilis Regis Edwardi Tertii, Roll Series 1889, Cohn, Norman, The Pursuit of the Millennium: Revolutionary Millenarians and Mystical Anarchists of the Middle Ages (1970).

< 104 >

Chapter Eight
The Present, The Past
July 1349
"Come back. Even as a shadow, even as a dream."
—Euripides

As he stood staring out the window, a cold wind chill across the back of his neck startled him. At first, it was a slight shock, but then the sensation changed as the hair on the back of his neck began to stand. Although the gust of wind had long dissipated, the feeling lingered and slowly merged with the new impression. He closed his eyes for just a moment and quickly opened them brightly. Someone was there, standing behind him, and he knew it. At first, he assumed it was Monson. He slowly breathed in a familiar smell, an intoxicating scent, most definitely not the aroma of Monson or any man. What seemed like minutes was only seconds. His mind raced, anticipating who he would see the moment he turned. He closed his eyes and imagined whom he would like to see at that very moment. Of all the people he knew, family, friends, acquaintances, who would he like to see standing behind him? He closed his eyes and again breathed in the aroma; it was familiar, fresh, yet faint. Unexpectedly the feeling on the back of his neck changed to goosebumps. It became cold and taut as if his skin was tightening to form a barrier of protection against some type of lethal penetration. Suddenly his capricious imagination came to an abrupt end. He stood tall, took a deep breath, and said, "I know you are there. What do you want?"

He waited a moment for a reply. Feeling more in control, he asked again, this time with more challenge in his voice.

< 105 >

"I know you are there, so I will ask you one last time, what do you want?"

He listened for a response. He again felt a shiver overcome him but dared not move as if he was in a trance. The presence moved closer. He felt something pierce his personal space; this being or person leaned so close behind his head and near his left ear that he could almost feel the warmth of a soul. Then he heard a silent whisper accompanied by a slight soft breath,

"You! Only you…"

Michael broke the trance and spun around, reaching for the sword at his side. With his hand gripped to the sheath and now facing the voice that spoke to him, he saw no one, nothing but a dissolving golden mist leaving millions of small sparkling speckles in the air. The mist disappeared, and the familiar scent with it. *"Who was it?"* He thought. *"Who was there?"* He found himself shivering almost uncontrollably, a feeling he struggled quickly to squelch. When he regained complete control, and the shivering stopped, he felt his heart racing and beating so powerfully that he could see his chest move with each beat. He knew someone was there but knew not who it was. He closed his eyes and felt a slight moment of dizziness. When he opened his eyes, he found himself again gazing out the window. He shook off the odd feeling, turned, and looked behind and around the room. Everything seemed normal, quiet, and untouched. He looked back toward the window. The dizzying feeling returned; this time, he reached for the side of the windowpane and braced himself from falling over. He did not know what had happened but supposed it was a daydream. He brushed it off, closed his eyes, opened them again, took a deep cleansing breath, hesitated, turned, and left the room. He started down the hall and then quickly stopped. The feeling returned, and he knew it was not a dream this time. He slowly turned and looked back toward his bedroom. He had not entered the room since the day Elizabeth was buried. He left

< 106 >

everything the way it was, the bed unmade, her clothing draped over a chair, and morning water still in the bowl on the dressing table. He realized that he had just come from the room but did not remember entering the room. The door was closed. He reached for the knob, attempted to turn it, and spun without releasing the door. His final instructions after taking the body of Elizabeth to her coffin were to lock the door so that no one would enter again. He held the nob and applied slight pressure against the door to ensure it was still locked. He thought for a moment; he tried but could not fight off the odd feeling that seemed to encompass his entire body. He felt something slightly pressing him toward the door. He had vowed never to enter the room again and did not want to open the door. The thought of opening the door and walking into the room caused an unwanted emotional feeling to well up in his throat. He held the knob and leaned his head against the door. He tried to force this feeling away, but the lure was too intoxicating, great, and confusing. He removed his hand from the knob and reached for the chain hanging around his neck. As he held it with both hands, he slid the fingers of his right hand down the chain until he felt the key. He lifted the key out of his tunic and slowly inserted it into the lock hole. As he did so, he heard the clicking sounds of the lock releasing the door from its fixed position. He closed his eyes as he slowly pushed the door into the room. He knew that he was not prepared to enter the room. Too much had happened, too much pain, too much misery, too much death, too much guilt. He doubted he could see her clothing, hairbrush, or the depressed pillow where she last laid her head before leaving him. The house was hauntingly quiet; he knew he was alone and far from Jillian or Monson. He knew that no one would hear or see him enter the room. He entered as if it was breaking some rule or committing some kind of sin. It felt liberating and condemning simultaneously, a mixture of pleasure and pain. When the door was fully exposed, he slowly lifted his head. With his eyes still closed, he breathed in the

< 107 >

familiar scent again. He imagined her sleeping stretched and swept across the bed as she so enjoyed doing. A smile formed on his lips as the memories began to tease his mind. He lost himself in the moment, standing in the doorway, still holding the door's nob. Suddenly he was shocked out of his musing by the most disturbing sound, the sound of a bird. To his horror, he looked straight ahead and saw an open window and a small yellow bird perched on the window seal. It was chirping at him and flapping its wings. He saw the bird mocking him in his mind, laughing at his shortcomings and his horrible mistakes. He ran toward the creature, stretched his arm as far as it would extend, and swung at it. Suddenly, it appeared that everything was happening in slow motion where space and time seemed to hesitate and fight against reality. He overlooked the changing table in front of him. His body slammed into the table, his chest over the water bowl, and he continued to move forward, overturning the table and the objects upon it. His focus was on the bird. He yelled as the tips of his fingers grazed and slightly brushed the very edge of the yellow feathers. With three up-and-down swooping motions, the bird extended its wings and navigated its way around the danger and out the window. When his motion stopped, he found himself on the floor awkwardly wrapped over the small dresser, the bowl overturned and upside down next to his head. He felt rage, anger, and hate welling up deep within him. Just as the emotions were about to erupt in some unknown manner, he heard a voice, a soft and frightening voice laughing from the other side of the room. He hurriedly gathered himself and sat up to see who it was. His eyes grew large. His entire body was filled with great anxiety and fear. He knew the woman. She walked closer to him, kneeled, and reached out her hand toward him. She smiled and slowly shook her head. Her eyes were light blue and illuminating streaks of brightness towards him. Her skin was shimmering white, almost fluorescent.

"Are you alright?" She asked, still laughing softly.

< 108 >

He did not know how to respond. He squinted, stretched his face, rubbed his eyes, and looked at her again.

"What were you thinking running across the room like that? She asked.

"It is you." He said, not believing what he was seeing.

"But it cannot be you. You're not here."

She laughed again and reached both of her arms out toward him.

"Of course, It is me." She said while shrugging her shoulders.

"Who else would it be? And I am most definitely here."

Suddenly the brightness evaporated from her hair and her skin. She looked normal, healthy, and alive. He continued to look at her in disbelief. He desperately wanted to believe it was her; he wanted to believe that she was real and right next to him. He wanted to touch her, embrace her, kiss her lips, and once again take her in, but he hesitated. She leaned into him, her face just inches from his. She cocked her head to the side and smiled. They were kneeling and facing one another. He slowly lifted his right hand, gradually extended his fingers, and moved his fingers toward her face. He stopped before touching her as he felt the warmth of her skin and her breath on his fingertips. He knew it was impossible; somehow, his mind was playing a trick on him, and his eyes were in on it. He thought. But how could his mind produce warmth and breath from someone or something that wasn't real? He thought. She looked deep into his eyes. He slowly allowed the tips of his fingers to brush against her skin. At first, he slightly jerked away, let his fingers touch her face, followed the curve of her jaw and chin, and then watched as they lightly crossed over her lips. She gently parted her lips and kissed his fingers. She reached up with her left hand and cupped his hand. He could no longer question what was happening or hold himself back. He quickly reached up both arms, had her face in his hands, and brought his lips toward hers, stopping shy of contact. She leaned in,

< 109 >

pressed her lips against his, and they both embraced into a long and passionate kiss. His mind no longer thought about reality. At that moment, life stood still and time hung in the air, void of motion. Elizabeth was back; she was with him, defying all reason and logic. It was good, extraordinary, and unexplainable, but for Michael, explanations could come later. After several minutes of passion, Elizabeth stood to her feet and reached for Michael to rise and follow her. He took her hand and began to walk across the room with her. He noticed that the room was clean and tidy, the dress she wore was no longer lying on the chair, and the bed was freshly made. He looked back toward the window where the bird had once again escaped and noticed that it was closed and the latch was secured. Elizabeth held onto his face and turned his head away from the window and toward her. When they reached the bed, he stopped and stood still as she began to undress him. He was mesmerized, a willing partner, a loving husband, and a wanting man. The next thing he remembered was lying in bed on his back, his arm under her head snuggled against his. The room was dark, but he could scarcely make out his surroundings by the moonlight shining through the window. He slowly surveyed the room as he felt fatigue set in. He struggled to keep his eyes open as something odd caught his attention across the room and under the window. The dressing table was again upright as if it had never moved, but more peculiar was the bowl. It was sitting on the white crocheted doily, still filled with water, and the empty pitcher sat next to it. He felt a brief moment of fear, and then exhaustion took over; his eyes closed uncontrollably, and he slept.

The sun began to brighten the room. Everything was quiet and serene. He hesitated to open his eyes, even though he knew he was awake. As he lay on his back, he tried to gather himself, but his mind was cloudy and hazy. He reached his left hand to his face and gently rubbed his eyes. He started lifting his right hand but noticed it was under something. He had a quick rush of clarity overcome his mind and clear away the fog

< 110 >

and haze. He remembered everything; it was Elizabeth, he thought. She was with him, he recalled. They shared a night of love and passion, an incredible night that ended too soon. His right hand reached for her shoulder to gently squeeze and caress it, but the large pillow seemed to get in the way. He leaned his head to the right to look at her face. Yet, as he turned, he realized the only thing on his arm was a large pillow. He threw the pillow off the bed, sat up, and yelled, "Elizabeth! Where are you?"

He looked around the room. He saw the dressing table, the bowl of water, the pitcher, and her dress draped across the chair. The room was as it was the day she died. Nothing had changed. He had slept in their bed, and although the night seemed genuine, he began to recognize that it was all in his mind. He turned on his side, facing her side of the bed and the spot where he believed he had laid with her. He felt a tear escape his eye and run down the side of his face. What a horrible trick his mind had played on him, he thought. Now he had to relive losing her again. As he looked at the spot where she had once laid her yellow hair-covered head, he felt a fleeting moment of joy just thinking of her. He rolled to his stomach, reached his arm, and began caressing where she had been. As his hand moved across the mattress and up to the top, it brushed over something odd. It felt like dust or dirt. He began to brush it off the bed as it created a small cloud of golden glitter inches above the bed. He abruptly sat on the bed and watched as the golden cloud slowly disappeared. Was he awake this time, he thought or was he still in a dream? For a moment, it did not matter as he recalled with fondness the memories of the night before.

After dressing, he tidied the room and carefully made the bed. He fluffed the pillows just as Elizabeth always did. He

< 111 >

held the last pillow a moment longer and slowly inhaled the faint aroma of her scent. It all seemed so real, from the chill in the wind blowing through the window to the touch of her soft fingers, the feel of her silky hair, and the back of his hand tracing the curve of her cheek to the edge of her chin. He squeezed the pillow and gently placed it on the bed next to his pillow. He backed away from the bed, looked around the room one last time, and promised himself he would never again enter the room unless she called him there. He stood in the hall, held the door's handle, and gently pressed it shut. He placed his right hand on the door above his shoulder level, leaned his head against the door, and slowly ran his hand down the edge. He closed his eyes and felt a tear escape and run down the side of his cheek.

The moment ended almost abruptly when he heard the soft sound of a woman's voice humming a familiar melody. He began to follow the sound down the long hall. After passing several rooms, he realized that the music was coming from the opposite wing. He stopped and listened more closely. He recognized the soft voice; it was Jillian. At first, he felt disillusioned when he discovered that the voice was not that of Elizabeth. He turned back toward the stairway, but something stopped him. He had heard Jillian quietly singing in her room many times since his return without William, but this melody was different from what she usually sang. He decided to walk to her room. When he arrived at the door, he slowly turned the handle and quietly opened it. As the door brushed into the room, he saw Jillian standing on the other side. She appeared to be holding a baby against her breast. Upon closer inspection, he could tell that there was no child but that she was again dreaming. She seemed happy, and he did not want to disturb her. He was about to leave the room when Jillian slowly turned and leaned over as if she was placing the infant into a crib. He watched as she carefully covered the imaginary baby.

< 112 >

She stood over the crib and whispered, "I love you, little Sarah." She then walked a few steps, leaned down, and kissed what seemed to be another child's head. She smiled and said,

"Sleep now, my little man, and Michael will be here to play with you when you wake."

Those words pierced his soul. He made a fist and held it to his mouth, forcing his lips and nose into the fingers of his fist. He closed his eyes and held them tightly shut while slowly breathing in. When he opened his eyes, Jillian sat in her rocking chair, staring out the window. It was all he could take. He slowly closed the door.

The morning was still young when Michael walked into the kitchen. He noticed Monson leaning over the fire pit stirring food in a large pot as he entered the room. The aroma was pleasant but unusual for a morning meal. Monson heard Michael enter the room, but he continued his meal preparation as if he did not notice him. Michael pulled one of the large stools out from under the large preparation counter. He climbed onto the stool and swung around until his legs were under the counter's overhang. Monson still ignored him as he tossed in the last ingredients from his hand. Michael noticed a freshly baked loaf of bread on the counter and wondered how he missed its smell, an aroma that usually filled most of the estate. Perhaps his mind was focused on other things, he thought. He tore off a piece of the bread and slowly began to eat it. Monson turned around, looked at Michael, smiled, turned toward the sink, and began to wash the few utensils and dishes he used while preparing the soup.

What is it?" Michael asked.

"What is what?" Monson replied.

"The pot, what is in it?"

"Bean soup," Monson said while washing the dishes.

"For the morning meal?" Michael asked.

< 113 >

"No, it is for the afternoon meal. I made some bread; milk and honey are on the other counter." He pointed as he spoke.

"I am feeling tired, Michael, and I did not know if I would have the strength to make the afternoon meal later, so I decided to make it now. I will raise it above the fire and reduce the flames; it will simmer till noon."

His answer was soft and thoughtful. Michael knew something was bothering Monson but did not want to ask yet.

"Do you miss Laurie?" Michael asked as he looked off into the distance. He continued before Monson could respond.

"I mean, since she is gone, you now do all of the cooking too."

"Of course, I miss Mrs. Collins, but not because of the cooking. Understand me, she was a wonderful cook, and I miss her because she was my friend. We worked together in this estate for many years. She is like a sister to me. I would gladly do the cooking for the rest of my life if I could exchange that duty for having her back."

"Do you miss Ernest?"

Monson stopped washing, turned toward Michael, and said,

"Michael, why do you ask a question when you already know the answer?

Michael thought for a moment. He swallowed, lowered his head, and responded.

"I am sorry, Monson; I know how much they both meant to you. I do not know why I am asking you these questions; perhaps I just needed someone to talk to."

Monson took a small towel, dried his hands, and walked over to Michael, putting his hand on Michael's shoulder.

"I miss all of them very much. We were a family; we loved one another, all of us."

He paused and then continued. "Sometimes, I wonder why they are all gone, and I am still here. Nevertheless, I am

< 114 >

thankful for you, Michael, and I am thankful for your mother. God has been good to us."

Michael closed his eyes, took a deep breath, and let it out slowly. He did not want to hear about God or his goodness.

"How can you say that after all that has happened? How has God been good to us?

Monson smiled and released his hand from Michael's shoulder. He pulled out another stool and sat next to Michael.

"Michael, sometimes you must look past what you think is bad to find what is good. People live and die; that has always been, and will always be, as long as people are here on this earth. Life can be difficult, it can be long, or it can be short. The time we have here is not what matters; what matters is what we do with the time God has given us. I will wager you that I could find ten good things God has given us for every one thing that you think is bad."

Michael continued to look down at the counter. He then asked, "How can you be so positive, so hopeful when there is little to be optimistic about and even less to be hopeful about?

Monson nearly cut off Michael with a quick reply that took no thought, "I suppose that is a matter of opinion. Maybe I choose to focus on the good instead of the bad. You might be surprised at how positive and hopeful you would become if you did the same."

Michael shook his head. Monson continued, "I find it interesting how often you blame God for the bad things in life, the heartache, the hurt, and the death. If you think he is responsible for everything, you must also credit him for the wonderful things in life, the joys, and the happy moments. We are God's children, not his toys. He wants us to be happy; he does not play with us and then toss us aside for another. God has many titles, but the title his son used more than any other when referring to him was Father. He does not make toys; he makes children, his children, the children of a perfect father. A good father lets his children learn and grow; he lets them

< 115 >

experience heartache and happiness, pain and pleasure so that they can appreciate and yearn for the good in this life, for the blessings God has for them. I believe that he has given us agency to choose, and sometimes our choices are wrong; sometimes, they lead to heartache and pain, and other times they lead to happiness and joy. Our lives are not pre-determined; it does matter who we are and who we become, God has given us that right, that freedom, and he expects us to use it and to hold it sacred." He paused.

"I know you're hurting Michael, but you are not alone. There are hundreds, even thousands, out there who are hurting. Many of them have more to be hurt about than you or me, yet many still love God, who still have faith in him, love for him, and yes, even hope, hope that he will save them and their loved ones."

Michael thought for a moment. He felt his heart beating in his throat. He knew his emotions were working their way from his stomach to his head, and he did not want to lose them. He took another deep breath. He felt a tear well up in his left eye and slowly and discreetly wiped it away.

"Monson, I have lost so much…."

He began to cry. He tried to hold back his emotion and struggled to finish speaking.

"My father is gone; it is my fault he is dead. I should have gone for him earlier."

Monson placed his arm over Michael's shoulder.

"Michael, it is not your fault that he is gone. There is nothing you could have done to keep him here if God wanted to take him home."

"But why would God take him home when I, we, all needed him so desperately?"

"Michael, did it occur to you that God knew that your father had already done all that he needed for you and that it was time for you to stand on your own, to become a better man?"

< 116 >

"How have I stood on my own? What have I done other than bring misery to the lives of almost everyone I have come in contact with? How have I become a better man?

"You have saved the lives of your loved ones on many occasions. You have made many difficult decisions, without hesitation, decisions that others would not have been able to make."

Michael looked at Monson, his eyes watery and his nose running.

"Difficult decisions, like burning my precious little sister alive because I thought she may have had the plague? What if I was wrong?

"What if you were right? You knew that Margaret had the plague, and your actions saved the lives of at least the three of us still here."

Michael lifted his head and looked at Monson, tears in his eyes, and he asked, "If God loves his children so much, how could he let Sarah die in the fiery house?"

"Did he?" Monson asked.

"What do you mean, did he?"

"Did you find her remains in the ashes?" Monson asked.

"How do you know about that?"

"I watched you from an upstairs window. I saw you carefully place Margaret's bones in a box. I watched as you looked for the remains of Sarah, but you never found them, did you?"

Michael shook his head. He thought about it for a moment, and he still had no answer for the mystery. It gave him an odd feeling of hope that somehow Sarah had escaped the fire.

"Monson, do you believe God took her from that burning building?"

"I do not know, Michael, but I do know that you did not find her remains, so it seems to me that someone took her, and if so, it was by the grace of God that they did."

< 117 >

Michael thought about what Monson had just said.

"Perhaps that is the mercy God has shown unto you, Michael. Perhaps he loves you much more than you are willing to accept."

"But what of Lucas and my father? God did not save them?"

"What evidence do you have of this, Michael? Do you know for sure that they are both dead?"

Michael quickly shot back. "Dead? Do I question the mortality of my father? I saw him on the floor, and he was not breathing. I tossed his lifeless body onto the death cart. I know that he is dead, and God did not do a thing to save him, not a thing!"

Monson waited for a moment until Michael calmed a bit.

"I question the mortality of everyone. It seems your father is dead, but I did not see him for myself. I did not see his lifeless body, and I do not know for sure if the death cart you believe you tossed him on was the thing that took him to his grave. Did you watch as men tossed his body into a grave? Did you see them toss dirt upon him and cover the grave? Michael, I do not question your honesty and the story you have told regarding the demise of your father. But if God wanted him to survive, it seems God may have miraculously saved him, just as he saved Sarah, assuming she is alive somewhere."

Michael thought about what Monson said. It had never occurred to him that there was any possibility that William was alive, but he also felt that he did not find the remains of Sarah either. He remembered choosing a burial plot for William next to the old oak tree by his light tower, and then he remembered that something stopped him from digging the grave. He would only know William was dead if he had heaped the dirt upon his body in the grave. He had never thought about any of this. Suddenly he experienced something that he had not experienced in a long while; in his heart, he felt hope.

< 118 >

"Do you think my father is alive, Monson?"

Monson smiled at Michael.

"Michael, I am not saying he is alive; I just want you to understand that things are not always as they seem. Sometimes we spend too much time looking at things with our physical eyes instead of our spiritual eyes. I trust that God will never leave us in times of trouble, and I believe that he leaves us on this earth until we have accomplished all that we need to. If your father is alive, I know that you will see him again, and I also know that if he is dead, you will see him again. Therefore, what difference does it make in the end? Either way, you must wait and be patient with the Lord. Heaven knows that he is patient with you."

"What about Lucas? Do you believe that Lucas is alive?" Michael asked.

"As a matter of fact, I do believe he is alive. I do not know where he is or why I feel this way, but the feeling is strong. And I have faith that God is looking out for him."

Michael thought about the conversation up to this point. He and Monson sat a few moments, simply looking straight ahead.   His mind began to process the things they had discussed.   He wanted desperately to believe that William, Lucas, and Sarah were alive; just the thought made him smile. Then the views of Elizabeth entered his mind. He did not question her mortality; he knew that she had died and their child Hope had also died. He felt the tears come again, but there was no need to suppress them this time. It was more important to him to talk to Monson than to be fearful that somehow Monson would judge him weak if he saw his tears. Michael broke the silence and asked,

"Do you believe in spirits?"

The question seemed unexpected. Monson thought for a moment and said, "Of course, I believe in spirits; we all have one."

"No, I mean, do you believe in ghosts?"

< 119 >

He thought for a moment. "I believe there are many things beyond my understanding, and I am just a child in the eyes of God."

Michael blurted out, "Last night, I saw Elizabeth."

Monson looked surprised but not shocked. He smiled at Michael and said, "How wonderful for you, Michael."

"That is all you are going to say; how wonderful? Do you not think I may be losing my mind to think such a thing?"

Monson shook his head.

"No, Michael, I do not think you are losing your mind because you saw a spirit. I think it is wonderful that God has seen fit to allow you to see Elisabeth."

"At first, I thought I was dreaming. I found myself standing in our room, looking out the window. Suddenly that obnoxious bird appeared and perched on the window seal and mocked me."

Monson asked, "What bird are you referring to?"

"You know, the bird that flew into the window when Hope died, it flew in again when Elizabeth died, and I saw it the day I was cleaning through the ashes looking for the remains of Sarah. It seems to mock me, to laugh at me. One day I will catch it and kill it." He stopped speaking and looked ahead in a daze.

"I am sorry, Michael, but I do not know the bird you are referring to."

Michael snapped out of the trance and said. "You saw it. You said you watched me looking for the bones of Sarah. It was sitting on the tree; it even dived at me several times. Do not you remember?"

"Sorry, Michael, but I never saw a bird."

Michael was frustrated but let it go.

"It doesn't matter anyway."

Monson said, "You were telling me..."

Michael continued, "I swung at the bird and then tripped over the table. When I landed on the floor, I heard her

< 120 >

voice. At first, I did not believe it. I thought it was something else. Then I heard it again; I turned, and there she was. She was beautiful, Monson, so beautiful. She was happy. She spoke to me as if nothing had ever happened. She spoke as if she was there. I was still unsure until I touched her face and felt the warmth of her skin. I kissed her lips, and we spent the rest of the evening together in love, in one another's arms."

He stopped. His eyes seemed to follow an image his mind projected on the wall in front of him. Monson was listening intently.

"Monson, do you think it was a dream or a vision? Was she there, or was she in my mind?

Monson thought for a moment and replied,

"What is the difference between a dream and vision? Is it not two different words that refer to the same thing?

Michael listened.

"Does it matter which it was, Michael? Would it be any less real to you if it were a dream?

"No, I guess not, Monson. I just wanted it to be real; I wanted her back so much that I wanted it to be real; I did not care what it was…only that she was with me."

"Then it appears to me that it does not matter whether or not I believe in ghosts or spirits. What I think of your experience should have no impact on how it affected you, now, should it?"

"No, it should not. I just wanted someone to confirm that it was real, that it wasn't just something in my head." He thought for a moment and continued. "Monson, do you think I saw with my spiritual eyes instead of my physical eyes? Has she been there all along, but I could not see her because I was looking with my physical eyes?"

Monson smiled and said, "Sometimes God parts the veil between this life and the next, and he allows us those precious moments to see through it. Yes, I think you may have been given that opportunity."

< 121 >

"Do you think it will happen again? I want to see her every day."

"I do not know if it will happen again, Michael. Maybe God gave this to you as a witness of his love for you. You see, Michael, he has not left you alone. When Jesus was with his disciples, he performed many miracles in their presence. He lived among them, and he taught them to live in the world but not of the world. He gave them miracles, but only according to their faith and needs. Moments, as you experienced, are precious and spiritual. They give us peace and hope, but they will not be with us daily. I believe God gives them to us as a crutch, something to lift us up until we can walk on our own."

Michael thought for a moment and said,

"Then it is better that I remain weak because I need to be lifted daily. I need her with me every day. I cannot walk on my own. If God will not do this for me, what he has given me is a tease, something to remind me that he has taken almost all that I love away from me and left me here alone. I do not need a crutch; I need to be with those I love. I need him to bring them back to me. If he does not, I know he does not love me. I am not his child. I am his toy." He began to cry.

"Sometimes God does cruel things. I heard singing this morning coming from my mother's room. I followed the familiar melody because it was different from what she usually hums. I saw her standing as if holding baby Sarah in her arms when I opened her door. I watched her place an infant not there into a crib and then tell the make-believe baby to sleep. She then leaned over and kissed the nonexistent head of Lucas, whom she imagined was sleeping in his bed. I could have dealt with it until she told him Michael would play with him when he awoke. What kind of God plays with people's minds and gives them false hope? Look what he has done to my mother. She will never be the same because God has placed her in a make-believe world!"

< 122 >

Although Monson had seen Michael unhinged before, he had never seen him overcome with tears and grief. As Michael attempted to collect himself, a thought came to Monson.

"Michael, what you perceive as cruelty from God is, in reality, mercy and love. If God were cruel as you have charged, he would not allow your sweet mother to remain in such a state of calm serenity. Perhaps he is sheltering her from things that would destroy her. Perhaps his love protects her from reality until she is ready to perceive it."

Monson started to speak again, but Michael cut him off.

"I am sorry, Monson, you are a good and much better man than I could ever be. I appreciate all that you have done for me and all you have tried to do, but this is something that I must figure out on my own. Besides, there is work to do today, and I must be off to attend to it."

Michael stood. Monson grabbed his arm, holding him back, and said, "Michael, God does love you. He is with you every day. Be careful; the moment we think we know better than God is when pride takes over, and pride has been the downfall of many a good man. Michael, I wish you could see yourself the way God sees you. One day, one day, you will."

He released Michael's arm. Michael nodded at him and left the room. Monson sat on the stool, contemplating the conversation they had just had. He wished and hoped that something said would pierce Michael's soul. He wished he could have told him more. He knew that he would tell Michael his secret one day, the secret that he had never shared with anyone at the estate. Today was not the day, he thought to himself; perhaps tomorrow.

< 123 >

Chapter Nine
Angels Among Us

"When the Angels arrive, the Devils leave."
Egyptian proverb

July 1349
Escape from the monastery.

She felt dizzy and heavy, her head pounding. She slowly opened and closed her eyes several times, regulating the light until her pupils could focus. She was lying on her back. She looked at the ceiling and noticed three beautifully painted angels with hands stretched outward. Flying around the Christ child, she felt a moment of peace and tranquility. Still, the moment passed as she focused on the baby and suddenly realized she had a baby, a little girl. She sat up quickly, causing more pain in her head. She placed her hands on her head, looked around, and screamed.

"Faith! Where are you? Where is my baby?"

The room was large and ornately decorated with religious symbols, statues, and numerous crucifixes. She knew that she was in a bedroom of some type of sacred shrine. She heard voices outside the room. The door flew open, and she saw a large round monk enter, holding her little girl. Faith leaped from his arms and shouted,

"Mommy!" as she ran to Angelia.

Angelia opened her arms, still sitting on the bed, as the little girl climbed onto the bed and wrapped her tiny arms around her mother's bosom. Angelia held her tightly, closed her eyes, and began to cry.

< 124 >

"Oh, my dear child. I thought I had lost you. Thank God that you are alive..." She hesitated, pulled the child away from her, surveyed her body from head to toe, and continued, "...and well."

She pulled her in tightly, began rubbing her head, and ran her hands through her hair. After a few moments, she looked up and acknowledged the monk.

"Dear Sir, where am I and how did I...we, get here?" Brother Richard slowly walked into the room.

"Madam, I am Brother Richard, and you are at the St. Jude Monastery. Are you feeling better?"

"There is some pain in my side, but overall I am feeling well, thank you. How did I get here?" She asked.

"We found you in a ditch on the side of the road." He noticed that she looked confused and in disbelief. "Do you not remember?"

She thought for a moment and then put her right hand on her forehead. Frustrated, she said, "I am afraid I do not remember. Faith and I were riding upon a horse, and...." She closed her eyes, shook her head, and tears began to flow from her eyes.

"We were attacked by an evil man...he knocked me to the ground." She stopped, opened her eyes, and looked at Brother Richard. "There was a small boy. I do not remember his name. Do I know him? Have you seen him?" She asked.

Brother Richard shook his head. "No, Madam, there is no small boy. The only child is your little daughter. Perhaps you should rest a while longer." He reached for Faith. "I will happily care for your child, little Faith. What a beautiful name for such a beautiful little girl." He smiled as Faith reached for him.

"Yes, she is our little angel." She hesitated and thought for a moment. "My husband. Have you seen my husband?" She asked. "His name is Percival."

< 125 >

"I am sorry, but there is no one else. Were you traveling with your husband?"

She thought for a moment. "No, we were alone. It seemed like there was a little boy with us. However, I cannot remember. Maybe there was not. My husband went to find his parents; they live in a small village." She thought for a moment until the town's name came to her. "It was Elkenshire, the town of his parents. He went to save them."

She noticed that Brother Richard gently shook his head.

"There is a sickness quickly moving closer." She squinted and rubbed her forehead. "It is deadly, but I do not know how I know this. Someone told me so, and I think it was the boy. Why cannot I remember? How long have we been here?"

"Three days, my lady, three days."

"No, he should have returned by now. How far are we from the Shire?"

"We are about a half days journey by horse. Is that where you are from? Where were you headed, and why were you traveling alone?"

"I do not know where we were headed, and I remember that we seemed to be running or escaping from something. Oh, my dear man, why cannot I remember?"

She tried to stand, but the pain was too much; she leaned over and held her stomach. Without warning, her body began to convulse with nausea. She vomited on the floor.

"Oh, please forgive me. What have I done?" She asked as dizziness overcame her. She sat on the bed, and the monk placed Faith on the floor and rushed to Angelia.

"My lady, please rest. Moreover, never mind the mess. I will clean the floor. You must rest. I am sorry to tell you this, but we found you alongside the road severely beaten. I fear that the man who did this defiled you."

< 126 >

Angelia laid back on the bed and began to cry. "Oh, dear God, what has happened to me? Where is my Percival? She rolled her head from side to side and continued to cry.

Dom Gordon entered the room. He walked toward the woman, but Brother Richard motioned him to stop with one hand while placing the index finger of his other hand over his lips. Dom Gordon stopped and then noticed the vomit on the floor. Brother Richard acknowledged the mess and mouthed,

"I will clean the mess. Can you take the child?" Dom Gordon stepped forward and took Faith from Brother Richard, and faith began to cry.

"Hush, child, all is well." Said Dom Gordon, to no avail.

"The child's name is Faith." Said Brother Richard. He smiled at her and continued.

"It is well, Faith. He is a good man. Let him hold you while I clean the floor and help your mother."

Faith stopped crying and smiled at Brother Richard. Dom Gordon was surprised at Brother Richard's bond with the child. As he held the child, he looked at Angelia, who continued to cry.

"May I have my baby, please" Dom nodded and gently handed the baby to her mother. He leaned in and said,

"Dear woman, you will recover. We have taken care of your wounds. You must be hungry and thirsty and have not eaten or drunk in days."

Angelia responded. "Yes, Father, that would be nice."

Brother Richard left the room and returned with a bucket of water and a mop. He began to clean the floor as Dom Gordon spoke to Angelia.

"What is your name?" He asked.

"Angelia. My name is Angelia." She attempted to regain her composure.

"I am Dom Gordon; I am the Father of this Monastery. I do not know how much Brother Richard has told you, but I

< 127 >

know that it is a miracle that we found you and that God has saved your and your child's life."

"Thank you for your kindness." She replied while cuddling Faith next to her. "I do not remember much. I know that I was beaten...." She stopped. She began to cry. "He had his way with me." She cried more and found it difficult to speak. "He defiled me and made me dirty. Can I be forgiven, Father?"

"My child, you are not the one who needs to seek forgiveness. It is the bastard who attacked you. God have mercy on his soul!"

Angelia was surprised at the plainness of the monk's language.

"Forgive me, child, for my words, but God does not look the other way when a man defiles a woman. His wrath is kindled, and his anger is justified as justice is served."

He caressed her head. "Let us talk no more of this. God has brought you here. You and your child are safe with us, and we will care for you until you are healthy enough to continue your journey."

"Thank you, Father." She thought for a moment and said, "But I do not know where our journey was taking us." She attempted to remember but could not. "My mind seems foggier as I try to remember things."

"Rest, you must rest; we will talk more later. For now, let me fetch you food and water."

He reached for the child, but she turned and snuggled against her mother. He smiled and left the room. Brother Richard finished cleaning the floor a while later. Angelia and Faith had both fallen asleep. He looked toward the bed and heard the faint whisper as Angelia quietly said,

"Thank you, God, for placing angels among us.

< 128 >

Dom Gordon gathered the priests together around the large table. As they ate the evening meal, he said, "My brothers, I fear that something wicked is coming. I do not know what, but God has spoken to my spirit and told me that we must prepare ourselves."

"What is it that you fear, father?" Asked one of the monks.

"It is not fear that concerns me; it is not knowing that concerns me."

"Father, I told you about the town of Elkenshire just two days from here. Do you remember?" Asked Brother Simon.

"Yes, I believe it is the town where Angelia's husband's parents live. What about it?"

The monk wrinkled his forehead as he spoke, "Did she not say the name of her husband is Percival?"

Dom Gordon thought for a moment and replied, "Yes, I believe she did say that. But, why do you ask this?"

"I heard his name as we were escaping the town."

"What do you mean you heard his name?"

"An old woman was shouting his name?"

"Did you see this woman?" Asked Dom Gordon.

"No, but I believe she was boarded in one of the houses, and Percival was there with her. I heard a man's voice trying to calm the woman."

Dom Gordon leaned over the table, placed his left elbow on the table, dropped his head into his hand, and, shaking his head, said, "Oh dear God above, how much more pain will this woman bear?" He lifted his head and asked, "Brother Richard, you seem to have developed a kinship with our visitor Angelia. Do you believe you can break the news to her in the morning?"

Brother Richard looked at the priest, slowly breathed in, and replied, "Father, oh, that I might have another task; nevertheless, I will speak with the woman."

Dom Gordon smiled, "I know it will not be easy for her to hear, but she should know now rather than wonder each day

< 129 >

when her beloved will come home." Each of the monks nodded in agreement.

"Now, we must make plans if we are to protect ourselves and this monastery. I want every window and door bolted shut at all times, and no one leaves the building alone, always at least two or more at a time. And take some type of weapon with you."

"Excuse me, Father." Asked one of the monks.

"Yes, Brother Thorley, go on." Said Dom Gordon.

"What is it that we are protecting ourselves from? The closest town is nearly a day's ride from here, and no one ever comes here."

"Brother Thorley, have you not listened? Have you forgotten about the young woman amongst us who has been sorely beaten?" He asked in a kind yet frustrated manner.

"Yes, Father, I have listened, and of course, I am aware of the woman's condition, but is it not possible that a strange man passing by caused this crime and that it is not related to anything else?"

Don Gordon took a breath and hesitated before speaking. "It is not my intent to cause fear among us. It is possible that the attacker did so with a random act of evil, but what of the town of Elkenshire that Brother Simon spoke of?" He looked around the large table and asked, "Brother Simon, who else was with you in the town of Elkenshire?"

Another monk spoke, "It was I, Father, Brother Andres." He stood near the end of the table and shook as he said, "I testify to the words that Brother Simon has spoken. We fled for our lives. It was as though the people there had all gone mad. Officials were boarding up homes while some were even trying to get out! They were clubbed, kicked, and beaten back into their homes. Fires were then set. It was awful. We even noticed the Pennington estate ablaze as we rode away from the town. It was as though hell had released its demons who flew

< 130 >

from house to house, throwing balls of fire into wood and thatch!"

He breathed heavily and continued. "It was the most awful thing I have ever seen; as we rode beyond the town, I could feel the heat of the flames behind us, and I feared to turn around lest I become a pillar of salt fleeing Sodom and Gomorrah!" He slowly sat back in his seat.

Dom Gordon spoke, "It is not for us to fear but to prepare. Remember the letter that I received from the Holy Father? He spoke of a deadly disease moving throughout the land, even abroad. If this disease were causing men to lose their minds and do unspeakable things, it would explain the events in Elkenshire and what happened to the woman. For this reason, we must prepare for the worst and protect ourselves. Let us pray and then retire to our beds. Brother Sykes and Brother Ingles, I would like you to secure the windows and doors this evening."

They both acknowledged him.

"Now, we shall pray."

~*~*~

He found himself standing in a largely empty hall. It was dark, and his eyes struggled to adjust. He was able to make out a long table surrounded by many chairs. Dim light fought to enter the room but was quickly smothered out by a thick mist of black fog. Seeing became more difficult. He opened his eyes as wide as possible, closed them, and opened them again. Over and over, the darkness covered the room as the black fog began to rise. He looked down and watched as it rose like a tide coming in. Slowly at first, then quickly rising above his ankles, to his knees, his waist, and nearly to his chest. He breathed in deeply and lifted his hands from the blackness and above his chest. He turned around and could no longer see the table or chairs. He felt the black fog thicken around him; it tightened around his legs, hips, and chest. Breathing became difficult. He raised his hands above his head as though the fog was forcing his arms

< 131 >

upward. He tilted his head back as the mist tightened around his neck. Suddenly a sliver of light from above began to cut through the fog. It shined on his fingers raised far above his head. He struggled to breathe. It felt as though his lungs were being squeezed tighter with each breath. A sliver of light tore through the fog and looked like a rip in a painting. He closed his eyes at the brightness of the light above him. He opened his eyes, and his heart stopped when her face nearly touched his. Her powder blue eyes were inches from his, wide open, her lips parted, and she said, "They're here! Let them in!" The image and the light wrapped together and shot back into the tear as the darkness and thick black fog forced everything out, all black, all dead! Michael sat up in his bed. His heart was racing as drops of sweat dripped from his forehead. His breathing was deep and quick as he forced air in and out of his lungs. A few moments passed, and he realized it was only a dream.

He found himself standing in the middle of the large dining hall. The room felt freezing and musty. He looked around and saw no one. He felt a shiver, looked across the room, and noticed that the window was not latched at the end of the room. As he began walking toward the window, a black fog began to seep through the corners of the bottom of the window. He tried to move, but his feet became stuck in thick mud and slime. He looked down and realized that some type of mud had oozed over the entire floor, and it was quickly rising. He tried to force his feet to move faster toward the window. Suddenly the large wooden shutters flew open. A dark mist began to flow from the bottom of the window seal. He felt his heart race; fear became unstoppable. He fought against it but felt terror rising deep from within. The mud-like substance had risen to his knees, and moving was nearly impossible. He wanted to scream for help, but he had no voice. The mud continued to rise. He could no longer move. The dark mist turned to black water flowing into the room. His mind told him what he saw and was feeling could not be real, but his eyes and body fought with a

< 132 >

reason as reality seemed as confusing as his current surroundings. He felt a cold chill and rush of wind through the window. Darkness began to fill the room. He looked from wall to wall for something to focus on. A large wooden crucifix with the dying Christ caught his attention. Light began to shoot from the fingertips of the wooden figurine. The light bounced off the ceiling and began to dance from wall to wall, floor to ceiling, and side to side. Long streaks of light permeated the room with glistening streams that multiplied like a million silk webs. The darkness became more intense and began to quench the light. The streams of light began to disappear.

Millions of streaks became thousands, hundreds, tens, and then only two that led to the tearful eyes of the Christ figurine. He looked at the image; suddenly, the wooden head lifted, and the face turned toward his. The wooden mouth opened and whispered, "They're here! Run, Now!" He leaned his head back, throwing his chin upward as the black mud reached his ears and throat. His arms were pinned to his side. As the room gave in to the darkness, he felt the pressure forcing the air from his lungs. He closed his eyes and screamed, "Oh, Dear Lord, save us!" Dom Gordon sat up in his bed and panted like an exhausted horse. He swallowed and struggled to catch his breath. It was a dream, he thought, a horrible nightmare. Just as he regained his composure, he heard the voice again in his head whisper, "They're here! Run!" This time he understood the message. He jumped from his bed, pulled on a robe and shoes, and ran into the hall. He ran into the large sleeping room filled with his brothers. In a loud whisper, he yelled, "Wake up! Now! We must rush!" The monks began to wake. He continued to repeat the words of warning.

"What is it, Father?" Asked Brother Richard.

"I had a vision, evil is upon us, and we must leave now before it is too late! Quick! Clothe yourselves!" The monks scrambled to clothe. One of them yelled, "But the sun has yet to rise? Are we to run into darkness?"

< 133 >

"God will give us light, but there is no time to argue. We must go now!" He demanded.

"What about the woman and the child?" Asked Brother Richard.

Dom Gordon looked back at him and said, "Get them, bring them here. We will leave through the back entrance."

Brother Richard ran down the long hall and down the stairs. As he ran, he noticed streams of early morning light fighting to squeeze through the closed and bolted shutters. Finally, he arrived at the room. He slid into the room and spoke in a loud yet muffled voice, "Angelia! You must get up! Something is wrong. Dom Gordon had a dream, and we must leave now!"

Angelia jumped from the bed. She was still clothed in a robe. She leaned over to lift Faith from the drawer and felt dizzy. She felt the blood rush to her head but knew she had to raise her child. Faith awoke and began to cry, and Angelia lifted her and quietly said, "Hush, my child. You will be fine. We need to go now."

She turned with Faith in her arms and faced Brother Richard. He smiled and reached for her. The dizziness overcame her, and she fell toward him. He tried to catch her, but Faith flew towards him as Angelia's limp body fell. He grabbed the child with one hand and reached for Angelia with the other. His fingertips brushed against her face as her body slammed into a large table. Her head hit the corner of the table, causing a gouge to the side of her temple and face. She fell to the floor unconscious and bleeding. Brother Richard yelled for help. Moments later, three monks rushed into the room. Brother Richard handed Faith to one of them. She cried for her mother. Brother Richard asked another to help him lift her. The two carried her out of the room and into a long hallway. The other monks and Dom Gordon met them in the hallway. Dom Gordon placed his index finger to his lips and told everyone to be quiet. He motioned toward the large eating hall.

< 134 >

A noise rang from the room. It was the sound of the shutters opening. They heard voices and movement. He motioned for everyone to follow him. They quietly ran to the kitchen and left through the back door. When the last Monk left the building, Dom Gordon realized that the horse stable was on the other side. He and another monk slowly walked toward the corner of the building and peered around it. They saw a group of five men climbing into the dining hall window. Two other men stood holding several horses. He knew that their only escape would be into the woods by foot. He pointed toward the woods and motioned for them to leave. As the monks started walking into the woods, Brother Richard and the other, helping him with Angelia, carefully placed her onto the same wooden cart they had used to bring her to the monastery. Dom Gordon helped them push it into the woods. They had only walked for a few minutes when the morning sun began to lighten their path. After walking two leagues into the dense forest, Dom Gordon told the monks to stop and take a rest. He gathered the men. Angelia was still unconscious. Brother Richard had torn part of his robe and made a bandage for her head. The bleeding had stopped, which gave him hope that she would recover.

"I am not sure what we do from here." Said Dom Gordon. "I know Saint Gabriel's monastery is about a three-day journey from here."

"I am sorry, Father, but I do not believe Angelia will survive a three-day journey. Surely there is a town closer." Said Brother Richard.

"There is, but how are we to know this sickness has not overtaken it."

"What town do you speak of?" Asked Brother Richards.

"It is not a town; it is an estate near the city of Cardiff. It is most likely a full day from here."

"How do you know of this place?" Questioned Brother Richards.

< 135 >

Dom Gordon responded, "I remember going to the estate when I was very young. I do not remember the reason, only that I went there with a Bishop from Cardiff. I remember that the people there were good, kind people. Hopefully, they are still there." He paused and said, "And still alive."

"What is safer for us? Do we take our chances and journey toward a large city like Cardiff, or do we drive deeper into the forest to a monastery that is most likely far enough removed from the nearest town to be a safe haven from the sickness and evil roundabout? us?" Asked Brother Simon.

Dom Gordon looked at him and said, "My son, we must leave things in the hands of God. He saved us from those who surely would have killed us had we stayed at the Monastery. I do not believe he brought us this far just to let us die. It makes more sense for us to travel to Saint Gabriel's than an estate near Cardiff. However, I fear this woman cannot make a three-day journey."

"What are you suggesting? You believe that we should head toward Cardiff?" Asked Brother Andres.

"No, but I believe that Brother Richard and I should." Brother Richard looked at Dom Gordon, surprised and nervous at the prospect of traveling in a different direction than the others.

"You, Brother Simon, take our brethren to Saint Gabriel's and tell them what has happened. We will travel to this estate, and God willing, we will meet up with you soon. None of us knows what we will find, either at St. Gabriel's or the estate outside of Cardiff."

Brother Simon acknowledged him.

"Tell them what has happened to us. Tell them to be careful and to protect themselves as much as possible."

Dom Gordon put his hand on the shoulder of Brother Simon and said,

"My son, if you find the monastery in good health, stay there until we return; even if the days turn to weeks or months,

< 136 >

we will find you again, I promise." The men embraced one another, and the two groups parted.

"How will we survive without food and water?" Asked Brother Richard.

"There is a stream not far from here. Also, the path is lined with berries. We will journey until sundown. We will rise early, and, hopefully, if we keep moving, we can make it to the estate by tomorrow morning."

< 137 >

Chapter Nine Notes

During the plague, monks were dying as often as anyone else, and it was not uncommon for entire monasteries to be empty or, worse, filled with the corps of dead monks. Those surviving the plague often joined together, pulling their resources and hiding from others to avoid plague infestation.

< 138 >

Chapter Ten
Whispers From The Dust

July 1349

*"And thou shalt be brought down, and shalt speak out
of the dust, and thy voice shall be, as of one that hath a
familiar spirit, out of the ground, and thy speech shall whisper
out of the dust." Isiah 29:4.*

Michael placed the basket of eggs on the counter.
Monson walked into the kitchen. His face was still wet, and
strands of hair dripped after he had washed his face in the bowl
in his room just next to the kitchen.

"Good morning Michael. How was your sleep?"

"I slept well, but I must admit, this is the first time since
I have been here that I made it to the kitchen in the morning
before you. Are you feeling well, Monson?" Michael asked,
with a concerned look on his face.

"Thank you for your interest, my son, but I believe that I
am just getting older and moving slower." He looked at the
basket of eggs and then at the milk pail.

"It seems that the chickens are laying more eggs than
usual. He looked at Michael for a response.

"I agree. Maybe it is because the chickens are banning
together for comfort

Monson smiled and said, "Is not it odd how we assume
that only humans can get attached to a companion and that an
animal cannot? Nevertheless, we now have more eggs than we

< 139 >

need for just three of us, and it will be a shame to lose some of them."

Michael listened in agreement. Monson walked over to the cooking pot, still hanging over a long since the extinguished fire.

"I guess I could toss a few of them into the stew today and try something new?" He laughed mildly. Michael smiled and then sat on one of the stools. He picked up a piece of carved wood lying on the counter; he had left it there the previous evening.

"What are you making there, Michael?" Monson asked as he began to place straw and wood in the fireplace.

"I am not sure. At first, I thought I would make an arrow, but now it looks more like a person than a weapon." Monson acknowledged the comment and lit a fire. Michael watched as Monson patiently blew on a single blade of dry timber, enriching the red ember until a small flame was born. He watched as the flame began to grow and finally overtook the wood. Monson carefully placed the flame into the piled kindling and poked it around with an iron fire rod that hung from a nail in one of the bricks. Monson lifted the pot and placed it on the counter. He then removed a large wet towel from the other end of the counter. It covered various vegetables that Monson had picked from the garden the day before. He took two large onions and placed them on the counter next to the pot. He bent down, opened a cupboard door, pulled three large beats from a basket, and then put them on the table. Michael watched as Monson continued what had become his morning ritual of meal making. Monson walked to another counter and lifted a dry cloth covering over assorted herbs. He placed the plants next to the other items on the counter. He then put four eggs next to the items and asked, "What do you think, Michael? Do eggs have any place in my vegetable stew?" Michael shrugged his shoulders and continued to inspect the piece of wood. "Well, I may get creative today.

< 140 >

Besides, we have been eating the same stew for weeks, and I am looking for something a little different."

He continued to collect other items from various areas of the kitchen, bread from another cupboard, dried meat, and ground spices from another. He began to chop the vegetables. He lifted a large pail of water that Michael had fetched from the well earlier, something Monson usually did.

"Thanks for fetching the water, Michael."

Michael smiled and nodded. Monson noticed that Michael appeared to be deep in thought. He asked, "Is something troubling you this morning Michael?"

"Nothing more than usual, I believe."

"You seem quieter than normal, so I thought I would ask."

Michael slowly shook his head. Monson continued to prepare the stew. He lifted the pail and slowly poured water into the pot. He then began to chop and add pieces of beets, carrots, and dried meat.

"Would you mind cutting one of these onions for me, Michael?" Monson asked as he slid a knife over to him. Michael placed the wood on the counter, took the blade, and then the onion.

"I would be happy to." Responded Michael.

He cut the onion in half and began to tear away the layers. The pungent odor of the onion caused his nose to run and tears to form. Monson looked over at Michael and playfully asked,

"Are you sure nothing is bothering you? You look quite emotional to me."

Michael turned toward him and shook his head, and said,

"Actually, something is bothering me."

"Then the tears have a purpose," Monson stated.

Michael smiled and said,

< 141 >

"No, they have no purpose other than to remind me that I am peeling an onion."

He placed the peeled onion on the counter and began to slice it and toss the slices into the pot.

"Last night, I had the strangest dream." He hesitated.

"Go on," Monson said.

"I dreamt I was standing in a large room, a hall of some sort. I believe there was a long dining table in the center. The room was very dark. Suddenly a fog-like substance began rising from the floor. It made it difficult to move. The dark fog began to rise until it reached my chest. I lifted my arms above my head, and the fog continued rising to my neck. I looked up toward the ceiling with my hands stretched upward. Suddenly a face appeared from the ceiling and flew towards me. It was Elizabeth. She said, "They're here! Let them in!" It shocked me, and I woke up. What do you make of it, Monson?"

Monson looked at Michael and then off into the distance. He thought for a moment and said, "I do not know what it means or if there is any meaning."

"No meaning at all? Surely you must think it has some meaning?" Michael insisted.

"I do not know, Michael, sometimes I dream of flying like a bird, but when I wake up, I do not think that one day I will sprout wings and start flying."

Michael smiled and shook his head.

"Here I am, serious and trying to have an intelligent conversation, and you are talking about flying like a bird. Maybe I should not have said anything."

Monson laughed and said, "Michael, Michael. I am not mocking you; it is just that I do not assume that every dream must have some type of meaning. Sometimes we dream about stupid and dreadful things because of the state of mind when we retire to bed. Perhaps there is meaning to your dream. What do you think it could mean?"

< 142 >

Michael thought for a moment and said, "Do you think Elizabeth may be trying to tell me something?"

"Are you asking if I believe that Elizabeth is speaking to you from the grave?"

Michael looked into Monson's eyes and said, "Sure, why not?"

Suddenly the conversation became serious. Monson took a deep breath and forced it out. He could tell that the dream had influenced Michael, and he did not want to say something that would cause him more pain.

"What do you think the dream means, Michael?" Monson asked.

"I think that Elizabeth is trying to prepare me for something…." He hesitated and then continued, "…something difficult, but important. Maybe someone is headed to the estate, and I am supposed to let them enter."

Monson stopped Michael in mid-thought. "I am sorry, Michael, but we both know the danger of letting anyone, much less a stranger, into the estate. What if they have brought the plague with them? What then?"

"Do not be concerned, Monson; I have no intention of simply letting anyone enter the estate. But it is possible that others could find the estate, especially since others did, and we know how that ended."

"Yes, we do, and it did not end well. I fear that the only souls that will come here are those on a quest for mayhem and plunder. I believe that we must be vigilant and protect the estate from anyone who may arrive."

"I could not agree with you more, Monson, but what if my dream does have meaning? What if people are coming here? Should we turn them away, or should we let them in?"

"Michael, you are asking a hypothetical question that forces me to respond according to what the scriptures teach. We are to act according to Christ; we are obligated to let. That is the part that worries me."

< 143 >

"But would Christ want us to let someone in who could bring death to us?" Michael asked.

"Not necessarily, but he will only protect us if we use wisdom in our choices. He will not stop an arrow headed for your chest if you purposefully jump in the path of an archer, now will he?"

"Then how are we to know if strangers arrive if we should let them in?"

Monson, without hesitation, said, "We must pray about it, and God will answer our prayers."

Michael closed his mouth. He did not want to entertain such an act. He waited a moment and said, "All this talk of God and Christ, and truthfully, I've had many conversations with both of them in the past, and look at where that has gotten me."

Monson smiled and said, "No, my son, a conversation only happens when people listen at least as much as they speak; anything else is a lecture. I, for one, avoid lecturing God or his only begotten."

Monson patted Michael on the shoulder and turned back to the pot of stew hanging over the fire. Michael stood. He said nothing and started to leave the room. Monson said, "Michael, I trust you. I trust that God has preserved you for some great purpose, and I will follow your lead. If we find visitors to the estate, I will support whatever decision you make regarding them."

"Thank you, Monson." Michael walked toward the back door and opened it.

"And Michael?"

"Yes, Monson."

"For what it is worth, I believe that Elizabeth lives in the spirit and that God could allow her to speak to you." Michael hid a half-smile and nodded as he walked out the door.

< 144 >

They had traveled just under three hours. The dirt path became narrower and more challenging to pull the wagon across. Dom Gordon stopped and leaned against the wooden handle he had pulled the last hour.

Brother Richard asked, "Are you alright, Father?"

Don Gordon gently nodded his head, breathed deeply, and, yawning, said, "Yes, my son. I will survive, but at this moment, my aging body needs rest."

He slowly bent down and sat on a fallen tree log near the grassy edge of the dirt path.

"I am afraid this path has not been crossed in quite some time, and it is becoming much more difficult to traverse."

Brother Richard walked to the cart and inspected the bandage on Angelia's head; Faith slept quietly beside her in the hay. He asked, "Do you believe that Angelia will survive this journey?"

"Of course, I believe she will survive; why else would I have suggested we separate ourselves from the others and journey to an estate that may or may not be infected with this plague?

Brother Richard raised his eyebrows. Dom Gordon smiled and continued, "I apologize. It is just that it never occurred to me that I would find myself in such a precarious situation. I never thought we would one day abandon the monastery while running from criminals. And how could I have ever entertained the thought that a severely beaten woman and her child would end up on our doorstep?" He shook his head. "It is not that I do not thank the Lord for saving us as he has done; it is that I am now heading to a destination with faith that we will be welcomed by kind and healthy people when we arrive. Also, I worry and hope that the others will arrive at Saint Gabriel's without harm or incident. I have accepted great responsibility as the leader of our monastery, and I love each of those in my care. Thank you for being such a good and faithful friend."

< 145 >

Brother Richard walked over to Dom Gordon and sat beside him.

"Father, you are a man of God, and I will follow you to the ends of the earth. I have great confidence and belief in you, and I also believe that God will allow us to take this woman and her child to safety. I have hope that God will straighten this path and lead us to new friends."

Dom Gordon put his arm around Brother Richard and said,

"Thank you, my son, my friend. Now, let us find some berries." They both stood.

"I believe there is a bucket in the cart that we can also fill with water." Added Brother Richard. "You sit and rest and let me find some berries and fill the bucket."

He put his hand on Dom Gordon's left shoulder and gently pushed him back on the log. Brother Richard carefully and quietly began to rummage through the hay to not wake Angelia or Faith. His hand brushed against something hard and sharp. He stopped, ran his fingers along the sharp edges, and realized it was a pitchfork. He remembered that there were two pitchforks in the hay. A moment later, he found the bucket. He took the pail and walked a few feet to the other side of the dirt road. He looked into the thick brush and pulled back a large section of thicket until he could see the stream. The water looked terrific; it gave him a sense of calm. He made his way through the brush creating a train to the stream. When he reached the shore, he bent down and began to wash out the bucket in the cold running water. After dumping it a few times, he filled it until the water spilled over the top. He lifted the bucket to his lips and took the first drink. It was refreshing and frigid. He stood with the full bucket and looked at the trail he had forged that led back to the dirt road. Suddenly he heard a sound a few feet from him, upstream. He slowly turned his head toward the sound but did not see anything. He waited a few moments but did not hear it again. Although he appeared

< 146 >

alone, something felt peculiar and made him uneasy. He tried to brush off the odd feeling and started up the path.

When he reached the top, he noticed Dom Gordon had fallen asleep leaning against the tree next to the log he was sitting on. He was excited to share the water but knew that Dom Gordon needed to rest, so he quietly placed the bucket of water into the cart. As he lowered the bucket, the edge of it hit the other pitchfork. He quickly lifted the bucket to keep it from spilling. He removed the pitchfork and rested it against the cart. He looked around for berries but did not see anything nearby. Then he remembered seeing something red near the stream. Indeed, it must have been berries, he thought. He turned and started to walk, and then it occurred to him that it might be easier to make his way through the brush if he used the pitchfork. He lifted it and made his way to the edge of the brush. The afternoon sun attempted to break its way through the thickly wooded forest, but only thin streaks of sunlight penetrated in scattered spots, here and there. Brother Richard stopped for a moment and breathed in the warm, clean air, noticing the damp, crisp fragrance of the rustling stream ahead of him. He looked up through the trees and marveled at the beauty of God's creations and the bright sunlight that gave life and warmth to the earth. After the pause, Brother Richard continued to make his way through the brush, swinging the pitchfork from side to side. Suddenly he saw it. The red that had caught his attention earlier.

In the distance, only feet from him was a large red apple tree on the other side of the stream. He smiled and thought how odd the tree was off by itself, with no other fruit trees nearby. He looked at the stream and noticed a crooked path of various-sized rocks protruding inches above the flowing water. It created an approach almost directly to the tree. He lowered the pitchfork and began to make his way across the rocks. As he stepped onto the first rock with his right foot, he felt the cold rushing water sting along the top and sides of his foot. The hem

< 147 >

of his robe began to absorb the water. He swung his left leg another two feet and placed his foot onto the next rock. He repeated the pattern until he had walked about two-thirds of the distance over the stream. The next stone was much smaller than it appeared on the other bank of the stream. He knew it was less than a quarter of his foot in circumference. He slowly lifted his right foot and lowered it to the stone. He slowly pressed his weight onto the stone. His foot slipped, but he regained his position. He paused and looked at the next stone, which was much more extensive and flatter. It looked like a good goal and a safer rock to stand on. As he shifted his weight and lifted his other leg toward the larger stone ahead, he lost his balance and began falling toward the water. Instinctively, he raised the pitchfork and shoved it into the water to brace himself. It sank less than two feet into an extended, sandy bottom. He was able to steady himself and regain his footing. A few more steps, and he made it to the other side. Standing on the other shore, he looked up at the apple tree. Its limbs were drooping with large, heavy red apples. He knelt down, folded his arms, bowed his head, and began to pray.

"Oh, dear God above. Thank you for your kindness and mercy. Thank you for leading me to this beautiful tree of life tree."

He stood, made the sign of the cross, and began to pick the apples. He lifted his robe's apron and began filling it with apples. A few moments later, the apron was filled. He pulled it upward and wrapped the long tie several times around the bundle, creating a closed pouch just over his belly. The apple pouch looked like a large lumpy stomach. When he turned, one of the apples fell from the left side of the apron pouch. As he bent down to pick it up, he was startled by a flock of birds that abruptly scattered from the brush on the other side of the stream. He spun around toward the commotion and discovered four large, hungry wolves. As their yellow eyes met him, their attention turned from the escaping lunch of birds to the prospect

< 148 >

of a much hardier lunch of humans. The lead wolf looked back toward the other three as if to give them new orders. It then looked back at Brother Richard. It began running toward the water in his direction; two others followed. Without thought, Brother Richard reached into the side of his apron, pulled a large apple, and flung it as hard as he could at the charging wolf. The airborne Apple struck the creature directly on its head and between its eyes. The impact obliterated the apple and knocked the wolf into the water. It yelped in pain at the unexpected blow. The blow startled the other wolves, each turning and changing direction but still toward Brother Richard. He again grabbed another apple and then another as he hit the animals with the red pellets. The first wolf, disoriented, turned and ran back toward the shore. The other two attempted to dodge the flying fruit successfully at first, but eventually, they too began to feel the pain of impact from high velocity, large red apples. Brother Richard successfully detoured the wolves. They all ran back into the woods. He bent down and picked up his pitchfork. A few more apples fell from his apron. He tightened the tie, looked around, and began to retrace his steps back across the stream, seeing no other wolves. His heart raced as he realized that he had averted death at the numerous fangs of vicious animals. He slowly followed the trail he had forged earlier, constantly looking ahead for any sign of the animals. Then a more terrifying thought occurred to him. The wolves ran back toward Angelia, her child, and Dom Gordon. He began to run as fast as his body could maneuver through the trail and heavy brush. A few minutes into the trail, he heard screams. He knew the voice; it was Angelia. He heard Dom Gordon yell, "Get down!" He heard the child scream. Finally, he made it through the brush and onto the road. As he broke through the brush, he saw the cart. Two wolves were inching their way up the cart as Angelia held Faith and kicked at them. He saw Dom Gordon on the other side of the cart fighting off another wolf with the other pitchfork. Brother Richard started

< 149 >

running and yelling to attract the attention of the wolves. One
of the wolves saw him; it turned away from Dom Gordon and
began running toward Brother Richard. When it was within feet
of him, it leaped into the air, opened its mouth, a growled,
pointing its long fangs upward in an attacking position. As the
flying wolf came down, Brother Richard stopped, dropped to
his knees, and held the pitchfork in front of him, bracing the
back end into the dirt. The animal had no time or ability to
change its direction as its fell into the sharp forks, piercing
deeply into its body just below its neck. Death was instant.
The weight of the animal knocked Brother Richard over. He
jumped back to his feet and struggled to remove the prongs of
the pitchfork from the animal. After a few attempts, they began
to loosen from the dead flesh. Screams continued from
Angelia, Faith, and Dom Gordon. Brother Richard raised the
bloody pitchfork and continued running toward the cart,
screaming to distract the other wolves at the top of his lungs.
Dom Gordon had snared one wolf that hobbled off into the
woods. He was fighting with another when Brother Richard
reached him. The two men swung and jabbed at the animal, but
it successfully dodged each blow. Finally, Dom Gordon shoved
his pitchfork into the head of the wolf; it dropped to the ground.
Angelia's screams grew louder as she tried to fend off the last
wolf with her feet. It had bit her legs and feet several times, but
she kicked at the animal as blood rushed from her feet and
ankles. Brother Richard ran toward the back just as Angelia lost
her balance, fell off the cart, and onto the ground. The wolf
seized Faith's dress, lifted the little girl out of the cart, and
began to run toward the woods dragging her. Faith Screamed
and cried as the beast carried her by the edge of her garments
like a rabid stork. Brother Richard raised his pitchfork above his
head, pulled his arm back, and thrust the pitchfork into the air
toward the animal with all his strength. Just before it reached
the edge of the woods, the tips of the forks contacted the back
of the wolf's neck and pierced into the back of its head. It

< 150 >

instantly fell dead to the ground, landing on the crying girl. Angelia stood and ran toward her daughter. She and Brother Richard and Dom Gordon reached Faith at the same time. Brother Richard rolled the dead animal off the girl while Angelia lifted Faith into her arms, pulled her to her breasts, and began to cry as she hugged and caressed the child. Dom Gordon hugged Brother Richard and thanked him for his bravery. They turned, held Angelia, and returned to the cart. When they reached the cart, Dom Gordon noticed the blood running from Angelia's ankles. He tore some fabric and began wrapping her ankles, feet, and legs. The blood loss was extensive; within moments, Angelia fainted. They carefully laid her back onto the hay and covered her with a blanket. Brother Richard laid Faith next to her mother. He helped Dom Gordon lift the yoke of the cart, and the two men began pulling it down the path. Brother Richard looked down and realized he still had several apples wrapped in his apron. He loosened the apron, pulled out an apple, and gave it to Dom Gordon. He then took another apple, bit it, broke it in half, and gave it to Faith. The little girl eagerly ate the apple. An hour passed, and not a word was spoken. Finally, Brother Richard spoke,

"What do you think will happen when we reach this estate you know about?"

"What do you mean?" Asked Dom Gordon.

"What if the residents will not allow us to enter? Then what?" He said, feeling apprehensive and nervous.

"They must let us in. We have a severely unhealthy woman who has had to endure two vicious attacks within four days. The last attack nearly cost her her life, and I do not believe the bleeding has stopped yet."

Brother Richard acknowledged the comment and asked, "But what if they do not let us in? What if they, too, know of this plague and are taking steps to protect themselves, including fending off unsolicited visitors? Then what do we do?"

< 151 >

Dom Gordon looked at Brother Richard, shook his head, and said, "I do not know, my son; I can only hope and have faith that God has led us here and that he will not abandon us now."

A clearing opened ahead as the sun began to set, revealing a large roofline with many chimneys. As they got closer, the outline of the building appeared. It was a vast building, more extensive than either had ever seen. Dom Gordon knew that his instinct was correct. They had reached the estate. Now, they hoped and prayed that kind people would welcome them in. Dom Gordon looked down at Angelia. Although he had bound her wounds the best he could, the blood from one of the wounds on her leg continued to soak through the cloth. He knew that if they were turned away from the estate, Angelia would likely die within hours. He felt a surge of adrenalin, much as he had experienced fighting off the wolves, but this time the experience was different; this time, he was preparing for something he had never done in his life; if necessary, he was preparing to fight.

< 152 >

Chapter Ten Notes

A **pitchfork** is an agricultural tool with a long handle and long, thin, widely separated pointed tines (also called prongs) used to lift and pitch (throw) loose material, such as hay or leaves. Pitchforks typically have only three or four times, while dungforks have four or five, other types of forks even up to ten times with different lengths and spacing depending on the purpose. They are usually steel with a long wooden handle but may also be wood, wrought iron, bamboo, alloy, etc. In some parts of England, a pitchfork is known as a prong, and a sprong refers to a 4 pronged pitchfork in parts of Ireland.[2] The pitchfork is similar to the shorter and sturdier garden fork.

The pitchfork and scythes have frequently been used as weapons by those who could not afford or did not have access to more expensive weapons such as swords or, later, guns. Thus, pitchforks and scythes are stereotypically carried by angry mobs or gangs of enraged peasants.

In Europe, the pitchfork was first used in the early Middle Ages, at about the same time as the Harrow. The pitchfork was initially made entirely of wood; today, the tines are usually hard metal.

< 153 >

Chapter Eleven
The Past, Again

"Do not let a doubtful head fight a feeling soul; quite often, the Holy Spirit turns from a closed mind to an open heart."
July 1349

"Monson, let me take that to mother," Michael said as he reached out for the tray that Monson had lifted from the counter.

"Of Course, Michael. Your mother would enjoy seeing you." Monson added as he carefully handed the tray, which included a large bowl of soup, two slices of bread, and a hot cup of tea.

"Now be careful, Michael, do not trip and spill everything." Monson smiled. Michael looked at Monson and returned the smile. He left the kitchen and walked through the dining hall toward the large stairway. When he reached the bottom of the stairway, he paused to fight off a hideous memory. His mind quickly filled with the scene of Mrs. Chattingworth tumbling down the stairs, screaming for a moment, until her neck snapped as her head slammed against the wall, followed by the force of her body. Her lifeless body continued the fall like an old rag doll discarded by a child, tired of playing with it. Michael tightly closed his eyes, clenched his teeth, and forced the thoughts out of his mind. When all was clear, he breathed and began climbing the stairway. Since the tragic death of Mrs. Chattingworth, he had tried to avoid using the main stairway. Instead, he used either the butler's stairs off the kitchen or one of two other stairways' in other parts of the estate. For some reason, this time, he did not think to avoid the

< 154 >

main stairway. Another memory entered his mind when he reached the halfway point up the stairs. He stopped, gazed ahead as if in a trance, and allowed the memory to grow. He saw himself hurrying up the stairway in the Bristol estate. There was a lot of commotion at the top of the stairs and down the hallway. He heard voices, women giggling, and then the voice of William. "A boy, Jillian! It is a boy!" Michael shook his head, turned his head from side to side, and quickly finished the climb. When he reached the top, he turned and headed down the hall to Jillian's room. The door was closed. He gently knocked.

"Please, do come in." Said the soft voice of Jillian.

Michael slowly pushed open the door with his right elbow while balancing the tray in his hands.

Jillian rose from a chair as he entered the room. She smiled and cheerfully said, "Michael, my son, it is so good to see you." Michael smiled and looked toward the small table on the other side of the room. Monson had rearranged the room to look like a parlor with a small eating table and two chairs. Although Jillian was certainly free to move about the estate, Monson knew she mostly preferred to stay in her room. At first, Monson had supplied her with yarn and material, but after making a shoal one day, Monson entered the room at lunchtime. Jillian was sitting in her rocking chair, staring out the window, holding two make-believe knitting needles, and skillfully making a sweater with invisible yarn. From that day forward, he never brought yarn to her. Instead, he would pretend to take the finished clothing and either hang it in the wardrobe or fold it and place it in a drawer.

Michael placed the tray on the table and motioned for Jillian to come to him. She reached her hand out to him, and he took it and helped her to a seat. He slowly pushed the chair under her as she leisurely sat. Jillian looked at the soup, then at the large linen napkin. She picked up the napkin carefully and

< 155 >

adequately folded it in her lap. She then turned toward Michael, standing behind her and to the left.

"Michael, please take the other seat. There is enough food here for both of us."

Michael pulled the other chair from under the table and sat in it. "No, thank you, Mother. I have already eaten." Michael replied, even though he had not eaten.

"Well then, at least stay a while, will not you?" She asked, with a large smile on her face.

Michael could not resist her soft and comforting voice and simple charm. Besides Elizabeth, Jillian was still the most wonderful woman he had ever known. It made him feel peaceful and safe, just being in her presence.

"I would love to stay with you a while, Mother, and I think you will love the stew; Monson worked on it for hours."

"I am sure I will." She thought for a moment and then asked, "How is Monson? I've been worried about him lately."

"He is well, mother. What is your worry about?"

Jillian picked up a spoon and gently scraped it along the top of the stew, slowly curving it enough to scoop the liquid into the spoon. She lifted it to her lips, blew on it, and carefully placed it in her mouth. She savored the stew for a moment and then swallowed.

"Oh my, this is wonderful, Michael. Are you sure you do not want some?" She asked.

"No, thank you, mother. You were saying?"

"Saying what?" Asked Jillian.

"About Monson. You say you have been worried about him"

"Yes, of course," Jillian said as she struggled to gather her thoughts. She placed the spoon down next to the bowl and said,

"I am worried that he may be ill. Have you noticed any change in his behavior lately?" She asked with a concerned look on her face.

< 156 >

Michael was surprised by the question but more surprised that Jillian seemed coherent and controlled her thoughts. He considered her question and then quickly ran the last several hours, and the last few days through his head, looking for moments with Monson. The only thing that caught his attention was the brief conversation earlier that morning as Monson prepared the stew. Michael remembered that Monson did look tired and a bit rundown. Michael, however, had written off the odd behavior as simply age and exhaustion.

"He does seem more tired than usual."

"Perhaps that is it, but will you keep an eye on him?" She has asked me about him several times. We have all been under a lot of stress lately. I know I am finding it very difficult to be here, especially with people constantly coming to me asking about others, like the woman asking about Monson." She said.

It seemed odd to Michael that Jillian spoke about being under stress.

"What do you mean, finding it difficult to be?" Michael asked, his face wrinkled as he spoke.

Jillian placed her hand on Michael's hand as it lay across his lap. She continued, "Michael, there are moments when I feel completely wonderful, as if I've no care in the world. Then there are moments when I see things clearly, and I do not like what I see; it hurts, and it hurts too much, so I go back to the other place." She stopped speaking.

"What other place, mother?" Michael asked.

"The place where Elizabeth and Faith are."

Michael felt a sudden surge of discomfort. He did not expect to hear such things. He moved his hand out from under hers. She reached back and held onto it tightly.

She looked into his eyes and said, "Michael, right now, I am here with you. I know it with every fiber of my being. However, when I am not here, I am in another place. It is beautiful. It is white, gold, and purple and filled with colors

< 157 >

beyond description. There are others there too, many others." Tears began to well up in her eyes. She paused and continued, "Little Hope is there, and so is Elizabeth."

Michael again pulled his hand away from her and stood.

"I am sorry, mother, but I cannot listen to this. I want you to be happy, and if happiness for you requires your mind to retreat deep inside, so be it. But please do not speak of those who are gone and never coming back." His voice cracked, but he regained his composure.

Jillian stood, gently grasped his right hand with both of hers, pulled it to her chest, and said, "Michael, my mind is not retreating deep inside; it is looking deep outside. I have seen them; they are alive there and happy. I have seen others too. The woman's name is Ruth; she is beautiful with long red hair and emerald green eyes; she mentioned Monson. She is one of many that I do not know, yet they know me. I have also seen my father, aunts, uncles, and grandparents, whom I never knew in this life. I have seen Margaret. I have even seen my mother there, Michael."

Michael cringed at the mention of her.

"It is alright, Michael, even she is content there."

"Mother, why do you tell me these things?" Michael asked, trying to hold back his exasperation.

"Because I spend so much time there, Michael; it is as if my spirit goes there only to be pulled back here by my body. It is an unsettling feeling being torn between two worlds."

Realizing that she was more conscious of her current surroundings than he had seen in many months, he asked,

"Mother, do you know where you are, and all that has happened?"

Jillian began to sob.

"Yes, Michael. I do. I know all that has happened. At least I know it now, but fear that I will be pulled back there."

"You said it was a wonderful place. What do you fear?"

< 158 >

"Right now, Michael, I am here with you and like being with you. I have not been with you for such a long time. I want you to know how much I love you. I want you to know how much I appreciate all you have done for us. I know it has been hard, and you have been forced to make many difficult decisions, but your father would be so proud of you."

Michael cut her off, "Excuse me, mother, I do not mean to interrupt you, but you said you have seen them. Have you seen father and Sarah and Lucas?" Michael asked with guarded anticipation.

Jillian thought for a moment and then began to cry.

"No, Michael, I have not seen any of them. Why have I seen so many others that have passed, my parents, grandparents, and even sweet Hope and beautiful Elizabeth, but God has not allowed me to see my William, my Lucas, and my Sarah?" She leaned on his shoulder and began to sob. Michael wrapped his arms around her and tightly held her thin, frail body against him.

"I do not know, mother. I do not know why you do not see them, also." Suddenly, his eyes opened wide. A shocking realization swooped into his mind, just like the little bird that seemed to taunt him. He understood why God had shown her all of those she loved who had already died. As far as William, Lucas, and Sarah, he knew they must still be alive!

The sun was beginning to set as Michael returned to the kitchen with the tray. He placed it on the counter. There was a large pitcher of water next to the washing bucket. He noticed another pot hanging above a smoldering fire in the cooking pit. He placed the bowl, plate, and spoon into the bucket and then took a thick cloth, wrapped it around the hot handle, lifted the pot of hot water, held another fabric at the bottom, and poured some of it into the washing bucket. He then poured some cool water from the pitcher into the bucket. He scrubbed the dishes

< 159 >

and spoon in the water and then placed each on the drying rack. He looked around the kitchen, hoping to see Monson. He dried his hands and walked down the hall off the kitchen. The door to Monson's room was open. He noticed the flickering light from a burning oil lamp. He peaked his head into the room and asked, "Monson, are you awake?" He slowly walked into the room.

Monson was lying on his bed reading a book. He quickly placed it next to him and put a pillow over it as Michael's face met his.

"Yes, I am. Come in, Michael. How is your mother?" He asked.

"Mother is well, be she is concerned about your health."

"She is concerned about me?" He questioned.

Michael nodded.

"She actually spoke to you about me?"

"Yes."

"Are you sure, Michael?

"Of course, I am sure. Why do you act so surprised?"

"Michael, your mother hasn't spoken to either of us in months, at least not in the present tense."

"Yes, I know. But for some reason, she was fully in the present this evening."

"How is she now?" Monson asked.

"She is resting. We had a long conversation about the hereafter, which became too much for her. She returned there as she finished her meal and did not speak to me again."

"Back where? What are you speaking of?" Monson asked, somewhat irritated at the bits and pieces of information Michael was giving him.

"She believes she is trapped between this world and the spirit world. She claims to see those who have died and gone to the other side."

Monson thought for a moment and asked, "Does she speak of this place in gibberish?"

< 160 >

"Truthfully, Monson, I have not heard her speak with such clarity in months. She says it is a wonderful place with complete peacefulness and beauty beyond description. I know she believes what she says, and I am having trouble not believing it myself."

Monson shook his head. The story seemed far-fetched at first, but then he realized that he believed in a life hereafter and in a spirit world where the departed go and wait for judgment. He was intrigued by what Michael was telling him. He had many questions and searched for the best order to begin asking them.

"Wait a moment, Michael; why are you having trouble believing in such a place? She describes the paradise Jesus spoke of to the thief who hung on the cross next to him."

"Monson, you, of all people, know how I feel about God and these things. I want to believe, but my head is filled with doubt, while my heart yearns for it to be true."

"Do not let a doubtful head fight a feeling soul; the Holy Spirit always turns from a closed mind to an open heart."

Monson's words seemed to pierce Michael's mental barricade around himself. He knew the words Monson had spoken were true. The more he lowered the barrier, the more the feelings of doubt escaped back into the darkness, and faith filled the empty crevices of his heart.

"Did she say whom she has seen?" Monson asked.

"Yes, she has seen her parents; she says they are happy."

"Both of them?" Monson asked. Not revealing which of the two, Michael was surprised would have gone to such a wonderful place.

"Yes, Monson, both of them. She has seen others too. She spoke of her grandparents, aunts, uncles, a woman whose name escapes me, and even of Margaret."

"She has seen Margaret?" Monson asked. He smiled and gently wiped a tear without Michael noticing.

< 161 >

"Yes, Monson, Margaret is there, and mother says she too is happy." Michael held back the tears, relieved that Margret was happy and in such a wonderful place.

There was a moment of silence between the two, then Monson asked,

"What about your father, Lucas, and Sarah? Has she seen them?"

Michael breathed in deeply and then exhaled.

"No, she has not seen them."

At first, Monson was surprised. He then smiled and said,

"Michael, do you know what this means?"

"Yes, Monson, you were right. They are not dead; they are alive, and I must find them."

He could no longer hold back the tears. Monson stood and reached for Michael. The two embraced, and Michael only allowed a moment of emotion. This time he suppressed the emotion not out of fear, guilt, or anger but because he wanted to be strong and in control. He wanted to believe that God had not abandoned him after all.

"Monson, I am so sorry."

Monson released Michael, placed his hands on Michael's shoulders, and asked, "Sorry, for what?"

"I am sorry that I have been such a burden on you."

"Nonsense, I have no idea of what you are speaking. If there is a burden, it is me?"

"You have been strong. Your faith has not wavered. Thank you for believing in me even when I no longer believed in myself." Michael said.

Monson smiled at Michael.

"Michael, God believes in you; how could I not?"

Michael smiled and wiped away a tear.

"Michael, if, in fact, your father, brother, and sister are alive, how will you find them? I do not want to discourage you. The things your mother said about the life hereafter and a spirit

< 162 >

paradise where our loved ones go to wait upon the Lord are things we have been taught since we were children. I do believe in such things; I do have faith in them. But your mother's words regarding your family may still be wishful thinking."

"Monson, all of those thoughts entered my mind too. However, other thoughts came to me, like you asking me if I knew for sure if my father was dead since I never saw him buried or if Sarah somehow escaped the fire because her bones were not among the ash. All I know of dear Lucas is that a man stole him away from here. I have as much knowledge that each of them is dead as I do that each of them is alive. Why would I not want to find them?"

"I suppose I cannot argue with such logic. I just do not want your heart to be broken and you to be hurt if things do not turn out the way you hope."

Michael smiled and said, "Monson, my friend, I have already been hurt, and my heart has been broken, for I know that my beautiful Elizabeth and precious Hope are indeed gone from this world. There is nothing I can do to see either of them again in this life. However, God has given me hope to see my father, brother, and baby sister again. I now know that hearts can heal and hurt can go away, but only if we have something to live for. And I do."

Monson smiled in agreement.

"There is one more thing, Monson."

"What is that, Michael?"

"I know my dreams of Elizabeth were not just figments of my imagination. She is alive in Paradise, and I believe she is trying to tell me something. I know that I must be prepared for something."

"Michael, you know I love you and will do anything I can to support you. I do not know your plans, but you can count on me to help."

"I know that, Monson, and thank you. I will check on the animals; you need to rest. Mother also said that she was

< 163 >

concerned about you and your health." Michael walked back to the door, took the handle, and pulled the door behind him as he left the room. He then remembered something and opened the door.

"The woman's name was Ruth. It just came to me as I was leaving. Sorry to barge back in." He began to pull the door shut when Monson called out,

"What did you say?"

Michael stepped in front of the door and said, "The woman who asked about you. Mother said she had long red hair and emerald green eyes. I do not know if that means anything to you, but her name was Ruth. Good night Monson; I will see you in the morning."

Michael left the room and shut the door behind him. Monson stood next to his bed and gazed at the door. He felt a shiver overcome him. He slowly turned, walked back to his bed, and rehearsed the words Michael had just said in his head: long red hair and emerald eyes. He lifted the pillow revealing the letterbox. He lifted the letter he had read out of the box when Michael entered the room. He passed over all of the words and stopped at the valediction, and reread it,

With all of my love, dear Monson, till God brings us together again, yours eternally, Ruth.

~*~*~

Michael began walking through the large front door and toward the chicken pen on the backside of where the barn once stood. Suddenly something off in the distance caught his eye. Something was moving along the dirt path about a quarter league from him. He squinted to get a better look through the heavy tree and brush-lined road. Between a clearing in the brush, he could see two monks pulling a cart behind them for a short moment. He felt the familiar rage of terror overcome him. His first thought was that they were carrying a death cart, and somehow their route detoured them a considerable distance

< 164 >

from the nearest town. He quickly turned, ran back into the estate, and grabbed a crossbow. He was temporarily blinded by the beams of the setting sun shining directly into his face as he opened the front door. He lowered the bow and raised his left arm just above his brow. As he squinted, looking forward, something blocked the sun; it was the silhouette of two monks and a cart less than fifty feet in front of him. He raised the bow and yelled, "Stop! You are not welcome here! Turn around and leave now, or I will begin shooting!"

The monks stopped. Michael felt his heart racing; just the thought of shooting two monks seemed not only impossible but also unforgivable in the eyes of the Lord.

Dom Gordon yelled back, "We have come for shelter, food, and medical attention."

Michael, still yelling, replied,

"We have healthy people here, and we cannot risk that you may be bringing the pestilence with you. You must turn back now!"

He hoped his comments would cause the men to turn and leave. They did not. Dom Gordon yelled,

"We are clean!"

"What are we going to do now, Dom Gordon?" Asked Brother Richard.

"God had brought us here; he will not abandon us now. Lift the cart."

Brother Richard looked at him and asked, "Are you sure he has a crossbow?"

"Yes, I am sure. Moreover, we have God on our side. Lift!"

The men lifted the cart and began walking toward Michael.

"Stop! I command you! Do not make me fire upon you!"

The monks continued to walk. Brother Richard began to shake. To him, it seemed horrible that they survived being

< 165 >

attacked by wolves and a mob of robbers, and now they would be shot by a madman. Nothing seemed to make sense, but for some reason, he felt the courage to do as Dom Gordon had instructed. Although he was terrified, courage and faith gave him the strength to do what he was asked to do.

"I will fire upon you!" Michael yelled again. The men kept walking.

Monson heard the noise and came to the door to see the commotion. He walked up behind Michael and asked, "Michael, what are you doing?"

"We do not know who they are, Monson, but more importantly, we do not know if they are bringing the pestilence to us. I have told them to stop, and I am ready to shoot. Please stand aside, Monson."

Monson took a step back. He knew what Michael had assumed was most likely accurate, and he understood that the action Michael was prepared to take was the most prudent, considering all. Within moments, Michael could make out the details of the monks' faces. He could see that the monk speaking was an older man, about twice the age of the other.

"This is your last warning! Stop now, or you will die!"

Michael raised his crossbow and took aim. He placed his finger on the trigger of the loaded and cocked crossbow. His breathing became heavy, and sweat began to bead on his brow. After such an enlightening and hopeful evening, this was the last thing he had expected. He thought to himself. *"Oh God, why is it that you throw another decoy into my path every time I listen to my heart and turn back to you? Why do you do this to me? Please give me a reason to not kill these monks."*

He began to squeeze the trigger when suddenly he noticed two small hands grasped onto the cart's edge and a small head covered with thick wavy blonde hair peering up from the front edge of the cart. He immediately lowered his crossbow. He heard Monson exhale in relief. He yelled again, "Stop Now, or you give me no choice!"

< 166 >

They kept walking. He again raised the crossbow, placed his finger on the trigger, and began to squeeze it. Monson could see that he was going to fire, and he could also see a little girl's head staring right at them.

Monson yelled, "No!" at Michael just as Michael's finger pulled back the trigger, releasing the hammer cock and forcing the tight spring to flare back and fling the arrow down the track of the weapon's barrel. It was too late to stop the arrow that flew from the crossbow at high speed. Within three seconds, the arrow made an impact and slammed directly into the front of the cart, between the two men, and into the heavy wood, just below the child's body. The arrow made a loud thud as it stuck into the wood. Brother Richard let go of his side of the cart and fell to the ground. Dom Gordon did not expect the additional weight and tilt of the cart. He fell to his knees and then forward into the dirt. Michael was shaking and breathing hard. Monson had seen this site before. When he saw that the arrow had hit the cart, it was apparent that Michael had only fired a warning shot, but the next would not miss. The monks stood up, brushed themselves off, lifted the cart, and continued to walk toward the estate. Michael raised the crossbow, reloaded it with another arrow, pulled the hammer back, and aimed it at the monks again. Monson stepped forward to the side of Michael and yelled at the Monks,

"Have you lost your minds? He will kill you. Now stop
He will not miss a second time!"

The monks stopped. Michael was relieved that the monks had listened to Monson because he was prepared to shoot the speaking monk in the chest.

"Michael, may I speak to them?"

Michael, with his crossbow, pointed at Dom Gordon, nodded.

Monson yelled toward the monks. "Surely, you know of the great pestilence that has caused the death of many. We are

< 167 >

only trying to protect our loved ones, and we cannot risk the possibility that you have the plague."

Dom Gordon replied, "I can assure you, kind sir, that none of us have the plague, and we have not encountered anyone with such a sickness."

"Then why have you come?" Asked Monson.

"We escaped from our monastery at night as it was being overrun by heathens. There were twenty-two of us."

Michael looked at Monson. Monson looked back at the monks and asked, "Where are the others?"

"I sent them to Saint Gabriel's Monastery, it was about a two-day journey in a different direction, and we knew that the woman we have with us would not make such a journey?"

"What woman?" Michael asked, and he lowered his weapon.

"She is very ill." Replied Dom Gordon.

Michael raised his weapon again and yelled, "You cannot bring a plague victim here!"

"She does not have the plague; she was attacked and beaten by vile creatures; one was human, and the other werewolves!" Yelled Dom Gordon.

Michael and Monson looked at each other; Michael had a confused look on his face. He had no idea what the priest meant by such a comment. He had heard old childhood stories of half-man and half-wolf creatures, but he knew they were just stories made up to scare children.

"What nonsense do you speak?" Michael shouted back at them.

"It is not nonsense! A few days ago, we found her lying on the side of the road; she had been beaten and defiled. We did our best to nurse her back to health. Her condition had improved, but we were attacked by wolves not far from here, and though we have bandaged her, she is still losing blood. If we do not get her attention soon, she will die."

Monson looked at Michael and said,

< 168 >

"Michael, I believe that they are telling the truth. We cannot turn them away and risk that woman's death."

Michael thought for a moment and yelled,

"Does the woman have dark-colored bruises or pustules on her body?"

Dom Gordon hesitated to answer because he did not understand the nature of the question. Brother Richard quickly responded at the top of his lungs,

"No, she does not! I have seen every inch of her naked body, and I can assure you that she is as clean and healthy as a white dove!"

Dom Gordon frowned at Brother Richard. Brother Richard shrugged his shoulders. Michael and Monson looked at each other again, and Michael asked Monson in disbelief,

"Do you really believe these men are monks?"

Monson was unsure how to react; he surely did not expect such an answer from one who had made an oath of chastity and dedicated his life to serving God.

Monson yelled, "How do we know that you are truly monks and not the vermin who attacked this woman you speak of?"

"My name is Dom Gordon; I entered the holy priesthood of God nearly forty years ago. I can assure you that I speak the truth when I tell you that my brother Richard and I have been ordained to serve God."

Monson reached out and touched the crossbow's top, slowly pushing it down toward the ground and walking toward the monks.

"Monson, what are you doing?" Michael asked.

Monson lifted his left hand in the air, signaling to Michael that all was well. He continued to walk, and Michael slowly followed behind him. As they got closer to the monks, their bodies could no longer block the sun's rays. Michael continued to try to block the sun with his arm, yet Monson walked to the men. Dom Gordon began walking toward

< 169 >

Monson. Suddenly his face lit up, surrounded by bright red glistening rays of a setting sun. Monson smiled too. He lifted his arms toward the man and asked,

"Dom Gordon, is it really you?"

Dom Gordon smiled and asked, Father Monson, is it you?"

The men embraced. Both Brother Richard and Michael were confused, and Michael looked at Brother Richard, who lifted his right hand and made an awkward small circle wave at him.

"Hello, I am Richard…Brother Richard."

Michael did not notice what Brother Richard had said, and he was too interested in the relationship between Monson and the other monk. Michael looked at the cart. The little girl who had been hiding lifted her head smiled at Michael, and cheerfully declared, "I am Faith."

Michael smiled at her. He walked up to the cart and looked over into it. He saw Angelia lying on her back in the hay. He was startled at her thick, long wavy blonde hair and pale skin. It was like looking at Elizabeth. The men released their embrace. Dom Gordon looked at Monson and said, "I thought you were dead?"

Monson laughed and said, "Dead? No. I haven't been dead for years!"

The men laughed. Michael looked at Monson and asked, "Did he call you, Father Monson?"

Monson smiled and said, "Yes, he did."

Michael did not know what to think. These men were monks, telling the truth about having a woman in their cart who looked pretty beaten up but did not look like she had the plague. Michael lifted one of the cart's handles, and Brother Richard lifted the other. He looked at Monson and said, "Let us get this woman to the estate and tend to her wounds."

< 170 >

They all began to hurry to the estate pulling the cart behind them. Faith smiled at Michael and lay next to her mother. Michael spoke to Monson.

"I believe we have herbs and remedies to stop the bleeding. We also have proper cloth for bandages."

"Agreed." Monson nodded.

"And Monson," Michael paused, with a curious look," I mean Father, we will speak later."

"Yes, Michael, I am sure we will, my son." He winked and smiled.

< 171 >

Chapter Twelve
A Kindling Flame

"It takes a minute to find a special person, an hour to appreciate them, and a day to love them, but it takes an entire lifetime to forget them." —Anonymous

July 1349

Michael leaned over, placed his arms under her body, and carefully lifted her out of the cart. He gently tilted her head against his left shoulder to keep it from hanging unsupported. She tried to open her eyes but lacked the strength to focus. She exhaled and moaned quietly due to the pain in her ankles and her sore and bruised ribs. As he walked toward the estate with her in his arms, a slight breeze whisked her long blonde hair back and forth and tossed several strands over her face and forehead. She mustered enough strength to open her eyes. As her eyes opened, she caught Michael's eyes. Her lips parted, and she softly said,

"Percival, you've come back to me."

Her eyes closed, and she fell back to sleep. Michael understood that she thought he was someone else, perhaps her husband, he thought. Brother Richard leaned into Michael and whispered into his ear, "That is the name of her husband."

Michael nodded, "I see." He said, trying not to act interested.

Brother Richard leaned in again and said, almost matter-of-factly, "He's dead, and she doesn't know it yet."

Michael looked puzzled. He turned toward Brother Richard as they continued to walk toward the large front doors and asked, "What do you mean she does not know it yet?" It

< 172 >

seemed like a reasonable question, but it appeared even odder that the woman did not know about the death of her husband.

Brother Richard replied, "I will explain it to you later. Now is not the time to say anything." He looked at her and pointed, "I do not want to upset her anymore."

Michael nodded. As they approached the front doors, Michael had a flashback of carrying his beloved Elizabeth the day she was attacked by men in the barn. He remembered the intense rage at the abhorrent men who attacked her and the overwhelming love and concern for her, her health, and their unborn child's health. For a moment, carrying this woman created an uncanny Deja Vu. Monson walked ahead and opened the door. He motioned Michael in; Michael walked through the door first, followed by Dom Gordon, holding little Faith, and then Brother Richard.

"Take her to the first guest room up the stairs and to the right. I will meet you there with clean water, cloth, and herbs."

Michael nodded and began walking up the stairway. Brother Richard began to follow him until Monson said, "Brother Richard, I could use the help of both of you in the kitchen."

Brother Richard smiled and said, "Of course, of course," He and Dom Gordon followed Monson into the kitchen. Michael could tell that Brother Richard had some attachment to the woman; he was not sure what kind, especially after the naked body comment, but he figured there would be time to discuss that later. When Michael reached the room, he carefully pressed down on the doorknob and pushed the door open with his back, careful not to brush Angelia against anything. He backed into the room and turned around, facing the bed. He had never entered this room before. He was somewhat surprised at the difference in décor compared to the other rooms. He knew this was a special guest room, but it had not occurred to him that Lady Chattingworth had gone to such trouble to ensure it was fitted with fine furniture, wall coverings, and area rugs. He

< 173 >

walked to the bed and gently laid her on top of it. He slowly pushed her body toward the center of the bed to ensure that she would not fall off the bed if she moved. Both of her ankles were tightly wrapped with a blood-soaked cloth. Her feet were dirty, and it was difficult to see how much of the debris was dirt and blood. Since he could not see any dripping, it looked to him that the bleeding had stopped. He stood above her and looked down at her. He gently lifted some of the hair that had draped over her face and brushed it to the side. Her face had patches of dirt, debris, and small pieces of hay from the cart. There were a few streaks of splattered blood, which he assumed to be her blood as she was fighting off wolves. As he looked at her, he was impressed at what seemed to be her tenacity to fight off wolves, and then it occurred to him that she was not just fighting for her own life but that of her little girl. As he stood looking at her, he tried to suppress his desire to compare her to Elizabeth, but it was complicated to fight the obvious.

Elizabeth was one of the most beautiful women he had ever known, yet this woman looked so similar to her that it was uncanny. He waited for a moment to make sure she was breathing comfortably. He expected Monson and the monks any moment with water bandages and aid for her lacerations. His mind kept trying to take him to memories, but he fought the desire and focused on staying in the present. He knew that she was not Elizabeth and that it was inappropriate to allow himself to foster any feelings for a woman who was already married to someone else. Then a quick thought entered his mind as if a voice said, *"She's no longer married; her husband is dead."* He shook off the inner voice, and then another sharp thought and quick vision entered his mind; Elizabeth was staring down at him with pure blonde hair and glistening gold mist surrounding her. With her bright powder-blue eyes looking directly at him, she said, *"They're Here!"* Michael took a step backward and was

< 174 >

shocked by reality as a large hand pressed against his back. It was Monson.

"Michael, are you alright?"

"Yes, Monson, I am well."

"Fine then, please move aside while we tend to her wounds."

Michael stepped aside as Monson and Dom Gordon walked past him, carrying a large pitcher of steaming water, another of cold water, several towels, and a few bottles of ointment. Brother Richard came in behind, bringing little Faith two bowls, one for the water and one for the dirty cloth to be removed. He stopped, handed Faith to Michael, and said, "Here, Michael, please hold the baby for a moment?"

Michael accepted the little girl into his arms. As he held her, she looked up at him and smiled and said, "I am Faith," and pointed to Angelia and said, "she's my mommy."   Michael smiled at her and then looked back at Angelia.

"What is her name?" Michael asked Brother Richard.

"Angelia." Replied Brother Richard.

Michael stood back as the men carefully and modestly tended to her wounds. When all of the bandages were removed, they began to clean the wounds. Most injuries had stopped bleeding, all but one, as blood began to flow freely as the last piece of cloth was removed. Monson worked quickly to clean it. He then rubbed a thick save onto the wound and had Dom Gordon assist him in wrapping a thin cotton strip around the ankle, tight enough to bind the torn skin together but not too tight to cut off the circulation.   Eventually, the blood flow stopped.   Michael was amazed at the precision in Monson's hands and his knowledge of healing herbs and wound dressings. After about forty minutes, the men had finished washing her legs and feet and bandaging her wounds.   Angelia remained unconscious until shortly after the last bandage was in place. She slowly opened her eyes and surveyed the room and the three men standing around her.   She flinched, and Brother

< 175 >

Richard reached her hand and said, "You are just fine, my lady. These are friends; you are safe."

"Where is my Faith?"

Michael leaned in and handed the girl to her mother. Angelia smiled at him and said, "Thank you, sir."

With Faith in her arms, she closed her eyes and fell asleep. Monson began collecting the bowls, towels, and other items used for Angelia. Dom Gordon took the dirty dressings and placed them in a bag Monson handed him. Brother Richard noticed the pitcher and bowl across the room put on a large dressing table under a large gold-framed mirror. He walked to the table, leaned over the pitcher, looked down into it, and slowly moved his head in a circular motion as if tracing the top of the pitcher. He picked it up and ran his finger along the bowl's surface.

He put the pitcher down, wiped his finger on his tunic, and asked Monson, "Sir, do you mind if I take the pitcher and bowl down, clean them, and fill them with fresh water?"

"Of course not, it has been a while since this room has been used, and I am sure it is a bit dusty." Monson replied, then added, "And please, call me Monson."

Brother Richard smiled, nodded, and said, "Yes, Father Monson."

Michael had been looking at Angelia but looked up at Monson. Monson awkwardly smiled and looked at Brother Richard and said, "Just Monson, thank you!"

Brother Richard realized that he had stumbled into an uncomfortable area. He wished that he could have taken back his previous comments. He quickly responded, "Yes, Dom Monson, I mean Monson. That is surely your name, and I will not call you by any other name or title, sir."

He shook his head, realizing the more he spoke, the goofier he sounded. He quickly picked up the pitcher and bowl and left the room. Michael smiled at the folly of the situation. His eyes again met Monsoon's, and the two men turned away.

< 176 >

Monson continued to gather things until his arms were full. Dom Gordon looked at Monson and said, "It appears that you and I have everything. Shall we take these things back to the kitchen? Tell me where your garbage pile is, and I will dispose of the items in my arms."

Monson nodded, and he and Dom Gordon turned and walked to the door. Monson stopped, turned back to Michael, and said, "Michael, I almost forgot. The chamber pot is under the bed, and would you mind retrieving it and placing it on the small stool next to the changing table?"

Michael looked a bit puzzled. He had not thought a chamber pot would be necessary since the estate had several garderobes on each floor. Monson could tell that Michael was concerned.

"Do not worry; I doubt she'll need it. But if she does, at least she'll see it,"

Michael considered what Monson had said. He hesitated, and Monson said, "Go ahead." He looked down and pointed.

"It should be just under the foot of the bed." Michael looked at Monson, knelt at the foot of the bed, lifted that overstuffed spread, and began to slide his hand under the bed. It was too dark to see anything.

Monson continued, "Be careful, I think it is clean, but I cannot be sure."

Monson and Dom Gordon both quietly chuckled as they left the room. Michael stopped and withdrew his arm from under the bed. He realized that Monson was only teasing him because the room had not been lived in for many months or even years, and if the chamber pot were dirty, there would still be a stench in the air, which there was not. Next to the bed was an oversized, thickly stuffed cotton chair with a large back, wide fabric-covered arms, and sizeable wood-carved lion's feet. Michael stood, walked to the chair, and sat down. He thought for a moment about the chamber pot and the possibility that

< 177 >

Angelia may need it in the middle of the night.   It seemed primitive to offer a guest of the estate a chamber pot when the architect went to such trouble to build eighteen garderobes (toilet rooms), eight on the main floor, eight on the second floor, and two in the attic. Michael stood and then left the room. He walked down the hall, and after passing another bedroom, he came to a garderoom. He opened the door and looked into the room. He wondered if Angelia, in her condition, could walk to this room if she needed to relieve herself. The thought of requiring her to use a chamber pot now seemed revolting. Michael thought about how much his life had changed since William first brought him to the estate.   The first time he had seen a garderobe was at the Bristol estate.   He remembered walking into the immense cold, dark room, lifting the lid, and looking down the long slick rock chute that seemed to end somewhere in the depths of hell; at least, that's what he thought as a twelve-year-old boy.

After years of living with such niceties, Michael did not want a guest of the estate to be expected to use what now seemed to be ancient or peasant technology. Each room was built with stone, approximately ten feet by ten feet, with rounded corners. A built-in bench raised two feet high and one and a half feet deep at the back of the room. The bench was made of red mahogany carved with intercut vines and gold leaf. The top of the bench was rounded to a flat solid surface. In the center of the bench was a raised wood-carved seat with rounded edges.   The center of the seat had been cut out, leaving an elongated circular surface to sit upon. The seat was covered with a hinged lid made of the same wood and a four-inch jewel and gold-covered ring that ran the circumference. The top, when closed, sealed the seat to limit any odor derived from the floor of the cesspit. Each room also had an iron pipe hidden in the wooden bench, vented from the exterior wall. Since the rooms were all rock, including the floor, they were usually cold, especially in winter. Lady Chattingworth had included

< 178 >

sheepskin rugs in front of each bench and a folded blanket next to the seat. The other side of the seat had a shoe-sized box filled with a soft disposable cotton cloth. Next to each doorway, either to the left or the right, depending on the room, was a large wooden bureau carved of the same wood and with the exact etchings and adornment as the bench. Each bureau had a tall, built-in mirror. A bowl and pitcher are on the bureau, and a stack of small white hand towels is next to the bowl.

Michael walked back to the room and quietly sat in the oversized chair. He stared at Angelia, noticing her chest rise and lower with each breath. She seemed to be sleeping well. It had been about fifteen minutes since the men had left the room. He wondered how much longer Brother Richard would be fetching clean water. He looked at Angelia and then toward the floor at the foot of the bed. He shook his head, realizing that he had not solved the problem of the chamber pot or the garderobe. He smiled and thought how stupid it was to be so concerned about such a thing. It almost seemed out of character. He was used to the women of the estate, cooking, cleaning, and attending to guests or others who lived on the estate. This was the first time they had guests since he, Monson, and Jillian had been left alone. He had not had to think about such things. He looked at the bandaged ankles and feet of Angelia. The more he thought about it, the more obvious it became that it would not be possible for her to get out of bed and walk down the hall to the garderobe. Now the chamber pot seemed like the most logical solution. He got up from the chair, walked over to the foot of the bed, and kneeled down. He lifted the bedspread and leaned down to the floor, placing his head partway under the bed. It was dark and difficult to see. He reached in with his arm and began to wave it from side to side, trying to find the pot. Monson, Dom Gordon, and Brother Richard walked into the room.

< 179 >

"Michael, are you still looking for the chamber pot?" Monson asked while placing his fist to his mouth to cover his smile. The other two looked at one another.

"Come out from there, Michael; there is no chamber pot under that bed or any bed in the estate. In fact, there has never been a chamber pot anywhere in this home."

Michael lifted his head from under the bed, looked up at Monson, and asked, "Really, Monson? You had me looking for something that doesn't exist?"

Monson smiled, and the others laughed lightly.

"I do not see the humor in that?" Michael said as he stood from the floor.

"Michael, I thought you would know I was joking with you before I ever left the room. I did not expect you to spend all this time looking for an item that will not be found in the estate."

"I haven't been looking the entire time. In fact, I just now bent down to find it. I went to the garderobe down the hall to see how feasible it would be for the woman to walk to the room if she needed to in the middle of the night."

Brother Richard piped in, "Sir, I do not believe that Angelia is in any condition to be walking. It is best if we fetch the chamber pot."

Monson added, "As I have said, there is not one in the estate. We do not need one since we have many garderobes on each floor."

"Perhaps you could find a large bucket." Said Brother Richard.

"I did not think of that." Said Monson.

"A bucket would work." Said Dom Gordon.

Michael was frustrated that the men were making such decisions without even considering the woman's comfort.

"Nonsense!" Michael stated.

"We will not give her a bucket and tell her to use it as a common peasant!"

< 180 >

"If she wakes in the middle of the night, what other option do we have, Michael?" Asked Monson.

Michael, without thinking, said,

"I guess I will just stay with her through the night."

Brother Richard quickly spouted,

"Oh, I do not mind staying with her, sir. It would not be the first time."

Michael raised his eyebrows and looked at Dom Gordon, who seemed not concerned at the suggestion.

"It would not be the first time? Are you or are you not a monk?" Michael asked.

Brother Richard became embarrassed.

"On no, sir, it is nothing like that."

"I cannot help but question, especially when you commented earlier about how you had seen her naked body. I am still confused at how that could have happened."

Both Brother Richard and Dom Gordon began talking at the same time.

"No, it is nothing like that!" Added Dom Gordon.

"No, it was when she first came to us." Said Brother Richard.

"She needed attention." Said Dom Gordon. He started to speak again, but Brother Richard cut him off.

"She needed to be bathed." Blurted Brother Richard.

"Stop! I do not need to hear anymore. Please spare me the details." Michael said while raising his hands in the air.

"No, my son, it is not what you think." Replied Dom Gordon. Brother Richard interrupted him again, and Dom Gordon stopped him by saying,

"Brother Richard, hush, please. Let me speak." "Michael, all we did was tend to her wounds. Her clothing was torn and muddy. We discreetly removed her clothing and covered her in one of our robes, like the one she is wearing today."

Michael looked at the robe and then at the monks.

< 181 >

"I see." He said he was embarrassed at the conversation and wanted to change it immediately.

"Well, I think it best that we discuss this another time," Michael said.

"I would be most happy to discuss it with you again, Michael." Eagerly stated Brother Richard.

Michael shook his head and replied,

"Actually, I am not interested in ever discussing this again; thank you!" Michael quickly responded.

"No, I think it is best if I stay with her the night."

Brother Richard looked at Dom Gordon with a surprised look on his face. Michael could tell that his comment was misinterpreted.

"Over there," he pointed to an overstuffed leather chase on the other side of the room," I will sleep over there, where I can hear her if she wakes in the middle of the night."

The monks nodded in relief.

Michael continued, Monson would you be so kind as to show these OK rooms where they can retire for the night?"

"Of course, Michael." He lifted his right arm and pointed out the door, "Come, brothers, there are other rooms down the hall that I believe will suit you just fine."

The monks turned and followed Monson out of the room; brother Richard turned back toward Michael and said,

"If she gets chilly in the middle of the night, it is because she kicked the blanket off her feet."

Michael wrinkled his eyebrows at Brother Richard's comment. Again, it seemed like the monk had too much information about the woman.

"Thank you, I will try and be aware if such a thing occurs." Said Michael as he waved the men out of the room.

Michael walked over to the water basin and inspected the pitcher of water. He then walked back to the bed and looked at Angelia. She seemed to be resting peacefully. He looked at the bedding draped over her and then at her feet. Due

< 182 >

to how the bed had been dressed, it seemed impossible that she could kick her covers off. Michael shook his head and attempted to get the last comments out of his mind. He looked over to the large bureau on the other side of the room. He walked to it, slowly opened one of the drawers, and looked in. He found two blankets, took one, and laid it on the chase. He then walked back to the other side of the bed and carefully pulled the new pillow toward him.

Angelia turned her head toward him but remained asleep. He stopped for a moment and then began pulling the pillow again. Angelia turned her body and threw one of her arms over the pillow. Her hand lay across his. At first, he was startled but did not want to move too quickly and risk waking her. He waited a moment and began to slide his hand out from under hers. She squeezed his fingers, and he stopped moving. For a moment, it felt like Elizabeth's soft fingers. He felt his heart beating faster; he did not know if the woman was awake or asleep. He looked at her face; she had a faint smile. It appeared as if she was still sleeping. He wondered what she was dreaming, was it a dream of lying next to her husband, the man she loved, or was it some other memory. Michael felt sad for this woman, knowing she would never again see her husband and knew she had no idea he was dead. He understood the pain she was about to encounter and the feeling of complete loneliness, helplessness, and fear. His heart seemed huge now, filled with empathy and compassion for a beautiful young woman who would wake in the morning to another day of hoping to see her beloved. He knew she would not receive the news of her husband's death. He closed his eyes and internalized the words, *"Please, God, help her get through the pain."*

He carefully pulled his hand away, and her fingers ran from his palm over his knuckles and slowly along the length of his fingers. He stopped for a moment, closed his eyes, and pretended it was Elizabeth. He opened his eyes and continued

< 183 >

pulling away until the tips of her fingers fell from the ends of his. He breathed out with a feeling of success. He leaned over, lifted her arm, and removed the pillow from beneath it. He gently placed her arm back on the bed. He stood for a moment and thought about the night ahead. He hoped that she would sleep through the night but was concerned that she would not.

He turned and walked to the chase. He placed the pillow on the chair. He lifted the blanket and shook it out, unfolding it to the floor. He removed his shoes and his tunic, leaving him shirtless and barefoot. He began to remove his trousers, but it occurred to him that it would not be in his best interest to lie half-naked if Angelia were to wake in the middle of the night. He walked to the water basin, took a clean cloth, and slowly dunked it into the pitcher. He squeezed the excess water back into the pitcher. He looked up at his reflection in the mirror. His thick black wavy hair was longer than usual, covering his ears, curling around his neck, and ending at his shoulders. He knew that Elizabeth would disapprove of such a look. He noticed that his face and neck had dirt patches along with slight wrinkles and crevices. Michael rubbed the wet cloth around his face and neck, down his chest and arms, and around his waist. A memory flashed in his mind of the first day he spent at the Bristol estate as a twelve-year-old who felt utterly out of place. He remembered waking in the morning to the sounds of talking women. His mind forwarded to the moment he was stripped and placed in a large tub and all of the soapy hands and washcloths all over his body. At the time, it was terrifying and extremely embarrassing. However, he smiled and quietly laughed at that moment, realizing that many things in life are difficult, uncomfortable, or scary. Still, as time passes and one has overcome the situation and learned from it, one can look back and laugh that it ever happened.

Most of the water had left the cloth after washing his upper torso. He placed the damp cloth onto another small and dry cloth. He took one of the towels and slowly dried his face,

< 184 >

neck, chest, stomach, arms, and hands. He rolled the towel into a ball and dropped it into a basket on the floor that had been placed next to the dresser. He turned back toward the bed. He walked to each side of the bed and carefully extinguished the lamps. The last light was on a small table next to the chase. He pulled the blanket back, climbed onto the chase, covered himself with it, and then reached for the lamp and slowly extinguished it. As the light dimmed, darkness filled the room. The only light shone in from the opened window and half-moon in the sky. The long heavy curtain was parted, allowing a soft breeze to enter the room and swirl around him. He looked at the half-moon and smiled. It had been a memorable day. It was the first time in months that he felt calm and reconnected in part to God. It was also the first time since her death that he felt peace deep inside. As he gazed out the window, a smile parted his lips, and he quietly mouthed the words, *"I love you, Elizabeth ."* He imagined her face looking down on him from the bright moon, her hair waving in the breeze, and her beautiful lips saying, *"I love you too, Michael."* He breathed in the tender moment of love and gratitude.

He turned and faced the bed, which was now just a faint outline in the darkened room. He slowly closed his eyes and hoped he would not open them again until daylight came, but something told him he would open them much sooner. Within moments his mind slowed, peace overcame him, and he slept.

~*~*~

She opened her eyes and looked up at the ceiling. It was still dark and difficult to make out the surroundings. She knew she was in a different room, a place she had never seen before. At first, it startled her, but then she remembered being carried into the room and laid on the bed. She vaguely remembered the monks and another man cleaning her wounds and wrapping them with new cloth. She wiggled her toes and felt a slight twinge of pain in her left shin, where the wolf's bite made the

< 185 >

deepest incision, but her right ankle and foot felt fine. She moved her shoulders to the left, then to the right. Her ribs were still sore, but her extremities seemed healthy and workable except for her lower left leg. She adjusted her hips that had sunk into the stuffed fluffy mattress. She breathed in deeply and then exhaled. She listened to the room but only heard the soft snores of little Faith, lying stretched out on her back, arms over her head and legs spread out, leaving her body in an X shape. Faith seemed to be sleeping soundly. She carefully leaned over and kissed her on the cheek. Suddenly, she remembered what had awakened her, her bladder was full, and she needed to find a place to relieve it. She slowly sat up in the bed, braced herself by putting both arms behind her, and pressed into the bed. She slowly swung her right leg over the edge of the bed, uncovering her toes and bending her knee, allowing her leg to swing alongside the bed. She turned her body and carefully slid her left leg over the edge of the bed, leaving her in a sitting position with both feet barely grazing the floor. The darkness made it difficult to gauge her surroundings. She remembered several pieces of furniture in the room but could not remember their placement or configuration. As she sat on the bed, formulating a strategy to leave the room in search of a place to relieve herself, she noticed the window in front of her about ten feet away. She could make out the parted drapes and what appeared to be a long chair or high-backed sofa just under it. She could not see the door but knew it was at the end of the room facing the foot of the bed. She felt an ache in her bladder and knew she had better find a place to relieve it before losing control. She stretched out her right leg and attempted to stand as her toes touched the furry rug on the floor. Carefully and slowly, she slid her left foot to the floor. With both hands holding onto the bed on either side of her, she leaned forward, placing most of her weight on her strong right leg and very little on her left. In a measured manner, she lifted her body until she stood on both feet. It seemed possible to walk and feasible that walking

< 186 >

would allow her to search the room for a chamber pot. Still standing in the original spot, she looked to the right, squinted her eyes, and attempted to see through the dark room; her attempts were useless. She then looked to the left and repeated the same process, still without results. She lifted her left foot about an inch from the floor and moved it one step in front of her. Carefully, she lowered her weight onto the foot. A shock of pain ran up her leg, causing a major cramp in her knee and thigh. She leaned forward and attempted to brace herself by thrusting her right foot forward and firmly planting it in front of her. The reaction kept her from toppling over, but the habit of rhythmically placing one foot in front of the other caused her to lift her left foot and repeat the same right motion; this time, the pain caused her to fall forward. She tried to catch herself until she realized that she would fall regardless. She raised her hands above her head and took solace that she was close enough to fall onto the sofa in front of her. She leaped forward, springing off her right foot and allowing her body to fly toward the sofa. As her body was in midflight and unable to stop, she noticed a form on the sofa that caused a moment of terror. Suddenly, Michael, who had been sleeping soundly on his back, opened his eyes just in time to receive the full weight of her body. He instinctually tightened his muscles and wrapped his arms around her, pulling her arms inward and sliding her hands onto his naked chest as their bodies impacted. Angelia wanted to scream but did not want to wake Faith. Michael had no idea why a woman came flying through the air and landed on top of him. Still wrapped in his embrace, Angelia suppressed her scream to a soft whimper. The sudden impact of her body forced the air from his lungs up through his throat and past his vocal cords, causing a low voice heaving sound. She leaned to the left, pulling both to the edge of the lounge. Their bodies locked together continued to roll and fell to the thick rug-covered floor; this time, Michael's body was lying upon hers, with his arms still wrapped around her back. Up to this point,

< 187 >

the entire ordeal lasted only seconds, with neither party controlling the situation. Michael gathered his breath and looked down into the face of the woman below him. Enough light pierced through the window for the two to see the outline of each other's faces. Angelia continued leaning to the left, causing Michael's body to roll to the side, swapping the position until she was on top. As the bodies stopped, Angelia straddled over Michael and lifted her torso above him, bracing herself with hands on either side of his neck. Her thick hair fell over his face as he attempted to look at her. The door opened, and a man holding a lantern rushed through. It was brother Richard. He first looked at the bed and gasped, not seeing Angelia; he then moved to the other side, lifted the lantern above his head, saw Angelia straddled over Michael, and shouted,

"My lady, what in the name of all holy are you doing?" His voice woke Faith, and she began to cry. Angelia, able to see her surroundings, turned and looked up toward the light. Michael tried to open his mouth to speak but could not because his mouth was filled with the entire left side of her hair.

"Oh, brother Richard, you startled me." She said. "And your voice has awakened the baby."

Angelia realized the man under her was struggling to free himself from her hair. She rolled off him into a sitting position on the floor next to him, and Michael also sat up next to her.

"Sir Michael, surely God does not look down kindly at your intentions with this woman!" scolded brother Richard.

"Wait a moment, Sir!" Michael defended. "Do not assume that what you see here is what you see!" Realizing that his statement lacked continuity, he continued, "I mean, I was sleeping soundly over there," he pointed to the chase, "When suddenly I awoke to the sensation of a warm body heaped upon me and conjoining with mine."

< 188 >

Angelia, to explain herself, blurted, "Well, I mean, we did not exactly conjoin...."

Michael cut her off,

"No! We did not!"

Faith, whimpering louder, crawled to the edge of the bed. The monk reached down, lifted her with his right hand, and pulled her against his body. She snuggled against him.

"Hush, child, and turn away from this sinful sight. Hide thine eyes from such wickedness." The monk stated as he condemned what appeared to be an act of sinful behavior.

"Brother Richard! Stop it! Nothing happened here! I awoke in dire need of a chamber pot. It was dark; I did not know where I was; I tried to stand and fell onto the sofa over there." She pointed to the chase. Brother Richard raised his left eyebrow and looked at the chase.

"Yes, I know. The vile bed of fornication has twice been brought to my attention." He added.

Exasperated, Michael responded.

"That is enough, brother Richard! Nothing has happened here except an unfortunate accident."

"Yes, an accident, and there will be another any moment if I do not find a chamber pot!" exclaimed Angelia. She tried to stand, and Michael stood and helped her to her feet.

"I am sorry, but there are no chamber pots in this estate," Michael said.

Angelia felt her heart pound and her bladder ache.

"What do you mean you have none? Am I supposed to run into the woods?" She asked.

"Of course not!" replied Michael. "But we do have indoor facilities; they are called garderobes,"

Angelia looked confused and asked, "Indoor facilities?"

"Yes, indoor"

"At this point, I do not care; just help me get to one of these chamber pot rooms before another accident occurs!" She

< 189 >

tried to walk, but the pain in her left ankle was too much. Michael reached down and lifted her into his arms.

"Please hurry!" She asked.

Michael brushed aside Brother Richard and hurried through the door. Brother Richard began to put the pieces together, and he felt a sense of relief at the realization that nothing appeared to have happened.

When they arrived at the first garderobe, Michael pushed the door open with his foot. The room was pitch black, and Michael carefully felt for the bench with his feet as he carried Angelia into the room.

"Where are we?" Angelia asked.

"This is it," Michael responded. He found the edge of the bench. "Let me put you here while I find the lamp and light it." He sat her on the end of the bench. She felt a sense of urgency. Michael walked back toward the door that was letting in the faint light. He saw the lamp on the edge of the bureau. He lifted the globe from the lamp and placed it next to it. He felt around until his fingers touched the magnesium flint. He slid his hand further and found the metal knife. He raised the lantern wick, took the flint, and struck the blade against it until a spark lit the oil-covered wick. He adjusted the flame, replaced the globe, and turned back toward Angelia. Light filled the room. Angelia noticed the lid-covered seat next to her and asked, "What is that?"

Michael smiled and said, "That, my lady is the built-in chamber pot. Just lift the lid, sit on it, and...." He hesitated, "well, you know...." She looked at him, tilted her head, and raised her eyebrows. Michael realized that he needed to give her privacy.

"Oh yes, I will be just outside the door when you need me," he nervously gasped. He left the room and closed the door behind him. As he waited, he contemplated what had just transpired. He understood how things must have looked to the monk. He smiled at the humor in the situation and was relieved

< 190 >

that neither he nor Angelia had been hurt in confusion. The more he thought about it, the more humorous it seemed. He smiled and shook his head.

"Excuse me, sir? Are you still there? Hello?"

Michael recognized the voice and replied, "Yes, I am here. Are you finished?" he asked. He closed his eyes and clenched his teeth wishing that he did not ask if she was finished.

"Yes, thank you. But I am still in need of your assistance to make it back to the bed." She closed her eyes and clenched her teeth, wishing she had not added the word "bed." "I mean, I need your help to make it back to my room."

"Understood," said Michael. "I am coming in now."

He slowly opened the door. Angelia was standing next to the basin. The flickering light created a halo around her head, emphasizing her bright blue eyes, full reddish lips, and wavy blond hair. She smiled as he reached out to her, lifted her into his arms, and pulled her against his bare chest. She leaned over and blew out the lantern flame, again leaving them in the dark. Michael made out the surroundings and continued to carry her down the hall toward her room.

"I apologize for falling upon you like I did. Please know that I did not know anyone was lying on the sofa."

Michael chuckled, "No need to worry, no harm done."

"Why were you lying on the sofa?" She questioned.

"Well, believe it or not, it was for this purpose."

"What purpose?" she asked.

"I was afraid that if you woke in the night with the need to," he hesitated, "you know."

"Yes," she added.

"That you would not know where you were or where to find…" he hesitated again."

She completed the thought, "A place such as your in-house chamber pot room."

"Exactly!" Stated Michael.

< 191 >

"Thank you for your concern." She said. "That was very thoughtful of you."

Michael stumbled for a moment; she pulled her left arm tighter around his neck and pushed her open palm right hand over his right breast; he caught his balance. She awkwardly lowered her right hand, removed it from his chest, and allowed it to lie on her lap. When they reached the room, Michael carefully carried her through the door. Brother Richard had placed the lamp on the bureau. He was lying on the chase, asleep with Faith sleeping next to him. Michael gently placed Angelia on the bed.

"Thank you again." She whispered to keep from waking the monk or her daughter.

"You are very welcome, my lady." He looked around the room and then at the monk and said, "It appears that there is no longer a place for me to sleep." Angelia looked at the monk and smiled.

"I believe I will not need more of your services this evening," Angelia said. She then questioned the odd innuendo of her statement.

Michael nodded and turned to leave the room. As he turned, she noticed the strength in his physic and the muscular contour of his back and arms. She thought of Percival and wondered how he was getting along. She stopped Michael and said. "Would you be so kind as to extinguish the lamp?"

Michael turned back toward her. Suddenly embarrassed, she noticed his bare chest and quickly looked up at his face, seeing him for the first time. She discovered that he was quite handsome.

"I am sorry, but I do not know your name." She said.

He leaned over to blow out the lantern.

"It is Michael. My name is Michael."

He puckered his lips, breathed in, filling his cheeks with air, and slightly cocked his head toward her as he blew the air into the burning wick. As the flame dimmed, the last thing she

< 192 >

saw was the glistening of his large brown eyes looking back at her. She lay back onto the bed, threw a pillow over her head, and tried to think of Percival to muffle any thoughts of attraction to Michael. Michael left the room and slept in his bed for the rest of the evening.

< 193 >

Chapter Twelve Notes

A chamber pot was typically placed next to a bed so that a person could access it to urinate or defecate when needed. One servant's job was to empty the chamber pots in the home. During medieval times, it was common to toss the contents of the chamber pot out the window. This usually caused stains to appear on the side of most buildings. Cobblestone or dirt streets were typically not sanitary. Some larger towns had street cleaners who kept the human and animal waste cleaned from the streets. Most homes of the day did not have any indoor plumbing and certainly no modern-type toilets. A garderobe was the modern term for a restroom. Garde·robe 'gärdrōb was a lavatory in a medieval building. Wealthy people and royalty began to build toilet seats, a hole on a wooden platform, with a drain pipe that emptied into a waterway or a pit.

< 194 >

Chapter Thirteen
The Confession

"Blessed are the hearts that can bend; they shall never be broken." Albert Camus

July 1349. The Chattingworth estate, Cardiff, Wales

Michael rose early, just before sunrise, gathered eggs, took them to the kitchen, and then returned to the barn to milk the cow. He wanted to help Monson prepare a proper meal for their new guests. It seemed odd that he did not know if they would survive to see another soul just a day earlier, and now four healthy people had arrived. He was relieved not only that they were healthy but that he did not shoot any of them with the crossbow, and he knew the only thing that stopped him was Monson recognizing the Priest, an unusual coincidence that Michael wanted to learn more about.

The last several months had been some of the most difficult in his life, too much change, too much heartache, and too much death. He was grateful that his mother and Monson were still with him. As he sat on the stool milking the cow, his eyes stared off into space as memories flooded his mind. He remembered the first time he met Monson. He, Jillian, and the children had just arrived at the Cardiff estate; it was cold rainy, and dark when they arrived. Monson helped Jillian and the children and told Jillian that her driver could put the horse and buggy into the carriage house. Michael remembered the feeling when he thought Monson assumed he was part of the paid staff. He remembered begrudging Monson and what appeared to be his upper-class and even more offensive attitude because he was the butler and not an upper-class member. Ironically, now Monson had become more than just a butler; he had become a

< 195 >

trusted friend, a father figure to whom Michael felt great love. Michael no longer considered Monson the butler; he no longer thought about different classes or statuses in society. The tragedy for society had become the great equalizer, and just surviving and being alive made everyone the same. He thought about Angelia and Faith and how they miraculously survived when Percival, the husband, and father, did not. He wondered how Angelia would take the news of the death of her husband. Michael knew all too well the feelings of helplessness, anguish, and utter despair at losing a spouse. He also knew of the pain, anger, and loneliness when an only child was taken. He felt a tear running down his face. It had been a long time since he thought about the death of his daughter because he focused so much on the loss of his wife. It was easier to put little Hope out of his mind when she was with him for such a short time. However, seeing Faith, a beautiful and lively toddler, reminded him of what he had lost, of what he would never get to see--a future absence of a daughter who would never grow to adulthood. The cow turned its head and mooed at Michael to get his attention. The bucket was complete, and the udders were empty; the cow knew it as Michael's fingers pinched and hung on, and it wanted Michael to know it too. It mooed again and took a step forward, almost knocking over the bucket. Michael grabbed the bucket and patted the side of the cow.

"Sorry, Ma'lady, thanks for the milk; next time, I will be more thoughtful and attentive." He said as he lifted the bucket and ran his hand down the side of the cow.

He placed the bucket on a bench and then took another bucket to milk the other cow in the adjacent stall. He focused on the task and completed milking the other cow in half the time. It was still dark when he arrived back in the kitchen. He placed both buckets of milk on the back preparation counter and then took two large glass pitchers from underneath the counter and placed them on top. Carefully, he emptied each bucket into a pitcher, covered the pitchers with a damp cloth, and slid them to

< 196 >

the end of the counter. The cooking fireplace was on the other side of the room. The flames had been extinguished from the night before. The old black iron pot was clean and hanging on the hook from the pole stretched over the fire pit's right side. A brick oven a few feet high was on the left of the fire pit, with an iron rack next to it for frying. Michael placed wood and kindling into the pit and lit it afire. He moved the logs around with an iron poker until there was an even flame for cooking. He stepped back, walked to the other counter, and pulled a large stool from beneath it. He sat on the seat and waited for Monson.

Moments later, a faint, single beam of sunlight broke through the window and splashed across the counter and to the back wall of the kitchen, and right behind it was Monson. He did not notice Michael sitting at the bar as he walked past him and picked up the empty milk cans.

"Where are you going with those?" Michael asked.

Monson swung around facing Michael and nearly dropped the buckets.

"Michael! You just about caused my heart to stop!" Exclaimed Monson. Michael laughed.

"Sorry, Monson, I did not mean to startle you. It is just that I've already milked the cows."

Monson looked back at the counter and noticed the pitchers of milk.

"Why, thank you, Michael!"

"You are welcome, Monson. I guess it is something I should do more often. There is no reason I should not be more helpful around here, especially now that it is just the three of us."

"Three of us?" Monson asked.

"Oh, yes, I guess it is seven of us now," Michael added.

"I had forgotten about the two monks, the child and the lady."

Monson smiled at Michael.

< 197 >

"Seriously, Michael, after the events of yesterday evening and last night, you forgot about the other four people who have joined us?" He shook his head.

"Well, only for a moment," said Michael. "Considering those events and my experience last night, it would be unimaginable to forget any of it."

"Last night? What experience?" Monson asked.

Michael smiled, "I will tell you about it later, but now, I have a question for you."

"For me? What question do you have for me?" Monson anticipated the moment and was unsure if he was ready to give Michael the answer he was asking for.

"How do you know Dom Gordon?"

Monson took a deep breath and exhaled.

"Michael, I am becoming an old man, and I guess there is no need to hide it anymore; after all, besides you and your mother, there are only four other people in this home, and what I am about to tell you probably doesn't matter anymore anyway."

Michael had a strange look on his face. He did not know that the story behind knowing Dom Gordon would be so troublesome to Monson. He motioned for Monson to sit. Monson turned and picked up a stool behind him; he moved it to the other side of the bar opposite Michael; this placed the men four feet across from each other. Monson smiled at Michael.

"Michael, what I am about to tell you is known by only two other people in the world, and one is no longer in this world; God rest her soul." He made the sign of the cross.

I was an only child, born to young parents of fourteen and sixteen. My father, at eighteen, enlisted in the army of King Edward the first. He was loyal, fearless, and very well respected by the king. On his twenty-fourth birthday, the King Knighted him, which changed my father's and mother's status. Growing up, I often did not see my father because he served the king and

< 198 >

the many battles and conflicts the king had engaged in. Although my mother was never content with her life being married to a knight, she loved him and always prayed for his safe return. As early as I could remember, I would hear my mother exclaim, "It is a miracle," each time my father would return home from battle. Over the years, many of her friends became widows when their husbands did not return from war. This constant anxiety kept my mother on edge and sickly. Late one afternoon, when I was in my sixteenth year, a knock was heard at our door. My mother had just finished sewing a coat for my father and was excited to present it when he returned from the most recent skirmish the King had enlisted him in. I remember the fear when she opened the door revealing two of the King's men. One of them, a very tall man, looked down at my average-height mother and said, "My Lady, it is with great regret that we deliver this news from the King." We both knew precisely what news they brought; for my mother, it was the news she feared almost daily; for me, it was the news I expected would come one day, for obviously, every time my father left for battle, it increased the odds that he would not return. The men left her with a small gold box and a short note from the King. I was standing in the doorway behind her, but I was unsure if she had noticed me. The men bowed graciously, and she slowly closed the door. She turned and walked to the small table in our kitchen and placed the box on the table. I walked up behind her and put my hands on her shoulders. She lifted her right hand and gently caressed my hand that was on her left shoulder. She breathed deeply, looked at the box, and carefully released the hooked latch from the lid. As the lid opened, I noticed many shiny gold pieces, like a small treasure chest filling the box. On top of the gold was a single folded piece of parchment. She slowly opened the letter and ran her right index finger down to the wax seal of the King's signet ring. I believe that was her way of verifying the authenticity of the news she was about to read. The note simply read,

< 199 >

"Dear Lady Annabella, it is with great sorrow that I write this to you today. On this day, your husband, Sir Monson Frederickson, gave his life in service to the King. He was one of my most trusted knights and will be sorely missed. I share your grief at this time, and I assure you that God will reward his faithfulness and nobility. This box contains his wedding ring, the gold crucifix he wore around his neck, and one year of compensation to help you until you can find another until arrangements are being made for his funeral to be held in my court. A driver will be dispatched for you and your son tomorrow at noon. Yours faithfully, King Edward I."

She dropped the letter back into the box and leaned back in her chair. The news tore her apart. It was as if her will to live was taken at that moment. I was the only family she had, and the prospect of a thirty-year-old widow re-marrying in our little town was virtually non-existent. She bowed her head and began to sob. I so wanted to cry for my father's death and the significant loss of my mother, but I was afraid to yield myself to tears at that moment, for fear that my mother needed my strength in her time of weakness. She reached out with her left forearm and wiped the box off the table and onto the floor. Gold coins bounced on the wooden slatted floor as the letter gently floated across the room, landing on the floor like a feather carried by the wind. She leaned forward, placed her arms on the table, dropped her head into her arms, and wept. I gently held the back of her shoulders and felt the shaking of her body; it was difficult to remain strong for her. The truth is, I never really knew my father since he was never there.

Nevertheless, I knew how much my mother loved him. Her loss was much greater than mine was. I lifted her from the chair and carried her to her bed. I leaned down and kissed her forehead as I covered her with a blanket. I wanted so badly to say something to comfort her, but all that came to my lips was,

"Mother, he is not coming home, so no need to worry anymore. I do not know if she actually heard me speak; I hope

< 200 >

she did not. Those words haunted me for years; I do not know why I spoke them. I remember extinguishing the lamp next to her bed and watching as the last flicker of light illuminated her tear-filled eyes. I left the room, not knowing if she ever knew that I was there. I walked to my room, undressed, and climbed into my bed. I could hear her sobs. I prayed to God that he would heal her broken heart and remove her pain. Shortly after my prayer, her sobs stopped. I thanked God for answering my prayer and not letting her suffer her greatest fear and sorrow alone. I closed my eyes and tried to hide the emotion but could not. I wept quietly, mostly for my mother and the father I never knew. When I woke early the next morning, I found that God had taken my mother earlier the evening before to be with my father in his great mercy. I realized that the only way he could heal her broken heart and take her pain away was to take her home and reunite her with her first and last true love. I gathered the coins and the letter and placed them back into the box. I then walked down the street and knocked on the door of Mrs. Lansbury, a long-time friend of my mother. I told her the news and then gave her a gold coin and asked her to attend to my mother's dressing for burial. I told her about my father's death and that the King would send a driver to take my mother to his funeral. I asked her to notify the driver that my mother would attend the service and lay by his side as their bodies were placed in the grave. She agreed. I gathered my meager belongings, climbed atop our horse, and rode toward London, not knowing what would become of my life. During my journey, I thought about my father's great service to his country and his King. I thought about the service and care my mother took to raise me, nearly on her own. I realized that my parents had sacrificed much to provide a life and future for me. We lived in a small shire, and I knew no one my age. I did not know what I would do in London. I prayed again and asked God to reveal his will to me, to let me know his will for my life. I had traveled many leagues down an old dirt path I had never traveled before. The

< 201 >

sun was shining mid-day as the path turned to the right, and just a short distance ahead was a large monastery, secluded, leagues from the nearest town. I had received my answer. I knew that God wanted me in the Priesthood. I remember knocking on the large front door. A few moments later, it opened, revealing a stout man in his mid-forties, Father Mueller. He was a kind gentleman. He smiled and asked how he could help me. My answer surprised him when I told him God had led me there and wanted to enter God's ministry. He hesitated at first, looked around on either side of me, and motioned me in. I told him my story and asked what I needed to do to enter the Priesthood. He told me I would need to make a vow of virtue, chastity, and service to God. He said that I would be required to forsake the world and covenant to sacrifice all in service to God. I agreed and then remembered about the box. I told him I needed to gather my belongings tied to my horse. He nodded and then asked another young man who had recently entered the priesthood if he could help me gather my belongings. The boy's name was Alabaster Gordon."

Michael interrupted Monson.

"Wait, his name is Alabaster? Dom Gordon's first name is Alabaster. What kind of name is that?" Michael asked, a little surprised.

"Now, Michael, none of us are allowed to choose our given name; fortunately, those who enter the priesthood are allowed to replace it with a title instead."

Michael smiled and shook his head. "Well, I guess some have more motivation than others to enter the priesthood. Please continue, Monson." Michael asked, still smiling.

"My new friend Alabaster was kind and welcoming. We were both sixteen, and he was orphaned as a small child and was raised in the monastery. After I was shown to my room, a room I would share with Alabaster..."

< 202 >

Michael tried to hold back a chuckle and then covered his mouth with his right hand.

"I am sorry, Monson, but I cannot get over the name."

"Fine, I shall refer to him as Dom Gordon so I can finish my story," Monson said, mildly irritated.

"Please, go on. I will contain myself, I promise." Michael said.

"Very well, now where was I?" Monson asked.

"Ala--I mean, Dom Gordon showed you to your room."

"Yes, afterward, I met with Dom Mueller. I showed him the gold box. I opened it revealing the coins, and asked if God would accept my offering to sacrifice all my worldly possessions. His eyes grew so large I thought they would fall from the sockets. He smiled at me, took the box with one hand and wrapped his other arm around me, and said,

"My boy, I am certain that God will accept your offering, and I will arrange immediately for you to begin your studies. Welcome to the brotherhood of God."

I spent the next four years studying and learning the Holy Scriptures of God. In his position with the King, my father had arranged for me to be tutored by the local Priest from seven to fourteen. This gave me quite an advantage when I entered the priesthood at sixteen. Over the next four years, I studied alongside Dom Gordon. I was ordained a priest at age twenty and sent to a small parish outside Thebes. Dom Gordon stayed with the monastery, the only family he had ever known. We kept in contact with regular letters for the next four years. I found great pleasure in serving God. I worked hard to provide spiritual guidance for my congregation. I grew to love the people. They had become the family I never had. I performed many marriages and baptisms over those four years. Not once did I look back on my life, nor did I question or doubt God's plan for me. Everything seemed perfect; I was happy and content with the Church and my calling. Serving others brought me great joy and happiness.

< 203 >

I knew each of the parishioners and their children. I shared many private moments of council and consultation, helping many make their lives right with God. One day a widower named Augustus Leavesly and his sixteen-year-old daughter Ruth moved into the community. He was hired on to the Johnson estate just outside of town. Calvin and Andria Johnson, a baron and baroness, were good and charitable God-fearing people. They had three daughters, ages eleven to fourteen, and a seventeen-year-old son named Simon. Simon was a wayward child, always causing grief and embarrassment to his parents. He flaunted his excellent name and father's wealth, never appreciating all that God had blessed him with, but always wanted more, including those things he could not have, such as a beautiful young red-haired girl named Ruth.

One afternoon Ruth came into the chapel and asked if she could speak with me. She told me that she was very concerned about the health and strength of her father. She asked me if I would pray for him. Of course, I agreed. Ruth was beautiful, poised, and filled with a beautiful spirit. Over the next few weeks, the health of her father improved. She and her father stayed after a Sunday service and thanked me for the prayers on his behalf. I assured him that many had prayed for his excellent health. He thanked me nonetheless. Ruth began to stop by the Church several times a week, and we talked often. One day I realized that I was developing inappropriate feelings for her. I had never been acquainted with a girl before Ruth and had never known such feelings. I begged God to remove them from me, but it seemed as though my prayers were ignored. One day I wrote a letter to Dom Gordon and asked for his advice. His return letter simply said to sing a hymn whenever I thought of her or when she was in my presence. I tried his suggestion but soon found that I was constantly singing, even to the point that members of my congregation began calling me the melodic priest. Finally, I decided to tell Ruth that our relationship was headed in the wrong direction and needed to

< 204 >

focus more on my calling. I suggested that her time would be better spent making herself available for courtship with many young men her age. It was an awkward conversation, but she took it well. I know it was not her intention to develop feelings for her priest any more than it was mine to develop feelings for her. We agreed to limit our meetings to Church services and confession as needed. The following Sunday, Ruth and her father came to Church accompanied by Simon. I felt a wave of unexpected anger, even jealousy, toward him. I tried to brush off the feelings, but they were too strong.

I remember cutting my sermon short, telling the congregation I was not feeling well. I retired to my study and searched the scriptures for an answer to my condition. No answer came. Over the next few weeks, I saw Simon hand-in-hand with Ruth. She would smile at me when our eyes met, and I would quickly look the other way. I was concerned that Ruth had chosen the wrong boy to court. Late one afternoon, while sitting in the confessional, I heard a knock on the booth next to me. I slid open the small wooden screen to listen to the person who had come for the Sacrament of Penance. He spoke in a low soft voice and said,

"Father, forgive me, for I have sinned."

I asked for the nature of the sin. He told me that he had lusted upon a woman. I asked if he allowed his lust to overcome him, and he said no. I then counseled him to pray and strive to live according to the teachings of God. He promised that he would do so. He then said something that I knew was directed personally at me.

"Father, it is hard to be strong when her beauty and red hair make me so weak."

I knew immediately that he was referring to Ruth and that he was Simon. I tried to contain my anger as I internally pleaded with God to keep me calm and focused. I told him that if he asked, God would give him the strength to resist temptation. He said,

< 205 >

"Perhaps you are right. It could be worse; I could be a priest trying to suppress feeling like this."

I did not respond. He waited a moment and then asked. "Father, are you still there?"

"Yes, my son," I replied.

I knew he was toying with me and trying to get a rise from me, but I did not want to give him the satisfaction. I said you have made a covenant with God to live according to his teachings, he will help you, but if you break that covenant, he will curse you, even unto death. There was silence. I was shocked at what I had just said to this young man. I had never given such counsel or warning. I wanted to retract my statement because I knew that I had allowed my personal feelings for Ruth to get in the way. Before I could speak again, he said,

"Thank you, Father; we shall see how God helps me."

He then got up and left the booth. I sat there another hour just pondering the conversation. I was frustrated with what I had said and fearful that he would take advantage of Ruth. However, since our discussion was sacred between a priest and parishioner, I knew my hands were tied to keep me from further action. A week passed, then two, then three, and I did not see Simon or Ruth. After a month, the constant concern became too much, and I sought out a young woman in the congregation whom I knew was a friend of Ruth. I asked her if she had seen Ruth. At first, she shook her head and turned away. I reached out for her hand and asked her again. This time she began to cry. She covered her face and said,

"Father, please do not ask me again. It is not for me to say, and you should ask Ruth."

I asked her if Ruth was all right. She nodded and then scurried out of the chapel. Another month passed, and I still did not see Ruth. Late one afternoon, as I was sitting in the confessional, another person entered the confessional and knocked on the door. I slid open the screen and asked the

< 206 >

parishioner to speak. I immediately knew the voice, it was Simon. He started by saying,

"Father, forgive me, for I have sinned."

I waited for him to say more. He asked,

"Father, are you there?"

"Yes," I replied. "What is your sin?"

"There is a beautiful young woman in the shire. She has been a temptation to me since I first met her. At first, she ignored me. But I continued to lust after her."

I cut him off and asked, "Did you act upon your lust?" I am sure my anger came across in my question. I felt my heart racing and the anger building. He said,

"I will get to that in a minute, Father. Let me finish."

"Of course, please continue," I said.

He took a breath and talked slowly and deliberately.

"Well, you see, Father, the last time I confessed to a priest about this very same woman, he told me that if I acted upon my lust, God would curse me, even unto death. I was hoping you could get a message to that priest and tell him that I acted and God did not curse me; I am still alive." He chuckled and continued,

"One day, I discovered that she was more interested in a man of the cloth, and I told her there was no man under that cloth. I had my way with her not once but many times. And now she knows who the real man is."

I had never known such rage as I felt at that moment. The anger inside me caused my mind to blur, forcing my spirit aside as the natural man took over. I tore the collar from my robe, tossed it to the floor, and threw open the confessional door with such force that it shattered the wooden louvers into small pieces and splinters, bursting all over the floor. As I exited the compartment, I grabbed the handle of the other door and nearly ripped it from the hinges opening it. Simon was still sitting on the bench as I grabbed him by the neck and flung his body into the room. I remember him taking a quick breath and raising his

< 207 >

hands to protect his face. After slamming his body against the wall, I began to pound deep into his chest and stomach with both hands in a rhythm with such speed that it was impossible to defend himself. As his body started to slump forward, I pulled my right arm back as far as possible and then threw the entire force of my body into a face punch, which caused blood to fly from his broken nose and splatter on the body of Christ that hung upon a large crucifix on the wall. He fell to the floor, crying like a wounded animal. He never had the opportunity to defend himself or fight back. I leaned over him again, stretching my arm back for another blow, when I heard him scream, "Father, forgive me!" At that moment, I regained my senses. My spirit regained control of my body, pushing the rage-filled natural man out. Tears began to flow down my cheeks as I looked at a broken and beaten man whose sobs echoed into the sanctuary. What had I done? I thought.

What kind of monster had been released deep from within the bowels of my being? For a moment, I felt remorse, and then my mind returned to the puffed-up and contrived confession from a vermin of a man who took the chastity from a young daughter of God, not once but many times. As he lay on the floor on his back in agony, I lifted my leg, positioning my foot over his groin; I wanted to ensure he would never be able to take the purity from a woman again. Just as I began to tense the muscle in my leg in preparation to thrust it at him, a voice screamed from down the hall, "Father! Father, are you alright?" I lowered my leg to the floor, turned, and ran from the church. All that I could think of was Ruth, helpless and alone." Monson stopped talking and stared ahead in a daze. Michael tilted his head and softly asked,

"Monson, are you alright?" Monson looked at Michael and smiled.

"Yes, Michael, all is well." Michael anticipated that Monson was going to finish the story. He waited a moment longer and then asked.

< 208 >

"Well, what happened next?" He asked.

Monson exhaled deeply and shook his head.

"That is when my life changed forever. It is when my first love and calling to serve God in his Church ended. As I ran down the cobblestone street, passing the small buildings, stores, and businesses, filled with people and merchants I loved, I knew I would never return. I knew that nothing would ever be the same. I thought of the babies I baptized, of the hand full of weddings I performed, the funeral services where I presided, and the words of hope, peace, and comfort that I had spoken to many of the good people of that little town, tears began to flow down my cheeks. I loved each of them. I wondered what I would say and what people would think when their priest disappeared after pulverizing a parishioner and never returned. As I passed the last building, the stony street turned to mud and dirt. It was then that I fully realized all that I was giving up, a firm foundation to a slippery slope and a path with no return. I continued to run for almost two leagues until finally, I reached the home of Calvin and Andria Johnson, the parents of Simon. I knew that Ruth and her father lived in the small servant's home next to the estate. Realizing that no one had seen me, I walked to the small rock house and knocked on the door. No one came, and I knocked again. The door was ajar, and I could hear voices, one of an old man and the other of a young woman; it was Ruth. "Ruth, may I come in?" I asked. A moment later, she appeared at the door and said, "Oh dear Father, you have come, just as I had prayed you would. My father, he is ill," she cried. "I am afraid he is dying. Please come pray for him." She asked, took my hand, and led me to her father, lying on a small bed in the one two-room house. As I walked into the room, he looked up and lifted his hand to greet me. I walked to him and knelt by his side. His breathing was shallow, and it was evident that strength and life were leaving his body. His eyes kept opening and shutting, slower and slower. He looked up and motioned for Ruth to come to the other side of his bed. She

< 209 >

knelt on the other side and held onto his left hand as I held the right. He leaned his head toward me and said, Thank you for coming, father. God has answered my prayer. He then leaned toward his daughter and said, my dearest Ruth, you have been the greatest gift of my life, and I thank God for allowing me to be with you this long. Ruth began to cry; he tried to wipe her tears. Do not cry, my child, he said. God has sent his servant, and he will take care of you. He then looked back at me and asked if I would give him his last rights. I obliged and offered a prayer that God would accept him into his bosom. After the prayer, he took each of us by the hand and pulled our hands onto his chest, mine first and hers on top of mine. He turned my hand upward and placed hers into my open hand. He put both hands on top of ours and squeezed our fingers shut together. He looked back to Ruth and said, dear child, God be with you until we meet again. He closed his eyes, and the last breath left his body. Ruth began to sob, still holding my hand as the grip of her father's hands slowly loosed. I gently pulled my hand away, allowing her to grieve for her father. She leaned over and placed her head on his chest. I left her there for several minutes and then realized that it would not be long before Simon, with help, returned home to report the news of his beating at the hand of a priest. I stood, then bent over and helped Ruth to her feet. She embraced me and cried more. I pulled her head back and told her that all would be well. She shook her head and said it was too late for all to be well. I then told her that I knew what Simon had done to her. She pulled away from me and said, "Oh Father, I have sinned," and then she lowered her head. I placed my hand under her chin, gently lifting her head, and said, "No, my child, you have not. God has punished the sinner, but you are free of him now."

She looked at me, again shaking her head, and said, "No, Father, I am not free. There is a child in my womb, and the man who did this to me will come again this night and defile me once more." Her knees buckled, and I caught her and lifted

< 210 >

her before she fell to the floor. I looked into her eyes and said, "He may come, but you will not be here. Gather your things; we must go now."

"But where are we to go? He will find us in the Church?" She said.

"We are not going to the Church; we are never going back. However, I know a place we can go to. Gather your things." I told her.

"But, what about my father? We cannot just leave him here." She said.

She nodded when I asked if their horse and cart were behind the house. I lifted her father, carried his body to the cart, and placed it on the hay. A moment later, Ruth came with a small bag of belongings. I quietly ran to the horse stable, found her father's horse, and led it back to the cart. After hitching the horse, we quietly rode back down the road and followed it another few leagues into the forest. Ruth sat on the small wood seat next to me, leaning her head on my shoulder. Neither of us said a word until the monastery appeared off the road.

"Where are we?" She asked.

"We are safe; there are kind friends here who will help us."

I remember walking up to the large door, and my head flooded with memories of the first time I came upon this door eight years earlier. It had been four years since I left. I knocked on the door, and it opened, revealing a young monk with a smile on his face. The sun had just set, and he was holding a lamp, trying to position it to see my face. He asked how he could help, and I asked if Dom Gordon was still at the Monastery. The monk smiled and told me that Dom Gordon was now the priest and Dom of their order. He invited me in. I walked back to the cart and helped Ruth into the building. A few moments later, Dom Gordon walked into the entry.

When he saw me, his face lit up, and he stretched his arms wide and ran to me. He embraced me and told me how

< 211 >

wonderful it was to see me. I introduced him to Ruth and said that her father had died and we had his body in the back of the cart. He told three priests to take his body and prepare it for a funeral without hesitation. He offered Ruth a comfortable room for the night. I bid her good night and told her we would speak in the morning. I spent the next several hours telling Dom Gordon everything that had happened. Finally, he asked me what I planned on doing next. I told him that I could not leave Ruth alone with nothing or no one. I knew several small towns were closer to London, and I suggested we could head in that direction. He then told me that it was best that I stay far from London. When I asked why he said how some of the king's men had come to the Monastery several months earlier looking for me. At first, I did not believe the tale, but then he told me that after the death of my mother, and when her body was taken to the king to be buried with my father that the king was angry that I had taken the box of gold and had run away. I had no idea that he had been looking for me for eight years. I asked Dom Gordon what he told the king's men about me. He laughed and said to them that he did not know of such a lad. I asked why he did not tell the truth. He said he had told the truth because I was no longer that boy; that boy was gone. I asked what had happened to Father Mueller. Dom Gordon said to me that he died a year earlier. He wasn't much older than I am today, Michael."

Michael smiled and shook his head.

"Oh, Monson, you are young at heart and as healthy as an ox."

Monson shook his head, smiled, and continued with the story.

"At some point, our conversation came to a lull, and Dom Gordon told me that a better place for me would be toward Whales. There were many small towns in that direction, and most likely, I could live out my life without stirring suspicion.

"But what about Ruth?" I asked.

< 212 >

He smiled and said, "You must take her to wife."

Suddenly, I realized that I had no plan, and taking her to the Monastery was only a temporary solution to the problem. I told him I had not considered such an idea and did not know if Ruth would agree. He asked me to pray and sleep on it, and we would talk again in the morning.

The following day, we were fed a large breakfast and introduced to the other monks. They were all quite lovely and inviting. Dom Gordon escorted Ruth and me into his private study. After sitting us down, he asked Ruth if she knew factually that she was with child. She began to cry, and I reached over and held her hand. She lowered her head and said yes. He then told her that it was evident to him that God loved her and rescued her from Simon and her awful situation. He asked me if I had a plan, but he said he had prayed before I could speak, and God told him that it would not be wise for her to become an unwed mother. He said that wherever she went, people would talk, and she would become an outcast. He then suggested that we should marry and head toward Cardiff. Ruth lifted her head; she was surprised and caught off guard. She looked at me and said,

"Father, I would never ask you to do such a thing. Besides, you have made a vow and are a man of the cloth."

I looked at her and said, "Ruth, I will protect you and your unborn child. I made a vow to God that I would serve his children, and I am not breaking that vow by taking you away from evil and to a place where you can find peace and happiness. I will do this if you will let me."

Ruth began to cry, and at first, I thought that she would not agree to such a thing. She wiped her tears and said that her father had told her he saw me coming to save her in a dream just hours before I arrived at their home. She said that she knew it was God's will that we be together. We hugged and shared tears of sorrow and joy. Dom Gordon married us a few moments later. We buried her father behind the monastery next

< 213 >

to the grave of Father Mueller. I told Dom Gordon how much I appreciated his love and help. We turned to leave, and he stopped me and told me he had something for me. He asked if I still wore my father's cross; I pulled on my tunic and revealed it hanging around my neck. He smiled and said, "There is something else you must have."

He walked over to a large bookshelf and removed three books revealing a small compartment. He opened the case and pulled out the box that the king had given my mother. As he handed it to me, I smiled at the gesture, but I was surprised at its weight. I asked what was in it.

He smiled and said, "All that is yours."

I opened the box, shocked to discover that all the coins were still there. I asked him how it could be. He told me that Father Mueller had no intention of taking my money; he just wanted to know if I was willing to offer all I had in exchange for service to God. He kept the coins in the box on the shelf and said that if God ever needed them, he would take them, and if I ever needed them, God would freely give them to me. We each exchanged heartfelt love for one another and bid farewell, not knowing if we would ever see each other again. Ruth and I left as husband and wife, yet I was still a priest in my heart, and my only desire was to find a home for Ruth and her child. We left and headed toward Cardiff. We found a small town on the English side of the river separating England and Whales. It was a safe place where we could make a home. We bought a small house next to the river. I worked for a local merchant who sold general supplies at one of the many little shops lining the harbor. Ruth seemed happy, and her pregnancy progressed. She radiated with beauty, she was filled with light and love, but I never went unto her."

Michael stopped Monson and asked, "Wait, are you telling me she was your wife, but you never slept with her?"

"Michael, it was never my intention to marry Ruth. All I wanted was for her to be happy, but I knew, just as Dom

< 214 >

Gordon said, her life would be difficult at best if she were an unwed mother. I was a priest, and although I loved her deeply, I was torn between my vow to God and my vow to Ruth. I was stuck somewhere in the middle. I knew that she had been defiled by Simon, and I did not want her to feel uncomfortable if I came to her too. After her child was born, I told her that we would consummate our marriage, and God willing, we would bring more children into the world and have a family. I believed that if it was meant for us to have children that it would happen.

We made a few friends over the next few months. One friend was a lawyer from Cardiff who stopped in the store from time to time as he traveled to London for business. He was a few years my senior, but we became good friends over a few short months.

One afternoon when Ruth was in her eighth month, a young boy burst into the store and alerted me that she had gone into labor, and the midwives had asked him to fetch me. I ran to the little house and found her lying on the bed with three midwives at her side. She was in extreme pain, and I knew something was wrong. I knelt at her side and caressed her face. She smiled, put her arms around my neck, and pulled me to her. Our lips met, and we kissed for the first time as husband and wife. She then turned and screamed in pain. One of the midwives pushed me aside and told me to leave while they attended to her. Ruth looked up at me, smiled, and mouthed the words, "I love you, Monson."

Monson stopped and squeezed his eyes tightly shut, but a tear escaped. Michael leaned over the counter, placed his arm over Monson's shoulder, and said, "It is alright, Monson if you would rather not tell me anymore."

Monson shook his head and replied, "No, I want to tell you the rest of the story. It feels redemptive to speak of it again. Let me finish, Michael. As I left the room, I remember thinking that if God allowed her to bring this child into the world, I would devote myself to it and Ruth and be a good father. Even

< 215 >

though I was not the child's father, I was willing to raise it as my own and keep the secret safe with Ruth and me. Nevertheless, it was not meant to be. Over the next two hours, I paced back and forth in the tiny front room of our home, pleading with God to take the pain away from Ruth and allow this child to be born, all the time hearing the muffled words of the women telling Ruth to be strong and to push the child out.

I had never felt such emotion, fear, or anticipation before. Abruptly, I realized that the screams had stopped. I listened but did not hear the cry of a newborn child but the cries of women, weeping women. I ran to the room, opened the door, and saw two midwives standing in a corner holding one another and the other leaning over Ruth, holding something in her arms. Ruth was not moving. Her eyes were open and staring at the ceiling. Blood was all over the bed and dripping onto the floor. I did not want to accept what I was seeing. I ran to the bed, knelt over my beautiful Ruth, placed my head on her neck, and pressed my chest against hers. I begged her to speak to me even though I knew she was gone. I cried like a child and asked God why he had taken her. I then stood and asked about the child. The midwife lying at the foot of the bed leaned back, revealing a precious little boy in her arms. When I saw his face, I realized all I had lost. It was not just Ruth; it was our son. I gently took him from the woman and looked at his perfect little fingers and toes, his little sharp nose, and pale red smiling lips. One of the midwives managed to say the words, "He took a breath." I was not prepared for the possibility that God would take either or both back to be with him. I knelt on the bed and placed that precious little baby beside his mother. I kissed them both on the cheek and closed Ruth's beautiful eyes, looking at them for the last time. They were both buried the next day. I remember standing next to their graves after the people had left. I did not know why things happened the way they did. I did not know why God led me to the places he did. I did not understand why he allowed me to love Ruth the way I did. But I knew that I

< 216 >

could never love another in the same way. I knew that I was a Priest but that I had broken my vow to God the day I allowed my rage to beat Simon the way that I did. I wanted him to suffer for what he had done to Ruth, and I let my anger for his actions cloud my judgment. When I should have helped him find a way to repent and come unto God, I took that opportunity away from him and did not allow him to take advantage of the atonement of Jesus. God had allowed me to serve as a Priest to help his children. Instead, I hurt one of them. After all that had happened, I knew that I could not return to the priesthood and that I could not marry because of the vow I made to God.

The next day the man from Cardiff knocked on my door. He embraced me when I opened the door and expressed his sorrow for my loss. He had become the only true friend I had. I invited him in and told him the entire story and that I did not know what to do with the rest of my life. He asked if I would come and work for him. I agreed, and at seventeen, I began work in the employ of your grandfather, Baron Chattingworth."

Monson stopped talking to let Michael soak in the end of the story. Michael had no idea that Monson had lived such a difficult life. He was amazed at his courage and commitment and impressed with his desire to give up everything to help Ruth. He then asked, "Was it worth it to give up what you loved the most, to be with Ruth?"

Monson smiled and said.

"I never gave up what I loved most, Michael. I have spent the last forty-five years serving God's children just as he had planned for me to do. This is what I have loved most."

"But Monson, you have suffered so much, and your trials have been great. Would not it have been much wiser if you had asked God to take your trials away before you ever threw a punch at Simon?" Michael asked.

Monson smiled again and said, "Michael, wisdom is not asking God to take your trials away; wisdom is asking God to give you the strength to overcome them."

< 217 >

Michael understood. He was more grateful than ever to know Monson. His heart ached for the trials Monson had endured in life, and his love for Monson increased. He embraced Monson and whispered in his ear, "Thank you for confiding in me, and thank you for being my friend."

Just then, Dom Gordon and Brother Richard walked into the room. Dom Gordon asked.

"Are we interrupting something?"

Monson looked at the men and said.

"Not at all. I was wondering when you would be down for breakfast. Have you seen Angelia this morning?"

Dom Gordon started to reply, but Brother Richard cut him off and said, in a stern voice,

"No, we have not seen the lass, but I assume that she was still quite fatigued after her events with Michael last night!"

Michael looked at Monson, raised his hands, wrinkled his forehead, and shrugged his shoulders.

Monson replied,

"Oh yes, Michael. You were about to enlighten me about the events of last night. Do tell!"

Michael shook his head and smiled. He knew that Monson was only toying with him, and then another thought entered his mind; he realized that Monson did have the priesthood and the authority when he performed his marriage to Elizabeth. It was a comforting thought that brought peace to his soul. He smiled as the thought of Elizabeth slowly fogged his mind, the others continued speaking, but he heard none of them.

< 218 >

Chapter Fourteen
When The Spirit Speaks

The Chattingworth estate, Cardiff, Wales. July 1349

Michael was pleased that Angelia felt strong enough to join everyone for breakfast. As the meal began, she asked if Jillian would be joining them. Before Michael could answer, Monson said, "Lady Beorn is not well. She spends most of her days in her room. I will take her breakfast right after Dom Gordon thanks the Lord for it."

The monk smiled and obliged Monson with a prayer of thanksgiving. After breakfast, Michael took Brother Richards aside and asked him what had happened to Angelia's husband. He retold all he had heard from the monks who claimed to have discovered his outcome while leaving the burning town. He asked when he was going to break the news to Angelia, and Brother Richards only said, "When the spirit speaks, we must listen."

Michael was not exactly sure what the statement meant but nodded anyway. He assumed that the monk did not know the right time to tell Angelia, or he did not want to be the one to tell her. Either way, it was apparent to Michael that the monks did not want to reveal the bad news to her, at least not then.

Later in the day, Michael took the new guests to meet Jillian, but she was little interested in the monks or Angelia. She rarely left her room. She said, "Welcome," as they stood in her doorway. Still sitting in her rocking chair, she turned back toward the window and continued to knit her imaginary sweater. The others returned to the main hall of the estate.

< 219 >

After the evening meal, Monson took Faith and told the monks that he would like to tour the estate. Thus, leaving Michael to entertain Angelia. Michael and Angelia sat in two large chairs and waved as the others headed down one of the long halls. This was the first time that the two had been alone since the events of the night before. An awkward silence echoed in the room as neither knew how to begin a conversation both knew it would be nothing more than small talk.   Angelia decided to speak at about the same time as Michael opened his mouth.

"I am sorry--" Michael cut her off.

"No, I am sorry--" Angelia cut him off.

"I did not realize that you--" She started to speak, but Michael cut in again and said, "No, there is nothing to apologize about, please."

"But, I--" She said.

"Let's not talk about it," Michael asked. Angelia leaned back in her chair and turned her head toward the large front windows, and Michael looked the other way. They both wanted to talk but did not want to make the other uncomfortable with the subject. Angelia began to smile, and Michael noticed her smile but did not say anything. Her smile began to overcome her, and she pressed her lips together.

So, tell me about yourself," Michael asked.

Angelia looked at Michael and back to the window. She hesitated for a moment and spoke.

"Well, you already know my name and also the name of my daughter, Faith." She paused, "And my husband's name is Percival."

When she mentioned her husband, Michael remembered what Brother Richard had told him. He considered whether to tell her the news but decided to wait for the opportune time. Of course, he had no idea when that time would come, and he looked at her and said, "Yes, go on."

< 220 >

"We live in a small shire called Viernes, and it is a small place with only a few dozen homes. Just after we married, Percival built our home about five years ago." She smiled as she thought about Percival.

"He is a good man. And no doubt, he is home now and wondering where Faith and I have gone off to."

She looked back at Michael and shook her head. He tried not to make eye contact with her, and he knew it would be difficult for her to hear the news about Percival.

"What makes you think he is there waiting for you?" Michael asked.

Angelia cocked her head to the side, unsure what Michael's comment meant. He continued.

"I mean, why did you leave your home anyway?"

She thought a moment and realized that much of the past few days were a blank.

"I am not sure. I remember someone telling me about a plague in one of the bigger cities. But I do not remember who told me or even which city they referred to." She stopped and tried to remember.

"It is like it is all a dream, a bad dream. I remember the three of us riding my horse--" Michael cut her off.

"The three of you? Was Percival with you?" He asked.

"No, it was me, Faith, and…" she paused to remember. "A little boy."

"A little boy?" Michael asked. "Where is he?" Michael asked with a swell of hope that perhaps the little boy could have been Lucas.

"I do not remember. I do not remember his name. I cannot even remember his face."

"Did he live in the shire with you?"

"Yes, I believe he did."

Michael felt his heart sink and hopes dashed upon hearing that the little boy lived in the shire. However, it still

< 221 >

seemed odd that he would have been with Angelia and Faith instead of his own family.

"Where were his parents, and why would he be traveling with you?"

"I do not know. I do not know where his parents were. Michael, I do not know what happened to him either." She began to tear up.

"I remember we were in a hurry to get out of the shire. I was upset that we were leaving because of the noise,"

"What noise?" Michael asked.

"The noise of screams."

"Screams?"

"Yes, at first, there was one scream, and it came from a woman I knew. Then a few minutes later, there was another scream. I remember the boy telling me that the sickness must have arrived in our town and that we would all die if we did not leave immediately. I do not know where his parents were; perhaps they were already dead, which is why he was with us."

"I know something about this sickness you are referring to. It is not just a sickness; it is a deadly plague. When it arrives in a town, it is only a matter of days before everyone becomes sick. The sickness quickly attacks; it causes black spots and pustules under the arms and groin. The pain is horrible. But the discomfort typically lasts three or four days before death ends the suffering."

Angelia carefully listened to Michael. She remembered a small boy telling her something similar. She remembered feeling terrified shortly before leaving her home. She knew that if what Michael and the boy had told her were true, there was a chance that Percival had also succumbed to the sickness. She tried to brush off the feeling.

"Can I ask what happened when you were on the road?"

"I do not remember everything, just bits, and pieces. I remember us climbing onto the horse and riding for several leagues." She paused and searched her thoughts.

< 222 >

"Oh, Michael, that small boy, his mother, and father must have been terrified not knowing where he was, and I do not know…" she stopped. She stared straight ahead and began to shake and cry.

"Oh, dear God in Heaven! We were attacked! It was awful!" She dropped her head into her hands, and Michael gently put his arm around her shoulder as she cried.

"It is okay; you do not need to talk about it anymore if you would rather not," Michael said consolingly.

She looked up and said.

"No, I think it is better that I talk about it. Some of the details are beginning to come back to me. I remember him knocking me off the horse. I do not know what happened to the boy, and I hope he ran back to the shire and found his parents. But then, if he did, he too may be dead from the plague you speak of. It seems like the horse kept running with little Faith holding onto its main as it ran." She stopped and stared out the window for a minute and then continued.

"I believe there was only one man. It was dark, so I do not remember his face. He knocked me to the ground and started beating me. He laughed as he hit me. I tried to fight him off, but I was losing my strength. I felt myself losing consciousness, and then the next thing I remember was waking up in a monastery. Brother Richard and Dom Gordon told me how they had found Faith and me. It was surely a miracle from God that we survived."

"There is no doubt about that," Michael added. He then thought about what he had just said, and it seemed odd that he agreed that God still worked miracles in people's lives, especially when so many died of the Black Death.

"I am thankful that Faith and I were saved. I hope the boy made it back home." She hesitated and added, "I hope Percival made it back home too."

Michael desperately wanted to tell her, and he struggled for the right words.

< 223 >

"If your husband did make it back to your home in the shire, what do you believe he would have found there?"

"I do not know. Perhaps he would have found everyone dead."

"Have you considered that Percival may be dead?" Michael cringed that he asked the question. He did not want to upset her, but the words seemed to escape his mouth before he could bridle them. She began to sob.

"I have not given it much thought until this moment. If, in fact, that small boy was right, Percival may be dead, and I just cannot imagine my life without him." She began to cry again. "He means the world to Faith and to me." She wiped the tears from her eyes.

"But right now, I do not know what to believe after what we have gone through in the woods with the wolves. My heart tells me to believe he is alive, but my mind tells me he may not be."

Michael felt like it was his opportunity to tell her the truth.

"Angelia, Brother Richard told me something I think you need to know."

She looked at him, concerned, and asked, "What?"

"He said that other monks in the monastery had traveled to the town where your husband Percival had gone."

She began to shake her head.

"No, please do not tell me…" she stopped.

"The monks said that city officials began burning the homes in the town. Many homes were boarded up, trapping the residents inside as they burned. They did this to stop the plague from spreading. One of the monks heard an elderly lady from inside one of the homes scream out the name Percival several times."

"No, it cannot be!" She screamed. She turned and placed her head in her hands again, and Michael put his arm around her shoulders.

< 224 >

"I am sorry, Angelia, but I believe your husband died with his parents in their burning home."

Her sobs became more intense, and she fell to the ground. Michael knelt and wrapped his arms around her as she cried. He understood her pain, perhaps more than most. He held her for quite a while until her tears dried up.

"I wish it was not so, but I know that your heartache will pass with time, and you will deal with the sorrow."

Angelia looked up at Michael and asked, "What do you know of heartache and sorrow? How could you begin to understand my pain?"

Michael looked at her and said, "Over the last year, I have become intimately acquainted with heartache and sorrow. I have lost my father, little brother, sister, wife, and only child. I have rid myself of the heartache, but sorrow has been at my side ever since."

"Oh, forgive me, Michael. I did not know. But for now, could you please help me to my room? I need to rest."

Michael lifted her into his arms and carried her like a small child. Angelia leaned into his chest and sobbed back to her room. Her bedroom door was ajar. Monson had tidied the room and put clean sheets and bedding on the bed. The covers were turned down. Michael placed Angelia on her back on the bed. He carefully unlaced her shoes and removed them from her feet. He lifted the covers over her and put the edge just over her shoulders. He caressed her cheek. She held his hand and kissed it.

"Thank you, Michael. I am so sorry for the things I said to you."

"Angelia, there is nothing to be sorry about. I am fine. I understand your need to grieve. I will find Faith and ensure she has been fed and clothed for bed. You get some rest. I will bring her and place her beside you in a while after she, too, has fallen asleep."

< 225 >

Angelia turned to her side and sobbed softly. Michael left the room and found Faith clean, fed, clothed, and fast asleep in a large chair with Monson.

< 226 >

Chapter Fourteen Notes

*A **confessional** is a small, enclosed booth used for the Sacrament of Penance, often **called** confession or Reconciliation. It is the usual venue for the sacrament in the Roman Catholic Church. In the Catholic Church, confessions are only heard in a **confessional** or oratory, except for a just reason. The priest and penitent are in separate compartments and speak to each other through a grid or lattice. A crucifix is sometimes hung over the grille. The priest will usually sit in the middle, and the penitents will enter the compartments to either side of him. The priest can close off the other compartment by a sliding screen so that only one person will be confessing at a time. Kneelers are provided in the compartments on each side of the priest, sometimes a prie-dieu style kneeler or sometimes a diagonal kneeler built into the confessional walls. Confessions and conversations are usually whispered. Sometimes a confessional will be built into the church walls and have separate doors for each compartment; other confessionals can be free-standing structures where curtains conceal penitents (and even the priest in some confessionals) from the rest of the church.*

< 227 >

Chapter Fifteen
I need you with me

August 1349.
The Chattingworth estate, Cardiff, Wales

Several weeks passed, and the guests had become part of the survivors. They were no longer strangers or long-lost friends; they were now family. Monson organized the monks to help with work on the estate, and Angelia had taken over the cooking and much of the cleaning.

Early one evening, when Michael had finished feeding the chickens, he stopped to rest, leaned against a large tree, and watched the sunset. September was near, and the days began to get shorter. The air seemed crisper in the mornings and much cooler in the evenings. The bright, burnt orange sun slid behind a dark black outline of trees many leagues in the distance. It had been a while since he had taken the time to clear his mind and appreciate the beauty around him, especially amid such misery everywhere else. He wondered how the rest of the world was fairing, whether people were still dying, whether the suffering intensified, or if it had begun to subside. He wondered if it was possible that William, Lucas, and Sarah were still alive and, if so, where they were.

Had they found one another, were they alone, scared, helpless, and afraid? He wondered if he would ever see any of them again. He so wanted the little boy that Angelia met to have been Lucas. If it had been Lucas, at least he would know that somehow, he survived and was alive. Lucas was the only one Michael believed could still be alive; after all, Lucas was taken away on a horse by a man, unlike William, whom Michael believed had died of the plague, and Sarah, who died in

< 228 >

the fire. Although he was still haunted that he had not been able to find her bones or any trace of her after the fire had burned its last ember.   He wanted to believe that somehow each had survived. The thought gave him great solace, even if he would never see them again; maybe just knowing they were alive would be enough. He remembered the talk he had with Jillian weeks earlier. She told him she had gone to a beautiful place and saw her departed family and loved ones, including Elizabeth and Hope. She saw everyone she had ever known that had died except William, Lucas, and Sarah. He envied the opportunity she had, such a gift, to look into the other side and see life hereafter.

His contemplation was cut short by a voice calling his name.

"Michael, the meal is ready, and it is still warm."

It was Angelia.   The weeks had done as Michael suggested they would; she had begun to deal with the pain of losing Percival. Most days, she focused on cooking, cleaning, and mothering Faith and everyone else in the household, including Jillian, whom she had befriended. Occasionally upon hearing her voice or catching a quick glance at her face, he would see Elizabeth. At first, he cherished those moments and tried to hang on to them as long as possible. As time passed, the flashes became shorter, and the feelings of longing for Elizabeth lost their intensity.   Over time, they were replaced by unexpected feelings for Angelia. He took a deep breath, closed his eyes, and tried to see Elizabeth in his mind. He had been able to picture her usually without much thought or concentration. However, her image was fuzzy this time, and her face appeared and then dimmed in and out. His attempts to hold her image became harder. He called out,

"Elizabeth, I cannot see you. Where are you?" He felt fear and loneliness. "Please do not leave me," he pleaded, his heart beating faster and harder.

< 229 >

"I need you with me." He implored. Then a tiny spot of light appeared deep within his mind's eye. The light grew more prominent and appeared to be moving toward him. It took shape, and the light became a glowing ball of waving fire. The roundness elongated, and the object turned as the waves became long strands of sparkling blonde hair. The figure gradually turned until its bright glowing white face rested upon his gaze. There she was, the woman he loved, he missed and longed for. Elizabeth was back in his mind where he wanted to keep her. She smiled, her lips gently parted, and she whispered, "Michael, I will always love you, but you must let me go now. God has plans for you."

"No! I cannot let you go, Elizabeth!" Michael said as tears welled in his eyes and gushed down his cheeks.

"I do not want to be alone!" He managed to squeak out.

"Michael, you are not alone. God has never left you alone, and now he has sent someone who needs you as much as you need her. Go! Be happy and make others happy." She said as her image began to fade. Michael watched and resisted letting her go. He felt his mind reaching out and pulling her back toward him.

"Michael, please let me go. Everything is well, Michael. Trust me, trust your heart, and trust God. This is not the end. I love you, Michael."

With those words, her hand appeared on her lips. She gently kissed her fingertips and turned her fingers toward his face. He felt a soft sensation touch his lips as the last flicker of her face faded into a bright light and burst into millions of tiny shiny stars. He opened his eyes and took a quick full breath as if just raising his head out of deep water moments before drowning. He began panting for breath. He swallowed, looked around, wiped his eyes, and realized she was gone. At first, he was afraid, but then peace and comfort filled his mind and heart. He knew that all was well.

< 230 >

He glanced one last time at the large sun. Its fading rays extinguished and momentarily highlighted a bright red glow behind the black line of trees. He looked back toward Angelia and said, "Thank You! I am finished here, and I will be right in.

Angelia smiled and turned. As she did so, a bright white glow enveloped her exactly as he had seen Elizabeth seconds earlier. Michael closed his eyes and mouthed, "I will miss you, Elizabeth. Goodbye, my love."

< 231 >

Chapter Sixteen
The Courtship

"The best and most beautiful things in the world cannot be seen or even touched - they must be felt with the heart." Helen Keller

October 1349

Michael never thought it was possible to love again, especially so soon after the death of Elizabeth and little Hope. It did not seem real that he had found another or that someone had found him. Angelia was almost perfect because she was the closest thing to Elizabeth, from how her long blonde hair hung and blew in the wind to her piercing light blue eyes and powder white skin. Even her lips looked like Elizabeth's. Michael loved her more each moment, but he struggled to keep the thought of Elizabeth from entering his head. Angelia was warm, thoughtful, loving, and a wonderful mother, and Michael realized she was also potentially a wonderful wife. He watched from a distance as she swung in the old oak tree with Faith in her lap. He listened to her soft voice as she spoke to her child, caressed her hair, and held her gently as she slept. Angelia was almost perfect; she was almost Elizabeth.

Later in the day, they walked through the meadow and to the creek's edge. Michael removed his cloak and draped it over a low-hanging tree branch. He bent over, cupped his hand, scooped water, and raised it to his lips. Angelia drew close to him and smiled as he drank. She cocked her head, and he knew she was also thirsty. She bent down next to him; he cupped his hand and repeated the process lifting it to her lips as drops of water slipped through his fingers. She gently supped the water. He watched her lips press against his hand; the sensation caused

< 232 >

him to miss a breath. She noticed it. She smiled at him and said,

"May I have more, please?"

Michael smiled at her, gathered his senses and composure, turned back toward the stream, and drug his hand into the water. He lifted his cupped hand to her lips. She reached out to him with her left hand and pulled him closer as he raised his hand to her lips. His face was at eye level with her face. She placed her right hand under his. He almost flinched at the touch of her soft skin. She smiled as the water's edge touched her lips, and then, with no warning, she shoved the water into his face with her right hand under his. He did not expect the wet chill and fell backward. She stood and began to laugh. She turned to run away, but after one step, he climbed to his knees and grabbed the hem of her dress. She started moving and noticed the tug on her dress. While laughing, she tried to slap his hand away, but he grabbed her hand and pulled her to the ground. As they both fell, she ended up on her back, and he fell beside her, both still laughing. He climbed over her, wrestled, and pinned her arms down over her head. She wiggled and squirmed and threw him off balance, rolling off toward the stream. He pulled her with him, and they rolled side over, ending with her on top of him. She attempted to pin his arms but was no match for his strength. He pretended to weaken, allowing her to push his arms down to the sides of his head. As he did so, her face came within inches of his. The laughter stopped. He closed his eyes and slightly puckered his lips in anticipation of their first kiss. He felt her hair brush against his neck and cheeks. He felt her body move as she took in a deep breath. He dared not move for fear of missing a perfect moment. But the moment did not come, and he opened his eyes just in time for her to scoop a hand full of water and toss it in his face. He attempted to shake it off as she jumped to her feet and turned to run. Without hesitation, he stood and leaped toward her wrapping his arms around her from behind.

< 233 >

As he made contact, he leaned with his entire weight toward the stream, throwing both bodies into the water. Angelia screamed when the water completely submerged them in a four-foot-deep section. Michael made sure he turned to protect her from the bottom or any possible debris with his back entering the water. Moments later, they emerged.

Angelia stood and tried to pull her hair back while brushing water from her face and eyes. Michael stood and continued laughing as he watched her drenched in a long heavy wet dress. He was laughing too hard to notice the chill of the water. Angelia cleared her eyes, looked at Michael, and started to laugh, but then realized how cold she was. She began shaking uncontrollably. Michael reached out and pulled her close to his body. Her arms were raised in front of her, her fists clenched and pressed against her chest and his. She wanted to laugh, but the cold water would not let her. Michael held her tightly and brushed his arms up and down her back. His laughter died down.

"It is alright! It is alright! Let me get you out of here."

She nodded as she shook. Michael looked to the left toward the shore to scope the best area for footing. He looked back at her to tell her he had found the best place to climb out of the water. As his face met hers, she lifted both hands, cupped either side of his face, and pulled his lips to hers. Although Michael did not expect the kiss, he did not fight it either. As they kissed, he felt incredible warmth overcome his freezing body. He felt calm, strong peace, and security that he had not felt in a long time. Her lips felt perfect as they pressed against his. He did not want the kiss to end. After a few moments, he broke away. He looked at her to speak when she suddenly pulled his face back to hers and continued the kiss. Obviously, she did not want it to end either, Michael thought. As Angelia kissed Michael, all her cares seemed gone; she once again felt safe, loved, and protected. It was a powerful feeling that overcame the chill of the water; nothing else seemed to matter

< 234 >

at this moment. They both felt an uncontrollable passion rushing through their veins, spiritually, emotionally, and physically connected, an unbreakable coupling that felt more natural and predestined than they had ever felt before. As the kiss ended, both breathed heavily, neither wanting to say anything. Although both had hoped for this moment, neither knew what to say after it happened. It was like being young schoolchildren experiencing their first kiss, awkward but wonderful at the same time. Michael smiled and looked into her beautiful blue eyes. She gazed at him for a moment and then began to shake uncontrollably.

"Let's get out of this water before one of us freezes to death."

Michael said as he turned and reached for a low-hanging branch. Angelia tried to laugh, but her teeth chattered away her ability to do so. Michael pulled their bodies closer to the stream's edge and moved Angelia around him.

"Grab onto the branch and pull yourself out while I push you up."

Angelia held on to the branch and began to pull herself hand-over-hand until, with Michael's help pushing her, she could climb out of the water. Michael quickly climbed out after her. Getting out of the cold water helped warm her slightly, but her long wet dress kept the water close to her body. Michael reached for his cloak hanging next to the tree and wrapped it around her shoulders. She turned, looked at him, and said, "Thank you, Michael."

Michael smiled. He wanted to kiss her again but restrained himself. She could tell that he felt a connection to her by the look on his face. She had hoped for some type of friendship or connection but did not anticipate things to happen so fast or in such a unique way. Suddenly, Michael felt the cold overcome his body. He reached the bottom of his shirt and pulled it over his head, ripping it from his body. He felt his temperature rise almost immediately after the wet garment was

< 235 >

removed. Angelia continued to shake and tried not to stare at Michael's muscular, naked torso. Michael wrapped his arms around her pinning her cloaked arms to her side. Her shaking slowed.

"There, let the warmth of my body warm you," Michael whispered in her ear. Angelia smiled and tried to relax. After a few moments, the shaking stopped; she breathed deeply and exhaled.

"Thank you, Michael; I am feeling much warmer now. I think we should return to the estate and get out of these wet clothes and into warm and dry clothes."

"Of course," replied Michael as he released her.

She turned toward him. Moved her face close to his and closed her eyes to kiss him. Michael closed his eyes, too, in anticipation of another moment of unexpected thrill. Just as her lips pressed against his, he felt both of her hands touch his shoulders. Suddenly the moment was ripped away as she pushed him back into the stream. He saw her laughing as his body again entered the cold water, this time alone with no hope of comfort. Still laughing, Angelia turned and ran back toward the estate. As she ran, the oversized cloak got tangled in her legs. Her focus was to outrun Michael, who she knew would not be too far behind. Michael climbed out of the water, grabbed his shirt, and started running after her. After several yards, she could not maneuver her legs in and out of the cloak; she miss-stepped and tripped. Michael was gaining on her as she fell. He heard her laughing and screaming as she fell; he too laughed as he knew this would be his opportunity to catch her. She rolled several times and ended up on her back. Michael reached her. She was holding her left arm and crying in pain. Michael knelt beside   her.

"Here, let me look at that." He lifted her arm, and she screamed out in pain. He moved it up and down.

"Nothing broken, but you may be in pain for a few days."

< 236 >

He lifted her and continued carrying her to the estate. Michael kicked it open with his right foot when they reached the front door. As the door opened, Brother Richard stood in the doorway. He looked at Michael, bare-chested, and Angelia soaking wet with hair hanging on her face, and said, "Michael, what in the name of all holy?"

Angelia tried not to laugh as she held her arm. Michael moved around the monk and said, "Trust me, she's definitely not holy!" The monk gasped and pressed his hand to his lips. Angelia slapped Michael's chest and blurted, "Michael!"

He laughed as he carried her to her room. He gently stood her in the doorway.

"Do you need me to help you change?" He asked, with a devious and joking smile on his lips.

"I am sure I will manage from here, thank you."

"How is your arm?" He asked.

"It is feeling much better. I will change and be down for dinner in a while."

Michael turned. "I am glad your arm is feeling better, and it would have been challenging to swim tomorrow with just one arm."

"Swimming? We're going swimming tomorrow?" she asked, somewhat concerned, knowing it wasn't the season for swimming.

"Did I say we?" Michael asked, smiling as he closed the door behind him.

< 237 >

Chapter Seventeen
The Swarm

November 1349.

The Chattingworth estate, Cardiff, Wales

The sun had not yet risen when Michael finished milking "Mable the Cow," as Sarah had lovingly named her. The barn was barely lit by the small lantern he had placed on a large barrel a couple feet from the cow.

"Good girl, Mable. Sorry to have to do this to you every morning, especially since we hardly know each other, but it is either the old man or me; either way, your options are limited."

He stood and gently stroked and patted her forehead and side. He looked around the empty barn but did not see Bertha, the "other cow," as Lucas used to call her. He lifted the lantern and stretched his arm out while moving it in several directions but did not see the other cow. Michael was not comfortable in the barn; there were too many bad memories there. After he had buried the man he killed, who had attacked Elizabeth, Michael had taken the horses from the barn and placed them into the buggy house. It wasn't as convenient as the barn, but he did not have to spend much time in the barn. The two cows were the only animals stabled in the barn. Monson usually milked the cows, and Michael did not have to go into the barn. But this morning, Monson wasn't feeling well, so Michael offered to milk the cows. After a few minutes of searching the barn, Michael took the lantern and headed outside, hoping to find the animal nearby. He walked the barn's length and then entirely around it but never saw the other cow. He picked up the bucket of milk, closed the barn door, and returned to the estate. When he entered the kitchen, he saw Monson standing over a large pot of stew hanging over the fire.

< 238 >

"Monson, what are you doing here? I thought I told you to stay in bed and let me take care of the morning chores?"

"It is fine, Master Beorn; I feel much better."

Michael placed the milk on the large counter. He then picked up the basket of eggs he had already gathered from the hen house.

"You know, Monson, there are just a few of us here now, and we are a handful of people alone in the forest, far from others. You cannot do everything you have done in the past, and you need to let others help, at least until...." He hesitated, and Monson looked at him.

"Until what, Michael?" Monson asked in a soft voice.

Michael hesitated, "Until we decide that this plague has passed."

"And then what, Michael?"

"Monson, I do not know what is next, and I just know that you must let me help more."

"Thank you for your willingness to help Michael. I appreciate all that you do around here. It is a big estate and nearly impossible for a few of us to attend to everything. But, we need to keep ourselves busy, so I am cooking the afternoon meal. But, if you would like to crack some of those eggs, I would be happy to cook some breakfast."

"What about Angelia? She should be up anytime and in here to make breakfast?"

"She was up late last night with Faith, who hasn't been feeling well. I already checked in on her and told her to sleep while I make the morning meal." Added Monson.

Michael took a large bowl from the cupboard below and began to crack eggs into it.

"Did I tell you that Bertha is missing?"

"Missing? What do you mean?"

"After I milked Mable, I looked around the barn but could not find Bertha. I walked around the barn and held out the lantern but never saw her."

< 239 >

"You know Michael, she is an old cow, and I would not be surprised if she went out into the pasture to die. Perhaps you can look for her later this morning when the sun rises."

"I surely will, Monson. I surely will."

After Michael cracked a few eggs, Monson took the bowl and prepared the breakfast. Looking out the kitchen window, Michael waited for the sun to rise. Although it came up as it always did each day, it seemed unusually long before its rays finally broke over the horizon. A fine mist hovered a foot or two over the grassy fields. Michael left the estate searching for the missing cow when the darkness gave way to light. Monson took breakfast to Jillian.

Michael found the cow trail the animals had been treading over for years, in the same spot stretching from the barn towards the end of the large fenced pasture. It was a trail that most livestock had created over years of grazing. He walked over a mile and stopped as his nose caught the smell of decay in the air. He suspected that perhaps Monson was right, and the cow had wandered off to die. He continued walking; the grass was taller, almost covering the dirt trail. The mist began dissipating, leaving behind the cold chill that clung to the ground. Suddenly something caught his eye. It was the carcass of a large animal, just a few feet ahead. He thought it must be the cow, but it had only been gone for a few hours; how could it already be in such a state of decay, he thought. He stopped when he reached the body. He held his forearm over his nose to block the overwhelming stench. He turned his head away from the remains, took a deep breath, and then looked back at it. He wasn't prepared for the grizzly sight. He jumped back from the carcass as he discovered that it was the missing cow. Its flesh and entrails were gone, leaving only bone and hooves. The sight was so grotesque that his body convulsed; he turned and heaved his entire breakfast. After a few moments, he regained his composure and looked upon the sight again. The more he studied it, the more terrifying it became. He noticed teeth

< 240 >

marks on one of the bones, then another. Not only did it appear that something had attacked the large animal, but that it feasted upon its flesh. He continued to survey the bite marks and realized that it would have been impossible for one creature to overtake, kill, and devour this unfortunate cow. As he tried to determine what could have done such a thing, he quickly jumped back when he saw a tiny mist of heat rising from what used to be the animal's midsection. He realized that whatever had done this had done it quickly and recently. The bite marks were many, too small for a coyote or a wolf, he thought, but definitely by some type of beast with long sharp teeth. He quickly jerked his head from side to side and surveyed his surroundings to make sure he was, in fact, alone. Seeing nothing, he looked at the ground and noticed hundreds of small footprints that appeared to be scattered everywhere. Obviously, the creatures attacked the cow repeatedly until they brought it to the ground and then devoured it in an unrelenting frenzy. Michael had never heard of or seen anything like this before. He knew of wolf attacks, but whatever did this was a smaller and more agile animal. He decided to walk further up the trail, following what appeared to be a scurried procession of tracks leading to where the cow's remains were discovered. Although he still did not know what he was looking for, it was evident that direction had come. He had walked a few yards when he noticed something ahead in the tall grass a few inches off the trail. He stopped, waited for a moment, and tried to determine what it was; it looked like a large black cat lying in the grass. He bent down and brushed his hand over the dirt until his fingers came upon a small rock. He picked up the rock and threw it at the animal. The stone hit the creature and bounced off of it. The creature did not move. It must be dead, Michael thought. He yelled at it and then tossed another stone, all with no reaction. He began to walk towards it, knowing that whatever it was, it was dead. It occurred to Michael that this creature was still covered with skin and hair. He wondered why

< 241 >

it, too, had not been attacked. When he was within a few inches of the body, he looked down and noticed a large bulging pustule. He stopped immediately and stepped away from the creature. He knew the site; it was the plague! He felt his heart begin to race. He turned and started running down the trail back toward the barn. He ran off the path several feet to avoid the cow carcass, and he kept running until he reached the barn. He stopped outside the barn, looked in, and noticed Mable quietly standing over the trough. Dizzying thoughts ran through his mind. He wondered what had killed and eaten Bertha. He sat on the small stool next to Mabel, reached his hand out to her, and caressed her side. Although she was just a cow, to Michael, she was part of the diminishing life still living at the estate that deserved to be protected.

Monson left the monks in the kitchen to clean up while he took breakfast to Jillian. Angelia and Faith were still sleeping. It was a good morning. Jillian was coherent and somewhat talkative, although her conversation with Monson revolved around her hallucinatory plans to go picnicking with William and the children. At least she was talking to him, Monson thought, and he did enjoy seeing her happy, even if her happiness was based on imaginings. After she had finished her food, Monson bent down and took her plate. Jillian looked up at him, held his hand, and said,

"Monson, you are so good to me. Thank you for being my friend."

Monson smiled and replied, "Madam Beorn, it is a pleasure to be your friend. Thank you for allowing our friendship to grow as it has for many years."

Jillian smiled, leaned her head down, and gently kissed his hand. Monson smiled and held back his emotions and the lump in his throat. He loved Jillian. He remembered her as a small child. She was a beautiful, loving child who grew into a wonderful, gracious woman. And now it all seemed unfair that

< 242 >

she had lost so much and spent most of her time elsewhere. He bent over, gently kissed her cheek, and said, "My dear Jillian."

Another thought occurred to him. Maybe God gave her these visions as a tender mercy of his love for her. At least this way, he thought, she was not burdened with the torture of missing or dead loved ones. A scripture came to mind, "Come unto me all ye that labor and are heavy laden, and I will give you rest." Monson smiled, looked upward, and reverenced God for his great compassion and unyielding love, especially for Jillian.

"Monson, could you help me to my rocking chair next to the window? I want to be the first to see William and Michael when they arrive?" Jillian asked.

Monson looked at Jillian, breathed in, exhaled, and was pleasantly surprised when for the first time, he did not feel sadness for her but relief. He knew that she had no idea that William would not be coming down the road but that God had allowed her to retain a measure of hope that allowed her to have peace. It was an odd feeling but a good sense. He smiled, helped lift Jillian from her chair, and walked with her to the rocker in front of the window. She thanked him as she sat in the chair. She leaned over to the side of the chair and reached down to pick something up. Monson looked but did not see anything next to the chair.

"Is there something I can get you, Madam?" He asked.

"I cannot seem to reach my needles, which are just beyond my reach. See them right there, in the basket? They are on top of the sweater I've been knitting for William."

Monson looked for a moment and then realized that there was no yarn, needles, and sweater, just another imagination to occupy her mind. He bent over, mimed picking up a basket, and held the imaginary basket next to her. She smiled, lifted the sweater, and stretched it open for him to see.

"What do you think?" She asked.

"It is beautiful. I am sure he will enjoy it."

< 243 >

"I agree; I think it will be his favorite," Jillian said as she laid the garment in her lap, leaned over the basket, picked up her needles and ball of yarn, and continued working on the sweater.

"You enjoy the view Madam, and I will clean up your breakfast dishes." Monson turned and walked back toward the small table next to her bed. He began to pick up the dishes and place them on the large serving tray when Jillian excitedly exclaimed, "Oh, look, Monson! I think I see them." She pointed toward the road as she looked through the window. Monson hesitated to acknowledge her. It was not the first time she insisted that she saw the carriage headed toward the estate. She squinted and moved her head closer to the window.

"They must be moving fast because there is a trail of black dust rising before them. Do you see the carriage, Monson?"

He started to acknowledge her with his typical reply agreeing with her statement, when suddenly, his mind hung upon the words, "trail of black dust rising before them." She had never mentioned a trail of black dust. With the tray of dishes in his hands, he turned and walked over to the window. While standing next to her chair, he looked out the window toward the dirt road. He wasn't surprised not to see a carriage, but he saw the trail of black dust that appeared to be hovering a foot above the road and moving in an erratic yet forward direction. Jillian stood next to Monson and grabbed onto his right arm.

"What on earth is that?" He said, still not able to clearly render the object.

"It is William and Michael, I tell you. The carriage must be moving quickly to stir such a storm before them." Jillian excitedly stated.

"Do you see the carriage? Jillian asked.

"No, I am afraid I do not," Monson added.

< 244 >

Suddenly, his eyes grew large as he was able to extract an identifiable object in the mist, and then another, and another.

"Oh, dear God above!" He exclaimed.

"Jillian, stay here! Do not move! I will return shortly." He declared. He turned, ran back toward the bed, attempted to toss the tray onto the table but misjudged its position, and the contents crashed to the floor.

"Never mind the mess; I will clean it when I return!"

He shouted as he ran out of the room, closing the door behind him and down the long hall. He continued running, panting for breath as adrenaline filled his veins. It was the only thing giving him the energy to move as swiftly as a young man. He reached the winding stairway and began trailing down it two to three steps at a time. He gave no thought to his enhanced ability to maneuver quickly and efficiently. He reached the bottom of the stairway, ran to the main entry, threw open the large door, looked toward the barn, and yelled at the top of his lungs, "Michael! Michael!"

Michael was still sitting on the stool next to Mabel when he heard Monson. At first, it did not register, but then he recognized the voice shouting his name; more astounding was that it came from Monson, in a terrifying cry that Michael had never heard come from his lips. Michael jumped up and ran to the doorway of the barn. He saw Monson standing on the front steps of the estate. One hand clutched a closed umbrella from the top, and the other held onto one of the columns as he tried to catch his breath. When Monson saw Michael, he yelled again.

"It is a swarm, and they are headed this way! He yelled.

Michael paused; he had never seen Monson so terrified. He attempted to look beyond the dirt road horizon but saw nothing at first glance. Suddenly, he saw black dust moving over the top of the slight rise in the road about a quarter-mile off in the distance. He strained to see what caused the phenomenon that appeared to be moving irregularly down the road. Astonishingly, his eyes began to decipher individual

< 245 >

movements just behind the dust. Accompanying the chaotic movement was a loud, high-pitched, screeching sound, resonating in and out of unison. His mind decoded the spectacle faster than he could mouth. "RATS!" As the word fell from his lips, he saw hundreds of monstrous cat-sized wild black rats running full speed toward the estate. Their sharp, long fangs appeared to be leading their way to their next meal. Michael immediately visualized the final, torturous demise of the timid milk cow whose scattered remains to lie off in the pasture.

He yelled at Monson, "Monson, go inside and close the door!"

Monson turned back toward the door as the front line of vicious varmints reached the front porch.   Their speed was swift but cluttered as the creatures banged against one another in a frantic attempt to keep moving at the same velocity and in the same direction. Monson heard the screeching noise as the rats began to pass the porch in their continued trajectory toward the barn. It appeared as if they did not notice him. As his hand touched the large door handle, he turned his head back toward the swarm just as one of the rats was pushed up the steps and rolled onto the porch, landing on its feet directly in front of him. It lifted its head, revealed its long sharp teeth, reared back, and lunged at Monson. Monson, still holding the closed umbrella in his right hand, leaned back, lifted his left arm, and shielded his face as he swung his right arm and umbrella in a long, scooping motion at the creature. The crook of the umbrella made contact with the rat, lifting it into the air and flinging it back into the swarm of running rats. Monson turned, opened the door, ran inside, and slammed it shut as several more rats thrust their bodies against the door.

Michael watched until Monson was safely back in the estate. Within seconds the anterior swarm was upon the barn. Michael swiftly closed the large door as bodies of rats were hurled into it. He heard thud after thud hit the door. The screeching noise amplified as rats began to scratch at the door,

< 246 >

shrieking louder and louder like wild animals in a feeding frenzy. Michael turned and rushed the cow toward one of the stalls. He then noticed that the back door of the barn was still open and turned to close it when he heard scratching sounds on the door and saw several claws digging under it. He grabbed a pitchfork and rushed back to the closed door. One of the digging rats pushed its head underneath the door. As it lifted its head, it saw Michael, opened its sizeable elongated jaw, and retracted its gums, revealing its long fangs and jagged, sharp teeth. Michael lifted the pitchfork and thrust it down upon the head of the rat, killing it instantly. No sooner had he killed the creature than another rat dug its way into the barn. Michael repeated the motion several times, killing five or six more rats. As the dead rats plugged the holes, Michael ran to the back of the barn to close the other door. The cow followed him. When he reached the door, he discovered that the rats had begun to run to the back of the barn. He lifted the pitchfork and started flinging them away from the door. The cow had followed him. He yelled at the cow and motioned for it to go back into the barn. One of the rats broke its way past Michael and jumped onto the cow. The rat startled the cow, and it ran back into the barn toward the last stall. Michael realized the entire swarm was headed directly toward him as he stood outside the barn door. He braced himself with the pitchfork in front and started swinging as the rats came. The terrorized cow began to shriek to fend off the attacking rat. Michael tripped and fell backward, and the swarm ignored him and turned into the barn. He slid on his back several feet away from the door, realizing the horrible fate of the unfortunate milk cow. The cow's screams ended within seconds, and Michael knew its pain was over. When the tail end of the rats entered the barn, Michael jumped up and quickly closed the door. He ran to the front of the barn to ensure all the rats were inside. He then headed for the estate. The front door opened, and Monson emerged with both monks and three burning torches. They leaped from the front porch, ran to

< 247 >

Michael, and handed him one of the torches. Michael motioned Monson and the monks to the front of the barn as he ran to the back.   Without any verbal communication, the men began torching the barn. Within seconds the wood caught fire, and the structure was engulfed in flames.   Monson and the monks backed away from the front of the barn as Michael moved away from the back. They listened as frantic and disoriented rats screeched in pain and hysteria, not knowing how to exit the building. After a few minutes, the noise began to die as rats died from the flames or smoke inhalation. Michael walked to the front of the barn and stood next to Monson. Monson leaned over and embraced Michael.

"Thank you, Michael, and thank God you are alive."

Michael held Monson for a moment as he watched the burning structure. The roof began to cave in, and the walls fell one by one. The men released one another and stood staring at the flames with the monks. Dom Gordon looked at Brother Richard, who had repeatedly repeated the cross sign so many times that he had a temporary indentation on his forehead. The screeching had stopped; the creatures were dead. As Michael started to feel relief, he noticed something moving toward him from the burning rubble. It lifted its head, opened its mouth, and screamed at him. His mind was taken back to the fire in the cottage.   He was looking into the window at his helpless, precious little sister. She was screaming at him. "Help me!" Michael began to walk toward the fire. He saw a figure of a man carrying a child. Monson grabbed his arm and tried to hold him back. Michael was too strong for Monson, pulling away as Monson clung to his tunic.

"I have to save her!" Michael yelled.

"Michael, stop! She is not there! Listen to me, Michael! She is not there!"

Michael stopped, shook off the odd memory, closed his eyes, opened them, and was back in the present. He looked back

< 248 >

at Monson and said, "Monson, she's not there! She was not in the fire! Someone saved her! Sarah is alive!"

< 249 >

Chapter Seventeen Notes

There are numerous stories of wild rats attacking people during the plague of 1348. When the plague began to cause massive death in late 1348, the King, believing that witchcraft may have been involved, sent decrees to kill all cats since cats were known to be companions of witches. This act may have increased the rat population as fewer cats meant fewer mortal enemies for rats.

"Many wild rats carry several diseases and parasites, but which diseases and what percentage of the rat population is infected vary with the population under study. Some parasites may have interesting effects on rat behavior, benefiting the parasite." http://www.ratbehavior.org/WildRatDisease.htm

< 250 >

Chapter Eighteen
Desolation

April 16, 1350.

The Chattingworth estate, Cardiff, Wales

8:00AM

"That's the last of it," Angelia said as she dumped the flour bag upside down, pouring its contents into a large mixing bowl.

"I thought we had been using it sparingly, Michael. I surely expected it to last longer than this," added Monson as he looked into the bowl. "What will we do now?"

Michael thought for a moment and asked, "Have you looked throughout the storage room to ensure there are no other bags?"

"Yes, unfortunately, we have no more." Responded Angelia.

Angelia looked at the men and said, "Running out of flour is not the worst thing. We still have eggs, milk, dried meat, and vegetables. I can make broth from the meat. We will survive."

"Yes, but for how long, Angelia? Even though the estate had great supplies, no one expected anyone to be here for over a year without replenishing them. It will be at least a month to six weeks before the garden will produce vegetables, and we will have enough for another two weeks if we are lucky."

"What do you suggest we do, Michael?" Asked Monson.

Michael thought for a moment. He and Monson knew that there was only one solution to the dilemma, but neither was ready to consider it.

< 251 >

"I will hook a wagon to one of the horses and go into town. Hopefully, there is still life there, and if we are lucky some flour."

"I will go with you." Added Angelia.

"Nonsense! We all know the danger that is out there. I will not expose you to it. Besides, you have a child that needs her mother."

Angelia placed her hand to her mouth as tears began to fall from her eyes.

Monson interjected, "Michael, you cannot go alone. You do not know what you will find out there. You will need at least one other person, someone to drive the horses, and someone else to watch for looters. I will go with you."

"Monson, I appreciate your offer, but you are in no condition to drive or ward off bandits. You coming with me is out of the question."

"Then who will go?" asked Angelia, still trying to hold back the tears.

"I will go!" stated Brother Richard, who had quietly walked into the room unnoticed. Everything looked at him.

"Are you good with a knife or a crossbow?" asked Michael.

"Neither, Sir. But I do command a mean whip over horses."

Michael raised his eyebrows.

"You do realize that what you are volunteering for is extremely dangerous? We do not know what or who we will find once we get past the estate. It has been months since I traveled to Cardiff, and back then, the plague had just begun its terror."

"Yes, I understand the risks, but it seems to me that it is better to risk our lives than give them up to starvation."

Michael looked at Brother Richard and then at Monson and Angelia.

< 252 >

"What about Dom Gordon? Will he agree to let you do this?"

Just then, Dom Gordon entered the room; he had overheard the last part of the conversation.

"Brother Richard is free to choose for himself." He then looked at Brother Richard. "Are you sure you are willing to take this risk?"

Brother Richard took a deep breath and let it out forcefully. He looked at Dom Gordon and spoke with conviction. "It seems to me that if God protected us from hungry wolves along the countryside on our journey here, he would protect us as we journey into a city."

Michael interjected, "This is not just a Sunday ride into the city. No doubt the plague will be all around us. I've seen what happens to some who get this sickness. Some lose their minds and become evil; others become delirious and wander the streets. Either type is hazardous if you were to come into contact with them. If you are going with me, you must understand where our journey will take us and the dangers we will face." Everyone remained quiet, contemplating what Michael had just said. Angelia spoke up.

"Michael, perhaps the journey is too dangerous."

"Regardless of the danger, we have no other choice, our food supply is depleted, and unless one of you Monks has a special relationship with God and can ask him to rain down manna from Heaven, we are going to the city to see what we can find," Michael said.

Angelia spoke again. "How will you protect yourself from the sickness?"

Michael reached over the counter behind him and yanked a clove of garlic from a long rope of garlic hanging over the counter.

"With this?"

< 253 >

Brother Richard looked surprised. "Michael, surely an arrow from a crossbow will do more harm than throwing garlic at people."

"Brother Richard, I have no intention of throwing garlic at anyone. We will wear it in our pockets, the hem of our robes, and our socks."

Brother Richard became even more shocked. He shook his head and raised his hands as he spoke.

"For the love of all that is Holy, what type of wicked incantation are you suggesting we engage in?"

Michael wrinkled his face, looked at Monson, and then back at the monk.

"Brother Richard, perchance, do I look like a witch?"

The monk shrugged his shoulders.

"Really?" Asked Michael.

The monk slowly shook his head.

"Thank you. Now, let me explain. My father taught us that garlic repels fleas, and he and I believe this plague is transmitted by fleas."

Angelia then asked but did not you also say that people can get it from the breath of those infected?"

"Yes, Angelia. However, garlic also has incredible healing power and is known to cleanse the body of sickness. I watched as one of the servants of my father's estate in Bristol was healed of the Black Death by drinking garlic juice."

Brother Richard mumbled, "Holy Father, above what have I volunteered for?"

"Do not fret, my friend; we will not need to drink it. But it would be wise to eat a few cloves before our journey, just in case we come in contact with the foul air."

Monson chimed in before Brother Richard could speak.

"Brother Richard, I will roast the garlic, and you can spread it on the bread that Angelia and I will make today."

The monk nodded his head. Michael looked at him and asked,

< 254 >

"Are you still with me?"

He again nodded.

"When will we leave?" he asked.

Monson said, "We can have the bread ready by noon."

"Thank you, Monson," Michael said while patting him on the back. He then put his hand on the shoulder of the monk and said, "Come, Brother, let us go outside and practice our incantations."

The monk began to puff his chest, and Michael smiled and added, "I mean, practice shooting the crossbow. Besides, something tells me my safety stands a greater chance of you shooting arrows at rogues than it does with you throwing garlic at them." The others quietly laughed as Michael and Brother Richard left the room.

Monson turned back toward the mixing bowl.

"Angelia, would you mind fetching more water from the well out back?" Before she could answer, Dom Gordon spoke.

"Please, let me. I would be happy to." He reached for the water bucket. Monson handed it to him and thanked him. For the next few minutes, Angelia helped Monson mix the bread dough. Neither said a word for ten minutes. Dom Gordon returned with the water. Monson scooped a large ladle into the water and filled a tall glass. He handed the glass to Dom Gordon and asked,

"Would you mind taking this to Lady Beorn and checking on her?"

"Of course not. I would be happy to."

He left the room with the glass of water, and Monson turned back to Angelia and continued to work with her. As they needed the bread, she asked, "Monson, is it safe for Michael and the monk to go to Cardiff?"

"Absolutely not." Replied Monson.

Angelia knew it wasn't safe, but she had hoped for a more consoling answer.

"Well then, you cannot just let him go now, can you?"

< 255 >

Monson smiled and asked, "You mean Michael or the monk."

"Michael, of course!" She added without hesitation.

She then caught herself and said, "I mean both of them, not just Michael, but the monk too."

Monson continued to look at the dough he was working with.

"Angelia, it is very dangerous, but there is something special about Michael. I have seen firsthand how God had preserved this young man. I do not know what they will find when they get there or what they will encounter along the way, but something tells me they will survive, and God will bring them home safely, with whatever we need to survive."

Angelia did not say anything. She continued to work the dough. A few moments passed, and she said, "Is it that obvious, Monson?"

"Is it obvious that you care for Michael?" Monson asked.

"I guess you just answered me with your question."

Monson laughed mildly. "Angelia, Michael is a very handsome man, and he is a good man. He is not the man he was nearly two years ago when he first came here. He had been through many trials, much like yourself, except he was quite the hard stone with many rough edges; you were already a diamond when you arrived. Michael still doesn't realize how much faith or wisdom God has blessed him with. But one day, he will. He came here as a boy, and now he is a man. He came here very prideful, and now humility has become his friend. Michael will be the first to tell you that it is better to humble yourself than to be humbled by God."

"Monson, you have been a good mentor for him, I can tell."

Monson took a deep breath and let it out.

"I do not know how much truth there is to that, but I do know that we have learned a lot from each other. If I were to

< 256 >

have had a son, I would have wanted him to be just like Michael. I know God has a great work for this man, and I know he will discover it for himself one day."

Tears began to flow from Angelia's eyes. She tried to wipe her eyes on her shoulders to keep from touching her dough-covered hands to her face.

"Monson, I feel so blessed to be here. It is hard to know that I will not see my husband again and that Faith will never know her father, but I know God has led us here, and I am most grateful for that." She tried to hold back her emotions.

Monson leaned closer to her, and she laid her head on his shoulder and cried.

"My child, I think it is obvious that you care for Michael." He paused. "And it is also obvious that he cares for you. Give it time, and if God brought the two of you together, you both will soon discover it for yourselves."

"Thank you, Monson," Angelia said as she lifted her head and gently placed her right hand on his left cheek. He lifted his right hand, bent his fingers, and wiped the tears from her eyes with the back of his knuckles. He then placed his left hand on her cheek. There was a short pause as they looked at each other. They each lowered their hands, and both looked back at the bread.

Dom Gordon walked back into the kitchen and said, "Lady Beorn is doing well this morning. She even spoke to me for a moment or two. Of course, I do not know what she was speaking about, but she seemed happy."

Both Monson and Angelia turned and looked at Dom Gordon. Neither noticed that their faces were covered with flour, Angelia with a handprint on one side of her face and ghostly white streaks under both eyes, and Monson with a handprint on his right cheek. Dom Gordon flinched backward and said, "Holy Father, save my soul!"

The two were surprised at his comments. He pointed at their faces, and they looked at each other and began to laugh.

< 257 >

The Priest shook his head and joined in the laughter. Monson thought to himself at that moment how wonderful God was to bring all of these people together during such a terrible time. What a joy it was to be reunited with Dom Gordon, how much he enjoyed getting to know Brother Richard, and what an answer to prayer was Angelia for Michael. He felt for an instant that they just might survive the pestilence. He had learned to treasure the special moments in life because he knew it could be long before they would share such a moment of frivolity again.

12:00 PM

Everyone but Jillian gathered in the kitchen shortly afternoon. Angelia removed the hot bread from the oven and placed it on the counter. The aroma filled the room and most of the house. She picked up a knife and began cutting the bread. She put a few slices on plates. Brother Richard reached out for one of the plates, and Monson said, "Stop! Not yet!"

He turned and lifted a small wire rack hanging above the cooking fire. He dumped it upside down, and many roasted garlic cloves fell upon the counter. He took a fork from a drawer and began smashing the roasted garlic into a paste. He then took a knife and lightly spread a thin amount of garlic onto one of the slices of bread. He repeated the process until he had covered five slices of bread. He then handed a plate to each person.

"Dom Gordon, would you mind asking God to bless this bread?" Monson asked.

"I would be honored to thank you, Monson." The priest replied.

After the prayer, everyone lifted the bread to their lips. Monson quickly grabbed the plate from Brother Richard and said,

"Wait, yours is not ready yet!"

< 258 >

He took the bread and slathered it with triple the amount of garlic. Brother Richard squinted and made a face as Monson spread the garlic onto the bread. Monson paused, and Brother Richard reached for the plate again.

Monson pushed his hand away and said, "Brother Richard, you are about to embark on a perilous journey, and unlike Michael, your body is not used to a daily regimen of roasted garlic. I am afraid you will require more to give you the protection you need."

He then spread more garlic until the top and crust of the bread was no longer visible. Everyone held their clenched teeth to keep from laughing. Monson raised the plate up to Brother Richard's nose. Brother Richard slowly took the plate, lifted the bread to his lips, opened his mouth, closed his eyes, and slowly placed the bread in his mouth. He bristled as his teeth came down on the bread, tearing it apart in his mouth. He chewed slowly, focusing on the bread's flavor and not the mound of garlic covering it.

Michael and the others finished eating the slice before them, and one at a time, they placed their empty plates back onto the counter. Brother Richard was the last to do so. Michael spoke,

"Monson, I believe that we are ready to leave. Before we do so, I would like to say a few things. Although I am confident that we will succeed on our journey, there is always the possibility that something--he hesitated, "will not turn out as planned. It is not a long journey into the city, and I hope to return within three hours. If we do not return, you must prepare for the worst."

"What do you mean, the worst?" asked Angelia.

"The estate has survived with very few outsiders crossing our land. It is possible that there could be heathens, like all of us have experienced, who discover the vulnerability of the estate and attempt to take it for themselves. You must

< 259 >

each arm yourselves and be prepared to fight for your lives, if necessary."

The thought of failure entered the minds of each person. Angelia began to tear up.

"One last thing," Michael added. "If either Brother Richard or I get exposed to the plague and begin to show any sign of sickness, we will not return and bring it here."

Angelia reached out to Michael and embraced him. She cried as she spoke.

"Michael, you must return! You must!"

Michael held her tightly against him.

"God willing, God willing."

Angelia looked up at him and quickly kissed his lips. Michael raised his right hand behind her head and held her as the kiss continued for an uncomfortable length of time for the others. Brother Richard cleared his throat, and the kiss finally ended. Angelia looked at Brother Richard and then at the others. Brother Richard cleared his throat again.

Angelia looked back at him and asked, "What?"

He cleared his throat again. Still looking at the monk, Angelia became irritated and said, "It is over!"

Brother Richard shook his head, held his throat, and struggled to mouth the words, "It is not over. I am still choking!"

Angelia began to pat his back. Dom Gordon joined in as the others stepped closer to see how they could help. After a few moments, Brother Richard coughed up a mouth full of garlic and spat it on the floor. Everyone moved back a step. He took a deep breath and said, "Alright, now I am better."

Everyone looked away as Monson said, "Well, Brother Richard, let me get you a spoon for that."

Brother Richard looked disgustedly at Monson as everyone laughed. When the laughter died, Monson asked, "Dom Gordon, would you mind offering a prayer that God might protect our friends as they journey?"

< 260 >

"Of course, thank you," He replied.

He began the prayer, 'Oh dear God, Father above. We give thee thanks for all that thou hast so graciously given each of us. We thank thee that we can be together at this time, buoy one another, and renew friendships. We give thee thanks for the love we have for one another. Please, dear Father, keep thy sons safe on their journey, let them find flour, and return to us that we might all live. And let us be safe here until they return. Let us—" he paused. Several uncomfortable seconds passed, and he began speaking again. "Let us have the courage and the strength to defend all we have been given, should the occasion require it. And Lord, please bless and protect those we love who are not with us. Please let us one day reunite with them. As we end this prayer, Father, help us to keep a prayer in our hearts and know of thy great love, protection, and great mercy. Amen." Everyone quietly added, "Amen."

After the prayer, everyone walked outside, where two horses had been hitched to a cart. Michael helped Brother Richard climb onto the cart, and then he followed. Each looked and verified that a loaded crossbow was near their feet. Two other crossbows and twenty arrows were placed in the front of the cart, just behind the seat. Michael lifted and snapped the reigns, commanding the horses to begin the journey. As the cart headed down the dirt road, everyone waived, and Monson said,

"Godspeed, my friends, Godspeed."

After traveling some distance before the road turned, Michael looked back to see the estate. Although large, it looked small from a distance. He could barely distinguish the three small human figures watching as the carriage disappeared. For a moment, he felt peace, and then suddenly, the foggy image of a man spun around in his head. Seconds later, the spinning stopped, and the face turned until it looked directly at him. The fog dissipated slowly, revealing a terrified pale face surrounded by thick black hair. A flash of yellow flames momentarily blinded Michael. The flames encircled the face, and thick black

< 261 >

smoke covered the image. Michael leaned forward into the vision just as the face burst through the smoke and stopped eye to eye with him. A quick flash of perfect clarity revealed the face. It was William. The vision ended as abruptly as it began. Michael's heart raced at the unexpected vision. He tried to control his heavy breathing. "Only a dream!" He thought. "Only a dream!" Michael knew that something wasn't right. He knew that their journey would not be without struggle. Michael remembered the words of Monson, *"God speed, my friends, Godspeed."* He clung to hope and prayed for faith, hoping God was with them.

1:00 PM

An hour had passed just as they arrived on the edge of town. Up to that point, the trip had been quiet and uneventful. It occurred to Michael that he did not notice birds or any wildlife on the trail, which was eerily atypical. As the city became closer, the horses reached the edge of a cobblestone street. Their hooves clicked as they walked. The storefronts on the edge of town were mostly boarded up. There was no sign of life anywhere.   The grass had grown nearly two feet tall between the cobblestones and next to some of the buildings. The wind was slightly blowing the aroma of a stale stench. Michael looked at a third-floor apartment, noticing an open window with curtains waving outside the building. The only sound was the sound of the horse hooves and the wheels of the cart. Neither man had spoken for the last thirty minutes, and both were in awe of the condition of the city. They each looked down intersecting streets as they passed, still seeing no sign of life. It seemed unbelievable that a city the size of Cardiff could be uninhabited. They were about six blocks into the city and nearing the harbor when suddenly Michael noticed a large ship anchored and men standing on it speaking to one another. He

< 262 >

whipped the horses, and the cart quickly moved closer to the ship. Michael stopped the horses when they reached the edge of the dock next to the ship. Several men were unloading the vessel.

"Brother Richard, stay here. I will only be a moment; I want to see the condition of things." Michael said.

The monk nodded in agreement. He then picked up a loaded crossbow and gently laid it on his lap.

Michael walked toward the men and yelled, "Where is your captain?"

The men noticed him, and one pointed toward another man who turned and faced Michael.

"I am Captain Wall. What can I do for you, sir?"

To Michael, the men appeared to be healthy and unusually comfortable, considering all that had happened with the plague.

Michael yelled. "Are you clean?"

The captain smiled and asked, "Do you mean are we carrying the pestilence on our ship or bodies?"

Michael nodded.

The captain continued, "Yes and No!"

Michael leaned back a bit. The captain smiled and said,

"Yes, we are clean, and no, we are not carrying the pestilence on our ship or bodies."

Michael walked to the man and reached out his arm to him. Their arms clasped hands wrist to wrist.

"My name is Michael Beorn. We have come into town to purchase wheat, but until seeing you, we thought the town had become uninhabited."

"Much of it has, but there is still quite a bit of life here. In fact, it seems that this plague is dying out," he hesitated, "Excuse me, poor choice of words. It appears that the plague has run its course. Especially from the places I've been of late."

< 263 >

The words *"run its course"* echoed in Michael's head; It did not seem real that the plague was coming to an end. He wanted to believe the news but still felt cautious.

"What do you mean, run its course?" Michael asked.

"I mean that it seems to be over."

"Over?" Michael questioned in obvious disbelief.

"Well, sir, it may seem strange to you, but my guess is that I get around much more than you, and I can tell you from the places I've been, the plague seems to be gone, and life is returning."

Just then, one of the workers dropped a bag of flour. The captain turned and screamed at him.

"Pick it up, you fool. Any losses will come out of your wages!" He turned back to Michael. "This is my third trip to Cardiff this week, and even this little town looks better than it did a couple of weeks ago."

Michael looked around and, seeing no one except for the workers and a handful of men receiving the goods, said,

"I do not see people. Where are they?"

"Most of the town to the east was hit hard, but some merchants and townspeople on this side have fared much better. It is strange that wherever I travel, those directly amid this pestilence seem unable to contract it. We load and unload as quickly as possible, just in case, and then head out to our next port. Unlike my fellow trade competitors, I never let my men off the ship to waste time and money in the towns. It seems to have been a good decision. So where did you say you were from?"

"We have come from a place far from town. We need to purchase flour."

"Well, I will tell you what, I will give you a good deal on the bag that one of my irresponsible employees just dropped. I doubt I would get a full price from the merchant, considering there is a tear in the burlap, and some of it has spilled onto the dock. What do you say? Half price of what you'd pay retail?"

< 264 >

"Sure, I will purchase the bag."

Michael reached into his coin purse draped over his neck and under his left arm and removed a small money pouch. He pulled some coins from the pouch and handed them to the captain. The captain waved at the man who had dropped the flour bag and pointed toward the cart. The man placed the large flour bag onto the cart.

"Thank you, sir. Nice doing business with you. Now, excuse me, I have a ship to sail." He turned and began to walk away.

"Wait, captain, I have one more question." The captain stopped and turned toward Michael.

"Yes, what is it?"

"You said that you have been to many places. Is Bristol one of them, and if so, what are conditions like there?"

The captain shook his head and responded, "Sir, if there is a devil, he lives in Bristol. I haven't stopped in Bristol in months, and I do not know if I ever will again. The air stinks of rotten flesh, human flesh, and the harbor is filled with sunken ships. As a matter of fact, it is quite tricky just maneuvering through the Frome on the way to the open sea."

Michael felt his heart sink. It did not seem real that Bristol could be so devastated. He wondered how the estate on the hill had managed and if any of his friends were still alive.

"Thank you, captain. And thank you for the flour."

"My pleasure, sir. Be safe and stay away from the other side of town."

Michael acknowledged the remarks. He climbed back onto the cart.

"Did he say to stay away from the other side of town? Did not we just come from the other side of town?" Asked Brother Richard.

"Yes, he did. And yes, we came that way. There is a shop a few blocks back and two streets where my family does

< 265 >

business. Let's head in that direction. Hopefully, the merchant is still alive, and his shop is still open."

They turned the cart and began heading back from the way they came. When they reached the merchant shop, Michael noticed a sign on the door. The sign read, "PLAGUE." Michael felt the hair stand on the back of his neck. "Brother Richard, we need to leave quickly."

Michael snapped the horses' reins and ran them near full speed until they left the cobblestone street. He felt a sense of relief as the carriage entered the forest back toward the estate. He felt a great urge to return to the estate as quickly as possible. They had planned on more than one bag of flour, but the feeling of peril was too strong to ignore. He knew that if he could keep the horses running at their current speed, they could make it back to the estate in under an hour. Michael remembered the last time he had ridden into Cardiff and the terror that awaited him when he returned to the estate moments before evil men would have ended the life of his beloved Elizabeth and the kidnapping of Lucas. He tried to shrug off the memory and the feelings of uneasiness. He glanced at Brother Richard, holding so tightly to the crossbow that his fingers turned red. He looked forward as he held to the reins of the horses. The animals seemed determined as they galloped, clicking their hooves on the cobblestone street. The buildings appeared to blur on either side as Michael focused toward the edge of town several streets ahead. Michael focused on, ignoring his peripheral vision. Brother Richard, however, noticed a tattered awning of a storefront, a block ahead and to the right, his side of the vehicle. Something was moving along the edge of it. He squinted his eyes to improve his vision.

He yelled, "What is that?"

Michael shook off his daze and looked to the right just as the horses galloping at full speed were within feet of the awning. The horses pulled to the right just enough for the front passenger side wheel to clip the edge of one of the posts holding

< 266 >

the awning. Michael jerked the reins to the left, forcing the horses back toward the middle of the street. As the post collapsed, the awning fell onto the cart covering Brother Richard. He quickly pulled the awning off and tossed it out of the cart. Michael looked at Brother Richard, but before speaking, a large creature jumped from the back of the cart towards the back of his head. Brother Richard lifted the crossbow that was still firmly in his grasp, raised it toward Michael, and without hesitation pulled the trigger, releasing an arrow into the creature's side a second before it reached Michael's head, knocking it out of the cart and onto the street. The incident happened so quickly that Michael was not sure if he was more shocked at some unknown creature jumping toward him or Brother Richard pointing a loaded crossbow at him and successfully shooting the thing. Michael started to say something, but Brother Richard reached down to the floor next to his feet, grabbed another arrow, and quickly loaded it into the crossbow. Michael felt his heart racing and his head spinning. He quickly looked over his shoulder back into the cart to see other unwanted passengers. While holding the reins with his left hand, he raised his right hand toward Brother Richard and questioned, "What are you doing? There is nothing else in the cart!"

Brother Richard finished loading the crossbow, held it tightly while pointing it toward the road, and said, "Sorry Michael, I did not mean to startle you, but I could not let that thing attack you, now could I?"

Still unnerved by the experience, Michael said, "No apology necessary. I appreciate your help, and I thank God you have a good aim!"

Suddenly several rats being chased by cats ran in front of the cart. Screeches resonated as the horses trampled on some, and others passed under the cart and under the wheels. Brother Richard stood, struggling to maintain his balance, and swung around toward the back of the cart with the crossbow

< 267 >

raised in front of him. The cart hit another bump, and his finger squeezed the trigger, releasing an arrow into the bag of flour. Michael pulled Brother Richard back down to his seat and then grabbed the crossbow and placed it on the seat between them.

"Brother Richard, I believe it would be a good idea to leave the crossbow on the seat and take a deep breath before you kill one of us!"

"Forgive me, Michael. I do not know what happened. It happened so fast when that creature fell from the awning and onto the cart that something inside of me caused me to point the weapon at it, and I did not mean to pull the trigger."

"What do you mean, you did not mean to pull the trigger? I am still shaking at seeing you pointing the crossbow toward me, but I am grateful that you pulled the trigger. Of course, I am more grateful that you hit the creature and not me, but you may have saved my life. "He then added, under his breath, "But then I probably lost at least a year of it during that split second when I thought you were going to shoot me."

"I am sorry, Michael. It will not happen again, I assure you. I will contain myself until we get back to the estate." He paused, "And then I will find a quiet place alone and regurgitate the last piece of garlic from my stomach!"

Michael shook his head and smiled. He patted Brother Richard on his back and said, "All is well, my friend. You are still alive, and by the grace of God, so am I."

They both chuckled at the experience that seemed to be far behind them. The edge of town was just ahead, and both looked eager to get as far away from Cardiff as possible. Although Michael felt relief surviving an unexpected situation, his moment of relief was overshadowed by a sick feeling that a greater evil was approaching. Michael knew they could make it back to the estate shortly after 2:00 PM if they could keep the horses running at full speed. He silently prayed, *"God, please, I beg you, do not let evil reach the estate before I do."* He paused, *"At least let me be there in time to defend those I love.*

< 268 >

And God, let them know of my love." He began breathing quickly but tried to hide his nervous feeling from Brother Richard. It was now 1:45 PM.

< 269 >

Chapter Nineteen
The Enemy Cometh

April 16, 1350.
The Chattingworth estate, Cardiff, Wales

1:45 PM

Angelia had just finished hanging the last sheet on the line. She stood back and wiped the sweat from her brow with the sleeve of her right hand. It was early afternoon; the sun was warm and drying the laundry. She picked up the linen basket and was startled by an unusually cool breeze that rushed by her. At first, she thought she saw something, but looking in all directions determined no one was there. She waited a moment until the odd feeling left her. She stood holding the basket and again looked from side to side. Suddenly she saw the face of Michael in her mind. He was looking over her shoulder. It gave her a moment of comfort. She closed her eyes, smiled, and pulled the basket against her as if holding him close. Suddenly his face jerked toward her and stopped with his eyes wide, looking straight at her. She flinched at the unexpected change. His face quickly looked over her shoulder and then back at her and yelled, "RUN!" She opened her eyes, dropped the basket, lifted her dress a few inches, and began running toward the kitchen door she had left slightly ajar.

The laundry line was about forty yards from the house. She ran as fast as possible, not knowing if she was being followed. She wanted to scream but did not want to alert her assailant or the others in the estate, especially if it was just her mind playing tricks on her. The faster she ran, the further away the house seemed. A feeling of terror entered her mind. Her body began to weaken, and she felt dizzy. She wanted to fall

< 270 >

but knew she had to make it to the house. She kept running, not looking back, only focusing on the door. When the door was within her reach, she raised her right arm and opened her hand, extending her fingers and facing her palm toward the door. She felt a sting as her palm and fingers slapped against the heavy solid wood door, thrusting it open. She flung her body through the doorway and into the room. She slid a short distance on the wood floor and spun around as her right hand tightly clutched the handle and swung her body back toward the door. When she came to a stop, she threw her weight against the door and slammed it shut. Immediately thereafter, she swung down the metal brace securing it shut. She fell to the floor, sitting with her legs stretched in front of her. She panted a moment for air, dropped her head, and began to sob uncontrollably. Dom Gordon had been reading in the study when he heard the commotion. He dropped the book he was reading, ran into the kitchen, and knelt in front of Angelia. He reached his right hand, touched her shoulder, and gently held her. He leaned in toward her and carefully pulled the long hair to the side to see her.

"My dear child, what has happened? Are you all right?" He asked.

Angelia tried to respond but could not get words out of her mouth.

"Are you hurt? He asked again while looking for visible signs of blood or bruise. Finally, Angelia was able to speak.

"It is Michael!" She blurted.

"Michael? Is he here? Have they returned?" The Priest asked, even more concerned.

She lifted her head and pulled the hair from her face.

"Father, I am sorry. I thought someone was out there; I thought someone was chasing me."

"You thought Michael was chasing you?" Asked the Priest.

< 271 >

"No, of course not. I had just finished hanging the last of the laundry when I felt a cold whisk of air that startled me. I turned and saw no one. But then, in my mind, I saw Michael's face. It was a peaceful thought in my mind, but his face looked terrified, and he yelled at me to run. So, I ran."

The Priest smiled at her, still concerned at her agitated state, and said, "Angelia, I think we are all on edge. I am sure your mind is playing tricks on you, and there is nothing to worry about." He leaned in and kissed her on the forehead. He helped her to her feet.

"But it was so real, Father. It was so real. I have never had an experience like that."

"I understand. Perhaps you should go and lie down for a while. I am sure the men will return shortly."

Angelia smiled and hugged the Priest.

"Thank you, Father. I am sure that a short rest will do me some good."

She turned and walked to the stairway. The Priest watched her as she climbed the stairway. He felt saddened that she had been through so much and continued to have moments of fear and trepidation.

1:50 PM

Monson lifted the teapot and placed it on the tray. He looked at Jillian and smiled. He enjoyed their time together. He told her how Michael and Brother Richard had gone to town for supplies. Although he had spoken to her for over an hour, she never responded. Every now and then, she raised the cup to her lips and slowly sipped the hot tea. She then put it on the saucer that had been placed on her lap. Monson made it a point to sit with Jillian each day and talk, hoping that she understood what he said, with faith that her faculties would return one day. He would take her by the hand on warm days and walk with her

< 272 >

through the garden to get her moving so that her body would get some exercise. Each day she seemed to be melting away. Her arms and legs were so thin and frail that she looked much older than her years. She flinched with a shiver. Monson looked toward the fire that had begun to die down. He kept her room so warm that the temperature was almost unbearable to others, but Jillian needed the additional heat to maintain a normal temperature. Monson looked over and, seeing her cup was empty, asked, "May I take that from you?"

The edges of her lips slightly turned up, creating a half-smile, but she said nothing. Monson reached down and lifted the cup from her hand. He placed the cup next to his on the tray. Jillian began to slowly rock her chair as she stared out the window. Monson rose and walked to the fireplace just a couple of feet from her chair. He placed his hand into a heavy sheepskin glove, lifted the fire poker, and jabbed at the smoldering logs until he could see a small flame in the middle of the pile. He placed another log onto the fire and waited until the flames encircled it. He jabbed at it a few more times, causing the fire to rise. He looked back at Jillian and said,

"You know, I believe that Michael has feelings for Angelia."

He waited, hoping for a reaction. Nothing came. He continued, looking back at the fire and poking at the burning wood,

"And I am certain that she has feelings for him. In fact, they both made it quite clear as they kissed right there in the kitchen today, in front of all of us."

He looked at Jillian again. She seemed to be in a daze. He wondered where her mind took her during these times. He looked back at the fire, and suddenly the sound of a shattering cup quickly drew his attention back toward Jillian. It seemed that her empty cup had fallen to the floor. He laid the poker down on the edge of the hearth, leaving the end of it still in the fire. He removed the glove and walked over to Jillian. She

< 273 >

hadn't moved and seemed not to have noticed that she had knocked the cup from the small table next to her. Monson bent to his knees and began to pick up the pieces. He looked up and noticed that Jillian's cup was still on the tray next to his. He did not remember placing the third cup on the tray before bringing the tea into her room. He felt a chill run up his spine. And then Jillian pointed at the window and cheerfully said, "Look, William is coming, and he has brought friends!"

Monson quickly stood and ran to the window. Although he had always hoped by the Grace of God that William was alive, he knew that if he did come, he would come alone and not with friends. He looked out the window and saw three men carrying crossbows over their shoulders. His greatest fear had come true. He knew that William was not among them, and they were not coming for a cup of tea.

He looked back at Jillian, held each of her hands, and said, "My dear Jillian, you must understand me. William is not here, and those men are not our friends. They have come here to do us harm. Please stay in your room and do not leave until I return. Do you understand?" He tried not to shake as he held her hands. She looked at him, leaned her head to the right, and smiled as a tear ran down her left cheek.

"Oh, Monson, my dear Monson. You have been so good to me. William is coming, but I will not see you again. Please tell my dear Father and Mother how much I love them when you see them." She lifted his right hand to her lips and kissed it. "Now go and do what you must."

Monson leaned in and kissed Jillian on the cheek. His thoughts were focused on the terrifying situation, and he did not try to make any sense of her comments. He ran out the door and shut it behind him. He ran across the large hall and into the bedroom on the opposite side of the house. He ran to the window, pulled back the draperies, and looked through the window. He saw four other men armed with weapons walking toward the front of the house. He turned and ran out of the

< 274 >

room and toward the stairway. He yelled at Dom Gordon as he ran down the staircase.

"Alabaster! Come quick! I need you now!"

Dom Gordon heard his name, ran from the study, and simultaneously made it to the bottom of the stairs with Monson.

"What is it, Monson?" Dom Gordon pleaded.

"There are at least eight men out there with weapons, and they are coming this way."

"What?" Dom Gordon asked in disbelief.

"You heard me! They are coming this way. Are all of the doors and windows locked?" Monson asked.

"Yes, they are!" Dom Gordon exclaimed. "What do we do now?" He asked, obviously rattled and terrified at the pending situation.

"Follow me!" Monson ran back into the study, and Dom Gordon followed. He ran to a large bookcase on the inside wall. He raised his hands and leaned his body into the bookcase. He looked back at Dom Gordon and said, "Help me push!"

Dom Gordon leaned next to Monson and applied his weight until the large bookcase moved into the wall. The men continued to push until the bookcase revealed a hidden stairway leading down to another room.

"Follow me!" Monson stated as he walked to the darkened stairway. With Dom Gordon behind him, Monson began to walk down the stairway into a darkened room. As the light from the study above began to fade, Monson reached for a torch placed in a hanger a few feet above the stairway. He took the torch from its holder and then reached in and found a piece of flint. He ran the flint along the rock wall until it sparked. He held the torch close to the flint, and a flame began to grow on the torch. Suddenly the room below was lit, and both men could see its contents. The walls were covered with all types of weapons; some were ancient, some more modern, bows, crossbows, swords, and hundreds of different shapes and sizes

< 275 >

of knives. There were also several basket-like shelves filled with arrows and small crossbow arrows. Monson found another torch leaning from a holder on the wall. He placed his torch to it until flames erupted on the other torch. The room became light, and Dom Gordon was overwhelmed at the immense weaponry everywhere, including six metal knight suits on stands all around the room.

"What is this place?" Asked Dom Gordon in disbelief.

"Sir Chattingworth, my former employer, was an avid collector of weapons of every kind. He was especially intrigued with newer weaponry and experimental weaponry such as black powder that is highly flammable." He pointed to a table with two large wooden pots filled with black powder.

"He also collected Chinese fire candles" He pointed to a shelf on the other side of the room filled with various sizes of odd-shaped candles tied to sticks.

"We'll need some of those. Grab an arm full!" He stated.

Dom Gordon ran to the other side of the room and began to load as many candles into his arms as he could hold. Monson took a crossbow and a basket of arrows and flung them over his shoulder. He took too small knives and placed them in his sash. He noticed a small wash bucket against the wall. He picked up the bucket and scooped it into one of the black powder kegs. He turned to another shelf, took a bag of sizeable marble-sized metal balls, and hung it over his arm. He then found a long odd-looking hollow stick and added it to his collection. When the men had taken all they could carry, they headed back up the stairs. When they reached the study, they both leaned into the bookshelf closing it back into its original position, completely hiding the stairway and room below. Monson ran to the staircase and began running up the stairs.

"Hurry, Alabaster! Follow me."

< 276 >

Dom Gordon struggled to hold all of his items while running up the stairway. He yelled, "Why are we heading upstairs?"

"Because it will be easier to attack them from above!" Monson yelled between breaths.

It finally occurred to Dom Gordon that he would be helping Monson attack and kill the intruders. Just the thought of taking the life of another human being made him sick to his stomach. However, he understood the magnitude of the situation and the reality that these men had surrounded the estate armed with weapons. If for no other reason, he thought, they must protect the women and the child. When they reached the top of the stairs, Monson pointed to a room facing the back of the estate.

"You go and set up in there, and I will be across the hall in this room facing the front of the estate. Light one of the lamps in the room; you will need the flame."

Dom Gordon nodded in agreement and entered the other room. Both doors were opened, and the men could see one another. He placed his armload of weapons onto the bed. He walked over and lit the lamp on a small table beside the bed. Monson did the same in the other room. Both men pulled back the curtains and looked out the windows. Dom Gordon saw three men standing below. He could see that they were attempting to open the wooden shutters covering the windows on the main floor. The men did not notice him looking down at them. He saw another man further down the building yanking on the locked doors. Monson pulled the drape aside and saw four men standing in front of the house; two were holding unlit torches. One of the men stepped forward, lifted the large iron door knocker, and pounded it against the door. Monson opened the window and yelled down at the men,

"What do you want?"

The men looked up at him. The man who had pounded on the door stepped back to see and yelled,

< 277 >

"We are here to take everything you have." The other men laughed. Monson could see that they were dressed in tattered, dirty clothing. Some had shiny gold chains hanging around their necks; one was wearing a cross. One wore a large hat with a feather, and another held a walking cane in one hand and a sword in the other.

The man continued, "So, as I see it, you have two choices, open the door and kindly let us enter, or two; we'll just burn the place down and take what is leftover in the rubble. So, what do you choose, hospitality or ashes?"

Monson looked across the room at Dom Gordon and asked, "How many are out back?"

"I see four men."

"Bring an arm full of those Chinese candles in here."

Dom Gordon scooped up the candles and brought them to Monson's room. Monson pointed to a small table.

"Lie them on the table next to each other. And get the lamp over there."

Dom followed the instructions and laid out ten of the candles next to each other, ensuring that the fuses hung off the end of the table. Monson helped Dom Gordon move the table next to the window.

The man yelled again, "We do not have all day, and I know there aren't many of you in there. Now, are you going to open the door, or do we have to start lighting fires?"

Monson took the hollow stick and stuffed a small linen cloth into the end of it. He then turned it and placed five metal balls into the barrel behind the fabric. Afterward, he scooped a hand into the bucket of black powder and poured it into the barrel. He took a long stick and began to pack the contents into the barrel. He moved his lamp to the edge of the table, looked at Dom Gordon, and said. "Ready?"

Dom Gordon had no idea what would happen, but he nodded in agreement anyway. Monson parted the drapes and shouted back at the men, "You are vastly outnumbered. It

< 278 >

would be wise of you to turn around and go back to where you came from."

The man yelled back, "No, old man, you are the ones who are outnumbered!" He whistled, and the four men behind the house came running and stood next to the other four.

"Now, I am going to give you one more chance. He paused and then screamed, "To save your lives! Open this door now!"

Monson pulled the curtains back, slid the table to the edge of the window, and motioned for Dom Gordon to light the fuses. The large clock in the main hall chimed; it was 2:00 PM. Dom Gordon removed the glass vase from the lamp and held the flame against each fuse until they lit. Monson yelled out the window, "Alright, we'll be right down!"

The men began to laugh, and the leader said, "That's more like it."

The men all looked up at the window. The room began to fill with smoke. Dom Gordon watched as the fuses quickly burned toward the end of the candles.

"Now?" he asked.

"Almost." Replied Monson, "Almost."

Dom Gordon covered his mouth and nose with his sleeve to keep from breathing in the smoke. One of the men noticed smoke from the window and pointed to it.

"Now!" Shouted Monson, and the two of them lifted the table's backside, causing the candles to slide toward the edge of the window. Suddenly the spark of the fuses began to reach each candle, and almost simultaneously, the candles took flight directly at the small crowd of eight men. Some held their crossbows in front of them as the fiery flying objects headed toward them; others did not react fast enough. Within seconds ten large explosions scattered the group of men. Most could deflect the things, but one was killed instantly as a candle entered his screaming mouth and exploded on impact. Angelia ran into the room, holding Faith in her arms.

< 279 >

"What on earth is happening?" She screamed as Faith cried and clung to her rag doll.

A fiery arrow shot through the window and lodged in the wall next to the open door. The flames began to burn the wall. Dom Gordon ran to the wall and started pounding the fire with a pillow from the bed. He pulled Angelia and Faith to the floor and motioned them to stay still. Monson cautiously looked out the window and saw the surviving men reloading their crossbows. He placed the packed barrel on the window seal and aimed it at one of the men. He then touched the burning lamp to the end of the barrel. The black powder ignited, making a loud popping sound that momentarily deafened everyone in the room. The weapon fired and hurled the metal balls at the man striking him in the head, neck, and chest. The impact knocked him over, and the metal balls killed him instantly. The leader of the men yelled for the men to spread out and surround the house.

Monson turned toward the others and said, "Alabaster, grab one of the small crossbows and the basket of arrows!" Dom Gordon stood and followed the instructions. Angelia stood, still holding Faith, who was crying.

"Angelia, take the child and go to Jillian's room. Bolt the door behind you!" She turned and headed for Jillian's room. Monson and Dom Gordon followed her.

"What is happening, Monson?" Asked Angelia. "Why are those men attacking us?"

"They want what all looters want.... everything of value," Monson replied.

When they reached Jillian's room Dom Gordon opened the door and ushered them in; Monson headed down the staircase, his arms filled with weapons.

As Dom Gordon was leaving the room, he said, "Angelia, move that bureau over in front of the door and do not let anyone in. Do you understand me?"

< 280 >

Angelia nodded. Jillian was still in her rocker when she entered the room, looking out the window through the wavy glass. Angelia sat Faith in Jillian's lap, then pulled the heavy wood shutters shut and snapped the latch over the knob, securing them. She looked at Jillian, who looked up at her and smiled. Faith stopped crying and wrapped her arms around Jillian. Jillian smiled, looked up at Angelia, and asked, "Can I hold her for a while?"

"Of Course, you can hold her. I need to move that large bureau in front of the door so no one can enter." She ran to the furniture and pushed it until it was in front of the door. She then sat in the chair next to Jillian, where Monson always sat. She reached out and held onto Jillian's hand. Jillian squeezed her hand and said, "Everything will turn out fine. Now, do not worry."

Angelia wanted to believe Jillian's comment, but the reality of their predicament did not provide much hope, especially since Michael wasn't back yet. She whispered a silent prayer begging God to save them and to bring Michael and Brother Richard home.

***

The horses were tiring as the cart came around the last bend revealing the estate beyond the last line of trees. At first, Michael felt a sense of relief to be home, but then he noticed a large plume of smoke from the far end of the estate. His heart sank when he realized that the closed-off section of the estate was a blaze of fire and smoke from the second floor. Also noticing the smoke, Brother Richard said, "Oh Michael, I hope we are not too late!"

Michael steered the horses toward the back of the house. He saw two men slamming a large tree stump against the wooden shutters on the lower level. The stump finally broke the shutters, and one of the men began to climb into the window. Due to the banging noise, they did not hear the horses and cart

< 281 >

heading toward them. Michael handed the reins to Brother Richard. The first man fell into the house, and the second climbed into the window behind him. Michael stood up, pulled a knife from his sash, and jumped off the moving cart and onto the second man, pulling him out of the window and onto the ground. Michael wrapped his arms around the man, and they rolled several times on the ground. Their bodies separated and landed a few feet from one another when they came to a stop. The man jumped to his feet before Michael could get his footing. He yelled like a wild animal and ran toward Michael with full force. Michael rose to one knee and stretched out his arm, pointing the knife at the man, who unexpectedly ran directly into it, shoving it deep into his gut. His body stopped, and his eyes came inches from Michael's. Michael pulled his knife out of the man and pushed his body onto the ground. He looked around and saw that Brother Richard had stopped the cart and ran toward Michael with a bag of arrows hung over his shoulder and a loaded crossbow in his hands.

"Are you alright, Michael?" Shouted Brother Richard.

"Yes, I am fine. We need to get in there, now!" Brother Richard ran toward the kitchen door. He pushed against it, but it would not budge. Michael motioned for him to follow Michael into the house through the open window. The two men cautiously climbed in through the window. When they entered the room, they could hear the crackling sound of burning fire on the other end of the estate. Michael knew it would not take long for the fire to reach the other side of the building. They looked down the hall, and not noticing anyone, Michael motioned for Brother Richard to follow him as he ran toward the main entrance. They only took a few steps when another man jumped in their path, holding a loaded crossbow at Michael. The man raised the weapon while Michael raised his arm to through his knife at him. Before either could execute their weapons, Michael heard a whip sound and felt a swish of air pass next to his left ear, and a small arrow pierced his enemy's

< 282 >

throat. The man fell to the ground. Michael looked back and saw Brother Richard behind him, still holding the spent crossbow. Michael shook his head, and Brother Richard shrugged his shoulders; neither said a word. Michael motioned for Brother Richard to follow him. Brother Richard followed behind while reloading his crossbow. They were not far from the main hall when they heard voices behind them. They turned but saw no one. Michael realized that others were in the house; he assumed they entered through the sealed-off section and had broken through.

He looked at Brother Richard and said, "Follow me." They continued walking toward the main entrance of the home. Michael called out as they moved closer to the main hall, "Monson, Dom Gordon, Angelia! Are you alright?"

"Michael!" Yelled Monson.   "Everyone is alright! We're in the dining hall, and I think some men have broken into the house!"

"Stay where you are; we'll be right there!" Michael responded. He and Brother Richard began running into the main hall and toward the dining hall. Monson and Dom Gordon greeted them with open arms as they came around the hall and into the room.

"It is so good to see you, Michael!" Said Monson as he embraced him. "I knew that God would not leave us alone."

"What is happening? Do you know how many there are?" Michael asked.

"I counted eight, but we took two of them out," Monson stated with pride in his voice.

Brother Richard added, "And we took two more!"

"That means that there are four men somewhere in the estate. It will not be easy to find them. They have started a fire on the upper East level, and it will not take long before the flames make it to this side. Where are Angelia, the child, and my mother?" Michael asked.

< 283 >

"They are in your mother's room." Responded Monson. "I told them to move that large bureau in front of the door so no one could get in." Added Dom Gordon.

"Do they know how many of us are here?" Asked Michael.

"We never told them, but if only four of them are left, then we are evenly matched, and we have weapons to defend ourselves." Answered Monson.

Dom Gordon quickly interjected, "Yes, there are four of us and four of them, but I would not say that we are evenly matched, for I know that Brother Richard has never fired a crossbow in his life, and this is all new to me as well."

Michael looked at Brother Richard, who smiled and quickly lowered his head. He then looked at Dom Gordon and said, "Excuse me, Father, but are you referring to this man?" He asked while pointing to Brother Richard.

"Yes! There is no other." He stated.

"Then God is his guide because I have never seen a more skilled marksman than Brother Richard!" Said, Michael.

Dom Gordon looked shocked by Michael's statement and looked at Brother Richard in disbelief. Brother Richard awkwardly pointed upward with his left index finger and mouthed the word "God." Dom Gordon wanted to be irritated to know that one of his monks was engaged in battle and carnage but then realized that there were many times in the scriptures when God led the Israelites into battle. Somehow, their situation seemed more palatable, believing God was leading them. He reached out, embraced Brother Richard, and whispered in his ear, "Thank you for sharing your talent."

Brother Richard smiled but did not know how to respond to such a compliment. He had spent all his adult life as a Monk, teaching children, copying scripture, and earnestly trying to uplift the lives of the downtrodden. He graciously and willingly did these things because he loved seeing the joy it brought others, but he always wondered what truly unique talent

< 284 >

the Lord had bestowed upon him. He wasn't sure how to react
to the realization that he had been blessed with the keen eye of
an archer; more importantly, if he and the others survived this
ordeal, how he would use that talent as a Monk to bless others.

Michael broke the thought and said, "The east wing of
the estate is on fire. I do not know if any intruders are up there,
but I know that the women and child are not safe there.
Monson, you and Dom Gordon look equipped to fend off our
attackers. I want the two of you to head back into the main hall,
down toward the East wing, and exit the house from the
ballroom. Avoid the men if you can. I will take Brother
Richard with me up the stairs. We'll get the others and meet
you outside the carriage house. "

The men nodded in agreement. Michael reached Dom
Gordon and asked, "May I have the extra crossbow you are
carrying?"

"Of course, and here, take this sack of arrows; I have
another." He handed the crossbow and arrow sack to Michael.

Monson put his hand on Michael's shoulder and said,
"Michael, I knew that God would bring you back to us, he
always does, and I thank him for it. Please be careful." His
eyes welled with tears, but he held them back.

Michael embraced Monson and said, "You too, my
friend. We'll see you outside shortly."

~*~*~

The leader of the intruders had made it into the house.
He instructed two of his men to shoot fire arrows into the upper
windows of the East wing. He and another man entered through
a door in the lower East wing. They climbed the East stairway
and began making their way toward the main entrance, stopping
in each room and taking anything of value they could toss into
burlap bags tied around their waists. The flames had only taken

< 285 >

a couple of rooms on the far end of the estate as the men continued running from room to room. They came to a hallway, and the leader said to the other,

"You go that way, and I will go this way." The men parted directions. The leader was heading directly toward Jillian's room at the end of the hall. He stopped a few rooms away and cautiously peeked into the room from where he knew he and his men were attacked. Seeing no one, he passed by and headed to the last room. He attempted to turn the doorknob, but it was locked; he leaned against it and tried to push it. Angelia heard the noise against the door and jumped to her feet.

The man outside heard the movement and yelled, "Open the door now, and I may let ya go. But if I have to break it in, I will be in a nasty mood, and who knows what I will do."

Angelia recognized the voice. She placed her hands to her mouth and backed up next to Jillian. Faith reached for her, and Angelia lifted her from Jillian's lap. The man continued to shove against the door. After several attempts, his weight against the door began to push the heavy bureau back into the room. Angelia handed Faith back to Jillian, ran to the bureau, and began to push against it, trying to keep the man from entering. Her strength did not match his; the door continued to open until he could reach through with his arm and sword in hand.

He swung the blade around the front of the bureau and yelled, "Now I am very mad, and someone is going to get hurt!"

He swung the sword again, and the blade tip nicked along the side of Angelia's face creating a narrow slash from her chin to her cheekbone. She fell backward and onto the bed. The man flung into the room, swinging his sword from side to side. One of his wild swings slashed through the right bottom bedpost, leaving a sharp, jagged edge. Angelia screamed. Jillian held Faith close to her. The man turned and saw Angelia lying on her back on the bed.

< 286 >

He smiled, revealing his black teeth, and said, "Well, if it is not my lucky day. Look who we have here. This brings back fond memories, now, don't it?" He laughed. Dropped his sword and removed his shirt, exposing his filthy dirty torso. "But this time, we have a nice bed to make it more comfortable." He fell onto Angelia, grabbed her hands, and shoved them on either side of her head, pinning her to the bed. Faith   screamed, Mommy!"

Allard looked toward Faith, still in the arms of Jillian, and said, "Now, ain't that sweet. Your little girl gets to watch. And who's the old lady in the rocker?"

Angelia managed to free one of her hands. She dug her fingernails deep into his face and pulled, dragging flesh and blood behind her nails. Allard yelled, slapped her face with his right hand knocking her away from him, then stood, turned toward Faith and Angelia, and snarled, "I changed my mind. I don't want nobody watching. I am gonna kill that little brat and the old lady too!"

Angelia jumped onto his back and wrapped her arms around his neck, choking him as tightly as she could. He reached around behind his head and began to pull her arms apart. She screamed! Michael and Brother Richard had just started up the stairs when they heard her scream. Michael ran past Brother Richard up the stairway. Suddenly an arrow whisked by him and stuck into the railing. He stopped and ducked, missing another arrow. Brother Richard was right behind him. He pointed his crossbow in the direction the arrows had come and pulled the trigger. Michael stood again and was nearly hit by another arrow. He heard Angelia scream again. The adrenalin began to flow through his veins. He knew that Angelia was in Jillian's room, and so was Faith. He knew they were in danger, but he was at a disadvantage against the man hiding at the top of the stairs.

< 287 >

Allard broke the grip of Angelia's arms and flung her off his back and against the wall knocking the wind out of her lungs. He picked up his sword and walked over to Jillian and Faith. Jillian was still sitting in her rocking chair, holding Faith with her left arm, and her right arm was dangling on the right side of the chair. She had quietly slid her hand into the heavy wool glove. Allard walked toward them.

He leaned down toward Jillian and pressed his bloody cheek next to her face, and whispered, "Too bad you and the kid do not get to watch; it would have been very entertaining, just like it was the last time I was out in your barn with the blonde girl and the little boy." He snickered.

Jillian turned, glared into his eyes, and softly said, "I have something for you from my daughter-in-law and my little boy."

Allard pulled away from her, lifting his head and shoulders. Suddenly, Jillian leaned back in the rocking chair, tightened her grip, swung her right arm over her chest, and slammed the hot fire poker into the side of his face. Faith began crying and dropped her doll. The pain of a fractured jaw and burning flesh caused him to stumble backward. He howled an ear-piercing agonizing scream that resonated out of the room and down the hall. He lifted his arms above his head, still holding the sword in his right hand, as his body fell against the jagged bedpost that gutted his spine and exited his stomach.

Michael heard the scream and yelled, "Mother! Angelia!" He leaped and ran up the stairs without regard to the danger of the archer at the top of the stairway.

Brother Richard fumbled to load another arrow onto the crossbow. He saw the man step forward and raise his crossbow at Michael. He knew he did not have time to aim and shoot, so he flung the entire crossbow as hard as possible at the man. The spinning crossbow came between Michael and the flying arrow from his assailant. The man dodged the flying crossbow, and Michael went down the hall and into Jillian's room. Brother

< 288 >

Richard began to run up the stairs toward the man who was quickly loading another arrow. The man pulled the lever back, raised the crossbow, and began turning toward Brother Richard. The monk heard the words of Dom Gordon echo in his head, *"thank you for sharing your talent."* Without delay, he pulled a knife from his sash and threw it at the man. As the blade entered his chest, the man took a few steps forward, fell against the railing at the top of the hallway, and fell to the entry floor below. Brother Richard hurried toward Jillian's room.

Michael burst into the room and saw Angelia lying on the floor. He looked up and saw Allard impaled on the bedpost, and faith was still in Jillian's arms, crying.

Michael looked at Jillian, who said, "We are fine, Michael. How is Angelia?"

Michael leaned down, scooped her up in his arms, and laid her on the bed. Her face was bruised and bleeding. He moved her hair from her face and leaned in, placing his ear near her mouth and nose; he realized she wasn't breathing. He sat beside her, put his hands on her shoulders, and shook her.

"Angelia! Wake up! Wake Up!" He demanded. He began to sob. No God! No! Not this time. Do not take her away too!" He pleaded. He pulled her face and head against his. Suddenly a memory flashed into his mind. It was William in the barn, holding Martha, who was feverish with the plague. He remembered the words William spoke *"You can warm your hands by the fire of my faith. For I believe God will heal this woman!"* Michael opened his tear-filled eyes, looked up, and said, "Yes, God! I have fire in my faith, and I believe you will heal this woman! Please, I beg you, bring her back to me!"

Angelia began to breathe and cough.

Michael pulled her head against his and said, "Thank you, God! Thank you!"

Brother Richard entered the room. He saw Jillian standing near the fire, holding Faith. He flinched and took a

< 289 >

step back when he saw the impaled body at the foot of the bed. He then noticed Michael sitting on the bed, holding Angelia.

He rushed toward them and asked, "Is she alive?"

"Yes, Brother Richard, she is very much alive," Michael responded.

Smoke began to enter the room.　Brother Richard shouted,

"Michael, we need to leave now!　The fire is getting closer."

Brother Richard ran over to Jillian and put his arm around her.　Faith reached for him; he pulled her into his left arm and kissed her on the cheek.

"I am so happy to see you, my little butterfly.　And Lady Beorn, are you well?" He asked while quickly surveying her head to toe.

She smiled and said, "Yes, I am well. And William will be here soon."

Brother Richard smiled and ignored her last comment. He helped her out of the room and into the hall.　Michael lifted Angelia from the bed.　She wrapped her arms around him, kissed him on the lips, and said, "Oh Michael, I prayed to God that you would be safe and that he would bring you back to me. He answered my prayer!" She began to cry.

"Yes, he did. Yes, he did."　Michael responded. With tear-filled eyes, he looked at his mother and said, "Oh, dear mother, I thank God you are safe! I love you so much!" He paused, then added, "Now, we need to get out of here."

He carried Angelia out of the room as he walked behind Brother Richard, Jillian and Faith.　Smoke had filled the hallway, making it difficult to breathe.　They made it to the open balcony just before the stairs and saw large flames coming down the hall.　Michael told Brother Richard and the others to walk faster as they began down the stairway.　Angelia told Michael she had the strength to walk, and he placed her on the steps in front of him.　She held to the handrail and followed

< 290 >

Jillian and Brother Richard, who were nearly halfway down the stairs.

Michael was walking just behind Angelia when Faith looked back and said, "Mommy, my dolly. I want my dolly."

"We will get you another one, I promise," Angelia said as she smiled at Faith.

"But I want her. Please, mommy, save her too!" Faith pleaded.

Michael looked at Angelia and said, "You keep moving. I can run back and get her doll."

"No, Michael! It is too dangerous, and the flames are too close."

"I will be fine. Now keep moving." He yelled down to Brother Richard, who was almost at the bottom of the stairs,

"Take everyone out through the kitchen door and meet the others at the carriage house out back. I will be right behind you."

Angelia pulled Michael's hand and said, "Please be careful, Michael."

"I will. Now go quickly."

Michael rushed up the stairs. Angelia made it to the bottom as Michael made it to the top. Just as he turned and began to run down the hall to Jillian's room, the fire reached the room next to the stairs where Monson and Dom Gordon had left the stash of weapons, Chinese fire candles, and a bucket of black powder. As the flames entered the room, the fire candles and the black powder ignited and caused a tremendous explosion that blew the door into the hall and a massive hole in the wall next to the stairway. The impact of the blast threw Michael against the wall at the end of the hallway next to Jillian's room. Flames engulfed the staircase, and fiery debris flew into the hall and down onto the floor in the entry. Brother Richard, Jillian, Faith, and Angelia had just passed the dining hall when they heard and felt the explosion's impact. Angelia turned and began to run back as she screamed, "Michael!"

< 291 >

Brother Richard ran after her, wrapped his arms around her, and yelled, "There is nothing you can do! We must get out of here, now!"

He pulled her back, and they joined the others who escaped through the kitchen door. Angelia continued to sob as they ran toward the carriage house. When they reached the carriage house, Monson and Dom Gordon ran towards them and helped them into the building. Monson asked, "Where is Michael?"

Angelia yelled out, "He's dead! He did not make it!"

Monson looked at her and then at Jillian, who had tears running down her cheeks. He exclaimed, "I do not believe it! He is not dead! He cannot be dead!"

Through tear-drenched eyes, Angelia shouted, "There was an explosion and wood, and fire was everywhere. It completely engulfed the stairway. When it happened, he was on his way back to Jillian's room to get Faith's doll. I do not see how he could have survived, and if he did, it would surely be a miracle."

Monson shook his head. "God would not let this happen!"

They all looked up at the burning estate. It was an unbelievable sight that none had ever anticipated. Monson had spent most of his life in that home, and Jillian had been raised there as a child. None of it seemed real to Monson, and even though Angelia could not be consoled by Jillian, Monson would not accept that Michael was dead unless he saw Michael's lifeless body.

Michael lay on the floor and began to cough as smoke filled his lungs. He could feel the heat of the fire. He lifted himself up and fell into Jillian's room. He crawled back and closed the door behind him. He stood to his feet, shook off the dizziness and loud ringing in his ears, and opened the window. Fresh air blew in, and he quickly filled his lungs. He saw the doll on the floor and picked it up. He looked at the doll and

< 292 >

then placed his hand on the wooden door. He could feel the heat behind the door and knew the fire would overcome the room if he opened it. He walked back to the window and looked at the ground below. He knew that it would be impossible to survive a 30-foot drop if he were to jump. He noticed the large oak tree and a branch about 15 feet from the building. The branch did not look sturdy enough to hold his weight, but the tree looked close enough to jump. He tucked the doll into his shirt. He climbed onto the edge of the window seal and stood looking at the ground below and the nearby tree.

Suddenly the door blew open into the room, forcing in a massive wall of heat. The immediate air pressure change forced Michael out the window, causing him to jump sooner than he had anticipated. As he leaped through the air, flames shot through the window and followed him half the distance to the tree. He stretched his arms out and wrapped them around the branch. The impact cracked a rib. He felt the instant pain in his chest, but he felt relief that he had made it to the tree. He pulled himself up onto the limb of the tree. He began to climb down the tree. When he was within a few feet of the ground, he jumped from the tree and landed on his feet. The carriage house was just around the corner from where he landed. He looked back and, not seeing anyone, began sprinting toward the carriage house. Monson was standing in the doorway looking toward the burning house when he saw the figure of a man running toward them. He yelled, "Someone is coming!"

Dom Gordon and Brother Richard jumped up, ran to the doorway, and poked their heads around the door to see what Monson had seen. Angelia stood, and Monson told her to stay back. Dom Gordon lifted his armed crossbow and raised it to the running figure. Suddenly Monson realized that it was Michael. He shouted, "Michael! It is Michael!"

Angelia and Jillian ran to the door. Both sobbed in relief. Angelia attempted to break through the group, but

< 293 >

Monson held her back and said, "There may be others out there; you must stay back!"

Just then, two men came running behind Michael, holding a crossbow. Monson yelled, "Run, Michael! There are men behind you!"

Michael was less than fifteen yards away, and the men chasing him were only a few yards behind. Monson stepped out of the doorway and raised his crossbow at one of the men. The man changed his aim toward Monson. Both pulled the trigger almost simultaneously. The racing arrows passed by each other in an instant. Monson's arrow pierced into the man's chest almost when the man's arrow entered Monson on the side of his torso. The impact knocked both men to the ground.

Michael screamed, "NO!" As he saw Monson fall to the ground. Michael knew that he could not outrun the arrow of the man behind him. Brother Richard pulled Monson into the carriage house; the others hid behind the door. Michael saw Dom Gordon step out of the doorway with a raised and loaded crossbow. Michael leaned forward, allowing his body to fall to the ground and roll. Just as he bent down, Dom Gordon took aim and squeezed the trigger of his crossbow. It seemed to him that the arrow and the entire scene traveled slowly. He saw Michael rolling on the ground, and the man chasing behind raised his crossbow while gritting his teeth and screaming. Dom Gordon watched as his arrow flew over the top of the man's crossbow and struck him between the eyes, bringing him down instantly. The scene ended in real-time.

Michael stopped rolling and jumped to his feet. He ran to Monson, propped up against a stable wall inside the carriage house. Brother Richard was on one side of him, and Jillian was on the other. The arrow was sticking out of his side, and blood flowed freely. Angelia ran to Michael and threw her arms around him. He kissed her forehead, gently moved her aside, and walked to Monson. Michael knelt in front of him. Monson reached out with his right hand and grasped Michael's wrist.

< 294 >

Michael said in a broken voice, "You're going to survive, Monson. You're going to survive."

Monson smiled and said, "I have survived, Michael. We all have, and look what we have been through together."

Tears began flowing down Michael's cheeks as he spoke. "Monson, God cannot take you now. I need you here much more than he needs you there."

"It is well, Michael. My journey in life is coming to an end, but yours is just beginning. "Michael shook his head as Monson spoke.

"God has great things in store for you, Michael. I know; I have seen your future." He struggled to speak as he became weak from the loss of blood.

"You have saved me, Michael. Before you arrived at the estate, I was an unhappy old man. But you helped me remember how much God loves me and what he has done for me. You gave me purpose. You, Michael, are the son I never had."

He took another breath. His grip on Michael's wrist loosened. "Promise me that you will be happy and trust in God so that he can show you your potential."

"I promise! I love you, Monson! And yes, I thank God for you. Again, you've saved my life and sacrificed yours for mine."

Monson smiled at Michael and said, "The disciple John said, *"Hereby perceive we the love of God, because he laid down his life for us: and we ought to lay down our lives for our brethren." (1 John 3:14).*

"Now, Michael, a beautiful red-haired woman, is standing in front of me with her arms stretched out. I must go to her. And you must go to that beautiful blonde-haired woman standing next to you. All is well, Michael. All is well."

Monson leaned his head back, released his grip, smiled, and was gone. Michael leaned over, gently closed Monson's eyes, kissed him on the cheek, and wept.

< 295 >

Chapter Nineteen Notes

The earliest medieval European clockmakers were Christian monks. Medieval religious institutions required clocks because daily prayer and work schedules were strictly regulated. This was done by various types of time-telling and recording devices, such as water clocks, sundials, and marked candles, probably used in combination. When mechanical clocks were used, they were often wound at least twice a day to ensure accuracy. Important times and durations were broadcast by bells, either by hand or mechanical devices, such as a falling weight or rotating beater.

*As early as 850, Pacificus, archdeacon of Verona, constructed a water clock (*Horologium nocturnum*).*

The religious necessities and technical skills of the medieval monks were crucial factors in the development of clocks; as the historian Thomas Woods writes:

The monks also counted skillful clock-makers among them. The future Pope, Sylvester II, built the first recorded clock for the German town of Magdeburg around the year 996. Much more sophisticated clocks were made by later monks. Peter Lightfoot, a 14th-century monk of Glastonbury, built one of the oldest clocks still in existence, which now sits in excellent condition in London's Science Museum.

The appearance of clocks in writings of the 11th century implies that they were well-known in Europe during that period. In the early 14th century, the Florentine poet Dante Alighieri referred to a clock in his Paradiso, *considered the first literary reference to a clock that struck the hours. The earliest detailed description of clockwork was presented by Giovanni da Dondi, Professor of Astronomy at Padua, in his 1364 treatise* Il Tractatus Astrarii. *This has inspired several modern replicas, including some in London's Science Museum and the Smithsonian Institution. Other notable examples from this period were built in Milan (1335), Strasbourg (1354), Lund (1380), Rouen (1389), and Prague (1462).*

Salisbury cathedral clock, dating from about 1386, is the oldest working clock in the world, still with most of its original parts. It has no dial, as its purpose was to strike a bell at precise times. The wheels and gears are mounted in an open, box-like iron frame, measuring about 1.2 meters (3.9 ft) square. The framework is held together with metal dowels and pegs, and the escapement is the verge and foliot type, standard for clocks of this age. The power is supplied by two large stones hanging from pulleys. As the weights fall, ropes unwind from the wooden barrels. One barrel drives the main wheel, which is regulated by the escapement, and the other drives the striking mechanism and the air brake.

Peter Lightfoot's Wells Cathedral clock, constructed c. 1390, is also of note. The dial represents a geocentric view of the universe, with the Sun and Moon revolving around a centrally fixed Earth. It is unique in having its original medieval face, showing a philosophical model of the pre-Copernican universe. Above the clock is a set of figures, which hit the bells, and a set of jousting knights who revolve around a track every 15 minutes. The clock was converted to pendulum and anchor escapement in the 17th century and was installed in London's Science Museum in 1884, where it continues to operate. Similar astronomical clocks, or horologes, *can be seen at Exeter, Ottery St Mary, and Wimborne Minster.*

< 296 >

One clock that has not survived is the Abbey of St Albans, built by the 14th-century abbot Richard of Wallingford. It may have been destroyed during Henry VIII's Dissolution of the Monasteries, but the abbot's notes on its design have allowed a full-scale reconstruction. As well as keeping time, the astronomical clock could accurately predict lunar eclipses and may have shown the Sun, Moon (age, phase, and node), stars, and planets, as well as a wheel of fortune and an indicator of the state of the tide at London Bridge. According to Thomas Woods, "a clock that equaled it in technological sophistication did not appear for at least two centuries." Giovanni de Dondi was another early mechanical clockmaker whose clock did not survive but has been replicated based on the designs. De Dondi's clock was a seven-faced construction with 107 moving parts, showing the positions of the Sun, Moon, and five planets and religious feast days. Around this period, mechanical clocks were introduced into abbeys and monasteries to mark important events and times, gradually replacing water clocks that had served the same purpose.

During the Middle Ages, clocks were primarily used for religious purposes; the first employed for secular timekeeping emerged around the 15th century. In Dublin, the official measurement of time became a local custom, and by 1466 a public clock stood on top of the Tholsel (the city court and council chamber). It was probably the first of its kind in Ireland and would only have had an hour hand. The increasing lavishness of castles led to the introduction of turret clocks. A 1435 example survives from Leeds castle; its face is decorated with the Crucifixion of Jesus, Mary, and St George.

Clock towers in Western Europe in the Middle Ages were also sometimes striking clocks. The most famous original still standing is possibly St Mark's Clock on the top of St Mark's Clocktower in St Mark's Square, Venice, assembled in 1493 by the clockmaker Gian Carlo Rainieri from Reggio Emilia. In 1497, Simone Campanato molded the great bell that every definite time-lapse is beaten by two mechanical bronze statues (h. 2,60 m.) called Due Mori (Two Moors), handling a hammer. Possibly earlier (1490 by clock master Jan Růže also called Hanuš) is the Prague Astronomical Clock that, according to another source, was assembled as early as 1410 by clockmaker Mikuláš of Kadaň and mathematician Jan Šindel. The allegorical parade of animated sculptures rings on the hour every day.

Early clock dials did not use minutes and seconds. A clock with a minutes dial is mentioned in a 1475 manuscript, and clocks indicating minutes and seconds existed in Germany in the 15th century. Timepieces that indicated minutes and seconds were occasionally made from this time on, but this was not common until the increase in accuracy was made possible by the pendulum clock and, in watches, the spiral balance spring. The 16th-century astronomer Tycho Brahe used clocks with minutes and seconds to observe stellar positions.

Sourced By: http://en.wikipedia.org/wiki/History_of_timekeeping_devices

< 297 >

Chapter Twenty
Ashes to Ashes

April 16, 1350.
The Chattingworth estate, Cardiff, Wales

It did not take long for the fire to engulf the entire estate. Even though the carriage house was almost thirty yards from the house, the heat of the flames was so intense that it made the side of the building hot to the touch from the inside. Michael and Brother Roberts found a large horse blanket and wrapped Monson's body. Michael looked toward the family cemetery, but the flames and debris from the house were falling all over it. He looked around and noticed a large oak tree near the stream, and he remembered that it was a favorite spot of Monson's.

"There! We'll bury him there." He pointed to the tree.

Michael held Faith in his left arm and held Angelia's hand with his other. Angelia walked alongside Jillian. They followed Brother Richard and Dom Gordon, who carried Monson's body. The Monks dug a shallow grave next to the tree using shovels they found in the carriage house.   They discussed burying him after the fire ended but decided it was best to bury the body sooner rather than later.

Brother Richard and Dom Gordon placed the body into the grave. Michael held Faith and stood next to Jillian, with Angelia on his other side. Brother Richard and Dom Gordon stood on the opposite side of the grave. Dom Gordon asked, "Michael, would it be alright if I were to say a few words before we cover his grave?" Michael nodded. He remained quiet and strong.

< 298 >

Dom Gordon began. "Dear Father, we call upon thee to accept this good man into thy bosom. We thank thee that we were blessed to have known and associated with him. We thank thee for his goodness, courage, faithfulness, charity, gratitude, friendship, and love. He was a giant among men. His wisdom and kindness will always be remembered. Like all of us, he came into this world with nothing but leaves with a legacy of love. His body will lie here until the great resurrection we all shall long for, but his spirit has returned to thee. His body was created from the dust of the earth, and to the dust, it returns, ashes to ashes, dust to dust. His spirit sent here from thee, and to thee, it returns. Oh dear Father, receive our friend and help us always be worthy of calling him friend even as we call thee. We offer this prayer in thy holy name, Amen. "

Michael put Faith on the ground between him and Angelia. Everyone except Jillian reached down and took a handful of dirt. Jillian lifted her right hand and said, "Wait."

She walked a few feet and picked a single yellow flower. She then turned and picked a single red flower, the only flowers in the field as far as the eye could see. She carefully wrapped the stems together. She then bent down and picked up a handful of grass and placed the flowers in the middle of the grass. She leaned out and released the grass and the flowers over the grave. The flowers remained intertwined and landed on the torso, but the blades of grass spread all around the body and the grave. She said, "The yellow flower represents Monson, and the blades of grass represent all of the people whose lives he touched and have changed for the better."

After a moment, Michael stretched his hand over the grave and released the soil from his fingers. Angelia followed then Brother Richard and then Dom Gordon. Michael and Brother Richard each picked up a shovel and slowly covered the grave. It only took a few minutes to cover the grave. Afterward, Angelia said, "It is terrible that we do not even have a marker for his grave."

< 299 >

Jillian pointed to the tree and said, "Right there."

Angelia looked at Michael, confused by the comment. Jillian said, "Look right there," pointing to the tree again.

Michael leaned over to the tree and noticed a small carving. Angelia leaned closer to see. She brushed some dirt from the tree and read the words, "Monson and Ruth Forever." She placed her hands over her lips and began to cry. Faith reached up to Michael, and he picked her up, held her in one arm, and placed the other around Angelia. Everyone stood in silence for a few more minutes. The silence was broken by the sound of a small yellow bird flying off a limb a few feet above their heads. Michael watched the bird disappear into the horizon. He thought about the many times when a small bird appeared either right before or directly after a tragic event in his life.

Michael remembered the anger he felt each time, as though he was being mocked. However, he felt calm this time, as if the bird was a sign of peace and not a tragedy. He realized that he had overcome great tragedy in his life, but he was a survivor, just as Monson had said. He wondered if God might have faithfully sent him a bird as a sign of peace during the most difficult times in his life. He then realized how often he mistook the tender mercy of God. He knew that even after the most tragic events of losing loved ones, God, his friend, gave him a sign that all would be well, just as Monson said with his last breath, "All is well, Michael. All is well." Michael felt a tremendous burden lift from his shoulders; deep love and gratitude encircled his soul. He understood what Monson meant when he said, "Your life is just beginning." He remembered the promise he made that he would trust in God. He knew the journey ahead would not be easy. He knew there would be more trials along the way and that he would still have his moments of weakness. Among all these things, he also knew that God had not left him alone but continued to bring others into his life.

< 300 >

Moreover, each had a specific purpose that helped him on his journey. Of course, he understood that each had a journey and that they were together to help one another as long as God kept them together. Michael felt his heart filling with love and gratitude for the many wonderful people in his life who had come and gone and those who were still around him. He wondered what future God had shown Monson.

Dom Gordon broke the moment, "Michael, I am sorry to be the one to start the conversation, but what shall we do now that the estate is burning down? All we have left is the clothes on our backs. Other than that, we have nothing."

Michael thought for a moment. He looked toward the massive flames destroying the estate.

"We have each other. And considering what we have all experienced in the last hour, I am grateful for that." Michael responded. "Of course, I did not mean to sound ungrateful; it is just that —"

Michael cut him off. "Dom Gordon, no one thinks that of you. None of us could have seen something like this happening. Unfortunately, we were never prepared for anything like this. And right now, I do not have an answer for you. But I know that we at least have a place to stay until we determine where and what to do next."

"Are you referring to the carriage house? Is there a place in there for all of us? Will we be safe? He asked.

Michael had an unusually calm countenance. He knew their situation was extremely precarious, but he felt a peace that things would somehow work out.

He responded, "Not that we have a choice, but yes, there is a rather large room in the back above the stables. I believe there is some old furniture there, covered in sheets. And I am sure there are plenty of blankets used for the horses. Dom Gordon, would you take the women there? Brother Richard and I will fetch a bucket of water from the well and meet you there shortly."

< 301 >

"Of course!" Replied Dom Gordon. Michael held his mother for a moment and kissed her on the forehead. Angelia kissed Michael, smiled at him, and said, "Be careful out there, and do not be long."

"I will," said Michael as he turned and walked away.

Dom Gordon said to Angelia, "We counted eight, and I believe that's how many are dead. Unless the Devil has the power to lift them from the ground, we should be safe."

Angelia stopped and looked at Dom Gordon. He realized that he frightened her; he added, "Fear not. He has no such power. Only Christ has the power to raise the dead, and I am sure our Lord and Savior will leave the souls of those dead in the cunning care of the Devil for quite a while." He smirked.

Michael and Brother Robert went to the well and filled two large buckets of water. As they carried the water, Brother Richard said, "Michael, I am sorry about Monson. If only I had been able to get my crossbow soon enough, I believe I could have taken out that fiend before he could have placed his finger on the trigger."

Michael smiled. "There is no doubt that you, Brother Richard, could have done so. However, perhaps this is the way God wanted it. Perhaps it was time for Monson to go home."

The monk thought for a moment and said, "Oh, dear me. Listen to me. I am speaking as the heathen, and you are speaking as the Monk. What is happening to me?"

Michael bit his lower lip. He began to speak, but Brother Richard cut him off. "Oh, forgive me, Brother Michael, I did not mean to infer that you are a heathen—"

Michael cut him off. "I did not take it that way, my friend. I understand. But just because one is a holy man does not mean he cannot experience righteous indignation?"

The monk raised an eyebrow.

"I mean, Saint Peter lost his temper from time to time, and surely Saint Paul even more so. Yet, these were among the

< 302 >

holiest of men. And did not Jesus snap a whip and cleanse the temple of money changers?"

"I see. You are right. But, I need to control my anger and not allow it to control me." He thought for a moment and then added, "Maybe I should vow never to take up a weapon again."

Michael quickly responded, "I think that would be most appropriate, but please do not make that vow until we all know that we are somewhere safe."

The monk smiled and said, "Good enough." He added, "Michael, have you ever felt like you have known someone forever?"

Michael thought for a moment, "Yes, I have."

"And have you ever felt like you will be connected to that person forever?"

Michael smiled and said, "Most definitely."

"Good. Because I feel that way about you. When I heard Monson tell you that he has seen your future, I felt a strong impression that I will be a part of it."

"You are a part of it, Brother Richard; we are living in the future from when Monson made that statement."

"I know you are just trying to find levity in my comments, but I am talking about a future that may be many years from now."

"Brother Richard, I will gladly welcome that future. I consider you a great friend."

Brother Richard smiled.

Michael then added, "And an even better marksman."

"That was not funny." Said Brother Richard.

Michael smiled at him. It felt odd to have lost Monson and not feel totally lost. He had often considered how difficult it would be for Monson to die. In every scenario he had previously run through his head, he believed losing Monson would have made it too difficult to move on with his life. Now

< 303 >

that he faced that reality, losing Monson made him feel like he had to work harder and lead.

They took the water into the carriage house. Dom Gordon and Angelia had tidied up the room above the stables. It was much nicer than Michael had explained. There was even a large bed in one corner and plenty of blankets to make beds on the floor for the men. Angelia had turned down one side of the bed and helped Jillian lie down.

"Lady Beorn, you rest for a while, and Michael and I will go find some vegetables from the garden, and I will make soup."

Jillian smiled and said, "That sounds wonderful, but please do not call me Lady Beorn."

Angelia was not sure how to respond to Jillian's request. She asked, "What shall I call you?"

"You can call me mother."

Jillian smiled again. "I remember when you and Michael married and how happy it made William and me. But we were even happier when the baby came along."

Angelia felt like Jillian had come out of her daze and was returning to normal until that moment. Now she did not know what to say. She knew that Jillian had mistaken her for Elizabeth and Faith for Hope.

Angelia smiled and said, "I cannot think of anyone more wonderful than you to call Mother. Now lay back and rest, and I will bring you food in a little while."

Jillian kissed her hand and said, "William is coming. He'll be here soon." She closed her eyes.

5:00PM

Michael asked Brother Richard to dig a fire pit near the carriage house. After starting the fire, he found an old pot and

< 304 >

washed it with water from the well. Michael and Angelia went to the garden to see if they could find any vegetables close enough to be harvested. Most of the vegetables were not ready, so they gathered what they could. As they dug in the garden, Angelia spoke.

"Michael, I know this must be terrible for you, losing Monson and this beautiful home. I am so sorry this has happened."

"Yes, it is difficult to understand how things like this could happen. Nevertheless, I have tried to put things into perspective. What has happened is horrible, but we are alive, and as Monson said, we will survive. I have seen so many people die of this plague. They suffer unbearable pain, their loved ones are helpless to do anything, and when they try to help, they too become infected. The cycle continues until entire families and communities are all dead. We have experienced something terrible today, but none of us has been infected with the plague. I consider that a great blessing. We are all whole and well, and we have a place to stay, at least for the night, and food to eat. I truly want to be outraged and filled with anger, but I am filled with hope and peace instead. I am happy that you and Faith are here. Do you think something is wrong with me that I am feeling peace instead of anger?" Michael asked.

"No, Michael, I do not think something is wrong with you. I will admit, you are not acting normal, but perhaps it was time to change from your normal to something else."

"Something else? What do you mean?"

"Today, when you and Brother Richard headed to Cardiff, you were angry and irritated with just about everything."

"I was?" Questioned Michael.

"Yes. And overall, you are usually angry and irritated quite often."

"Sorry, I have been caught up in myself for so long that I have forgotten to appreciate the good things in my life."

< 305 >

"The good things that God has given you," Angelia added.

Michael thought for a moment. He had spent so much time doubting the goodness of God and blaming God for all that had happened that he had become angry and faithless. He was now experiencing happiness and faith that God would help them find a way to survive.

"Yes, Angelia, I am thankful for the good God has done for me and for all of us. Yes, I…" He paused, "we have lost much, but we have gained much more. I am not saying that I will never doubt God again or have unwavering faith, for I know I am weak in spirit; I am just saying that I feel new, as if somehow my soul has been cleansed. "Does that make sense?"

"Of course, it makes sense!" Angelia replied. "You are experiencing a change of heart. That is all God wants from us, to soften our hearts and trust in him. When I realized that my sweet Percival had died, I did not think I could live or ever be happy again. He was a wonderful man, just like you, Michael. However, I now know God has a plan for us; he wants us to be happy. I think God constantly puts situations and people in our paths to bring us happiness, but too often, we are so focused on our failures or heartache that we miss what He has put right in front of us. I think…"

Michael leaned in and kissed her. She did not expect it but welcomed it. She wrapped her arms around him and continued to kiss him. Michael held her tight and leaned his head over her shoulder.

"I knew when Brother Richard and I were in Cardiff that something terrible would happen today. I begged God to protect each of you. I specifically thought of you and little Faith; I begged God to protect you. I did not want to lose you again." He stopped and pulled his head back, and faced her. "I am so sorry, Angelia. I did not mean that the way it came out."

< 306 >

Angelia held the side of his face and kissed him. She looked into his eyes and said, "It is alright, Michael; I understand what you mean."

Michael continued. "It is just that when God took Elizabeth and Hope, my world collapsed. I did not believe that there was anything left to live for. I had my mother, Monson, and the hope that somehow Lucas was alive somewhere, but I had no assurance of anything. Then one day, God brought you and Faith into my life. I never thought I could love someone like I loved Elizabeth, and then I met you."

Angelia began to cry.

"I understand, Michael. I feel the same. But I thank God for knowing what is best for us and for bringing us together when we needed each other the most. I never knew Elizabeth, but I love her because I understand how much she loved you."

"I am sorry, Angelia. I do not mean to compare you to her."

"Michael, there is nothing wrong with that, as long as you do not call me Elizabeth."

Michael laughed, "I hope that I have never done that."

"Well, once or twice, maybe, but I am over it." They both laughed. "However, your mother thought I was Elizabeth a little while ago."

"What did she say?"

"She talked about when we, you, and Elizabeth got married, how happy she and your father were, and how much happier they were when Hope came along."

"I am sorry, Angelia."

"You do not need to be sorry, Michael; your mother is a wonderful woman trying to deal with all of this in her own way. I hope someday her mind can return to her, and she can return to us."

"We all hope for that. Monson sat with her daily for hours, talking to her. Every now and then, she would say

< 307 >

something, but usually, she would say that my father was coming home."

"Why do you think she continues to say that?"

"I do not know. Maybe the last thing she wants to remember about him is that he just left Bristol and is on his way." He thought for a moment and then continued. "Finding my father on the floor when I returned to Bristol was one of the worst moments of my life. I tried to wake him but realized that he was dead. I decided to bury him but could not bring myself to do it. I took his body to a death cart in the harbor. I always assumed that his body was loaded onto one of the carts, taken, and dumped into one of the large grave pits."

"What do you mean assumed?"

He took a breath and then exhaled. "For the longest time, I thought he was dead. But now I am not sure if he was dead."

"But you saw his body and placed him on a cart. Why would you now think that he wasn't dead?"

"I thought he had the plague. But I never saw any signs of it, and I never saw any boils on his face or hands. I am afraid that something else had happened and that he wasn't actually dead."

"Michael, why would you say such a thing? Of course, he was dead."

"I was sure at the moment, but as time has passed, my assurance has wavered."

"Perhaps it is only because your mother believes he is coming here. Do not torture yourself with doubt. Haven't you done enough of that already?"

He looked at her and smiled. He gently kissed her again. "Yes, I have. And I do not want to be doubting Thomas anymore. Monson has shown me that I have too much to live for. You and Faith have shown me that I have too much to live for."

< 308 >

Angelia smiled, kissed, embraced him, and said, "Oh, Michael Beorn, I love you!"

Michael closed his eyes as they embraced. He held her tighter and said, "And I love you, Angelia." He pulled his head back, faced her again, and asked, "Will you marry me?"

Angelia did not expect a wedding proposal, especially during all that had transpired over the last several hours. She felt her heart racing and tears welling up in her eyes. She cocked her head and said, "Michael Beorn, I thank God for bringing you to me. I would be honored to be your wife."

They kissed for several moments until a voice was heard at their feet.

"Mommy, is Michael going to be my daddy?"

Michael and Angelia both laughed. They reached down and lifted her between them. Angelia answered and asked, "Would you like that?"

Faith smiled and nodded. Michael and Angelia leaned in, and each kissed Faith on opposite cheeks.

April 17, 1350

Michael woke up to the early sounds of thunder and pounding rain. He walked to the main doors of the stable house and slowly opened one enough to allow light to get in. The intensity of the rain doused the remaining flames and left the smell of soot radiating with burning embers floating in the air. Most of the rock walls of the state had fallen inward as the timber burned. Six chimneys still standing dotted the outline of what was once a majestic landmark for decades. It was hard to believe that such a thing could happen. He watched the rain, wondered why it could not have started the day before, and put out the fire before the entire estate was destroyed. He thought it was God's way of saying that they needed to leave Cardiff and find their way back to Bristol for some reason. Perhaps, he thought. He spent so much time thinking about how to protect

< 309 >

his friends and family from the plague it never occurred to him that the plague would find a way to destroy the only safety and security they had left. The Chattingworth estate seemed impenetrable, yet at the hand of six thugs, born of the plague, it was obliterated within hours.

Dom Gordon walked out of the carriage house and stood next to Michael.

"I've been thinking, Michael. Now that the estate is gone, it makes no sense for us to stay here. Besides, Brother Richard and I only came here to find a safe place for Angelia and little Faith. We have many friends and brothers in the priesthood who are probably wondering what became of us. I sent them to a Monastery in the hills about a day and a half from here. I told them to stay there and that we would come and find them. I think it is the time that we do so."

Still leaning against the building and looking at the burning rubble, Michael responded, "I understand, Father. I cannot adequately express my appreciation for all you and Brother Richard have done for me." Michael turned and faced the priest. "My life has changed because of the two of you. And I do not just mean because you brought me, Angelia, and Faith. You have helped me to realize how good God has been to me. For those things, I will never forget either of you."

Dom Gordon reached out and hugged Michael. "Michael, you are a good man. I have always known that, and Monson reminded me of it nearly every day. He truly loved you."

"I cannot let you and Brother Richard travel alone into that forest. You and I both know that there are evil men out there just looking for an opportunity to attack a lost and weary traveler."

"What are you suggesting, Michael?"

"I am suggesting that we all go with you to the Monastery to find your friends, and afterward, My mother, Angelia, Faith, and I will travel back home to Bristol."

< 310 >

"How would it be any safer for you to travel with two women and a child to Bristol than it would for two of us men to travel into the forest?"

"You are right; I hadn't thought that all through. I just know there is nothing here for us, and if the plague has ended, it may be safe to return to Bristol."

"What makes you think the plague has come to an end?"

"When Brother Richard and I were in Cardiff yesterday, I spoke to a ship captain who told us that in his travels around the countryside, it looks like life is returning, and the plague has run its course."

"That is surely good news, but it doesn't mean that things have simply returned to normal in Bristol."

Michael did not want to tell Dom Gordon what the captain said about Bristol. He assumed that divulging such information would be received with great resistance. But something was drawing him back to Bristol, or at least away from the torched estate.

"I realize there are no guarantees out there, but we cannot stay here and simply wait for the next group of thugs to come and attack us either."

"I agree. Maybe we should all go find the estate, regroup with the others, and then decide our next move from that point. What do you think?"

"I think that is a reasonable plan. Let's go tell the others."

Michael and Dom Gordon went into the upper room in the carriage house and shared their conversation with the others. Brother Richard and Angelia agreed it was good to make the journey, but Jillian protested.

"I am not leaving. William will be here soon, and what will he think if no one is here to greet him?"

Her comment made everyone uncomfortable. They all looked to Michael. He knelt before Jillian and said, "Mother, we have been here almost two years, and father has not come.

< 311 >

He is not coming, mother. And there is nothing left here for us, and we must leave."

Jillian sat back in the chair and shouted, "Nonsense! We have plenty here for us! We have this beautiful home. It has been in my family for years! I grew up here. If we leave, William will not know where to find us when he arrives. I am not leaving without William!"

She folded her arms, leaned back, and closed her eyes. Michael stood up and reached for her.

"Mother. Please, come with me. I want to show you something."

Jillian reluctantly took Michael's hands as he lifted her from the chair. He placed his arm around her shoulder and walked her to the door. He opened the door and helped her down the stairs. The others followed. When they reached the dirt floor of the carriage house, Michael stopped and looked around the room.

"Mother, do you know where we are?"

"Of course, I know where we are." She looked around the room and then at the dirt floor. She began to tremble, and Michael held onto her. "We are...we are...."

She could not speak. Michael opened the large doors, and the sun beamed in. He walked her outside and stopped in front of the open doors. She fell back when she saw the smoldering building, but Michael caught and held her. She placed a hand over her mouth, and tears began to flow down her cheeks.

"This was my home. What has happened to it? Oh, Michael, I remember the fire and that evil man who came into my room. He tried to hurt Angelia and the baby, and I would let him. I hit him with the hot fire poker, and he fell onto the bedpost. What have I done, Michael? What have I done?"

"You saved Angelia and the child, mother. That is what you have done."

< 312 >

She sobbed. Angelia reached over and held her other shoulder.

"Oh, Michael, my head hurts. I cannot think clearly. It is as if I am being pulled back into another place. I do not want to be there, but I do not want to be here without William. "

"It is alright, mother. You are safe. We are safe, and we will stick together. You do not need to go to another place, and you can be with us. Please."

Jillian stopped crying. She smiled, looked at Michael, and asked, "How long will we be gone?"

"I do not know, mother."

"Let me pack a few things and leave a note for your father. Where shall I tell him we are going?"

Angelia covered her mouth and began to cry, realizing that Jillian had returned to the other place in her mind. Michael looked at the others and then back at Jillian.

"You can tell him that we are headed for London."

"Thank you, Michael. I will not be long."

She turned and walked back into the carriage house and up the stairs. Angelia followed her. When they reached the room, Jillian began to look for a quill and parchment.

"I know there is something to write a note with. It must be here somewhere because I know the stable boy was required by my father to keep a record of the comings and goings of the horses."

She walked to the back of the room and looked through a large case of shelves. She moved bottles, horse brushes, bridles, and other miscellaneous items until she finally found a corked bottle of ink.

"Ah-ha! I knew it was here somewhere. Now, where is that quill?"

Angelia helped her look. They could not find it. Jillian smiled and said, "My dear child, I do not require a quill to write a letter. We used sticks long before feather quills in the olden days, and I know that there are many sticks around here."

< 313 >

She turned and noticed a splinter on a board on the wall. She pried off the splinter. She then found an old book. She ripped out a white page and placed it on the table. She opened the ink, dipped it in the splinter, and began to write her note.

"My Dearest William, there has been an accident, and the entire estate has gone up in flames. We are all well. Michael, his wife and daughter, and two men of the cloth. Monson has gone to be with Ruth, and we are traveling to London. I am sorry we were not here when you arrived; we waited as long as possible.

Yours always, Jillian."

Angelia read the letter. At first, she wanted to make some corrections but then decided there was no need to do so since she believed William would not be coming to the estate.

"What a lovely letter. I am sure William will be most happy to read it."

"Thank you, my dear. Now can you help me pack a few things?"

Angelia did not know what to do since there was nothing to pack. But she pretended to receive garments as Jillian handed them to her.

Michael walked into the room. It was almost eleven, and the rain had stopped.

"Angelia and mother, we will see what we can find to take with us on the trip. We have loaded the buggy and that horse cart, and we'll hitch the horses when I get back and be on our way."

"We are almost done here, dear." Added Jillian. "I am almost packed, and then I can help…" she hesitated.

Michael leaned in and looked at her, then at Angelia, and then at Jillian.

"Angelia?" Michael asked.

Jillian stared straight ahead and said, "Oh dear, Elizabeth is gone. How could I forget?" She began to tear up.

< 314 >

Michael put his arm around her shoulder and pulled her in towards him. "It is alright, mother." He said as he held her.

"No, it is not alright." She looked at Angelia and lifted her free arm toward her. Angelia took her by the hand. "My dear Angelia. I know who you are. Please forgive me. I have prayed daily that God would bring my loved ones to me. He has not yet answered that prayer," She paused, then continued, "instead, he brings new loved ones to us to help us and prepare us to find those that are still separated somewhere among us." She pulled Angelia toward her and kissed her on the cheek. "Thank you for being so good to me. And thank you for discovering that God has brought you and my son Michael together. I've prayed for God to send him an angel, and my prayer has been answered."

Angelia hugged Jillian. Michael kissed Angelia and then his mother.

"Yes, mother, I have been blessed to meet and fall in love with an angel. Thank you for your prayers. We have decided to marry. May we have your blessing?" Michael asked.

Jillian smiled and said, "Of course, my son. When will the ceremony take place?"

Michael was not anticipating such a discussion at this time. He thought for a moment and said, "I do not know, mother." He looked at Angelia and asked, "When do you think we should marry?"

Angelia smiled and said, "Michael, I do not know what to say?"

Michael released both women and said, "Both of you wait here. I will be back in a moment."

He left the room and walked out to the buggy and horse cart. Brother Richard and Dom Gordon had just finished loading the food that had been gathered, along with some blankets, utensils, and two water buckets. They turned toward Michael when they saw him walking their way.

< 315 >

"Hello, Michael." Said Dom Gordon. "I think it would be wise to see if we can find anything of value in the rubble before we go."

"I agree, Dom Gordon. I know there is a seller room where my grandfather kept weapons and a room beside it where he kept quite a few valuables."

"Valuables?" Asked Brother Richard. "What kind of valuables?"

"Gold and silver pieces." Casually answered Michael as if the treasure had no specific value.

Brother Richard's eyes grew large. Dom Gordon nudged him in the side and said, "Brother Richard, keep thy head on thy shoulders. He could tell that Michael seemed to be preoccupied with something else. He asked, "Is there something else you wanted to tell me, Michael?"

Michael smiled and asked, "Have you ever performed a wedding ceremony? I mean, you are a priest; I assume you've done these types of things."

Brother Richard pulled his head back and looked at Dom Gordon, waiting for his reply. Dom Gordon was caught off guard and stumbled with his answer.

"Of course, I mean…I am a priest…um, I have been in the priesthood for many years."

"But have you performed a wedding?" Michael asked.

"Are you asking if I am willing and able to officiate in such an ordinance, Michael?" The nervous priest asked.

"Precisely!" Stated Michael with a big smile on his face.

Brother Richard smiled and said, "Why Michael, I do not believe I have seen you this giddy the entire time I have known you. Are you…." He stopped, and his eyes grew large. He asked, "Are you and Angelia speaking of marriage?"

Michael smiled and said, "I asked, and she said yes."

Brother Richard rushed to Michael and threw his arms around him. "That is wonderful, Michael! I am so happy for

< 316 >

you. Wait! When are you planning on the wedding, and where?"

Michael took a breath and said, "Here and now!" He smiled and looked back at Dom Gordon. "Well? Can you, will you perform the ceremony?" He asked.

Dom Gordon to a breath and began to speak, but Brother Richard cut him off.

"Do not be silly, Michael. Dom Gordon may be a priest, but he has never performed a wedding. We are talking about a man who has spent the last 30 years cooped up in a Monastery with as many as forty men. Marriage? That is certainly one opportunity that has never been afforded to him."

Dom Gordon glared at Brother Richard, cleared his throat, and huffed, "It would seem that my colleague is accurate in his assessment of my calling and surroundings of the last thirty years. However, I am a priest, have been ordained of God, and have the authority to perform such a holy ordinance as a wedding." He looked back at Brother Richard, who slowly turned his head downward and to the side.

"Wonderful!" Said, Michael. "I will get Angelia, my mother, and little Faith, and we can start the ceremony." He turned to leave, and then Dom Gordon stopped him and asked, "Do you mean I am to perform this ceremony right now, right here in front of livestock in a stable?"

Michael smiled and answered matter-of-factly, "Why yes! If a stable was good enough for the birthplace of the Son of God, it is more than good enough for the wedding place of an orphan boy and a stable maid."

He ran back into the carriage house to give the news to Angelia and Jillian. Dom Gordon, frustrated, turned to Brother Richard and asked, "What have you gotten me into?"

"Me?" Asked Brother Richard. "You are the one who so confidently stated your qualifications. I am just here for moral support," He smiled.

< 317 >

Dom Gordon shook his head. "Oh, dear me, what have I done?"

Moments later, Michael walked back to the monks with Faith in his arms, Angelia at his side, and Jillian holding Angelia's hand, walking beside her.

"We are all here and ready to do this," Michael said.

Dom Gordon looked at the group and replied, "What a wonderful and somewhat unexpected occasion this is." He stopped and looked around and then at the smoldering house. "Oh dear, I am not sure what I just said. I look around at all the destruction, including as many as eight dead bodies out there; we have loaded up what meager supplies we can find to make a journey to a place none of us have ever been, hoping to have safe passage. We stand here as I say; what a wonderful occasion." He put his hands to his head. "I am sorry." He stopped, looked back at the ruins, and then at the small group of people he had grown to love. With tears in his eyes and a stutter, he said, "Yes, this is a wonderful occasion. How wonderful amid such destruction, debauchery, pestilence, and ruin, that God has spared us, even if for a while longer, to appreciate and share in his love and the love we have for one another. What miracles we have seen, the great faith we have witnessed, and the great mercy God has shown us. Michael, do you love this woman?"

"Yes, with all my heart," Michael said.

"Angelia, do you love this man?"

Tears rolled down her face as she said, "Yes, more than I ever knew I could."

"Then by the authority and priesthood vested in me by the Holy Catholic Church, I pronounce you Michael and Angelia Beorn, husband and wife joined together by God as long as you both shall live." He smiled, and everyone hesitated. "Michael, this is the part where you kiss your bride. Go ahead!"

< 318 >

Michael handed Faith to Brother Richard. He took faith by both hands, leaned into her, and kissed her. She wrapped her arms around him and held him as they kissed.

Faith began to clap her hands and said, "Does this mean that you are now my father?"

Angelica smiled and placed a hand to her mouth. Michael smiled, reached for Faith, lifted her up in front of him, and said, "If you will have me, I will do my best to be a good father."

She smiled and said, "I will have you then."

Michael pulled her into his chest and kissed her on the cheek. Angelia embraced Michael and Faith. Michael turned and looked at Jillian. She had a faded smile, and her eyes were glazed. He handed Faith to Angelia and then stepped toward Jillian.

"Mother? Are you well?"

Jillian continued to stare ahead. Michael knew that she had gone back to her place of comfort. He hugged her and kissed her on the cheek. "I love you, mother. Thank you for being here with me." His voice trembled as he spoke. "Thank you for always being here for me. I wish that I had the faith that you do. I want to believe that my father is alive and out there somewhere and that Sara and Lucas somehow have survived. Oh, mother, I would give anything to have them all back with us. Anything."

He pulled away and looked at her. Jillian looked at him, wiped the tear from his cheek, and said, "They are alive, Michael, and we will be together again." She then asked, "What do you have to give God?"

Michael said the first thought that came to his mind, "My will. It is all I have left."

Jillian smiled and said, "And he asks for no more."

She turned her head, looked off into the distance, and returned to her other place.

< 319 >

Michael helped Jillian, Angelia, and Faith into the carriage.

"The monks and I are going to see if we can find a few things in the rubble. I believe we may get into the seller and find more weapons and arrows, just in case we need them. You stay here with mother and Faith, and we will not be long."

Michael and the monks walked up to the charred ruins of the estate. Most of the walls had collapsed as the heavy timber from the roof, attic, and floors collapsed with the fire. Michael led the way as they shuffled through ash, pieces of wood, rock, and mud. Michael stopped and pointed toward a half-wall.

"Look! Over there. I believe that is the entrance to the cellar."

He and the monks carefully made their way through the debris and toward the wall. Brother Richard was the last of the three. He tried to walk on the path in front of him as it was being cleared by Michael and Dom Gordon. As he walked, he looked around at the massive footprint of the estate. It was still overwhelming for him to think that such a large estate could be gone so quickly. It was eerie and nerve-racking to be walking in its aftermath. Suddenly, he tripped and began to fall. Dom Gordon turned too late to stop the fall. Brother Richard threw his hands in front of him to break the fall. He landed face down in a pile of rubble just out of the cleared path. His body landed with a thud. As he opened his eyes, he realized he was lying face to face with one of the dead robbers; its eyes were protruding from the sockets of a badly burned head. He screamed and screamed. Michael turned and yelled, "What is it, Brother Richard? Are you all right?"

Both Michael and Dom Gordon helped Brother Richard to his feet. He quickly brushed the dirt and char from his robe and face.

"Oh, dear Father in Heaven!" Exclaimed Brother Richard.

< 320 >

"I just saw the eyes of the devil, and I do not believe I will ever be the same!"

The other two looked over at the burned body. Dom Gordon held his hand to his mouth and closed his eyes to maintain his composure. Michael flinched and said, "You will be fine, my friend. Let us get what we need and get out of this place."

The three men continued walking toward the wall only a few feet away.

"What will we do with them?" Asked Dom Gordon.

"With who?" Asked Michael.

"The dead bodies of those who attacked us."

"We will not do anything with them," Michael stated matter-of-factly.

"We cannot just leave them there." Stated Brother Richard.

Michael thought for a moment and looked at Brother Richard.

"You're right. We cannot just leave them where they lie. Let us shovel up their remains and bury each of them. You start scooping that one up, and we'll split up and find the others."

Brother Richard looked at Dom Gordon, who had raised one eyebrow.

"On second thought, it is probably best that we do not attempt to move any of them. Besides, if God wanted them buried, he would have sent them to us in wooden boxes, I am sure of it." Said Brother Richard. Dom Gordon slowly shook his head. The men turned and continued toward the rock wall.

They lifted a few large timbers that had fallen across the top of the stairway. Most of the main floor was still intact. Michael had wrapped a long piece of wood with cloth from the stable, fashioning it into a torch. He lit the torch, and the monks followed him into the cellar. The rock stairway was still sturdy. They looked around upon reaching the bottom of the stairs.

< 321 >

They could see that most of the weapons were unaffected by the fire. Michael lit another torch that was still hanging on the wall. Michael entered another room as the monks began loading weapons and arrows into their arms. This was a room that he had never been in before. It was lined with shelves stacked floor to ceiling. The shelves were packed with boxes of old household items. Both rooms had been hidden and kept secret. Few people knew of its existence. Michael noticed two medium-sized chests in the center of the room. He walked to the first one and slowly lifted the hinged lid revealing hundreds of gold and silver coins. He closed the lid and lifted the other. It, too, was filled with a tremendous amount of gold and silver coins and various gems.

"Over here!" Michael called.

The monks quickly entered the room.

"What is it?" Asked Dom Gordon.

"It is the treasure of the estate. We must get these two chests and as many weapons as possible into the carriage."

Brother Richard carried a huge arm full of weapons as Dom Gordon and Michael lifted the first chest, took it up the stairs and loaded it into the back of the carriage. Afterward, they returned and retrieved the other chest and loaded it onto the carriage.

It was almost 11:30 AM when they left for the Monastery in the forest. They anticipated they could reach it in twenty-six hours, including stopping somewhere for the night. They all agreed that it would not be safe to be in the forest after dark, and they made plans to protect themselves with the various weapons they had assembled.

Michael sat upon the carriage top, and the monks followed behind in the wagon. The trail took them behind where the barn had been. Michael looked at the charred footprint, the only thing left of the structure. He remembered returning from town and seeing the man who had accosted Elizabeth and Lucas while in the barn. Flashes of the past raced through his head.

< 322 >

He saw himself aiming his crossbow and firing an arrow into the head of the one man holding Elizabeth. He watched as Elizabeth's eyes met his. She was terrified but relieved at the same time. Michael stopped the coach after they had traveled down the path to the end of the open meadow where the estate had once been.

The Monks stopped their cart. They all took one last look at what was left of the estate. Angelia looked through the coach's window; Jillian was on the other side of the coach and did not attempt to move to see through the window. Instead, she sat and gazed at the fabric-lined wall in front of her. Michael was overcome by a myriad of emotions. So much had happened in his life at the estate. The last two years of his life seemed to have whisked by like a strange breeze. He had experienced bitterness, hatred, fear, sorrow, terror, love, remorse, faith, and hope. He thought about the people who changed his life while living at the estate. His unkind grandmother, the various servants, Laurie and Ernest Collins, Margaret, the young lady who contracted the plague and died in the fire, his precious little sister Sarah, Elizabeth, his infant baby Hope, and of course, Monson. Each had played an essential role in his life. He made good and bad choices, some brought happiness, and others did not. In the end, he realized that all his experiences had led him to where he was at that moment and caused him to become a better man. He wiped away a tear and mouthed the words, *"Goodbye, my friends and loved ones. Thank you for being there for me. Please forgive me for not appreciating and loving you more than I did."* He turned forward, snapped the reins, and looked ahead as the horses led the way into another journey of the unknown.

It had been nine months since Dom Gordon, Brother Richard, Angelia, and Faith had left the monastery. Dom looked back at the last view of the charred estate just as the road turned into the woods. He remembered coming out of the woods on the same path and seeing the majesty of the estate peering through

< 323 >

the trees. It was hard to believe that he spent almost a year of his life in a place he never expected would see again, from so many years earlier. He thought about the experiences over the last nine months, the great friendships he made, and the rekindled friendship with Monson, the friend from his youth. He marveled at how God had led them to the estate. Although he had no idea they would have spent so much time there, Dom Gordon knew that he had made the right decision nine months earlier when he told Brother Simon and the others to go to St. Gabriel's. He remembered the last thing he said to Brother Simon, *"My son, if you find the monastery in good health, stay there until we return; even if the days turn to weeks or months, we will find you again, I promise."* The last two words, "I promise," echoed in his mind. He wondered if he could keep his promise and if God had given the same protection to Brother Simon and the other Monks that had been placed in his care. He wondered how they were faring in the midst of the plague.

The sunlight dimmed as they entered the forest. Dom Gordon felt a shiver of fear race through him. He knew that their journey would not be without trial, but his faith reassured him that God would not have brought them together nine months earlier, protected them from evil men, only to lure them into a dismal and hopeless conclusion. He knew that God was with them, and regardless of the trials ahead, he would not leave them alone.

< 324 >

Chapter Twenty-One
Back Again

April 17, 1350.
The Monastery in England, en route to Cardiff.

"William, do you know the path you will take to Cardiff? There are several routes to take, and the fastest is probably to follow the river," said Dom Friedman.

"Yes. I have a friend named Saxton Bentley who lives in a cabin in the woods, about a day's journey from here. I have a map." William pulled the map from his cloak and rolled it onto the table.

Dom Friedman looked at the map.

"I know this area, and there is not much there." He ran his finger along the map and stopped at one point. "This is a small shire called Havens Stop. It is deep in the woods; maybe thirty to forty people live there. You realize that going this route will take you, several leagues, off the most direct path to Cardiff?"

"Yes, but I believe Saxton will be able to provide us shelter for the first night of our trip. Besides, I need to enlist his help in getting whatever is mine behind that door in London. And it will be good to see him again."

"I understand. Do you have your things packed?"

"Yes, I believe that we are ready."

"Then let us go to the main room and ask that God protects you on your journey."

He motioned for the group to follow him. Those in the front knelt in a circle; the others stood in the back as Dom Friedman offered the prayer. After the prayer, William and Lucas began to hug each monk. Dom Friedman was the last.

< 325 >

As he and William embraced, Dom Friedman whispered into William's ear,

"My dear brother, I do have faith that God will protect you and that you will return. But remember that no matter what you find in Cardiff, God has not and will not abandon you."

William smiled and said, "Thank you, my friend, thank you for everything."

The monks followed William and Lucas outside to the horse that had been saddled and packed.

Suddenly, one of the monks raised his hand and said,

"Father, do not forget!"

Dom Friedman smiled and replied, "Of course,"

He motioned for the monk to come to him. The monk scurried to Dom Friedman and stopped in front of him. He then lifted the front of his apron, revealing a large crossbow. He handed the crossbow to William. Another monk came forward, lifted his apron, and gave William a large sheath of arrows. William swung the sheath around his neck and draped it over his back. He placed the crossbow on a double wood hook on the side of the saddle and secured it with a piece of leather string next to each hook. William turned back toward the crowd of monks and said,

"I guess I should have thought about protection on this journey. Thank you for recognizing that which I did not."

William lifted Lucas onto the horse. He then climbed up and sat behind Lucas. Another monk moved his way to the front of the group. He opened his apron and lifted a large knife up to William. William smiled and received the weapon, placing it in the leather belt around his waist. He raised his arm to wave at the men when one of the other Monks lifted a flail, holding it by its wooden handle as the spiked ball dangled from the iron chain. Before William could acknowledge it, another Monk raised a War Hammer and lifted a spiked Morning Star. Dom Friedman looked from monk to monk in disbelief. William stretched his arm and said, "Brethren, thank you very much for

< 326 >

your offering, but I believe we are sufficiently prepared to defend ourselves on this journey if any evil were to fall upon us. Perhaps it is best to keep those…" he paused," weapons if you are attacked by an unknown army."

Dom Friedman stood with his mouth open as he looked at the monks. He asked, "Where on earth did you acquire such things?"

One of the monks replied. "There is more to trade at the market than carrots and beats." The monk looked at another monk and motioned him to cover the shiny steel falchion he held in front of his robe. Another monk attempted to keep a large Lochaber ax covered. Dom Friedman looked at William and shrugged his shoulders.

William laughed and said, "I will miss you all. And I pity anyone who may attempt to overtake you while I am gone." William snapped the reins, and the horse galloped off into the woods.

As they entered the forest, William looked back toward the monastery on a hill off in the distance. He saw four small figures, Dom Friedman and three of the priests. He looked ahead at the tall tree-laden forest, took a deep breath, and directed the horse in. For a moment, he felt peace, and then suddenly, the foggy image of a man spun around in his head. Seconds later, the spinning stopped, and the face turned until it looked directly at William. The fog dissipated slowly, revealing a terrified pale face surrounded by thick black hair. A flash of yellow flames caused momentary blindness. The flames encircled the face of the figure, and then thick black smoke covered the image. William leaned forward into the vision just as the face burst through the smoke and stopped eye to eye with him. A quick flash of perfect clarity revealed the face. It was Michael. The vision ended as abruptly as it began. William knew that their journey would not be without struggle. He remembered the words of Dom Friedman, "No matter what you find in Cardiff, God has not, and will not abandon you." He

< 327 >

clung to hope and prayed for faith, knowing God was with them.

Michael and the others…

The world became very quiet as they entered the forest. No one spoke for the first league. Every now and then, a flock of birds flew from the treetops and then down again, creating a tear in the silence. Afterward, only the sound of horse hooves and rotating wagon wheels echoed between the tree-covered hillside and the winding dirt path. Dom Gordon spoke just above a normal voice and said, "Saint Gabriel's is about a four days journey from here."

Michael looked back at him and asked, "What is between here and St. Gabriel's?"

"A few towns, mostly small, except for a larger town, depending on the direction we travel."

Michael thought for a moment and then responded, "Perhaps it is wise if we avoid any larger towns." Dom Gordon nodded in agreement.

"Can you lead us to Saint Gabriel's from here?" Asked Michael.

"Well," said Dom Gordon, "It has been a long time since I've been there, but I believe I can get us there." "But can you get us there while avoiding any large towns?" Asked Michael.

Dom Gordon swallowed hard and replied, "With God's help, anything is possible."

Michael was unsure if that was Dom Gordon's way of saying he had confidence that he could find the way or if he relied on God to show him the way. Either option caused Michael a bit of trepidation.

< 328 >

"So be it!" Michael said. "We will travel until sundown and then find a secluded spot to stop for the night?"

William and Lucas...

It had been several hours since they left the safety and security of the Monastery. The sun would be setting soon, and William was anxious to find the cabin before nightfall. The road had become a narrow dirt path covered with trees and tight thickets, often challenging to pass through. William noticed an opening ahead. The trail blended into the grassy ground as they approached the opening and completely disappeared. A small stream lie ahead of them. William allowed the horse to stop and drink in the stream. He looked around and surveyed the area. There was no sign of human life anywhere. The forest had become dense and uninviting.

William felt the weight of Lucas, who had fallen asleep, leaning against him. William gave the horse a few more minutes to rest and drink from the stream. He lifted the reins and directed the horse to cross the stream. When they reached the other side of the stream, William heard a noise off to his right. He stopped the horse and listened. The noise stopped. He started the horse again and heard another sound a few moments later. He stopped the horse. He felt uneasy. According to the map, he knew they had to be close to the shire and Saxton's cabin. He directed the horse to continue moving ahead. A few minutes later, he heard the noise again. This time he saw something off in the distance, a stone's throw away. He stopped the horse and tried to focus on the movement. He remained quiet and still, allowing his eyes to move deep into the direction of the motion. Suddenly, his eyes caught the image. His heart began racing as he recognized a wild boar's large

< 329 >

frame and sharp tusks. The animal had not noticed the travelers. William hesitated for a moment. He realized the animal was off in the distance, and it may not have seen them, but he also knew that a boar could run fast and its territory, where William, Lucas, and their horse had entered. William's mind flashed back to the time that he defended King Edward II from a wild boar attack on the mountain above the estate in Bristol. It was his first and only encounter with the wild beast.

Although it ended well, he did not want to revisit a similar situation, especially when he had Lucas to protect. He decided to continue moving forward. William continued looking toward the boar as the horse slowly walked ahead. The animal appeared preoccupied with something, and then William noticed two other boars. Altogether, he counted seven. William shook the reins causing the horse to move faster. Suddenly, one of the boars saw William and the horse. It turned and began to run toward them. William kicked the horse on the flanks and yelled, causing it to run faster. The motion awakened Lucas. He cried, "Father! What is it?"

"Hold tight, son; we need to outrun a sounder of wild boars!"

William guided the horse through the dense forest. Several times, it jumped over fallen dead trees and small thickets. William held Lucas and leaned forward to avoid as much brush from slapping against his face as possible. At one point, he looked back and noticed all the animals were running toward them and gaining on them. He knew their only hope was to keep moving as quickly as possible. At times, it became difficult to stay balanced atop the horse. Another opening in the forest allowed the horse to run faster. Eventually, after about one-quarter of a league, the boars lost interest in the chase and let the horse run without them. William kept the animal running until he could no longer see the boar. He stopped the horse next to a large tree. They climbed off the horse and

< 330 >

stretched. William took a flask of water and offered it to Lucas. Lucas took the flask and began to drink.

"It looks like we made it, Father. I do not see them any longer. Why do you think they stopped chasing us?" Asked Lucas.

William thought a moment and then replied,

"I guess they decided we were no longer a threat to them."

Lucas looked at William, cocked his head, and asked,

"A threat? If they thought we were a threat to them, would they not be running from us instead of chasing us?"

"There is strength in numbers. One single boar would not have chased us unless he thought he could overpower us. But each boar was empowered by the other. It is like the difference between a bully in a crowd and a bully by himself; in a crowd, he feels power and draws his strength from the others who encourage him, but when he is alone, he feels vulnerable and becomes more timid, regardless of what he thinks of his own strength."

Lucas nodded. He thought about the time he had spent with Allard, and he understood the concept of a bully and that all bullies have vulnerabilities and weaknesses that, if found, would be their downfall. He thought about the scare they had as they outran the boars and how safe he felt being with his father.

"Father, thank you for protecting us from the boars."

"You are quite welcome, my son."

Lucas added, "Thank you for being such a good man and not being a bully."

William smiled and replied, "I have been blessed with much in my life to be thankful for, a life that has taught me the joy that comes from gratitude and the happiness that comes from helping others, not hurting them."

"Why do you think there are bullies in this world, father?" Lucas asked.

< 331 >

"I do not know, my son; perhaps it is their insecurity, hurt, lack of love, and desire to be loved. They feel adoration and recognition from others when they make someone else hurt. I would assume that even the worst bully is not a bully when he is alone because when he is alone, there is no one to impress, no one to shower him with praise or accolades. When alone, he becomes as vulnerable as the weakest person he bullies."

William had just finished speaking when an arrow whisked past him and stuck into the tree, just inches from Lucas's head. He pulled Lucas down to the ground. He looked around to see where the arrow originated. In the distance, he saw a man with an outstretched crossbow walking toward them. The man yelled,

"You are not welcome here. This is my land, and you are trespassing. Either leave now, or I will kill both of you!"

Still kneeling next to Lucas, William yelled back, "Sir, we mean you no harm!"

"Your words have no meaning here, and I cannot risk my family to the potential that you are carrying the plague. You must leave now; this is my last warning!"

"Wait! I assure you, we do not carry the plague, and we are healthy and free of the sickness."

"What is your purpose for being this far from the nearest town?"

"We are looking for a man, a friend of mine. His name is Saxton Bentley. Do you know him?"

The man lowered his crossbow. He attempted to get a better look at William and Lucas. He asked, "What do you want from this man?"

"Only to speak with him. I need his help."

"Who are you?" He yelled.

"I am William Beorn, and this is my son Lucas."

"The man you seek does not know a William Beorn or a Lucas. You must leave now!"

< 332 >

William stood, motioning for Lucas to stay low. He tried to get a better look at the man. He yelled back, "How do you know who he knows?"

"Because I am Saxton Bentley, and I do not know either of you." He again raised his crossbow. "Now, I have asked you repeatedly to leave.   I will not ask you again." William took a couple steps toward Saxton and asked, "Saxton, my friend. Do you not remember me?

Saxton lowered the crossbow and looked at William. The men were too far apart to decipher each other's facial features.

"It is I, William."

Saxton shook his head. Suddenly William realized that Saxton did not know him as William; he knew him as John.

"My name is William Beorn, but you knew me as John. We were at Newgate together."

Saxton lowered the crossbow. He took a few steps toward William. As he got closer, William's face became more apparent. He smiled. And said, "Well, if you are not the luckiest man in the world, you are definitely the apple of God's eye to still be alive."

Both men walked toward one another. When they were within arm's reach, they embraced one another.

"John, it is wonderful to see you. How did you find me?"

William released the embrace and, while holding the arms of Saxton, said, "My name is William, William Beorn. God has been good to me. I have regained most of my memory. I know who I am and from whence I have come." He looked back at Lucas and motioned for him to come."And this is my son, Lucas."

Lucas reached out his hand and said, "I am honored to become acquainted with you, sir."

Saxton smiled and said, "William is a fine name. Moreover, you have a son! How wonderful! I, too, have a son.

< 333 >

We were going to name him John, after you.   But we felt impressed to give him another name."

What did you name your son?" William asked.

Saxton smiled and said, "We named him William. His name is William."   Both men laughed, and Saxton embraced him again.

"It is so wonderful to see you again, my friend. What a blessing it is for you and your son to be alive."

"I too am very overjoyed to know that you," He paused. "and I assume your wife and son are alive."

"Yes, they are both very much alive. Come, let me take you to them."

"I would like that. We have much to talk about."
Saxton added, "And a lot of catching up to do."Saxton led the way as Lucas and William followed on their horse.

Michael and the others…

"It is getting dark, and we will not be able to travel much longer this day. It is time that we scout for a safe place to stop where we can hide or at least secure the carriage and wagon for the night."

Dom Gordon acknowledged Michael's comment.

"I agree." He noticed a bend in the road ahead and what looked like a small tell in the side of a large hill. "There!" He pointed. "Perhaps we can stop there."

Michael looked at the hillside.   It was covered with trees, except for the indentation on the side of the hill. It looked like the opening of a cave. When they got closer, they could see a very shallow cave with an opening large enough to get the carriage and horse and the cart and horse into it. The depth of the cave was approximately fifteen feet. It would provide cover

< 334 >

and safety for the night. The men agreed to rest there for the evening. They left the cart and carriage in the front of the cave and tied the horses to the carriage further in the cave. This created a barrier between the vehicles, the horses, and the people, who made camp against the cave's back wall. Michael helped Angelia gather some bread and various vegetables from the cart. They decided not to create a fire to cook anything, to keep from attracting anyone or anything that could harm their group.

"How are you fairing, Michael? Asked Angelia.

"I am well, my dear. And, how are you?"

Angelia smiled and looked around at the forest and the road they had traveled.

"Considering all we have been through, I am very happy."

"Happy?" Michael asked. "You are happy?"

"Well, I did not mean in a giddy fashion; I meant that we are all here, alive, and God has protected us from a terrible tragedy."

"I understand. I did not mean to insinuate that you were aloof to all that had happened, and I just meant that…." He thought for a moment, "I am amazed that after all, we have been through, you could be happy. We have lost nearly everything."

"Michael, we have lost things but have not lost each other." She gently kissed his cheek.

He smiled at her and added, "God has allowed me to suffer many great things, but he has never left me. He has allowed me to think and act according to my own will, and in doing so, I have made many mistakes, and I have even assumed and said things that were simply wrong. I have felt completely alone and deserted at times, yet he has never left me. Why do you believe this is so?"

Angelia wrapped her arms around Michael's waist and leaned against his side with her cheek snuggled against his.

< 335 >

"Because he never leaves us alone. He knows that we are too weak to be left alone and will wither and die if we are left alone. The only person he left alone was his son so he could perform his great sacrifice on the cross. He understood that Christ had to complete his mission completely on his own. Remember when Jesus looked up from the cross and said, "Father, why hast thou forsaken me?"

Michael nodded his head.

"God knew that Jesus had the strength to do it on his own, and he also knew that Jesus had to do it on his own."

"How do you know these things?" Michael asked.

"What do you mean? How do I know these things?" "Well, you were raised in a small Shire, not exactly the most common place to become educated."

"Are you insinuating that the only people who can be educated are the upper class, those who can afford to pay a Priest or a Monk to teach them?"

Michael thought for a moment and then added, "Yes, I believe that is exactly what I am saying."

"Before marrying Percival, I lived with my parents in a small town near his. My parents were not wealthy; our town had no wealthy people. However, there was an old monk who had parted ways with the Church. And in doing so, he had no way to provide for his living. Instead of begging, he opened his small one-room home to anyone who wanted to learn to read and write. Those who were interested paid him with food, clothing, and necessities of life. It gave him what he needed to live, and it gave us, a small town of simple peasants, the opportunity to become educated."

"But when did you have time to learn? Were you required to work for the landowners?"

"Yes, most everyone worked in the fields all day, but at night, many of us sat at his feet, and by candlelight, we learned to read from the Holy Vulgate."

Michael turned and looked at her.

< 336 >

"Wait a moment. Are you telling me that he had a copy of the Holy Scriptures in his possession? He would have been in grave danger if the Church had known. What about your priest? Did he know this?"

Angelia began to laugh. "Michael, our priest, knew about this; he was friends with the monk."

"But I thought you said the monk had left the Church."

"I did not say he left the Church. I said he parted ways."

"What is the difference?"

"Leaving means that a person no longer believes, parted ways means that he had a disagreement with something and decided not to affiliate with the Church."

Michael shook his head. "This is becoming confusing to me."

"Michael, he still believed in the Church; he simply decided that he could no longer follow the direction of the priest at his Monastery."

Michael raised an eyebrow.

"Could no longer follow the direction? He became an apostate?"

"No! Of course, not!" She insisted.

"If he could no longer follow the priest's direction, why did he not just transfer to another monastery?"

"He had fallen in love with a young woman in the congregation. He could not hold back his feeling for her, nor she for him."

"Oh, I understand. So, he left the priesthood and went to the young woman."

"No, he did not."

Michael scratched his head.

"Alright, this is getting confusing. Just tell the rest of the story."

"His priest told him to pray that God would take away his desire for this woman, that God would take away his desire to be with any woman."

< 337 >

Michael again raised an eyebrow. He began to speak, but Angelia pressed two of her fingers to his lips.

"Let me finish. The Priest told him that since he had made a vow to remain chaste, virtuous, and unmarried, God would take away any thought or affection for a woman."

Michael cocked his head and widely opened both eyes.

"Michael, it meant he would not have sexual urges or feelings toward anyone."

She removed her fingers from his mouth.

"Did it work?" Michael asked.

"Did what work?"

"Did God remove his desire for this woman or any other?"

"Unfortunately for him, no. His desire continued. He told the priest that nothing had changed. The priest told him to fast and pray longer. After several weeks, he returned to the priest and told him that his desire for this woman only grew stronger. The priest told him that he had given into his carnal desire and would not be worthy of the priesthood unless he could remove these feelings from his heart and mind. He told him that God did not intend for a priest to be with a woman; it was not natural."

Michael looked at her and asked, "Not natural? Seriously, that is what the priest told the monk?"

"Well, yes, it is." Angelia began to shuffle about as she realized how awkward the statement sounded. "I mean, it is unnatural for a priest to have feelings for a woman."

"Is it?" Michael asked.

"I mean if you really think about it. Why would God not want a priest to be married, to be a husband and a father? That way, he would better understand what his parishioners go through daily."

"Michael, now you sound like an apostate."

"For asking a question? Surely a person can ask a question without sounding like they are becoming a heretic."

< 338 >

"I suppose you are right."

"About what, that a priest should be able to marry or that asking such a question does not make one a heretic?"

"About asking the question. A priest should not marry, and it says so in the Holy Scriptures."

"Really? Where is it written?" Michael asked.

"Michael, neither of us has access to the scripture; therefore, I can't show you the actual reference."

"Or you do not know where it is written," Michael said.

"You are right. I do not know where it is written, but I am sure it is written somewhere."

"Truthfully, that is where I have an issue with the Church. Too many things are done, rules are made, and ordinances performed, and nobody except the priest, a monk, or the higher-ups know where these things are "supposedly" written."

Angelia looked away from Michael.

"I did not say I was going to leave the Church. I simply stated what bothered me. So, what happened to the monk?"

Angelia took a deep breath and then exhaled.

"Several more weeks passed, and the monk again met with the priest. He told him that he believed it was natural for a man to love a woman. The priest cut him off and said, "you are not a man; you are a monk!" The priest replied, "I am a man first and a monk second. God did not put a monk into my mother's womb; he placed the body of a boy he knew would one day grow into a man. God hoped that that boy would one day follow the natural desire to fall in love with a woman, and together they could do as he commanded Adam and Eve to multiply and replenish the earth." The priest was speechless. He shook his head and said, "then go, be a man. Go find this woman and ask God if he will bless your union with her to multiply and replenish." The monk opened his mouth to respond, but the priest cut him off. "But if you do this, you will

< 339 >

turn your back on God, and he will turn his back on you and those you believe you love!"

"That seemed harsh," Michael said.

"It was harsh. However, the monk understood the perspective of the priest. He left that night and went to find the young woman. When he arrived at her home, her mother told him she was sick with a fever. She asked the monk if he would pray for her. He agreed and went into the home. Her father was kneeling next to her bed, holding a cold, damp cloth to her head. She looked up at him and lifted her hand toward him. He reached out for her hand and knelt next to her father. She smiled when their fingers touched. She was too weak to speak. She smiled, lips parted, allowing her last breath to leave her body."

Michael cut her off. "Wait, are you telling me that she died at that moment?"

"Yes, she died."

"So, you believe that it was the fault of the monk for falling in love with her?"

"No, of course not. It was simply God's will."

"What did the monk do? Did he go back to the monastery?"

"No, he came to our town and began to teach, as I have already told you."

"So, he never left the priesthood and never married?"

"That is right. He believed that God had another purpose for him, that perhaps his life could be used in another way to fulfill God's purposes. Therefore, he taught until old age, and God took him."

Michael shook his head. "You see, it is things like this that confuse me. I understand the priest's frustration, but I also understand the frustration of the monk, and truthfully, part of me agrees with the monk that it is natural for a man to desire to be with a woman. It is not for evil but a spiritual purpose, to bring God's children into the world." He paused and then added, "So what do you believe?"

< 340 >

"About the priesthood?"

"No, do you believe that the monk was used in some other way to fulfill God's purpose?"

"Michael, I do not know the answer to that, and I can only speak for what the monk did for me and the many others in my village; he gave us a chance to become literate and learn God's Holy word. That must have been a purpose of God."

"I would agree. But perhaps there is more he has done. How many others know his story?" Michael asked.

"Everyone in the town knew his story. Of course, most of those who lived in my village are now dead from this plague."

"You are alive, and you know his story, and now I know his story too. Perhaps God wants his story to be remembered. Perhaps there is still purpose in his life, even after his death."

Michael smiled and put his arm around Angelia. Angelia looked ahead, and they both stood looking at the large full moon. The moment ended abruptly at the sound of a wolf howling in the distance.

"Come, we must prepare our beds for the night. I want you, Hope, and mother to sleep in the carriage, and I will sleep in the cart with the monks." Michael added.

They embraced for a moment, and then Angelia went to the carriage, and Michael opened the door for her, and she climbed in.

"Good night, Michael," Angelia said in a soft voice. "I love you!"

Michael smiled and said, "And I, you. Goodnight."

He closed the carriage door. Michael looked around at the area. The darkness had hidden most of the trees and brush. He felt a soft breeze as the air began to chill. He walked behind the carriage and into the cave. He was careful not to step on the sleeping monks who had already bedded on the ground against the cave's back wall. It seemed odd to be sleeping outside. The events of the last twenty-four hours began to seem less surreal.

< 341 >

He spread a blanket on a section of hay the monks had placed on the cold soil. He laid on half of the blanket and wrapped the other half over himself.

"Michael, please forgive me for disturbing you, but I cannot sleep. Said Dom Gordon.

"What is it, Father?" Michael asked, still lying on his back.

"I have been thinking about what lies ahead of us."

"What do you mean?"

"Well, Brother Richard and I have spent the last several months living with you and your family at the estate." Michael listened with his eyes opened, barely able to see the coved ceiling a few feet above him. The monk continued. "So much has happened in that time. I was reunited with my old friend Monson, whom I had assumed had already passed on to the next life. And I have had the blessing of becoming acquainted with Angelia, her blessed child, and you. It has been an honor to know you."

"You speak as though you are dying. Why are you telling me this?" Michael asked.

"My life had been rather quiet and uneventful up until the day that a baby on a horse showed up at the monastery. Everything changed from that day, and no one could have known the events that would transpire from there. My faith has truly been tested."

Michael thought about the words the monk had spoken. He added, "It would seem that the faith of each of us has been tested."

"There is no doubt about that." The monk said. He continued, "Tomorrow, we will reach the monastery where my friends have been since we parted so many months ago. It will be wonderful to see each of them again, but it will be difficult to part with you, Angelia, and the others."

Michael had not thought much that these two monks who had become part of his family would actually leave, and he

< 342 >

knew the plan was to take them to the monastery and then travel to Bristol. At that moment, he realized how difficult it would be to bid farewell.

He said, "Dom Gordon, you, and Brother Richard have become part of my family. I cannot thank you enough for what you have done for me, especially for bringing Angelia and Faith into my life. Tomorrow we will go our separate ways, but I can assure you that our paths will meet again."

"God willing, my friend. God willing." Said the monk.

"Good night Michael. Sleep well."

"You as well," Michael added.

He closed his eyes and attempted to sleep. With his eyes closed, his ears began to hear every sound of the night, the crickets chirping, small creatures wrestling in the brush, and the wind shaking leaves in the trees. Within a few minutes, the noises became a rhythm working together, and his mind could not distinguish one sound from the other. He felt his body begin to relax. His breaths became deeper and longer. He yawned, filling his lungs with air and increasing the oxygen to his brain. The noises slowly melted together as he felt himself begin to slip into sleep. He breathed in deeply, exhaled long, and slowly emptied the used air from his lungs. His breaths became short, shallow, and quiet. He was on the edge of unconsciousness when suddenly, he heard a stick break off in the distance. The sound of crickets stopped. He heard footsteps. His eyes opened wide. He lay there, listening for something, but only hearing the whisper of the wind. A few quiet moments passed, and he felt that whoever was out there was trying to be unnoticed. He heard it again. This time he rose to his feet, walked to the carriage, and carefully took the loaded crossbow from behind the seat. He aimed and held the weapon in front of him, anticipating another sound. The darkness made it nearly impossible to see into the woods. He looked over his right shoulder at the sleeping monks. Brother Richard was closest to him. He bent down, picked up a small stone, and tossed it,

< 343 >

hitting Brother Richard in the leg. The unexpected sting caused him to sit up quickly. He looked toward Michael with his mouth open. Michael placed his right index finger to his lips and told him to be quiet. Brother Richard could see that Michael had the loaded crossbow. He quietly climbed out from his bedding and walked to the cart. He carefully rummaged through it until he found his crossbow. It was not loaded. He found the quiver of arrows, pulled one out, and slowly loaded his weapon. He walked over to Michael as he pointed his crossbow off into the darkness. He leaned into Michael and asked,

"What is it, Michael? What is out there?"

Michael responded in a whisper.

"I do not know. It may be wolves."

Brother Richard flinched. The thought of wolves and the memory of his last encounter with wolves caused his heart to race.

"Are you sure?" He asked, with fear in his voice.

"No, I am not sure. But whatever it is, I think it knows that we know It is out there."

"What do you think we should do, Michael?" Asked Brother Richard.

Michael lifted his crossbow, pointed it toward the dark woods, and pulled back the trigger. The arrow quickly whisked through brush and then stuck into a tree several yards. When the arrow made contact with the tree, it startled whatever was out there. Brother Richard then shot an arrow a few feet from the first. Suddenly a rustling sound was heard as the unwelcomed visitors turned and ran. Michael reloaded his crossbow and said,

"Brother Richard, I believe we have scared away whatever was watching us. I think we should keep our bows loaded and return to our beds. Just sleep lightly."

Both men looked toward the dark woods for a moment and then returned to the others.

< 344 >

~*~*~

William and Lucas…

The cabin was much further into the woods than William anticipated. It took them almost an hour from their initial encounter with Saxton before arriving at the house. It was nestled between two very old and large trees, and thick foliage and numerous other trees almost hid the wood-built cabin. The trail became extremely narrow over the last league of the journey, making it impossible for a wagon to make the trip. The cabin was a simple rectangle-shaped building with a rock fireplace on either end. The front door was closer to the left side. They tied their horses near a trough on the right side of the house.

Saxton motioned to William and said, "Come, let us go inside, and I will introduce you to my wife."

William smiled and nodded as Saxton led the way. Saxton opened the door and entered the home first. As they walked in, William noticed a beautiful young woman holding a baby, standing next to the fireplace.

A bit startled, she turned toward the men and said, "Goodness, Saxton, I did not know we were expecting company." She smiled, pulled the baby close to her, and took a step back.

"My dear, all is well. Let me introduce you to my friend John." He stopped and then continued, "I mean William, William Beorn. And this is his son Lucas."

She smiled and said, "It is lovely to meet both of you."

Saxton added, "And this, of course, is my wife, Julianna."

William stepped forward and stretched his hand toward her. She looked at Saxton, who nodded with approval. She reached for his hand, and he leaned in and kissed her hand.

"It is a pleasure and honor to meet you, Mrs. Saxton."

< 345 >

"Oh, please, call me Julianna."

William smiled and said, "Yes."

Saxton offered William and Lucas places to sit. They spent the next hour talking about their time together in Newgate prison. Saxton had often spoken to his wife about William and their time together, and Julianna knew that William was a good man. William told Saxton all that had happened to him since leaving the prison. He explained what had happened to his family and how he and Lucas were reunited. The sun had gone down, and several purposefully placed oil lamps dimly lighted the small cabin. Lucas had fallen asleep.

Julianna stood up and said, "I am so sorry; we have spent all of this time catching up that it did not occur to me that I need to make a place for you to sleep."

William stood and said, "Thank you, but we do not want to be a bother. We would be fine to sleep outside."

"Outside?" Asked Julianna. "Nonsense! Do not be absurd; we have an extra room, and it will only take me a few minutes to make you both a bed."

"I do not want you to go to any trouble," William said.

"Trouble? This is a rare treat to have guests. In fact, we have had no one visit us the entire time we have lived here. It is no trouble at all. Besides, I need to put little Will to bed anyway." She held the sleeping baby in her arms. "I am happy to take care of it. Now you two keep talking, and I will return shortly." She left the room, and William returned to his seat.

Saxton smiled at his wife and then looked back at William. "So, tell me, John." He paused and smiled. "I am sorry, but it may take me a while to get used to calling you William. I still see you as John."

William smiled. "I understand, and I will not be offended if you call me John."

Saxton smiled again and said, "That will not be necessary. You deserve to be addressed by your original name, not the name you were given while in prison."

< 346 >

"Fair enough." Said, William. "Please continue with your question."

"Why have you come all this way from the Abby outside of London? Surely you knew of the danger when you left."

"Yes, I understood the danger, but I believe it was important for me to make the journey and find you. I cannot tell you how happy it is to be sitting here with you. It makes me even more grateful to know that you and your wife have a son, and you are all well and have been protected from this plague that has taken the lives of so many.

Saxton smiled and nodded. William continued.

"When my son returned to me, and my memory began to return, I realized that my family needs me, now more than ever. And I need to go to them and ensure they are still well."

"Of course," said Saxton. "But did your memory reveal how you became separated from them and then ended up on an abandoned cargo ship in Spain?"

"Not everything has come back to my memory, and it is as though the Lord only gives me a little at a time, just enough to increase my desire to find my family. I believe that in doing so, I will eventually regain all that I have lost, both figuratively and literally."

William spent several minutes telling Saxton the memories that had returned to him.

"I am here because I need your help with something in London."

Saxton raised an eyebrow and said, "You realize I have not been to London since leaving Newgate. In addition, I feel extremely blessed that I left when I did, and I consider myself one of the very few lucky ones who escaped with my life."

"I understand. "William said. "And I do not want to put your life in danger."

"Do you not believe that going back to London would be dangerous?" Asked Saxton.

< 347 >

"Yes, I understand there is danger in leaving this place, but I also know that you cannot continue to survive here indefinitely."

"That is true. We have survived on little food and a few vegetables that we have been able to grow. I have made a few trips to the closest town, but it has been a while since I traveled there. The last time I was there a few months ago, it was like being among the walking dead. Those who were not dead were pillaging and killing those who were barely alive. I found myself taking bags of flour from a small shop, where the keeper lay dead on the floor. I barely reached my horse when several thugs came from nowhere and attempted to accost me. I looked back while riding on my horse and was shocked that two of the men had faces covered with decaying flesh and limped after me like a wounded dog. One fell to the ground face down, and the others ignored him and continued moving toward me. None of it seemed real to me. It was like taking a tour of hell. Before I could make it to the edge of town, buildings on either side of the street rose up in flames. I saw townspeople torching buildings and houses, some of which had been barricaded with sick and infected people still inside. Not only did the place look like hell, but with the flames, weeping, and wailing, it sounded like it too. William, most of the handful of residents around me have died. I do not know why my wife, child, and I have been spared." He smiled, "Maybe some of it may have to do with the garlic cloves we carry in our clothes, thanks to a man I used to know named John."

William smiled. Saxton continued.

"William, we are down to the last of our flour, and I am not sure how much longer we will survive. I know we cannot stay here much longer, but I am not sure that traveling to London is the wise thing to do." Said Saxton.

"I understand your fear, but it does seem like the disease is retreating. Not all of London is dead; believe it or not, commerce still continues."

< 348 >

"So, what is there for you in London, and why do you need me to travel there with you?" Saxton asked.

William pulled the chain around his neck out of his tunic. He held the key in his fingers and said, "I believe this key unlocks a box that will change our future."

"What exactly do you mean, William?"

"I do not remember everything, but I do know that I, William Beorn, am a very wealthy man. I am from Bristol, a shipbuilder. Moreover, I have a substantial estate there. I intend to find my family who is with my wife's mother in Cardiff, then return with them to Bristol."

"What does this have to do with London or that key?" Saxton asked.

"I believe this key will unlock a box filled with coins, jewels, and notes. I cannot get my family back to Bristol without money."

"I do not understand where I come into this."

"I need you to go back to London with me and help me get into the shop where the box is hidden," said William.

"Why me?"

William explained what had happened with the monks when he found Lucas. He explained that the local authorities may be looking for him, and it would be difficult for him to retrieve the box without help.

"Saxton, the fact that God has spared your life tells me that he wanted me to find you and your family, to help me continue my journey. If you come with us, I will give you half of whatever is in the box. Surely, it will provide a new life for you and your family."

Saxton stood. He looked at William.

"William, there is no doubt in my mind that God loves you, and I also believe that he has sent you here. We will run out of food within a couple of weeks. If you are correct, I know our prayers have been answered. Your offer is more than generous, but I could never take half of all you have."

< 349 >

William smiled and placed a hand on Saxton's left shoulder.

"My friend, half of all I have greatly exceeds the contents of one small box. It would be my honor to divide that box with you."

Julianna had been standing in the hallway within hearing distance of the conversation. She stepped into the room.

With tears in her eyes, she spoke. "Saxton, this man is an angel from God, sent to answer our prayers." She began to cry, and Saxton embraced her.

"Thank you, Julianna; I am but a man. A man blessed with wonderful friends."

"What do you think of this proposal, my dear?" Saxton asked Julianna.

"I realize there is danger leaving the shire, but I also know we cannot survive here much longer. I believe God has led William to us, and we would be foolish to disregard such a blessing." Julianna said.

Saxton looked at William and said, "I will go with you, but I cannot leave my wife and child alone."

"They can come with us. There is room for all of you at the monastery."

"It is settled then. When do we leave? Asked Saxton.

"I must first find my family in Cardiff. I believe that it will be a three-day journey from here. My son and I will leave in the morning. I want you, your wife, and your son to travel to the monastery. When you arrive, tell them I sent you. We will return to the monastery within a week. Here, take this map; it will lead you to the Monastery."

Saxton and William shook hands. Julianna hugged William, kissed him on the cheek, and said,

"Thank you so much for coming. I have made a place for you and your son to sleep."

< 350 >

William turned and noticed Lucas curled on the bench next to him. Both Saxton and Julianna smiled as William said,
"It looks like he has already found a place."

William bent over and lifted Lucas. He took him to the room, placed him on the bed, and bid good night to the Bently's. William knelt next to his sleeping son and offered a prayer of thanksgiving to God. After the prayer, he lay on the bed, closed his eyes, and looked forward to the journey. His heart warmed at the thought of seeing his dear Jillian, Michael, Sarah, and his friends at the Cardiff estate.

< 351 >

Chapter Twenty-One Notes

*The term **flail** refers to two weapons: a two-handed infantry weapon derived from an agricultural tool and a one-handed weapon. The defining characteristic of both involves a separate striking head attached to a handle by a flexible rope, strap, or chain. The two-handed variant saw use in a limited number of conflicts during the European Middle Ages.*

*A **morning star** is any of several medieval club-like weapons that include one or more spikes. Each used, to varying degrees, a combination of blunt-force and puncture attack to kill or wound the enemy.*

*A **falchion** is a one-handed, single-edged sword of European origin, whose design is reminiscent of the Persian scimitar and the Chinese Dao. The weapon combined the weight and power of an ax with the versatility of a sword. Falchions are found in different forms from around the 11th century up to and including the sixteenth century. In some versions, the falchion looks somewhat like the weapon-seax and later the saber, and in some versions, the form is irregular or like a machete with a crossguard.*

*The **Lochaber ax** is a type of halberd. The Scottish highlanders employed the weapon. The ax is similar to tools used with crops, such as the scythe, which is designed for reaping. The hook on the back bears a passing resemblance to a shepherd's crook, although, within agriculture, a smaller hook such as this may have been used to lift and carry tied bundles of a harvested crop or pull down tree branches. Early Lochaber axes, like the billhook, served a dual purpose as building instruments and farming tools.*

< 352 >

Chapter Twenty-Two
The Parallel Path

April 18th, 1350.

In the forest, en route to the Monastery.

Michael awoke early, just as the sun was rising. He looked around and noticed that the others were still sleeping. He gathered his bedding, rolled it up, took his crossbow, draped it around his shoulder to carry, and loaded the other items behind his seat on the carriage. He quietly peeked into the carriage. He saw Jillian, Angelia, and Faith lying stretched across the padded seats, still asleep. He turned to walk back into the cave when he noticed a carrot lying on the ground in front of him. He picked up the carrot and then walked to the cart. When he reached the coach, he noticed that the bag of vegetables had been opened, and some of its contents were gone. He felt a shiver run up his spine at the thought that someone had been there sometime in the evening while everyone was sleeping. He looked at the cart, into the woods, up and down the trail they had taken, yet saw no one. He lifted a blanket that had covered the flour and other food. Nothing was missing. It is evident that whoever had taken the food had done so quickly, not noticing the flour and other items. He walked over to the monks and woke them. Dom Gordon opened his eyes, looked at Michael, and said, "Good morning. Did you sleep well?"

Michael held out the carrot and said, "Someone has robbed us of some of our vegetables."

Dom Gordon quickly rose to his feet.

"Did they take everything?" He asked, concerned about the missing supplies.

< 353 >

"No, they did not take much. They quickly grabbed what they could and then ran off before getting caught."

Brother Richard opened his eyes. He heard most of the conversation.

"Do you think they are still nearby?" He asked.

"I doubt it," said Michael.

"I would guess whoever did this had no desire to cause us harm. They only wanted to eat."

Dom Gordon said, "You do realize, Michael, that this means that there are people out in these woods who have obviously left their homes and towns, either for lack of food or to escape the plague.

"Or both!" Added Brother Richard.

"How far do you believe we are from the Monastery?" Asked Michael.

"It depends on the route we travel. My plan was to travel through the small town of Berkshire, it is probably only a few leagues from here, and I believe it is the closest town from here."

"That means whoever stole from us must have come from Berkshire, which is not good."

"Are you suggesting that the town of Berkshire has been decimated and its population is dead?" Asked Brother Richards.

"It would be an obvious conclusion." Added Michael.

"If you are right, Michael, it would not be a good idea to travel through Berkshire, and the detour would probably add another hour to our journey." Said Dom Gordon.

"I would rather add an hour to our journey than risk the potential of taking our loved ones into the heart of the plague." Responded Michael. The others agreed.

"Dom Gordon, how far would we need to travel before the detour?" Asked Michael.

Dom Gordon looked down the road, thought for a moment, and said, "There is another road about two leagues

< 354 >

from here, and it will take us about three leagues away and around Berkshire."

Michael nodded and said, "Alright. We will take the alternate route. I will wake the others while the two of you pack your things and prepare for the journey." He turned and walked to the carriage, knocked on the door, and Angelia opened the door and smiled at him.

"Good morning, my love. Did you sleep well?" Angelia asked Michael.

"I slept well enough. How about you?"

"It was cramped here, but I felt safe." Said Angelia. She could tell that something was wrong. "What is it, Michael?" She asked.

"It is probably not as bad as it sounds, but someone was here last night, and they took some of our vegetables."

Angelia covered her mouth with the four fingers of her left hand.

"It is alright. They did not take everything, and they surely are far from here now."

Suddenly, a sound from underneath the carriage spooked the horses, and one of them jerked forward, moving the carriage a couple of feet. Angelia fell back into the carriage as Michael jumped away from it. Michael dropped to his knees and pointed the loaded crossbow underneath the carriage. He anticipated seeing a wild animal of some kind. He leaned toward the right, and his eyes made contact with another set of eyes. He felt his finger touch the trigger as the hair stood on the back of his neck. It had been an uneventful trip, and he was caught off guard by the possibility of a dangerous intruder. He had long ago determined to protect his friends and family at any cost, even if it meant taking another life. The moment seemed to move slowly as his finger began to squeeze the trigger. In his mind, he saw the face of a wolf with its golden glowing eyes. He justified that pulling the trigger and sending the sharp arrow into its chest would end the danger and protect those he loved. As his finger

< 355 >

pulled the trigger to the point of no return, his eyes focused on the target under the carriage; it was a small boy, a terrified human, looking at the weapon that would end his life. The time to think had passed. At that moment, Michael knew that it was too late to stop the mechanism from releasing the arrow. However, something strange seemed to give him enough time to lift the crossbow upward, just enough that the arrow raced over the crossbow and into the undercarriage. The boy screamed and quickly crawled away from the other side of the carriage. Angelia jumped from the carriage next to Michael, yelling, "Michael!"

She assumed that Michael had just shot the boy. Michael jumped to his feet with the crossbow hanging at his side. He turned and took two steps toward the back of the carriage. He reached out and grabbed the boy tossing him to the ground. Angelia was relieved to see that the boy was not injured. She ran towards him, and Michael thrust his hand toward her and commanded,

"Stop, Angelia! Do not come any closer! This child could have the plague!"

Angelia stopped. The boy lay on the ground and began to cry.

"Please, Sir, do not kill me. I have only taken one carrot. Please, sir."

"Young man, I have no intention of hurting you. But I cannot risk that you may be infected with the sickness." Michael said.

The boy attempted to speak as he sobbed. "But sir, I am not sick; only hungry and tired."

"Where are your parents?" Asked Michael.

"They are dead. All of them are dead!"

Michael looked back at Angelia. Dom Gordon and Brother Richards came from behind and stood next to Angelia. Dom Gordon leaned toward Michael and said, "Careful, Michael, surely this boy has the plague."

< 356 >

"I am not sick!" Yelled the boy. "They were all sick. My parents and my older sisters. But I did not get sick!"

Michael looked back at the others and then at the boy.

"How old are you, young man?"

"I will be ten years old in two months."

"Where are you from?"

The boy turned and pointed. "I am from Berkshire. That way."

"What are you doing out here in the woods?"

"My father told me to run?" He began to cry again.

"Why?" Asked Angelia.

"Because the men were coming to burn the houses."

"Why were they burning the houses?" Asked Brother Richards, even though he knew the answer.

"They were burning the sick people, so they did not get more people sick."

Angelia felt tears roll down her cheeks. Dom Gordon placed his arm around her shoulder, and she leaned her face into his shoulder. She remembered the monks telling her how the house of her husband's parents was boarded up, and they were all burned alive.

"My father told me to run. I ran into the woods and watched as the men came with torches. They burned our house. I could hear my father and sisters screaming, and my mother was already dead. The others were sick, but I begged God to save them, but he did not." He cried as he continued.

"He did not. When the screaming stopped, I saw that one of the men with a torch had fallen to the ground. He was sick too. The other three men turned their torches on him. He began to scream and roll as the flames covered his body. I turned and ran. I ran as far as I could. It was dark when I found your cart. I am sorry that I took a carrot. I promise I will not follow you if you let me go."

Michael took the crossbow from his shoulder and laid it on the ground. He walked toward the boy and said, "Young

< 357 >

man. None of us wants to hurt you. However, we need to be sure that you are not sick. I need to look at you closer. Will that be alright with you?" Michael asked in a soft voice.

The little boy nodded his head.

"Lift your arms so that I can see them?" Michael asked. Michael looked at the arms of the boy.

"Now turn in a circle while holding your arms above your head," Michael said. The boy slowly turned.

"Would you please remove your tunic?" Asked Michael.

The boy slowly pulled the shirt over his head and tossed it to the ground. He then turned in a circle. His skinny little torso did not show any signs of the plague. Angelia and the monks looked on, relieved that the boy did not have visible signs of the plague.

"How do you feel, young man?" Michael asked.

"I am not sick, sir. I do not know why God has spared me and taken my family. But I am not sick."

Michael could see that the boy seemed healthy, dirty with pale white skin and thick messy black hair, but nevertheless, healthy.

"Wait here just a moment, young man," Michael said as he turned and faced the others.

"What shall we do with him?" Michael asked.

"Well, surely, we cannot leave him here!" Stated Angelia.

Dom Gordon looked at Brother Richards and then at Michael. He said, "Michael, it is possible that this child has not been infected with the plague for some reason. Look around; neither have we, yet we have all been exposed to it in some manner. Perhaps it is God's will that we find this child."

Michael looked over his shoulder at the boy, who was obediently standing in the same spot.

Brother Richards chimed in. "If we leave him here, he would most likely die in these woods if he wasn't first eaten by wild animals."

< 358 >

Michael raised his eyebrows and cocked his head to the right.

Angelia began to speak when suddenly another voice said from behind them. "It would not be wise to reject a gift from God."

They looked back and saw Jillian standing on the top step of the carriage. Angelia walked toward her and said, "Mother."

"I am fine, child. I have most of my family with me, but this child has no one but us. Unlike him, I know that all of my family will be reunited soon. When God gives, we must receive."

Angelia turned back toward the others and said, "She is right, Michael. We are no more than travelers now, and this child is a traveler too. We cannot leave him or ignore the thought that God has led him here to be with us. We are all family now, and I believe he was meant to find us, his new family."

Michael sighed. He knew that she and Jillian were right, and the boy seemed healthy, and leaving him alone seemed unethical and wrong. Michael turned back to the boy standing in the same spot.

"What is your name, boy?" Michael asked.

"My name is Kemp."

"Kemp is a good name," Michael said. He then asked, "Would you like to go with us?"

"I do not know. Where are you going?"

Michael looked surprised by the response. He said, "Seeing that you have no other options, does it matter where we are going?"

The boy thought for a moment and said, "I suppose it does not."

He hesitated and added, "If I go with you, can I have another carrot?"

< 359 >

Angelia smiled and walked to the boy. She leaned down toward him and said. "Young man, if you are with us, you can have anything we have." She embraced him. "We are happy God has spared you and brought you to us."

The boy dried his tears. Angelia took his tunic from the ground and helped him put it on. The monks each greeted him. Michael looked down at him and said.

"Of course, we will expect you to do your part. There is no free ride, and we must all do our part."

"I will be faithful, sir."

"And one last thing, Kemp. Please, call me Michael."

"Yes sir, I mean, Michael," said the boy.

Angelia prepared a light meal. They ate, packed the vehicles, and headed down the dirt road an hour later. Michael kept his loaded crossbow on his lap. Kemp road in the cart with the monks.

Michael felt more tension than he had the day before. Although he saw no one, his eyes continued to dart in different directions for the next hour.

Their path led them to a large lake. They could see smoke on the other side as they approached the lake.

"That is Berkshire." Said Dom Gordon. Angelia looked at Michael and placed her hand over her mouth. She leaned in toward Michael and nestled her head on his chest. Michael caressed the back of her head as he looked toward the smoke.

"You know what that means, do you not, Michael?" Asked Dom Gordon.

Michael nodded. "They are burning the infected, just as Kemp has said."

Brother Richards quietly added, "I wonder how many are left?"

"What difference does that make? There is nothing we can do for them. We must keep moving and get to the monastery as soon as possible." Michael said as he looked up the path.

< 360 >

Dom Gordon nodded and motioned for Brother Richards to shake the reins. The horses continued down the trail. Each wondered what they would find at the Monastery, but none dared to discuss it.

~*~*~

William and Lucas had been traveling less than an hour when they noticed smoke rising from trees a league in front of them. It did not look like a single fire but many fires. The path opened up to a wide road as they got closer; William realized something was wrong.

"I have seen this before, father." Said Lucas.

"To what do you refer?" Asked William.

"They are burning the town." Said Lucas.

"What?" Asked William.

"They are burning the town to stop the plague. I saw this once before when I was with Allard. Remember, I told you."

William thought for a moment and then remembered when Lucas told him about his experience with Allard, the man who had kidnapped him. It occurred to him that Berkshire was a large town, and a larger population meant more people with the plague. He was not sure what to do. There was no other path to take. If they turned back, they would have to find another way to Cardiff that could take them hours or even days. He stopped the horse and asked Lucas,

"Lucas, I believe that we should continue through Berkshire. It may be dangerous, but we are prepared with weapons if we need to use them."

"I understand, father."

William pulled the knife from his belt and handed it to Lucas.

"Take this and place it in your belt, just in case you need it."

Lucas took the knife and did as his father instructed. William felt odd giving his small child a knife, but he knew it was a necessary precaution.

"Hold tightly to me if I need to cause the horse to run."

Lucas wrapped his arms around William and continued their journey into Berkshire. The road continued up a small hill and then turned toward the right. As they reached the top of the hill and finished the turn, they began to see the outskirts of the town. William was shocked to see remnants of burned homes and buildings on both sides of the road. He did not see any people for the first several blocks as the path turned into a cobblestone street. Most shops were boarded up, and some had signs in the window that read, "PLAGUE." He felt Lucas tighten his grip as he held close to his father. Just as they reached the center of the town, a yellow dog darted in front of them, spooking the horse.

William calmed the animal, and they continued the journey through the town. They passed a section of town with multi-story buildings of shops with housing above. Many windows were open, and the drapes blew in the slight breeze. A foul stench of death and burning human flesh began to flow in the air. William noticed a jog in the road ahead. It looked like a road that continued out of the town. He saw a large lake off to the right as they followed the road. It appeared to be about two leagues in length and less than half a league across. He could see a parallel road on the other side of the lake. He felt a great relief as they passed the last row of buildings and began their journey next to the lake. He looked over his shoulder and marveled that they had traveled many blocks and never saw another human. He was relieved that defending them was unnecessary but still puzzled that at least this section of town seemed to be abandoned. As he looked back at the town, his eyes caught something on the other side of the lake. *"People."* He thought as he noticed a carriage with horses and a small horse cart behind it. Although they were traveling in the

< 362 >

opposite direction, it gave him hope that there were still others who had survived the plague. He noticed that one of the men riding on the back of the cart saw him. As he looked closer, he saw that the man was a monk. He waved at the man. The monk also noticed him and waved back. Dom Gordon was in front, driving the cart. He looked back at Brother Richard, sitting on the back of the cart, and asked, "To whom are you waving?"

"Just a man and a boy on a horse. They are traveling toward where we have already been. I wonder if they have any idea what lies ahead for them?"

Dom Gordon added, "God be with them."

< 363 >

Chapter Twenty-Three
Dead or Alive
April 20th, 1350.

The remainder of the day yielded no surprises. They traveled slowly but without incident. They found a place for the evening, and Michael, Dom Gordon, and Brother Richard took turns keeping watch throughout the night. The following day, they packed, ate a small breakfast, and continued back on the path to the Monastery. Michael had Kemp sit next to him in the front of the carriage. Kemp had not said much since joining the group and was quiet and polite. Michael looked at him while holding the reins and wondered how such a young boy could maintain his composure after losing his family horrifyingly. He looked at the path and then back at the boy. He wanted to say something but waited until the right words came to him.

"Kemp?" Asked Michael.

"Yes, sir," he hesitated and said, "I mean, Michael."

"How are you fairing?" Michael.

Kemp thought for a moment and said, "I am getting along well, thank you."

Michael did not expect such a confident answer.

"Are you sure?"

"Yes, I am sure." He added, making it evident that he did not particularly want to talk. Michael thought for a few moments and then said, "I know what it is like to lose loved ones."

Kemp continued to look forward. It was apparent that he heard Michael, but he did not want to lose self-control.

Michael continued. "It hurts. And there are times when you want to blame God. You even get mad at him and ask how he could let such things happen. Sometimes your anger

< 364 >

becomes difficult to control, and you want to lash out at others. It took me a very long time to stop blaming God for the bad times in my life. I promise that your pain will eventually lessen, and you will begin to recognize the many blessings God has given you and continues to give you each day." Michael smiled at Kemp and then looked at the path ahead.

"I do not blame God, Michael. God did not kill my family; the plague did. I love God and thank him. God allowed me to survive and to find you and the others. How could I be mad at God when he has been so good to me?" Kemp said.

Michael continued to look forward. He was amazed at the attitude of this young boy and wondered how he could have such love for God after such tragedy in his life. He thought about the years he blamed God for all the bad in his life and how he struggled to make sense of heartache and death. He knew he was in a much better place than he was a few months earlier, and he hoped he would never allow himself to return to the dark place that only presented anger and justification for bitterness and hatred.

"Good for you, my little friend. I hope your thoughts never change and your heart always remains soft with the love of God." Said, Michael. He thought for a moment and then asked, "Why do you have such faith in God?"

Michael continued to look ahead as he guided the horses on the path. Kemp looked at Michael and said, "My father and mother taught me about God when I was small, and our priest taught me to read from the Holy Vulgate. My father told me that he believed that I would live to see wonderful things in my lifetime."

"Wonderful things, that is a great thought." Added Michael.

Kemp looked at his lap and continued to speak softly. "I know that he did not mean seeing my family die. But I do believe in my father, and I believe in God, and someday I will know when my father's promise comes true." He wiped a tear

< 365 >

from his eye. It was the first sign of emotion that Michael had seen from the boy since he joined them. Michael felt a love for this young man, and he knew there was something special about this boy. He silently prayed, *"Dear Lord, help this boy to live to adulthood and see his father's wish come true."*

Michael reached over and ruffled the hair on Kemps' head.

"I believe your father knew what he was talking about. You will see wonderful things in your lifetime. Of course, that does not mean that you will not also see many not-so-wonderful things along the way."

Kemp smiled at Michael and looked back at the road. He was beginning to warm up to Michael and the others. He did not know what lay ahead for him on life's journey, but he knew that God was in control and that as long as he trusted God, he could endure anything.

~*~*~

Lucas's last hour of the journey became very uncomfortable as he remembered the last time he had traveled this path. He remembered Allard stealing him away from the barn, tying him to the horse, and beating him. He had flashbacks of escaping Allard, hiding, sleeping alone, and walking the path by the river. Many of the thoughts caused his tension, but being with his father, even retracing where he had been before under such difficult circumstances, brought him great comfort. None of it seemed real at times. William pointed to an opening in the trees and said,

"Do you know what that is, my son?"

"Yes, father, it is the path to the estate. We are almost there."

"It will be wonderful to see everyone again." Said, William.

"I am sure it will be a surprise, father, because everyone thinks you are still dead."

< 366 >

"Still dead?   Let me remind you, Lucas, that I have never been dead."

Lucas laughed and said, "You know what I mean?"

William smiled and said, "Of course I do.   I hope my arrival will not be too shocking to your mother."

"Actually, father, she is the one person who always believed that you were still alive."

"Really?" William asked.

"Yes.   She sits in her room in a rocking chair in front of the window, most every day, waiting for you to come."

"I am happy that she has such great faith," William responded, knowing that the description Lucas gave of Jillian was evident that she had lost her sense of reality. William felt a pit in his stomach at the thought of Jillian losing her mind, and he hoped that his return would also bring her back.

A ray of setting sun beamed across the opening out of the forest and onto the path to the estate. William and Lucas held their arms in front of their faces as they rode down the trail on the last jog of their journey. William squinted his eyes while looking in the direction of the estate, and the sun made it difficult to see. Every now and then, he caught a quick glimpse of something that looked like the estate.   Lucas held tight to William and planted his right cheek against William's back.

"Can you see it, father?   Can you see the house?" Lucas asked excitedly.

William continued to look toward the estate, unsure what he saw.

"Not yet, Lucas.   The sun is too bright.   Just a bit further, and the sun will be behind the trees.   I suspect that your sister will be running toward us any minute."

He hoped that Jillian and Michael would also be running.   As they got closer, he began to notice the smell of burning embers.   His first thought was that Laurie Collins, the housemaid, and chief cook, must have been cooking, but the scent was much too harsh for a chimney fire.   Suddenly as the

< 367 >

large trees behind the estate arose to block the sun's rays, a structure began to materialize. William closed his eyes and opened them again. Something did not seem right. At first, he thought he had gazed toward the sun too long, and his eyes played tricks on him. All he could see were the large rock corners of the estate rising high. He rubbed his eyes with his left hand while holding the reins with his right. He opened his eyes again. This time, he could see the remnants of what used to be the Chattingworth estate. He saw only a few large rock walls left of the estate, mainly in the corners. Smoke was still rising in various spots. He felt his heart race as he tried to determine what had caused this destruction and the terrifying thought that his family could be dead in the rubble of the estate.

"Dear Father, NO!" He said in a quivering voice.

Lucas leaned around his father and saw what William had seen.

"Oh, father! What has happened?" He screamed. "Mother, Michael, and Sarah, where are they?" He yelled.

William kicked the horse in the flanks, and they quickly rode to the house. William jumped from the horse, and Lucas followed. He ran toward where the front door had been and walked into the front hall's remains, with Lucas behind him.

He turned toward Lucas and put his arm in front of him.

"No, Lucas, you need to stay back. There is still smoke and burning embers and the floor could give way. Stay back, and let me look first."

"But father, I am afraid." He began to cry. "What has happened here? Who did this? Where is everyone?"

He began to yell for his mother, sister, and Michael, and William also yelled for each of them. After a few moments, he began to call out for anyone who could hear his voice. The debris from the collapsed second and third floors and roof made it impossible to walk further into the house's front. He walked back to the front porch where Lucas stood.

< 368 >

Lucas ran to his father, wrapped his arms around him, and said, "Oh, father. We have come too far, and too much has happened for the rest of our family to be dead. How could God allow this to happen? How could he?" Lucas cried.

William held Lucas and continued to survey the area.

"Lucas, we do not know if anyone is dead. All we know is that the house has burned down. Let us walk around and see what we can find."

They turned to the right of the estate and began walking. As they reached the front end of the estate, William noticed that the small cottage was also burned down. He walked with Lucas to where it had once been. He noticed there was no smoke or burned wood in that area. He realized that the debris of the cottage had been carefully removed, leaving only the outline of the rock foundation. He knew it must have burned down long before the rest of the estate. He tried to determine what had happened. He thought about the town they passed through, where many homes and buildings were destroyed by fire. He knew that the only reason to burn a building was to stop the plague by burning those who lived in the building. His mind began to rehearse all he knew about the plague. His loved ones succumbing to the plague, and being burned made him sick. They continued walking around the estate. When they reached the back, they noticed the fire had destroyed the barn. They stopped, and William looked toward the barn. He saw it was also cleared of debris, which told him it had also been burned sometime before the estate. It was obvious that whatever happened to cause the fire in the estate occurred recently, but the other buildings had burned quite some time in the past. They continued walking around to the back of the estate. When they reached the back of the estate, William noticed that the carriage house building was still standing. It gave him some hope. He said to Lucas,

"Look, son, the carriage house is still standing. Let us go there."

< 369 >

They picked up their pace and walked faster, hoping they would find someone. William began to run, and Lucas tried to keep up with him. William was a few feet ahead when Lucas tripped over something and fell. William looked back just as Lucas was falling. He stopped and turned, and Lucas began to scream. William ran back to him. He reached down to help Lucas and then noticed what had caused Lucas to cry. He had fallen over a dead body lying face down in the dirt.

"Help me up, father!" Lucas yelled. "It is a dead body! Who is it, father? Who is it?" William lifted Lucas and held him close.

"Are you alright, son?" William asked.

"Yes, father." Replied Lucas as he shook.

"Stay here, and I will see who it is," William said.

He slowly walked over to the body. The stench of seared flesh and human decay was nauseating. William held his left arm to his nose and mouth. He bent down to get a closer look when he reached the body. The face was buried in the dirt. He looked around and noticed a short flooring plank. He lifted the plank out of the debris and wedged it under the body. He knelt down, laid the plank over his right leg, creating a wedge, and pressed down on it. It took several attempts until he could slowly move the body. Lucas had taken a few steps closer. He leaned over and helped William push the plank down, and the body began to turn. They had the body on its side and continued to push until it began to fall on its back. The pressure of the limp body falling onto its back caused the lungs to expel the last cavity of oxygen, forcing air up the windpipe and past the vocal cords. This caused a loud moaning sound to escape through its mouth. Both William and Lucas jumped back. Lucas began screaming, "It is alive! It is alive!" believing that the dead person had somehow come to life again. William held him tightly and tried to calm him down.

< 370 >

"Lucas, there is nothing to fear. This man is dead, and air escaping from his lungs causes that sound. Calm down, son. Calm down."

Lucas began to regain his composure.

"Who is he, father? Do we know him?" Asked Lucas.

William noticed an arrow from a crossbow protruding from the dead man's chest. He looked at the face and noticed that the man was missing some teeth and others were rotting.

"He is no one we know, son."

William gathered that the man must have been an intruder and someone from the estate shot him with the arrow. The scene began to make sense. William surmised that the estate was attacked and burned down, He lifted Lucas, and they continued to walk to the carriage house. They had only taken a few steps when they noticed another dead body. This time it was lying on its back with two arrows sticking out of its chest. William got close enough to see that it was another stranger. He began to feel some hope that somehow his family and friends may have survived the attack and the fire. A few feet further and they discovered another body, this one more gruesome than the other two. Another man was lying on his back with an arrow between his eyes. Lucas turned, fell to his knees, and began to vomit. William walked toward him and placed a hand on one of Lucas' shoulders.

"I am sorry you have to see this, my son. None of these men belongs to the estate, and I am sure your brother Michael had something to do with stopping them from hurting our family and friends."

Lucas wiped his mouth with his right arm. He looked up at his father and said,

"But where is our family, father?"

William lifted Lucas to his feet, put his arm around his shoulder, and said, "We have not found them yet. That is all. I do not believe God would preserve our lives and lead us this far to find our family dead. Come, let us go to the carriage house."

< 371 >

William took the crossbow from his shoulders and loaded it with an arrow.

"Why are you doing that, father?" Asked Lucas.

"Because we do not know who or what is in the carriage house, and I want to be prepared, just in case."

They stopped at the front and opened the doors of the carriage house. William looked inside. The carriage, the horse cart, and the horses were gone, and he noticed fresh wheel tracks and horse hooves tracks.

"Lucas, someone has taken the carriage, the cart, and the horses. That tells me several people left the estate sometime after the fire." He paused. "I do not believe our family and friends died in this fire and battle. They are alive, and they have left the estate."

"Father, that would be wonderful. But where would they have gone."

"I do not know, son. Perhaps they have gone home. Come, there is a room over here; let us look inside. If it is safe, we will stay here for the night and figure out where to go in the morning."

They walked to the room. William opened the door. He pointed his crossbow into the room and slowly walked in. He looked around and saw no one. He noticed someone had slept in the bed and uncovered some furniture. It was the touch of a woman, he thought. A man would not take the time to tidy a room if it was for a short stay. Lucas walked to the bed and lay down. William felt a sense of relief. It appeared that those responsible for the destruction were dead, and his family was out there somewhere, still alive. He noticed a piece of parchment on a table. He walked to the table and lifted the parchment. His heart began to race as he read the words.

"My Dearest William, there has been an accident, and the entire estate has gone up in flames. We are all well. Michael, his wife and daughter, and two men of the cloth. Monson has gone to be with Ruth, and we are traveling to

< 372 >

London. I am sorry we were not here when you arrived; we waited as long as we could.
Yours always, Jillian."

He held the letter in his chest, and tears began to roll down his cheeks. It was the most beautiful end to such a difficult day. He turned to tell Lucas the good news, but the boy had fallen into a deep sleep. Not wanting to disturb him, he closed the door and secured it. He walked back to the bed, knelt on the opposite side, and began to pray in his mind.

"Oh dear, kind and loving Father. My heart is full. My soul rejoices to know that my family has been spared from this plague and the fire and destruction around us. I thank thee for thy overwhelming love and kindness to me. Thank thee for giving me my memories again so that I can be grateful for my loved ones and all that thou hast given me. Please help me to always remember thee and to give the gratitude for all that thou hast given me, including the difficulties and hardships that have humbled me and made me the man I am today. Please, father, continue to protect my family and loved ones and allow us to be reunited, including those whom I have left in Bristol. I love, revere, and thank thee with every fiber of my being. I pray in the holy names of Jesus, Amen!"

After finishing his prayer, he reread the letter. His happiness stalled as he realized that Jillian mentioned Michael, his wife, child, and two men of the cloth but did not mention Sarah. He hoped it was an oversight while writing a quick note. Still, it bothered him. He also realized that she did not mention any of the servants, and he felt great sadness when he realized what she meant by saying that Monson had gone back to Ruth. Where were the others, he thought, and who were the two men of the cloth? He lay on the bed next to Lucas and closed his eyes. He tried to relax and sleep. Just as he felt himself slipping off to sleep, an image appeared in his mind. It was a cart with

< 373 >

two monks, one waving at him. He opened his eyes widely and realized whom he had seen.

The long journey ended. Dom Gordon stopped the cart and yelled to Michael to stop the carriage, and he jumped from the cart and ran to Michael.

"Michael, look just above the hill and into the trees. There is the Monastery; can you see it?" He asked excitedly.

Michael looked in that direction and eventually saw the large building in the trees. He was surprised that it was so far off from any other town or village.

"Yes, I see it. Shall we continue?" He asked.

Dom Gordon nodded. He quickly returned to the cart and steered it in front of the carriage. This was the first time on the journey that the cart led the party. They traveled up the hill and were in front of the large rock monastery in a few minutes. Dom Gordon was surprised that no one came out to greet them. However, amid his excitement, he jumped from the cart and ran to the door. Michael also thought it was odd that no one had come out. He yelled at Dom Gordon, "Dom, stop! Wait!"

Dom Gordon stopped just before the big gate entrance into the compound. He looked back at Michael and waited until Michael walked to him.

"Something is not right," Michael said. "I have a bad feeling."

The monk looked at Michael and then at the gate. His excitement seemed to cloud his judgment.

"Michael, surely nothing is out of sorts. Perhaps they have all gathered for a meal, and no one has noticed us yet. Come, let us enter, and you will see."

Michael grabbed the monk's shoulder and said. "Dom Gordon, I know you are excited to be here to see your friends again, but we need to be cautious, especially after all we have seen and experienced. We are not going in there without

< 374 >

weapons. Tell Brother Richard to wait here with the others while you and I go in, just to ensure it is safe."

The monk agreed and told Brother Richard the plan. Michael followed as Dom Gordon opened the large wooden gate. When the gate was open, the men looked into the courtyard. Dom Gordon felt a shiver and breathed deeply as he assessed the courtyard. Everything was overgrown and unkept, entirely unlike a monastery. He knew that something was not right.

Michael grabbed his shoulder and said softly, "Dom Gordon, you and I both know something is wrong. We must use caution if we are to go any further."

Dom looked back at him and said, "If we go further? We have come too far to not go further."

"All I am saying is that we must be prepared for what lies ahead."

Dom Gordon knew that Michael was right. He also felt very uncomfortable; something told him he would not like what he was about to see. They slowly walked toward the main building. Michael could tell that the compound was beautiful and carefully manicured at one time. There were stone paved walkways lined with narrow streams and flowerbeds. He saw many statues, stone bridges, and sitting areas, but all had suffered a terrible lack of maintenance. This did not look like a lively and living monastery. Michael stopped as a foul order hung in front of them. He reached for the monk and stopped him too. The monk looked back at Michael, signifying that he, too, could smell the air. The monk motioned for Michael to look over to the right. Michael looked and saw the legs of a dead monk bobbing in a stream a short distance ahead and to their right. The monk covered his face and began to cry.

"Oh, dear God, please do not let this be so. Please let my friends be alive."

< 375 >

Michael walked to the monk and put his arm around him. Dom Gordon regained his composure and said, "We must go into the main hall and see if anyone is left.

The two walked up the stairs. They slowly pushed open one of the giant 15-foot doors. The door opened, revealing a massive hall with twenty-foot ceilings adorned with large chandeliers. The walls were covered with paintings, tapestries, and sculptures. A pungent odor, more intense than they had just encountered, hung in the stagnant air. They slowly entered the room and began to walk down the long hall. They knew that death was all around them. Dom Gordon started to tremble at the thought of seeing the dead bodies of his friends. Michael noticed parchment on a large table in the middle of the room. He stopped as Dom Gordon continued walking. Michael picked up the parchment, brushed away the dust, and began to read it when he was stopped by the squeal of Dom Gordon.

"Oh, dear Father above! No!"

Michael ran to the sound of Dom Gordon's voice. He had turned into the large dining hall. He saw Dom leaning against the doorway, vomiting. Michael looked into the room and counted forty decaying skeletons around the table. Most were slumped over the table, and some were slumped back in their chairs. Each had a goblet either in their hands or near them. Michael helped Dom out of the room.

"They are all dead! All of my friends are dead."

Michael did not know how to console the priest. He looked at the letter again and began to read it to himself, and he stopped when he realized who had written it. He smiled, looked at the priest, and said, "Dom, look! A letter addressed to you by Brother Simon.

Dom Gordon picked up the letter and read it aloud.

"Father Gordon. I am writing this letter in hopes that you receive it. We arrived at St. Gabriel's as planned. Unfortunately, we did not find it in the condition we had hoped

< 376 >

for. All the monks here are dead, and we discovered many bodies on the grounds and in some buildings.

Nevertheless, the most gruesome discovery was the dining hall. It appears that most monks took their own lives by poison to avoid the death around them. I know that those who acquire this sickness die a horrible death; I just pray that God will have mercy on the souls of those men who violated God's commandment to not kill by taking their own lives. We are all well. We have gathered anything of worth that we can carry. We are leaving for London, hoping to find better conditions and a place to continue our ministry. When we get there, we will leave word for you so that we can be together again. I pray that you and Brother Richard are alive and well.

Your brother in Christ, Simon."

Dom was relieved at the news. He and Michael quickly left the grounds. They told the others what they had found. After a short discussion, it was decided to leave the monastery and head for London. They knew they only had an hour or two before the sun went down and wanted to be far into the forest before stopping for the night. London was a few days away. Each hoped that the mother city was still living.

William awoke to the sound of a rooster crowing. The sun was still low on the horizon, slowly making it rise and shooting spring rays gently through the trees. He stood in the carriage house doorway and felt the chilly fresh spring air sting his face. He looked over the estate and tried to imagine what had happened. It did not seem real that such a beautiful home that had withstood generations of time could be gone. Nothing left but burnt timber and tall rock chimneys. He counted the majestic rock fireplaces peering through the rubble; none had been toppled. It gave him hope that somehow all of his family had also survived. He assumed that they must have headed back to Bristol. He wondered about the condition of Bristol,

< 377 >

was his home still standing, were his friends still alive. Had Bristol withstood the ravages of the plague? Another crow from the rooster interrupted his thoughts. He rubbed his eyes and turned to go back into the carriage house when suddenly, an idea entered his mind. He turned around and looked out into the forest. "The hunting house!" He thought. He remembered that Jillian's father had a hunting house a few leagues into the woods. "Could they have first gone to the hunting house?" He asked himself. He walked back into the carriage house and woke Lucas.

"Come, son, it is time to go," William said as he helped Lucas sit in bed. He shared Jilliana's letter with Lucas.

"Where are we going, father? Lucas asked. "Are we going to London to find mother and the others?"

"Yes, but first, we are going to the hunting house that your grandfather built. It is only a few leagues into the woods, and it will not take us long to reach it." William added.

They gathered their things, climbed onto the horse, and began the journey into the woods. Lucas rode on the back of the horse and looked behind at the embers of the estate. Fond memories of life there came to his mind. He turned back and held tight to his father. As they approached the forest edge, William noticed fresh horse tracks. He stopped the horse and loaded his crossbow. He wanted to be ready if there were any other pillagers on the path ahead. The forest became thick, and the wavy trail turned and headed downward and narrowed to the point that it was sometimes difficult to pass on it. William continued to look for the fresh horse tracks ahead of him. He noticed two sets of tracks, each going in opposite directions. He knew that someone had recently been on the estate. He felt a wave of nervousness brush through his body. It would have been much easier, and he would have felt more confident on the journey if he did not have Lucas with him. He was more concerned about protecting Lucas than himself. He said a silent

< 378 >

prayer that gave him a measure of comfort to continue the journey into the unknown.

They had traveled just over an hour when the trail opened up into a sizeable rounded clearing that stretched over forty feet in any direction. William stopped the horse and surveyed the area. He felt uneasy, as if someone or something was watching them.

"Father, can I get down for a moment to relieve myself?" Lucas asked.

William helped Lucas to the ground. "Do not go far, Lucas. I want to be able to see you," William said as he looked in all directions. Lucas stood next to a tree.

"Hurry, Lucas," William said. "We need to keep moving." Lucas nodded his head in agreement. Suddenly, William heard the sound of a branch breaking into the woods, and he turned toward the sound but saw nothing.

"Lucas!" William shouted in a loud whisper. "Come, now!" Lucas gathered himself and quickly scurried back. William leaned down and scooped the boy onto the horse, placing him on the back. William turned, but before he could nudge the horse, he heard another sound that seemed to come from the right a few feet ahead.

"What is it, father?" Lucas asked, speaking in a whisper into William's ear.

William did not want to answer because he knew that the odds were that they were being stalked by either a pack of wolves, a wild animal, or a remnant of the men who had attacked the estate. He ran scenarios through his mind, trying to determine the best way to out whit whatever was out there. He held tightly to the crossbow with his left arm. He felt his fingers itching to pull the trigger. Whatever was about to happen, he would not let his son die. He looked down at the quiver of arrows hanging from the saddle's left. He wondered how quickly he could reload. In his mind, he traced the location

< 379 >

of each weapon attached in various places on the saddle. He appreciated the monks who insisted he was armed with whatever means necessary to stop or kill anyone who attempted harm to him or Lucas. He gently lowered the reins, reached with his right hand into a leather pouch, and slowly wrapped his fingers around the handle of a knife. He could hear Lucas's breathing, arms wrapped tighter around William's waist. William, Lucas, and the horse remained still. William slowly looked toward the right and asked, "Who's there?"

He waited for a response and said, "I know you are out there."

Suddenly, a cracking sound to the left startled a flock of birds that flew directly toward William and Lucas. William pulled the knife from its holster and flung it as hard as he could in the direction where the birds had come. The flying projectile and wave of William's arm separated the path of the birds that abruptly flew up and out over the tops of the trees. William's eyes followed the knife as it suddenly stopped with a loud thud, mercilessly entering a tall tree's flesh. He lifted the crossbow, pointed it in the same direction, and began to squeeze the trigger, when unexpectedly he saw a dark shadow and heard a low voice screech and shockingly yell, "WILLIAM?"

~*~*~

Nearly an hour had passed without anyone saying a word. Kemp had fallen asleep and leaned his head against Michael's right shoulder. An eerie quiet seemed to overshadow the afternoon. Michael noticed the absence of birds or the sound of animals. The trail was long and desolate of life. Another hour passed, and the silence was broken by the soft sound of singing. Michael listened and realized that Jillian was singing a lullaby. He slowly slid open the window cover and looked into the carriage.

Angelia was sitting on the seat just under the window box. She was holding faith in her lap; both were asleep. Jillian

< 380 >

sat across from them. She was in a daze, her eyes half closed. She did not notice Michael looking at her. He watched as she held her arms in a cradle, slowly swinging an imaginary baby from side to side.

His heart sank as he listened to her sing the words, "Sleep child, sleep so deep, close your eyes, do not weep," over and over again.

She gently caressed the imaginary baby's face with the back of her fingers. The melody was strange and somewhat unnerving. It was a combination of tunes that she used to sing to Lucas and Sarah when they were infants. The notes were discordant, sharp, and then minor.

An uneasy feeling overcame him. He wanted to wake her but did not want to wake Angelia and Faith. He turned his head away from the opening and began to slide the cover when he noticed Jillian change the song's words.

"Sleep, child, no more breath; it will not hurt; it is only death."

The hair stood on the nape of his neck. He looked back and saw Jillian cupping her hand as if holding the face and nose of the baby. She shook her arm and hand as if restraining the struggling child. Michael felt sick. Jillian stopped and looked at the lifeless baby in her arms, her eyes half shut. She placed it on the seat next to her. She then turned forward and looked directly at Michael. He flinched and then realized that she was still asleep and did not actually see him as he witnessed the grizzly dream.

She continued humming the twisted tune. She cocked her head to the right, laid her left hand in her lap, slowly slid her right hand across her lap, and rested it on the seat next to her thigh. Michael felt anxious and nervous as he realized he had seen a glimpse inside her confused mind. He felt tears well up in his eyes. He again began to close the slider when he noticed her fingers tighten around something on the seat next to her.

< 381 >

She began singing again to the same melody but with a new verse.

"Death now, no more life; it is Michael's fault; I will kill his wife."

Michael sucked in a shock of air as Jillian slowly raised her hand tightly clutched around the handle of a shiny knife. Michael yelled, "MOTHER!"

His voice startled both Angelia and Faith awake. Angelia sat up and screamed as she saw Jillian leaning toward her with the knife. Michael jumped to the carriage's side and flung open the door. The scream and his quick movements startled the monks in the cart behind them. He hurled himself into the carriage between Jillian's knife, Angelia, and her crying child.

William released the trigger, and the man behind the voice stepped forward, lowering his loaded crossbow. It was Ernest Collins, a servant from the Chattingworth estate. He seemed shocked to see William.

"William? Is it really you?" He asked in amazement.

"Of course, it is me? William responded.

William looked closer and recognized the face. He knew that this was someone he knew. The memory was slowly coming to him. As the man's name appeared, Lucas shouted, "Mr. Collins! You are alive!"

Lucas jumped from the horse and ran to Ernest. Ernest dropped to one knee and threw his arms around Lucas. Ernest dropped his crossbow and held Lucas tightly. He looked at William and said, "We thought you were dead. How can you be before me?" He pulled Lucas away from him and looked at his face. Tears ran down his cheeks as he struggled to say, "My dear boy, you too are alive! What great mercy from the God of Heaven!" Held pulled Lucas to him and held him tightly.

< 382 >

"Ernest Collins. Yes, I know you." Said, William.

"Of course, you know me, Sir. My wife and I had served your wife's family since before she was born." He smiled at William. "But I have so many questions that I do not know where to start."

"Where are my wife and children? How many of the others survived?" William anxiously asked.

Ernest shook his head. William felt his heart sink. He could not bear to hear fateful news about his wife, Michael, and little Sarah. It did not seem possible that God would take him this far on the journey to have it end so abruptly. His face drooped.

Ernest looked up at him and said, "Oh, but Sir, all is well. All is well." He stood, turned behind, and yelled, "Laurie! Laurie! Come! Come quickly! Bring the child!"

William was confused. He looked into the forest and noticed a woman running toward them. As her face appeared in his sight, he recognized her, and she, him. He remembered Laurie, her cheerful disposition, and kindness. She placed her hand over her mouth when she saw Willian. He dismounted the horse, and she ran to him with arms raised. He opened his arms to greet her. She cried, tears streaming down her cheeks as she embraced him. She kissed his cheek and then held him tightly.

"Oh, William, you are alive! You are alive!" She cried profusely. William tried to comfort her as he brushed the back of her head. He was happy to see her and Ernest, but he still longed to see his wife and children. She looked back and saw Lucas, and she ran to him and bundled him into her arms.

"Lucas, my child." She could hardly speak through her sobs. "God has saved you, and he has brought you back. How can this be? How can this be?"

"Ernest and Laurie, it is joyous to see you. However, we would also like to see Jillian, Michael, and Sarah. Are they with you?" William asked.

< 383 >

Laurie stood and looked back at Ernest. He nodded his head. Laurie motioned to come, with her hand, back toward the forest. William could see another person running toward them. He was expecting Jillian but noticed it was a child running toward him. When the child broke through the forest's darkness, her bright blue eyes lit up, and strands of her auburn hair swung back and forth across her face. William raised his arms to her. She smiled and called out, "Father! Father, you came home!"

William was overcome with love and gratitude as he recognized the beautiful face of his precious little girl, Sarah. He embraced her tightly and swung her in a circle. At that moment, he could not imagine anything more wonderful God could do for him.

The knife pierced his tunic and continued into his chest just below his right breast. The pain was sharp and severe as the blade continued its entry between two of his ribs. His open hand clasped around Jillian's hand, stopping the blade. In a continuous motion, he reversed the direction of the knife, pulling it out of his chest. Angelia's screams woke Jillian from her trance. She was shocked to see her hand around a knife and blood coming from the wound in Michael's chest. She released the blade, and Michael brushed it to the floor of the carriage.

The noise had awakened Kemp. He stopped the carriage, jumped off the seat, and ran to the open carriage door. The monks were right behind him. Michael held his chest and fell backward out of the carriage into the arms of Dom Gordon and Brother Richard.

Angelia continued to scream. Jillian was now conscious. Angelia leaned out of the carriage while holding Faith. She looked back at Jillian and shouted, "What have you done? You crazy woman! You have killed your son! You

< 384 >

have killed Michael!" Her weeping and whaling echoed deep into the abnormally quiet forest.

< 385 >

Chapter Twenty-Four
Life and Death

Laurie cried as Lucas rehearsed the difficult trials he encountered during his abduction with Allard. They then told William about the events that caused them to end up at the hunting cabin.

"We understand why Michael did what he did. So much was happening at once, and it must have been difficult for him to manage everything thrust upon his shoulders." Laurie said as she watched William shaking his head.

"If only I had gone to Cardiff with my family instead of staying behind," William said while wiping away a tear.

Ernest put his hand on Williams' shoulder and said, "No one blames you, William. We all know that you had an estate to run and other than just your family to be concerned about."

William thought about the word "had" and estate to run. He wondered if the Bristol estate was still his. He wondered if his friends had survived the plague and all of the human tragedy and debauchery that came because of it.

"My heart aches for Michael. He is out there somewhere with my wife, his wife, and a child, trying to stay alive. And he has no idea that Lucas, Sarah, and I are alive." William said. He looked back at Ernest and asked,

"Why did you not go back to the estate and tell Michael and the others that Sarah was alive?"

Ernest and Laurie looked at one another and then back at William. Laurie spoke in a trembling voice. "Oh,   William, many times we considered taking her back. But we were not sure how Michael would react."

"We were afraid for her." Added Ernest.

< 386 >

"But what about Jillian? Naturally, it would have brought her great joy to know that her child was alive. Did you not think of that?" William tenderly asked.

"Yes, we thought about Jillian all the time. However, something changed with her after weeks, and you did not make it to Cardiff. She began to act oddly. Some days she would not leave her room, and other days she would talk as if you were arriving later in the day...." Laurie cut in, "And she believed that it had only been two days since they arrived at the estate. We did not...." She paused, "Do not believe that she is of sound mind, William."

William brushed both hands on his face, running his temples and then wiping his eyes. He did not want to believe that Jillian had lost touch with reality.

Ernest continued, "I believe her mind worsened when Lucas was taken. At first, she blamed Michael."

"Most everyone did." Added Laurie.

"But that didn't last long. Jillian loved Michael." Added Ernest. "Everyone loved Michael, and he worked hard to keep everyone and everything together."

"I don't believe he ever gave up hope that you were still alive." Said Laurie.

"Of course, that hope was dashed when he found you in Bristol and..." he paused... "assumed you were dead. I think that was the turning point for Michael too. Everything changed when he returned to Cardiff and gave the news to Jillian and each of us."

"We were afraid to come back after Lady Chattingworth banished us from the estate. It was hard being close enough that we could have come back, but we did not know how or if we would have been received if we did return. For this reason, we decided to stay away."

"Of course, all of that changed one day." Said Laurie. "Ernest was hunting in the forest, and I decided to return to the estate. I did not tell him my plans because I did not want him to

< 387 >

talk me out of it. I had a powerful impression that I needed to go back. It was a very long walk, and there were many times on the trail that I almost turned around, but something was pulling me to the estate. When the house was within my sight, I began to hear a lot of commotion. I hid in the brush, close enough to hear but far enough away to not be seen. It was awful. I saw flames from the cottage. I knew exactly what had happened because I remembered the last words Michael had said to me. *"Laurie, I will do anything necessary to protect my family and loved ones. I will make any necessary sacrifice if I am forced to."* I knew that those were the sacrificial flames that Michael had lit to save the rest of his family and loved ones. Nevertheless, I could not allow little Sarah to die. I never believed that she had contracted the plague. Obviously, I was right. I ran to the cottage, and while Michael was on the other side, I quickly opened the door, ran inside, and found Sarah. The heat and smoke had overcome her, and she was unconscious but alive. I picked her up and ran out of the house. The flames followed me and caught my dress on fire. I felt the heat on the back of my legs as I ran, but at that moment, nothing mattered but Sarah. I ran into the forest with her. After we had cleared the estate, I ran into the stream and doused the flames. We both fell into the water. The sudden chill awakened her. She cried and called out for her mother. I calmed her down, picked her up, and walked as quickly as possible toward the cabin. Ernest, who discovered my absence, met me about halfway and helped us both back to our new home."

"William, I am convinced that God spoke to my Laurie and told her to go to the estate to rescue this beautiful little girl from an unnecessary death," said Ernest.

William leaned over and wrapped his arms around Laurie.

"Thank you so much, you dear woman. Thank you for listening to the still small voice of the Spirit."

< 388 >

William held back the tears as he hugged her. Sarah ran to him, and he brought her into his embrace. Looking down, he noticed Laurie's dress had raised over her left calf. He could see discolored scarring along the back of her leg, which was a testament to him of her love for Sarah.

"You see, William, we were afraid to return to the estate, and we did not know how to do or how long to separate ourselves from our friends and loved ones. From time to time, I would ride to the edge of the forest, just close enough to see that all was well, but never close enough to been seen," said Ernest.

"We had concluded that we would spend the rest of our lives here. How could we have known that you and Lucas would show up here?" Laurie said.

William asked, "Do you know what happened to the estate? How did it burn down?"

"We do not know. We heard yelling and screaming, and then we saw the smoke and the flames later." Ernest said.

"But we were afraid that if we got any closer, the men would find us." Stated Laurie. "So we went back to the cabin and prayed that God would protect the estate's inhabitants."

"We don't know who did it. However, we do believe that your family survived. The day after the fire, I went to the estate. I discovered that the carriage house was still standing, and the carriage, a cart, and the horses were gone. The tracks were fresh. I knew it was your family who had left the estate because there were several dead bodies on the grounds around the charred remains of the estate." Explained Ernest.

"It was also obvious that Michael defended your family quite well."

"That, he did." Added William.

"William, we know that Michael is a good man. We were just not sure of his state of mind. That is the only reason we never went back with Sarah. We struggled many times with the desire to return. We prayed for God to tell us when, or if, we should take Sarah back. But the answer never came." Said

< 389 >

Ernest, with tears in his eyes. Laurie reached for him and placed her arm around him.

"Ernest and Laurie, I understand the dilemma that was yours. I do not hold any ill feelings toward either of you, and I have nothing but love and gratitude that you saved my daughter. I am eternally in your debt."

Laurie wrapped her arms around William and said, "Oh, William, this is a day we never expected. God has answered our prayers with a reply truly Heaven sent." She kissed his cheek and reached out for Lucas and Sarah, who each joined the embrace.

After another hour of catching up, Laurie fixed a straw bed in the main room. William, Lucas, and Sarah snuggled together. The children were asleep in moments; William, however, lay awake for quite some time thinking about Jillian and his love for her. He offered a prayer to God. *"Oh, dear Father, He who has been my friend and constant companion has saved my life numerous times; I thank thee for all that thou hast given me. I thank thee for reuniting me with my little ones. I thank thee for keeping them safe. I thank thee for my dear friends Ernest and Laurie. Please, dear God, bless them always. And Father, please, wherever they might be, please bless Jillian and Michael and all those who travel with them. Please keep them safe, and give me the guidance to find them. And Father, if it is thy will, please let my beloved wife return to me with all her cognizance, heart, and mind. My life, my gratitude, and my heart are in thy care. I remain thy loyal servant, in the name of thy Son, even Jesus Christ, Amen!"*

< 390 >

Chapter Twenty-Five
Devine Intervention

"Quickly! Help me get him on the ground." Dom Gordon yelled as Brother Richard helped him carry Michael to a soft grassy area. Angelia climbed out of the carriage, holding Faith in one arm, and walked behind the monks.

"Oh, dear God," Cried Angelia as she caressed Michael's forehead. "Is he dead? Is Michael dead?" She asked as the monks carefully placed him on the grass.

"No, he is not. He is still breathing." Said Dom Gordon. "Please, give me some room," He asked as he held his arm out, keeping Angelia back. He took the top of Michael's tunic and tore it below his chest, revealing the wound. Michael opened his eyes and began to breathe deeply. Angelia leaned over and kissed his face.

"Angelia, please give me some room to tend to his wound." Asked Dom Gordon.

She leaned back and smiled while still holding Faith.

"How bad is it?" Asked Michael. Dom tore a small piece of Michael's tunic and brushed it over the wound. Michael flinched and took in a deep breath. "Ouch! Said Michael as the cloth passed over the wound. Dom Gordon took Michael's hand and placed it on the fabric over the wound.

"Keep some pressure on it. There does not appear to be a lot of blood coming from the wound. I would guess the knife pierced between these two ribs and into your muscle perhaps two inches." Said Dom Gordon as he traced his fingers around the area. He looked up at Angelia and said, "There are some herb roots in one of the bags on the cart. Can you please retrieve them and bring them to me?"

Angelica handed Faith to Brother Richard and ran to the cart. She found the bag and gave it to Dom Gordon.

< 391 >

"Michael, keep the pressure on the wound while I mix up a poultice to place on the wound." He took a small bowl and poured some water into it, then broke some of the herbs and ground them into a thick dressing.

"Oh, dear Michael, I thought you were dead," cried Angelia. She knelt next to him and took his other hand.

"I will be fine, my love. Although the pain is intense, I do not believe the blade punctured anything important." He smiled. He looked up at the carriage and asked, "Where is mother?"

"Michael, it was your mother who did this to you." Said Angelia. She looked at Michael and frowned.

"Angelia, I believe that she was dreaming at the time, and she was not awake and conscious of what she was doing," Michael replied as he looked at Angelia, hoping that she would accept his reasoning.

"Michael, she tried to kill you!" Said Angelia as she looked to the carriage and then back at Michael. "She frightens me." She began to sob.

Michael lifted his right arm and touched Angelia's cheek. She placed her hand over his and nestled her head into her shoulder.

"Michael, I am so afraid. What if she does something like this again? Then what?" She asked.

"Angelia, I know that her actions could have taken my life, but what would you have me do with her? Shall we leave her here to fend for herself?" Michael asked, knowing that his questions were purely rhetorical.

"I know, Michael. I know." Responded Angelia, still holding her hand over Michael's. "But what are we to do? How can we ensure the safety of the others?"

Michael smiled at Angelia and said, "I suppose that we first must make sure that she does not have access to anything that could cause harm to another. I do not believe she was awake or aware of what she was doing. Surely you don't

< 392 >

believe that she would knowingly hurt me, or anyone else, for that matter?" He asked.

Kemp climbed into the carriage. He saw Jillian sitting back in her seat, shaking her head. She looked at him, her eyes filled with tears. "Is he dead? Is my Michael dead?" She sobbed as she spoke.

"No, he is not dead, Lady Beorn. He is alive?" Kemp said.

"Tell him that I am sorry. Tell him that I love him." She said. "I do not know how it happened. I would never hurt Michael." She said through continuous sobs.

Kemp reached out, took her hand, and kissed it.

"Michael knows that it was an accident. He will recover."

"Thank you, my child. Thank you!" Jillian said as she slowly pulled back her hand, held it with the other, and placed her hands on her lap.

As Dom packed the wound with the herbal poultice, Michael flinched. "I am sorry, Michael. I don't mean to hurt you."

"I will be okay, Dom. Thank you for your care."

"Hold the compress tightly against your chest while I fetch some more cloth to wrap around you, to keep it over the wound." Dom walked back to the cart and looked for more material.

"Brother Richard, can you help me to my feet?" Michael asked.

"No, Michael, you must not sit up yet." Said Angelia.

"I will be okay, Angelia. The pain has subsided, and I do not believe I am bleeding anymore either." He looked at Brother Richard and raised his right arm while holding the compress against his chest with his left. Brother Richard took his hand and gently helped him stand. Michael took a deep breath after standing, and he slowly exhaled. "Thank you, Brother Richard."

< 393 >

He looked at Angelia. "I do believe that I will be fine." She leaned in and kissed his lips. She carefully wrapped her arms around him and buried her face into his neck.

"Oh, Michael, I thought you were dead, and I am so happy I was wrong." She cried as she held him. He caressed her head and then pulled away from her.

"I love you, my dear. My life has again been spared, and I thank God for that." He said. He looked at the carriage and added, "I need to see my mother." He turned and walked to the carriage. Dom Gordon came running with some cloth.

"Michael, wait! I have found some more cloth. Let me bind the dressing so that it does not come off." He said. He wrapped the cloth around Michael's chest and back several times. He then tore it and tied it in place.

"How are you feeling, Michael?" He asked.

"I am feeling well. A bit dizzy, but well." Michael answered.

"I do not believe that you have lost much blood. You should be fine if we keep the dressing tight and constant pressure against the wound. The more pressure you apply, the less blood flow to the area. Do you understand? Asked Dom Gordon.

"Yes, I understand. Thank you very much for your help. Can you help me into the carriage to see my mother?" Michael asked.

"Of course," He helped Michael raise his leg to the first step. Michael lifted his other leg and slowly climbed into the carriage. Angelia climbed in behind him. Jillian was still sitting in her seat, looking out of the window on the other side. She did not seem to notice Michael. He reached over to her and touched her left shoulder. Angelia placed her hand on Michael's right shoulder.

"Mother," Michael said. Jillian slowly turned her head to Michael. She smiled.

< 394 >

"Michael," She said as if surprised to see him. She looked back to the window. "Do you see them?" She asked.

Michael shook his head. He looked out the window and asked,

"See who, mother?"

"The angels." She smiled, then frowned. "Oh, they are gone now." She said.

Michael looked back at Angelia. She shook her head, still concerned for him to be near Jillian. He looked back at Jillian, who had returned to looking out the window.

"Look, Michael!" She said. "The bird is still there."

"What bird?" Asked Michael.

"The white bird. It came with the angels. Do you see it? Still sitting on that branch." Do you see it, Michael?" She asked while touching her finger to the glass.

Michael looked out the window again. This time, he saw the bird. It looked at him and then flew away. He felt a chill and a flash of memory.

"Oh, there it goes!" Goodbye, little bird," said Jillian, as she waived. "See you next time."

Michael sat next to Jillian and asked, "Mother, are you feeling well?"

She smiled at him and replied, "Why yes, I feel just fine. And how are you, my son?"

She appeared to have no memory of the recent events. Michael wanted to talk to her about what had happened, but it was evident that she had, once again, gone to another place, a happy place in her mind. He thought about the bird and remembered so many times seeing a bird before or just after painful events in his life.

"I am fine, mother." He answered. "How many angels were there?" He asked.

"Just two. A man and a woman.

"Have you seen them before?" Michael asked.

"Yes, a few times."

< 395 >

Angelia tugged on Michael's shoulder. He motioned for her to sit on the seat across from him. She sat down and listened.

"Do you know why they were here?" Michael asked.

"I am not sure, Michael. But they have been with us since we left Cardiff."

Michael looked at Angelia. She frowned, slowly shook her head, and whispered, "I cannot do this, Michael. I cannot listen to this madness."

Michael smiled at her and whispered, "I understand; please give me just a moment." He asked. He turned to Jillian and asked, "Why are they following us, mother?"

She smiled, looked at him, and said, "They are protecting us!"

"Protecting us from what?" Michael asked.

"From the others," She said matter-of-factly.

"Which others?" Michael asked.

"The others who want to hurt us," She said.

"Michael, please, do not do this. Not now." Angelia pleaded.

Jillian looked at Angelia and said, "But they are protecting you too, my dear, and your unborn child."

Angelia placed her hand over her mouth and shook her head. "Michael, I cannot listen to this." She began to cry. Michael took her hand and held it tightly. He looked back at Jillian and asked,

"Mother, how could you know such things? Angelia is not with child?'

Jillian smiled and said, "I only know what I am told, Michael. God has placed your son in her womb. All is well now, and the angels are no longer needed here." She turned her head and looked out the window.

Angelia sobbed quietly and lowered her head. Michael kissed Jillian on the cheek and then sat next to Angelia. He

< 396 >

whispered in her ear, "I am sorry, my love, that my mother has made you uncomfortable."

"Michael, I am afraid to be in here with her. I fear for Faith. She could have killed you with that knife. Where did she get it?"

"It was placed in the slider next to her seat. My father put one in both sliders for protection." He leaned over her and slid open the small compartment next to her. "See, here is the other."

"Please take it, Michael. I will not feel safe knowing it is here, especially if she knows it is here."

Michael took the knife and slid it into a pocket in his tunic. "Do not worry; I will keep it safe."

Dom Gordon and Brother Richard walked up to the open carriage door and looked in.

"Michael, how are you feeling?" Asked Dom Gordon.

"I think I am going to be fine, Dom. Thank you for attending to my wound."

"What wound?" Asked Jillian.

"It is nothing, mother."

The monks looked at one another. Everyone knew Jillian was not in the right frame of mind and was getting worse.

"Can I speak to you alone, Michael?" Asked Dom Gordon.

"Of course," Michael replied. He climbed out of the carriage. Brother Richard handed Faith back to Angelia, and Michael and Dom Gordon walked behind the carriage to the wagon.

"Michael, you realize that she could have killed you if that knife was in a different spot or went further into your chest." Said Dom Gordon.

"Yes, Dom, I know that."

"What are we going to do with her?" He asked.

"What do you mean, do with her?" Michael asked.

< 397 >

"Well, we cannot leave her alone." The monk said, and he was surprised that Michael did not seem to understand the severity of his concern.

"She is not alone. Angelia and Faith are with her."

"Michael, does it not concern you to have your wife and daughter in the carriage with her?"

"No. It does not concern me. What happened was an accident."

"An accident?" Asked Dom with a scowl on his face. "She lunged at you with a knife? How is that an accident?" He asked incredulously.

Michael hesitated before responding. "She did not lunge at me," Michael answered.

"You have a wound in your chest, Michael! It is quite evident that she was aiming for you!"

Michael did not want to tell the priest that the knife was meant for Angelia. He knew that Jillian was only dreaming and that she would never intentionally hurt anyone. He also believed that there were no other weapons within reach of Jillian if she had another bad dream.

"She was dreaming, Dom. That is all. A bad dream."

Dom shook his head. "Michael, I know you love your mother; however, you must accept that she is dangerous and getting worse. We must do something."

"I understand that she is getting worse. Surely, the stress of all that has happened, and this endless journey also plays a role in her behavior. I can only hope that she will return to herself once we get situated."

Dom Gordon slowly shook his head and said, "Alright then. It was a nightmare. But are you comfortable with her being there with your wife and child?"

"Yes, I am," Michael responded.

"May I suggest that you also ride in there with them?"

Michael shook his head.

< 398 >

"Michael, it is only for a short time. Your body needs time to heal, and it would be much more comfortable in there than sitting on a hard bench in front of the carriage. I will have Brother Richard ride with Kemp. You need to rest so that your wound can heal."

Michael did not respond. "I insist, Michael!" He added.

Michael nodded. He climbed into the carriage and sat next to Jillian, who had fallen asleep on a pillow next to the window. Angelia held Faith, who was also asleep. Michael kissed her hand and leaned his head back on the comfortable upholstered seat. Brother Richard climbed into the carriage and sat next to Kemp while Dom Gordon took the reins of the cart behind. Their journey continued.

Michael closed his eyes and thought about the angels. He wondered if they were simply a figment of the imagination of his ailing mother or

if somehow God did send angels to be with them. He decided to accept the latter, which brought him a moment of peace until the white bird entered his mind.

< 399 >

Chapter Twenty-Six
The Search

The following day Laurie prepared breakfast. After the morning meal. While Laurie cleaned the dishes, Ernest asked,

"William, what are your plans from here?"

William shook his head and looked over at Lucas and Sarah sitting on the floor, playing with a small pebble, and laughing.

"I do not know Ernest. It all seemed so obvious as I traveled with Lucas to Cardiff. I imagined being reunited with Jillian, Sarah, Michael, each of you, and the others who worked and lived in my wife's childhood home. I never could have anticipated such a travesty."

Laurie looked at the men and offered a sympathetic smile. She turned back to the dishes.

"I know it is all quite a shock, William. No one would have ever anticipated such things could happen," said Ernest.

"I have seen much in the last two years, Ernest, things that I will never forget and some things that I would like to forget. Yet through it all, I have never felt alone. God has been with me, even in my darkest times." He paused, held back his emotion, and continued. "And I do not believe that he has left me or any of us now. I know my beautiful wife and son Michael are out there somewhere, and I must find them."

"But, where will you look, William? How will you find them?" Asked Laurie.

"I must have faith that God in his great mercy will lead me to them," William said. "Does it not seem miraculous that each of us is here at this moment, alive and well, when so many are dead?" William asked as he stared across the room.

< 400 >

He continued, "I have seen death and destruction everywhere I have traveled in the last two years. I thank God every day for my life and for the life of my family and loved ones. There must be a reason that he has allowed each of us to live."

Ernest nodded his head in agreement. "Do you believe they are returning to Bristol, William?" Asked Ernest.

"I fear what Michael will find in Bristol; I do not know the condition of things there," William stated.

"I assume that it is also a probability that they are heading to London, the largest city, and one might think that there is a greater chance that normalcy has returned to a town the size of London," said Ernest.

"I have a dear friend just outside of London. He is waiting for my return." Said, William.

"But what will you do in London? Your home is in Bristol. Shouldn't you return there?" Laurie questioned.

"It is my intention to return to Bristol. However, I have some belongings hidden in a lower room in London." William added.

"What kind of belongings, may I ask?" Said Laurie.

William thought for a moment and then remembered. "Gold, silver, and gems," William said as the memory came to him. "It is enough wealth to last for years. If I am to return to Bristol, I must ensure I have sufficient coinage for my needs."

If you traveled alone, you could make it there within three days," said Ernest.

"Ernest," William said," I have no intention of traveling alone. I have been reunited with my dear little ones; I cannot allow them to be separated from me again."

"But, how will you travel on one horse with the two children?" Asked Laurie.

"I had hoped that you and Ernest would come with us," William said.

< 401 >

Laurie looked at Ernest. Tears filled her eyes. She wiped her hands on a small towel, stood beside Ernest, and said, "Oh, William, we would love to go with you, but we are old and would be useless to you."

"Old? Useless? William questioned. "Nonsense! There is plenty of room on the estate in Bristol. Moreover, you are not old! Laurie, you have mothered my child for months. I could most definitely use your help back in Bristol. Besides, I cannot simply leave the both of you here, alone and unprotected."

Laurie and Ernest looked at one another and then back at William. Ernest said, "William, we would love to go with you, but we would slow you down. We can manage here."

"Ernest, you know as well as I that it is not safe for you here. Yes, I am anxious to find my wife and son, but I am willing to travel at whatever pace is needed to get my loved ones back to Bristol."

Laurie smiled and looked at Ernest. "It is your decision, dear. I will support whatever you decide." Said Laurie. Ernest looked back at William.

"We have a small wagon, one horse, a cow, and six chickens. Would you have a place for all ten of us on your estate in Bristol?" Asked Ernest.

William laughed and replied, "Well, it may be a tight squeeze, but I believe it would be able to accommodate all of you." They all laughed.

Laurie walked to William and wrapped her arms around his neck. "Oh, William, I am so thankful that God has spared your life and brought you back to us. I am so grateful," Laurie said as tears fell down her cheeks.

"As am I," William responded. "As am I."

Within an hour, they had caged the chickens, packed their meager belongings, hitched the horse to the cart, and tied the cow on a rope behind it. William rode in front on his horse, and Ernest, Laurie, and the children rode in the wagon. The sun

< 402 >

was shining, and the skies were clear as they started their journey home. William thought about his life in Bristol. He remembered the peace and comfort he had there. He remembered his friends and family, his light tower, and the time he spent there thinking and writing in his journal. He had forgotten about the journal, and the memory brought him great joy as he realized that he had many pages of his thoughts hidden behind a brick in the tower. He looked forward to returning to Bristol to read his journal and catching up and writing down all that had happened since the day he sent his beautiful wife and children to Cardiff. Life had changed in ways he never could have imagined. He was ready to return to Bristol, peace, safety, and the warmth and love of his God above.

"What do you think we will find when we get to London, Brother Richard?" Asked Kemp.

I hope we will find my brothers all alive and well." He said.

"But what if they are not alive and well? What if all of London had been destroyed by the sickness. Then what will we do?" Asked Kemp.

Brother Richard thought a moment and said, "I guess we will take whatever the Lord gives us." He sighed. "And nothing more."

Kemp was quiet for several minutes. He then looked at Brother Richard and asked, "Why do you put such faith in a God you cannot see?" He added, "But if he is real, in a God who is so merciless?"

Brother Richard did not anticipate such a question from Kemp. He replied, "My son, why would you ask such a question? Surely, you do not doubt the existence of God."

"If you had asked me that a few days ago, my answer would be that I do not doubt his existence. But today, I do not

< 403 >

believe in him anymore." Kemp said as he defiantly gazed forward.

Brother Richard took a breath and said, "That must be sad for God to hear because he still believes in you."

"If there were a God, he would not have let my family die, and he would not have allowed all the others to die."

"So, you tell me that you only believe in God when life is well and you are happy. But when things get tough, when you are hurt or sad, you no longer believe in him."

"I am telling you that if he existed that he would not allow people to die, he would not allow such pain and sorrow."

Brother Richard refuted Kemp's logic by saying, "My child, God knows pain and sorrow better than anyone. I can only imagine his pain and sorrow as his son was beaten by evil men, scourged by non-believers, and crucified by the people he came to save.   In fact, God's pain and suffering were so great that he caused the earth to shake and darkness to cover the land for three days. If he felt the pain and suffering of his only begotten son, why do you think he does not feel your pain and suffering?"

"But why does he do it?" Demanded Kemp. "If he loves us so much, why does he allow such things to happen?"

Brother Richard replied, "There is wisdom in everything God does."

Kemp began to tremble as he spoke. "What wisdom is there in taking away the family of a ten-year-old boy and causing him to be alone, to be an orphan?" He cried.

Brother Richard put his arm around the shoulder of the crying boy and pulled him close.

"Kemp, you are not alone. In God's wisdom, you have been placed with people who will love you, treat you with kindness, and consider you one of their own. I do not have all of the answers. Moreover, I do not have the answers you are looking for either. However, I do know that God never leaves us alone. I know that his ways are not ours, and sometimes we

< 404 >

can live an entire lifetime and still not completely understand his plan for us. I also know that your family is safe and happy in the arms of a loving God and king. They watch over you now, with the angels of heaven. Kemp, I believe God has a great work for you because it has been by his hand that you have been spared, surely for a much greater purpose than either of us can know at this time." Kemp listened. He sat back up, wiped his tears, and said,

"Thank you, Brother Richard. I want to believe in God again, and I want to be a good person. And I want to make my father proud."

"Kemp, your father is proud of you. He was proud of you the day he told you to run. He was pleased that you listened, were obedient, and that do to such, you will one day be a father, and in doing so, will continue the legacy that your father has given you."

Kemp cried. Brother Richard held him tightly and tried to console him.

"We cannot choose the situations that come to us in life, but we can choose how we react to them. When bad things happen, we can choose to be bitter and ungrateful and blame it on God. Alternatively, we can choose to learn, be humbled by our experiences, and ask God to help us understand and grow with each trial, setback, or tragedy. Too often, people think that life should be comfortable. But comfortable makes us weak. The farmer who did not have to plant, weed, water, and harvest would not appreciate the fruit if he did not labor for it. The King would become complacent if he never had to defend his kingdom. And from that complacency would come utter destruction if he decided that he did not need an army because there was never a threat to his kingdom. Opposition can make you stronger or weaker, but it is entirely your choice. Kemp, do you believe that you are the master of your soul? Do you believe that you can make your own choices?"

Kemp nodded. "I guess so."

< 405 >

"Then let that belief burn in your soul. Let that belief remind you that you are in control of your life and how you react to whatever comes your way. I promise you that as you do, your sorrow and heartache will always be temporary, and your happiness and gratefulness will be eternal.

"Thank you, Brother Richard. I am happy that God put you in my life. I hope that I can be just like you one day."

Brother Richard smiled and said, "Oh my boy, you will be much greater than I, and you will do much greater things. This I know. This I know." He smiled at Kemp and then focused on the long trail to London.

Several hours passed, and they stopped to rest for the night. Dom Gordon took the lead to allow Michael time to recover from his wound.

"When was the last time you checked on them?" Asked Dom Gordon as he stood next to the carriage.

Brother Richard slid the wooden panel back and looked into the carriage. Everyone was asleep.

"They are all sleeping. Should we wake them food to eat?" Asked Brother Richard.

"No, let them rest. We can prepare some food, and they can eat it if they wake in the night." Said Dom Gordon.

He looked at Brother Richard, "You do realize that the monastery is probably just a couple of hours from here?"

"If it is that close, should not we keep going?" Asked Brother Richard.

"No, the horses are tired; they have walked with little food and water all day. Besides, it is not safe to travel at night."

Kemp spoke up, "But we have not seen anyone all day. Why should we expect to see someone just because the sun has gone down?"

< 406 >

Dom Gordon smiled at him and responded, "My son, we have been blessed with many things this day. God has spared the life of our dear Michael, and he has given us safe passage. I do not believe in testing God. Our horses are tired, we are tired, and the Spirit tells me that we should stop and rest before going any further. Therefore, we will rest here until morning."

Dom Gordon smiled. Brother Richard nodded.

They found an open area off the side of the path and did their best to hide the carriage, the wagon, and the horses. After eating, Brother Richard said, "I will take the first watch."

"No, you will not. I will take the first watch," said Michael as he climbed out of the carriage.

"Michael, how are you feeling?" Asked Dom Gordon.

"Remarkably well. Thank you." He responded.

"How is the pain?" Asked Brother Richard.

"Actually, I do not feel any pain." He touched the padding over the wound and flinched. "Well, as long as I don't touch the wound, that is." They each smiled.

"You need to rest. We can handle the watch this evening." Said Dom Gordon.

"I have rested most of the day. I am feeling well and very much awake. Each of you needs to rest." Michael said.

Dom Gordon stretched and yawned. Brother Richard started to speak when Dom Gordon cut him off.

"There is no use arguing with Michael. If he has made up his mind, neither of us changes it. Come, we can make a spot to rest on the wagon."

Michael looked at Kemp and said, "Kemp. You can sleep in the carriage next to my mother."

Kemp looked at Brother Richard and then back at Michael. Michael could tell that he was concerned.

"You will be fine and safe. I assure you."

Michael helped him into the carriage. Dom Gordon turned and began to walk to the wagon. Brother Richard said, "Go ahead, Father; I will be there in a moment; I want to speak

< 407 >

to Michael first." The priest nodded and went back to the wagon. Michael and Brother Richard climbed onto the seat in front of the carriage.

"What is it, Brother Richard? What did you want to talk about?" Asked Michael.

Brother Richard looked into the carriage. He noticed that Kemp had fallen asleep on the seat next to Jillian. He looked at Michael and said,

"Michael, what happens if we make it to the monastery in London and find no one there, or worse, find our friends all dead? Then what?"

"Then we go to Bristol."

"That is it? We just go to Bristol?"

"Yes, that is it. Where else would we go?" Why are you asking me this?"

"It is the boy."

"Kemp?" Michael asked.

"Yes, he is struggling with his faith in God."

Michael smiled and said, "Then he is becoming a man."

"How do you relate lacking faith in God to becoming a man?" Asked Brother Richard. "I do not see the correlation."

"When I was a child, I did childish things. I also believed in God, not because of some great faith-promoting experience, but because it was the thing to do. But when I became a man, I began to question everything. If there was a God, I wanted to know him, not just be told such a thing. I have told you much of my life's difficulties, Brother Richard. You know what I have been through. Of course, I do not say that to diminish the trials in your life; we all have them. Nevertheless, God knows me, he knows you, and he knows that little boy in there. He knows when we are ready for the next trial in life. Sometimes he allows us to experience much more than we believe we can handle. In the moment, we think we have reached our limit and that either we will die or just give up. But God doesn't let either happen. Sometimes he has to take away

< 408 >

everything we love to leave us feeling alone and vulnerable. At that point, we realize that we are not alone but with God. It is at that point that we understand his great love for us. It is at that point that we begin to recognize our potential, and we readjust our goals to be in line with what God wants for us. I understand the pain that child feels. I know the vast emptiness he feels at the loss of his family. And I know that God has a plan for him. It does not matter what or who we find at the monastery. What is important is that we keep moving in whatever direction God takes us."

"I appreciate your thoughts, Michael. Your life is a testament to me that God can change hearts and minds. You are a much better man than you were when we first met months ago."

"Thank you, Brother Richard, for helping me on my life's journey. My spirit is weak, but I strongly desire to know what God has in store for my loved ones and me. The boy will be okay; he is family now; you need not worry. Now, go and get some sleep. All will be well."

"Thank you, Michael. I will see you in a few hours."

Michael nodded as the monk left and headed back to the wagon. He took a deep breath, leaned back, and looked up to the heavens. Michael marveled at the myriad of stars, the clusters of light in faraway galaxies. He looked for the moon but could not find it. He then thought to himself. *When the moon is full and shining bright, it hides the mysteries of the heavens. Although it provides light and beauty, it keeps us from seeing everything behind it. It is like walking next to God as his brightness and glory keep us safe from everything we cannot see.* It reminded him that sometimes God needs to step away so that we can see all that is out there and see our potential, along with trials, tribulation, and the unknown.

The heavens were beautiful and eternal, but the moon was what he longed for this night. The moon and its light. As he gazed into the dark night sky, he noticed a light rising above

< 409 >

the horizon, and its brightness began to outshine the stars. He smiled as the light started to take shape and quickly overcame the sky. It was possibly the largest full moon he had ever seen. He felt tremendous peace and love fill his soul as he watched God's glory shine above and around him. Tears rolled down his cheeks as he mouthed the words, "Thank you, Father, in Heaven. Thank you."

~*~*~

They ate a small breakfast of dried meat and fruit the next morning. They packed up and began the final leg of the journey. Jillian seemed to be content, although off somewhere in her own world. Michael was feeling strong, Angelia was excited at the prospect of sleeping in a real bed, and Dom Gordon and Brother Richard were hopeful about finding the monks alive and well.

Michael rode in the front of the carriage with Kemp while the monks rode in the wagon behind. Two hours quickly passed, and signs of civilization began to appear. Kemp pointed at a farmhouse ahead. He smiled at Michael when they noticed children playing. Michael saw a woman beating a rug hung on a line. The closer they got, the more life they saw. Houses began to appear on both sides of the trail. The trail became a road that led into the city of London. They came to a fork in the road; the left led into the city, and the right led away from it.

"Turn right!" Yelled Dom Gordon from behind. Michael acknowledged him and turned the horses to the right. Dom Gordon drove the wagon past the carriage and waved. "It is not far from here. I will lead us there." He said.

A few minutes later, the steeple of the monastery appeared through the tops of the trees.

"There it is!" Yelled Dom Gordon with the enthusiasm of a child in a candy store. He was relieved to finally be arriving at what he hoped would be his new home. More importantly, he was excited to be united with his friends and

< 410 >

brothers. The road curved, and another small drive led to the impressive building, which appeared intact. Dom Gordon stopped the wagon in front of the building. He and Brother Richard jumped off the wagon and motioned for Michael to come.

"You stay with the women until I come out and tell you if it is safe." Said, Michael. Kemp nodded. "And remember, the crossbow is under your seat; be prepared to use it if necessary." Kemp smiled at Michael, having no idea how to use the weapon but did not want Michael to know.

Michael joined the monks, and the three walked to the massive front door. Brother Richard lifted the large knocker and slammed it against the door three times. A few moments later, someone behind the door opened a small peephole and looked through it.

The person behind the door asked, "What is wanted?"

"I am Dom Gordon, with my friend Brother Richard and Michael Beorn of Bristol. We have come to see our friends and are looking for Brother Simon, Brother Andres...." The man behind the door shut the peephole. Several loud mechanisms clinked, and then they heard the sound of a giant thud. The door opened, revealing a large gathering of monks. Dom Gordon smiled as he looked into the doorway.

Standing in front of the monks was Brother Simon. He spoke first, "My dearest Dom Gordon and Brother Richard, where have you been?"

He raised his arms and walked forward, engulfing the men in the crowd of monks. Tears of joy and happy greetings rang out in the group of monks. Dom Gordon introduced Michael. Brother Richard and two monks went to the carriage, gathered the others and some of their belongings, and took them into the building. Brother Simon introduced Father Carrington, who officiated at the monastery. Michael and Angelia were taken to a room on the second floor and told that it would be theirs as long as they stayed. Faith and Kemp were put in an

< 411 >

adjoining room. Jillian was given a room across the hall. The monks spent the day catching up on all that had happened. Michael, Angelia, Jillian, and the children rested.

As Michael lay on the bed, Angelia snuggled next to him with her head on his outstretched arm. With his eyes closed, he thought about the journey and the things that had happened along the way. Although he knew it was possible there would be challenges along the way, he did not expect to add an orphaned boy to their family, nor did he expect that Jillian would attack him while having a nightmare and nearly take his life. The thought of the stab in his side caused him discomfort. He shifted a bit, and Angelia, now asleep, moved her position too. Kemp had become part of the family so quickly that it seemed odd he had not always been with them. Michael enjoyed a brief moment of having a little brother until the thought of Lucas entered his mind. He wondered if it was possible for Lucas to still be alive. *"Oh God, if Lucas is still on this earth and in thy care, please let us be reunited one day. Keep him safe,"* he thought to himself. He felt a tear run down the side of his face.

Memories of Lucas began to race through his mind. He remembered how Lucas always ran to him, hugged him, and held him tightly. He recalled Lucas asking Michael to tell him a story or to race him to the barn. The barn. He remembered Elizabeth In the barn being attacked by the evil men. He remembered his rage as he killed the man on top of her. He felt his heart beating faster and harder as the memories flooded his mind. And then he heard Elizabeth telling him that one of the men had taken Lucas. Michael opened his eyes, and the memories stopped. *"If only I had looked further into the barn instead of looking at the man attacking Elizabeth. I would have seen the other person taking Lucas. I could have stopped him."* He thought. He then realized the man would have killed her if he had not been focused on Elizabeth. He knew he did

< 412 >

the best he could, and although Lucas was taken, saving Elizabeth was right. He turned his head away from Angelia and toward the open window. His thought turned to Jillian. His heart ached for her. It seemed that everything that had happened affected her the hardest. At first, she was strong, determined, and self-sufficient. But now, her entire world turned upside down, had left her somewhere else, only to return for short periods before retreating again. He turned his back toward Angelia. He never thought he could love anyone like he loved Elizabeth. Losing her seemed to be his breaking point after losing so many others. He felt ashamed at the hardness he had harbored against God, in his heart, for so long, especially now that God had given him Angelia. Michael thought everyone had been through so much and lost so many, but no one as much as Jillian. He wondered if she would ever come back to this life. He pondered how he would cope if she got worse. He closed his eyes and asked God to help her return and return to those still left behind. He breathed deeply and smiled at the memory of how she used to be.

"That was an excellent meal, my friends," Michael said.

"We are joyful that you are here with us and that God has brought our brothers to us too," said Brother Simon as he looked around the table. "These are challenging times. We have each lost good friends. The world is in an uproar. I do not know if God is this plague's author or finisher." He added.

Father Carrington stood and said, "God is the author of all things. He creates, he destroys. He creates again. And we are but pawns in his eternal game. Our moves are his; we have no control, and only he knows the outcome. Who are we to question his ways or his means? We must accept what we have no control over. We must adhere to God's will, whatever it may be."

< 413 >

The room grew silent. The monks each lowered their heads in reverence. Michael sensed a little tension brewing in the chamber. The monk's comments seemed harsh and provided no solace for the loss that each had endured. Suddenly, Brother Richard lifted his head and pulled the hood back. Dom Gordon was seated next to Brother Richard. His eyes grew big, and he gently nudged Brother Richard and whispered, "Don't say it!"

The other monks looked up. Brother Richard looked at Father Carrington and said, "Father, although I appreciate your words, I must take issue with some of them."

The monk raised an eyebrow and slowly turned his head toward Brother Richard.

"Oh? And what is that?" He asked.

Brother Richard stood and spoke.

"If we assume that everything that happens in this world is by predesign, that no one has control over their own actions, that God is the grand puppet master who controls every jot and tittle, then there is no reason for you or me to do anything."

The monks slowly looked at one another, each afraid to participate in the discussion. Dom Gordon lowered his head and muttered a soft pleading to God to end the conversation. Father Carrington raised the other eyebrow and started to speak, but Brother Richard cut him off and picked up where he left.

"Why should I exert any strength or energy to help myself or help another if I have no control over my actions? Why should I think for myself if God does all of the thinking? Why should I try to do good if my actions are already predetermined? Why should I listen to you if there is no consequence for my belief or unbelief?"

"Brother Richard, that is enough!" said Dom Gordon.

"Is it enough?" asked Brother Richard. "I suppose God will shut me down when I have said all he wants me to say. After all, he is in charge, anything that happens is not only his will but his design, so there is nothing I can say or do that he

< 414 >

does not want me to say or do. At least your logic would dictate such a belief."

One of the other monks quietly chuckled. Father Carrington looked toward him, still maintaining a stern expression. He started to speak when Brother Richard cut him off again and continued, "Why must we always blame God when bad things happen? Is it not possible that sometimes bad things happen due to a series of events that were put into motion from a single starting point? Did God not put Adam and Eve on this earth and give them commandments? If there was no agency, then there could be no accountability? How could we blame Eve for being the first to sin if she was not responsible for her actions? Your logic would mean that her actions were actually God's actions and that God broke his own commandment, that God sinned."

Dom Gordon lowered his head. The others in the room slowly fixed their eyes on Father Carrington. It was apparent to them that Brother Richard had made a solid argument for his point of view.

Father Carrington slowly breathed in as if to temper his response. He spoke. "I suppose you have made a point. Perhaps I should clarify my remarks." Father Carrington said in an almost emotionless tone. "God is the author of the great plan. He knows the beginning from the end. He knows each of us personally and intimately. He knows the choices we will make in a given situation."

Brother Richard interjected, "Most likely make. He knows us like children. He knows that in a given situation, we will 'most likely' make a certain choice. But he does not take that choice from us and allows us to choose for ourselves."

Dom Gordon kept his eyes closed and slowly shook his head, not because he disagreed with Brother Richard but because of the boldness of his challenge to Father Carrington.

"Brother Richard," asked Father Carrington, "may I continue...uninterrupted, please?"

< 415 >

"Yes, of course. Forgive my impertinence. I'm not sure what came over me." Said Brother Richard as he slowly sat down.

Dom Gordon quietly muttered to himself, 'the devil, no doubt."

"As I was saying," stated Father Carrington, "God is in control. If we give him thanks for good in our lives, we must also give him thanks for the bad. For how can we know the sweet if we never taste bitter?" He stood; everyone else stood. Brother Richard began to speak again until he felt Michael squeeze his arm. Michael looked at him and winked, and gave a slight nod. He whispered, "He got your point. Let it alone."

Michael looked at the priest and said, "Father Carrington, we will be leaving in the morning. Again, I thank you profoundly for your hospitality and charity to my family and me."

"You are most welcome, my son." the monk replied. "But where will you go?" he asked. "There is no reason to leave so soon."

"We will continue to London, where we will make passage aboard a ship to Bristol, our home," Michael said.

"The mother city is not far from here, and I believe ships are sailing again. We will pray that your passage home is safe," added Father Carrington.

"Thank you, father." Michael graciously responded.

"Michael, thank you for bringing our brothers back into the fold. I am sure they will miss each of you." The priest concluded.

"They have become family to me." Michael looked at the others and added, "to us. It will be hard to part company."

< 416 >

Chapter Twenty-Seven
A Voice From The Dust

She awoke to his voice calling her. "Jillian! Jillian, my love, where are you? " the voice echoed in the wind. Jillian sat up in her bed, startled by the sound. She smiled and attempted to look through the darkened room of a moonless night but could barely make out the outline of the bedroom doorframe. She climbed out of bed, stepped into her slippers, and draped herself with the robe that had been laid across the foot of her bed. At first, she wanted to yell back at him but didn't want to wake anyone else. But then she thought it was only fair since William had returned that everyone would like to know. She opened her mouth to call out to him and wake the others until a thought entered her mind. She wanted to be the first to greet him. She wanted to be the first to throw her arms around him and feel his strong and comforting embrace. *After all, she thought, I am his wife and deserve to be the first person he greets after such a long and arduous journey.* She closed her mouth and quietly opened the door. She stuck her head into the hall and looked both ways but could only see a faint candle quite a distance in a holder near the stairway. She tiptoed down the long wooden hallway and past several other rooms as quietly as possible. She whispered, "William, I am coming, my love, I am coming."

Finally, she reached the end of the hall. She picked up the candle holder and held it in front of her to help illuminate the long stairway. She slowly and cautiously moved down each step, continually whispering, I am coming, my love. I am coming. When she reached the foyer, she looked around and back up the stairs to ensure no one had followed her. Seeing no one, she opened the large wooden door, slowly closed it behind

< 417 >

her,   and walked into the night. She raised the candle high above her head and in front of her.

"William?" she called out. "William, where are you? I am here for you." No answer came.

She looked to the left and then to the right. It was dark, with a thick fog all around her. She took several steps forward, staying on the cobblestone path that led to the dirt road they had traveled. When she reached the road, calling out to William again was safe. This time, she called louder, "William, where are you?"

Suddenly, she heard his voice. "I am here, my love. Come to me."

She squinted her eyes, still holding the candle high, and attempted to look through the fog and down the road.

"But I cannot see you. Where are you?" Jillian cried.

The voice came to her again, "I am here. Come to me."

Although she could still not see him, she began to walk in the direction from whence the voice seemed to travel.

"I'm coming, William! I'm coming!" She exclaimed as she began to scurry in excitement to the voice, she was hearing. She smiled. Her heart was filled with joy. She felt tears well in her eyes and roll down her cheeks.

"Oh, William, I have so much to tell you. So much has happened since we were last together."

She felt courage and strength and began running through the fog and down the road to meet her William. It became cumbersome to run with the candle, and she dropped it, grasped the sides of her robe, and lifted it above her ankles so that it didn't hamper her speed as she ran.

"William, I am coming for you. I've missed you, and now, finally, you are here!"

The candle holder rolled along the middle of the road, discharging the candle as it came to a stop. The fragile pleas of Jillian's soft voice slowly merged into the thick, dampness of the night.

< 418 >

~*~*~

Michael didn't sleep well. The morning seemed to come just moments after nightfall. He sat in bed and watched the sunbeams pass the curtains and into the room. Angelia woke and smiled at him. She lifted her hand, caressed his cheek, and said, "Well, my love, it is a new day. Let us pray that it is a good day."

He leaned over and gently kissed her lips. He looked into her eyes and replied, "Yes, let us pray it is."

He looked forward to a new day that would finally take him back to Bristol. He quietly climbed out of his bed and knelt beside it; Angelia knelt next to him. He began to pray.

"Dear God, thank you for allowing us to arrive here. And thank you for keeping these good monks safe and enabling us to bring two of their friends back to them. Please keep them in thy care. Please be with us as we travel this day so that we may avoid those who would do us harm and that we can make safe passage back to our home in Bristol. Amen!

"You head down, and I will be down with Faith in a minute." Said Angelia.

Michael nodded, dressed, and went down to the great hall where all the monks had already gathered. The smell of a fresh hot meal permeated the air around him. He smiled at Kemp, who sat eagerly at the table, ready to eat when food appeared.

"Michael!" called Dom Gordon. "Come! Sit here next to me. Where is Angelia?" he asked.

"She will be down shortly. Everything smells wonderful, my friends. You are making it very hard to leave." He smiled as the others smiled and whispered amongst one another. A few moments later, Angelia arrived with Faith and sat next to Michael.

"Where is Madam Beorn?" asked Brother Richard.

< 419 >

Michael looked around the room and then toward the stairway. It wasn't uncommon for Jillian to stay in her room for days at a time. Michael shrugged his shoulders and said,

"I assume she is still in her room waiting for something wonderful to happen, as she does each day." Brother Richard smiled. "Perhaps I will make her a plate and take it to her."

Angelia touched Michael's arm and said, "Why don't you eat first and let mother rest for a while. There is no reason for you not to enjoy this meal with your friends."

"You are right, my love. Let us eat."

Several of the monks began serving the food. It was blessed, and everyone started to eat. Michael quietly ate as the others engaged in conversation. His mind was elsewhere, so he didn't hear anything being said. Michael thought about Jillian. He wondered if her life would ever return to normal and if taking her back to Bristol would be helpful, or make things worse, being back in the home where she had lived with William. A half-hour passed, and he finished his meal. He asked one of the monks to make a plate for Jillian. The monk obliged and returned with the plate. Micheal thanked him, excused himself, and headed up the stairs to Jillian's room. He softly knocked on the door.

"Mother, are you awake?" he asked. No answer came. He knocked again; this time, the door opened as he knocked. He realized that it had not been shut all the way. He looked into the room and said, "Mother, it is Michael. Are you awake? I have food for you."

As he reached the bed, he realized she was not on it. He looked next to the bed, placed the dish on the bed, and quickly moved to the other side and looked but did not see her. He looked around the room and called, "Mother, where are you?" He walked around the furniture and pulled back the drapes, but she was not there. He ran into the hall and began calling for her. Angelia and the others heard Michael and the concern in his voice. She headed up the stairs, and they followed her.

< 420 >

When she reached the top of the stairs, she saw Michael at the end of the hallway, opening doors looking into rooms, and calling for her.

"Mother is gone, and I don't know where she is." He said in a panicked and frustrated voice.

They searched the monastery for nearly an hour and did not find her. Everyone tried to recount the last time they had seen her. No one remembered seeing her after she retired to her room the evening before. They searched the grounds but did not find her. Michael knew that something was terribly wrong. The fog was lifting, and he noticed a shiny object a short distance ahead. He rushed to it, bent down, and picked up the candlestick holder. He saw the candle lying just a few inches away. Angelia placed her hand over her mouth and shook her head. The monks gathered around. Michael looked down the long dirt road and yelled, MOTHER!"

~*~*~

The old man rode the gray horse pulling a small wagon filled with hay, carrots, and beets. As the fog began to clear, he noticed the silhouette of a woman walking down the road about fifty feet in front of him. He looked on either side of the road and saw nothing but forest. He wondered who she was and why she was walking alone, far from anything. When he was within a few feet, he called out to her, "Excuse me, madam?" She kept walking as if she did not hear him. He called to her again, "Ma'am? Hello? Hello," She continued walking and looking ahead. He pulled the horse next to her. She slowly looked up at him and smiled.

"Hello." He said again.

This time, she acknowledged him. She smiled and said, "Good morning, sir."

'Good morning." He replied. He noticed she was wearing a nightgown and slippers. How she was dressed

< 421 >

seemed odd, and he did not know of any homes within at least a league of their current position.

"Are you lost, madam?" He asked.

"Oh no! I am with William." She said as she smiled at him and then looked ahead as she continued her brisk walk. The old man looked around and then over his shoulder but saw no one else. He asked, "Where is this man you refer to? I see no one but you and me."

"He is just ahead. If you look very carefully, you can see him ahead." She said while pointing straight ahead. The old man looked but saw no one.

"I am sorry, madam, but I do not see anyone in front of us or behind us." Jillian kept walking.

"He is there; I just need to walk a little faster," Jillian said as she sped up her pace. The old man started to speak again and realized that the woman was not well. He looked down at her and asked, "Would you like to ride on the back of my wagon? You will be safe, and I can get you to your William faster." He smiled at her.

Jillian looked up at him and replied, "Oh, thank you, kind sir. That would be lovely."

The old man stopped the horse, dismounted, and helped Jillian onto the cart. He pushed back a section of hay, making a comfortable indentation that allowed her to lay back as her feet dangled over the end of the wagon.

"There, how is that?" The old man asked as he backed some of the hay next to her."

"Oh, this will do fine. Thank you!" Jillian replied.

The old man smiled at her and nodded. He turned to get back on the horse and then stopped. He looked behind the wagon at her and in front of the road. He breathed in, exhaled, and said, "I am sorry, ma'am, but I do not see anyone but you and me. Does this man, William know that you are following him?"

< 422 >

"Of course, he does. He called me and told me to follow him."

The old man realized that the woman was not thinking clearly. Considering how she was dressed and her conversation, he realized that she must have found her way out of the asylum. He knew the place; it was only a few leagues ahead on the outskirts of London.

Jillian smiled and said, "I am sorry, but we have not been properly introduced. William will be pleased that you have so generously agreed to assist my journey to him. However, he surely will want to know the name of the man who offered such kindness to me." Jillian smiled and raised her eyebrows in anticipation of his response.

The old man smiled, and his tongue pressed between his missing front teeth, filling the gap. "Excuse me." He replied. "My name is Beeves." He said with a slight lisp.

"Oh, what a lovely name. Is that your given name or your surname?" Jillian asked.

He looked at her, thought a moment, pressed his lips together, and replied, "Just Beeves. It is just Beeves. And what is your name, madam." He asked while slightly bowing his head and cocking it to the right as if presenting himself to a dignitary.

Jillian smiled again. She opened her mouth and realized that she could not remember her name. She thought for a moment, but nothing came. At first, she was alarmed, but then she brushed it off as a lack of sleep.

Jillian looked at Beeves and said, "Please forgive me, Mr. Beeves, but I am afraid that my journey has made me…" she yawned, "…very exhausted. I think I will lie back and rest while you help me find my William."

She laid her head back and closed her eyes. Beeves walked around and climbed onto the horse. He looked back at the wagon and the sleeping woman. He knew his duty was to get her back to wherever she belonged. He slapped the reins,

< 423 >

and the horse began to travel down the road again. He wondered how the woman could have walked so far from the facility. As they headed down the road, he occasionally looked for the man she had spoken of. Eventually, he realized there was no William, and his duty was to return this pleasant and mild-mannered woman to where she could be safe and cared for.

~*~*~

Michael looked at Angelia and said, "Gather the children; we must leave now. My mother is out there somewhere, and I must find her." He choked back tears as he said, "She is all I have left of my family." He sobbed. "I have lost everyone else; I cannot lose her too." Angelia embraced Michael and pressed her head against his chest.

"We will find her, Michael. I know we will find her."

The monks helped Michael, Angelia, and Kemp pack the carriage. They were ready to leave within thirty minutes, and all of the monks had gathered around to bid them farewell.

"Father Carrington, I do not need the cart; I want you to have it," Michael said as he pointed to it.

"Thank you, my son. We will find a use for it. Michael, we will pray that you find your mother alive and well. Have faith; God is not finished with you."

Angelia stood next to Michael, Faith in her arms and Kemp at her side. They looked at the monks who had been so kind to them.

Angelia smiled at Father Carrington and said, "Father, thank you for your kindness to us." She began to cry. "May God continue to bless each of you." She looked at Dom Gordon and said, "And you, my friend, I am alive today because of you. There is no way I could repay your kindness and charity." She walked over, held him tightly, and kissed his cheek. "And you, Brother Richard. You are my knight. God has gifted you with strength and courage. May you always be a

< 424 >

hero." He reached for her; she embraced him and leaned her head on his shoulder. He could not hold back the tears as they embraced. He tried to speak but was too choked up.

Michael hugged Dom Gordon, who whispered, "God will lead you to your mother; this I know. You are a good man, and he has preserved you for a purpose. Never forget that." Michael smiled at him and nodded.

Michael looked at Brother Richard, who was visibly overcome with emotion. "And you, my friend, it has been an honor fighting at your side." They both smiled. "Thank you for helping me see things more clearly," Michael said.

Brother Richard was still too emotional to speak. He held Michael tightly and then placed his hand against the side of Michael's head, pressing it against his. Michael helped Angelia and Faith into the carriage. Kemp stood next to the carriage, looking at the monks, confused at the situation and the future.

Brother Richard walked to him, knelt before him, and placed his hands on the boy's shoulders. He said, "Kemp, you be strong and have courage." Kemp nodded as tears began to flow. "God has a plan for you, this I know, and your father knew it too."

Kemp started to cry. He wrapped his arms around Brother Richard and said, "I want to stay with you, Brother Richard."

Brother Richard held him for a moment and replied, "My son, God has given you a second chance at life. I can think of no one better to raise you than Michael and Angelia. Go, and be happy."

He released Kemp. Michael lifted his arm toward him. Kemp smiled at the monk and turned toward Michael. Michael said, "Come, my son, let us go."

Michael helped Kemp onto the driver seat above, climbed up, and sat next to him. He waved at the monks and said, "Thank you! Thank you again!"

< 425 >

Michael lifted and snapped the reins, and the horses began to move. They traveled a quarter of a league down the road to London when Kemp noticed something behind them. He motioned for Michael, who looked back and saw a horse pulling a cart galloping toward them. As it got closer, he recognized the two men in the vehicle. Kemp smiled, looked at Michael, and then back at the men. Michael brought the carriage to a stop. The cart pulled up behind them. The men jumped from the cart and ran alongside the carriage.

One of the men spoke to Michael and said, "Our journey is not over, Master Beorn. We believe we must continue with you if you will have us." Said Dom Gordon.

With an enthusiastic smile, Michael said, "You will always be welcome, but what of the others?"

"Father Carrington, lead us in prayer. Afterward, he stated that God spoke to him and that we were to help you find your mother. London is not far, and if she walked down this road, that is where her journey would lead. Let us help you find her."

Michael smiled and said, "Thank you, both."

Brother Richard quickly added, "And after we find her, we will journey with you to Bristol. After all, you will need a teacher for the children."

"Brother Richard!" Said Dom Gordon. "We have not been invited to Bristol."

Angelia poked her head out of the carriage and said, "I accept your offer, Brother Richard. You are both family."

"Michael, if your mother makes it there before us, it is possible that someone would notice her and take her to one of four asylums in London. We can help you find them." Said Dom Gordon.

Michael agreed, and they continued toward London.

< 426 >

Michael stopped the horses at a fork in the road and looked in both directions hoping to see some sign of Jillian.

"Which way should we travel, Dom Gordon?" He yelled to the monks on the cart behind him.

"Let us go to the left." Came the voice of Dom Gordon. "There are two facilities relatively close in the direction." He added. Michael slapped the reins and turned the horses to the left. He could see the outline of the mother city ahead. Michael felt a lump in his throat thinking about Jillian being alone somewhere. He offered a silent prayer, *"Oh dear God above. Please keep my mother safe, and let us find her so we can take her home."* Michael looked at Kemp, who had been silent the entire journey.

Kemp looked at him and said, "I, too, offered a prayer. We will find her, Michael."

"Thank You, Kemp," Michael responded.

"Why do you think she left, Michael?" Asked Kemp. "Was she not happy with us?" He added.

Michael looked ahead as he spoke. "Kemp, my mother always found happiness, even after losing my father and two of her children."

"How?" Asked kemp.

"She found happiness within. In some ways, I envy her. Most of us focus on the outside, especially after losing a loved one. But, somehow, she could focus on the inside, the memories, and all the things that brought her joy. By doing so, she could find happiness even amid great loss."

"But hasn't her focus on the inside caused her to overlook life around her?" Asked Kemp.

"Yes, that is the drawback. By not letting go of the past, she cannot enjoy the present or look forward to the future," Michael replied as waves of memories of the difficult past rushed through his mind.

< 427 >

~*~*~

William stopped his horse, allowing Earnest and Laurie to catch up to him. He waited a few moments until they arrived.

"William, I told you we would be a drain on you."

"Nonsense!   I was not paying attention and allowed my horse to run too fast." Said, William. "The fork to the left leads to the main part of town, but to the right is the way to the monastery. It is only about a league from here. Come, we are almost there." He smiled, and they all continued down the right fork in the road, not knowing that just a league ahead toward the left were Michael and the others.

< 428 >

Chapter Twenty-Eight
If I Were Lost...

"Though lovers be lost, love shall not."
Dylan Thomas

Beeves passed the first Asylum in the city only because he did not know anyone who worked at the facility.   He decided to continue a few blocks to Bethlem Royal Hospital. He stopped the horse, dismounted, and walked to the back of the wagon. He found Jillian soundly sleeping. At first, he thought of waking her but then decided to find someone from the hospital to help. He tied his horse to a post and quickly climbed the front door stairs. He opened the door and walked into the main hall. A young woman greeted him.

"Beeves, welcome! It is wonderful to see you. How have you been," she paused, cocked her head, and winked at him, "my friend?"

"It is good to see you again too, Miss Mable." He gently bowed his head. She smiled, revealing her missing front teeth.

"How can I, I mean, we, help you today?"

Beeves looked back toward the door. "There is a sleeping woman in the back of my wagon."

Mable opened her mouth, raised her eyebrows, and said in a surprised and agitated tone, "A woman sleeping in your bed?"

"I did not say bed. I said wagon. I found her on the side of the road a while back."

His clarification did not settle Mable.

"What? I am baffled. For what purpose did you take this woman?"

"Miss Mable, I only brought her here because she seems very confused. I thought this would be the best place for her."

< 429 >

Mable smiled with relief. She then stated, "You cannot just leave her here. Who shall pay for her stay?"

"It did not occur to me that someone would need to pay for her," Beeves answered. He seemed frustrated and unsure of what to do.

"Well, the hospital is not a charity; we have bills to pay, you know." Another woman walked into the room, and Mable turned and acknowledged her.

"Hello, Sister Compati; I did not see you there."

A tall, slender Nun with large eyes and soft, delicate features stood next to Mabel. "My friend, Beeves, has a sleeping woman in his wagon. He found her near a brothel." Beeves cut her off.

"That is not correct. I found her earlier this morning. She was walking along the road, dressed in a sleeping gown. I asked where she was going, and all she would say was that she was looking for a gentleman named William."

"Uh, Hmm! Brothel!" stated Mable.

"Mable, please, there is no reason to assume such a thing. Please continue, Beeves. Did she tell you her name or where she came from?" asked Sister Compati.

"I am afraid that she did not give me much more information. I gathered that this William must be her husband. Of course, I never saw the man the entire time we traveled, and I assume he is a figment of her imagination." Said Beeves. "She fell asleep almost immediately after I helped her into the wagon. I did not know what else to do besides bringing her here. I do not have much, but I am happy to give you what I have to help pay for her accommodations."

Sister Compati smiled and replied. "Beeves, please take me to her."

Beeves opened the door and waited for Sister Compati to walk through it. He stepped into the doorway before Mable and followed her to the wagon. Jillian was still sleeping. Sister Compati looked at her and could tell she was dressed in fine

< 430 >

apparel. She knew the woman was not a peasant but a woman of means. She leaned down and gently brushed her hand against Jillian's hand. Jillian opened her eyes, looked up at the Nun, and smiled.

"Hello." Said Sister Compati.

"Hello. Where am I?" Jillian asked as she nervously tucked a few strands of hair into the scarf covering her head.

The Nun helped her stand. "You are in London."

"Wonderful!" Jillian responded with a significant smile. "Is William here?" she asked.

"William?" asked the Nun.

"Yes, William, my husband. Has he arrived yet?" Jillian asked.

Sister Compati smiled at her and, in a soft voice, asked, "I do not believe so. Did he tell you what time he would arrive?"

Jillian thought for a moment. She looked around at the building across the street and other structures. "I am sorry, but I do not know your name," Jillian said.

"Oh, please forgive me. I am Sister Compati."

Jillian smiled and said, "You are a Nun."

"Yes, I am."

"Did you choose your name?" Jillian asked. Beeves and Mable looked at one another and then at Sister Compati, confused at the question.

"Why do you ask?" Questioned the Nun.

"Because Compati means compassion, and I think it is a lovely name for a sister of the Lord."

"Thank you. And what may I ask is your name?"

Jillian thought for a moment and said, "For some reason, it escapes me. Of course, I know my name; I do not remember it now. Do you think that is odd?"

"Not particularly; I have known many people who cannot remember their name." The nun said in a soft smiling voice.

< 431 >

Mable smiled and suppressed a laugh.

"But that is fine because some would rather choose a different name," said the nun.

Jillian smiled and added, "Just as you did."

"Exactly.   And what name would you choose for yourself?"

Jillian thought a minute and said, "I choose Pati." Mable and Beeves looked confusingly at each other.

"Pati, I believe that comes from the word patient. Why would you choose that name?" Asked Sister Compati.

"Because I have been very patient for quite some time waiting for my William to come back to me." She smiled.

"Patience is a virtue.   I would be honored if you came into my home, and I can offer you some hot food and tea while you wait for William.   What do you say?"   asked Sister Compati.

"I would like that." Said Jillian.

"Wonderful! Let us help you."

Beeves helped Jillian into the facility.   Sister Compati took her to a small private room with a large window in front of the bed.   There was a rocking chair next to the window.   Jillian quickly sat in the rocking chair, began to rock, and gazed out the window.   Beeves witnessed the entire process.   Sister Compati knelt before her and asked, "May I take your scarf so that you can be more comfortable?"

Jillian agreed and helped remove the scarf, revealing her long auburn hair.

"My new friend Pati, you have the most beautiful red hair I have ever seen." Said Sister Compati.

"Thank you, sister.   It is a lot of trouble to keep brushed and cleaned."

"Would you allow me to brush it for you?"

"Yes, that would be lovely.   Thank you." Jillian added.

The Nun took a brush from a drawer beside the bed and gently brushed Jillian's hair.   Beeves stood in the doorway,

< 432 >

watching and marveling at the kindness and gentleness of the Nun. When she finished, she put her left hand on Jillian's shoulder. Jillian placed her right hand over Sister Compati's hand and whispered, "Thank you, my dear."

Sister Compati placed the brush back in the drawer and walked to the doorway where Beeves was still standing. They left the room, and Beeves asked how much he needed to give for her stay. The Nun smiled and said, "My good man. I ask nothing of you."

"But Sister, I understand she cannot stay here free of charge."

"Beeves, this woman is lost, and I am confident that her William will find her. Besides, she is a woman of means; he will gladly pay for whatever costs she has incurred when he comes."

"But what if he does not come?" asked Beeves. "What if there is no William?"

"He will come, of this I am sure. Thank you for your kindness; remember, God, rewards all acts of kindness. Please make sure that Mable provides you with some food before you leave."

"Thank you, Sister Compati. You are too kind."

"No one is too kind, but I appreciate your words."

Beeves bid her farewell and left the room. Sister Compati waved at him and then turned back to the room. She noticed that Jillian was sitting in the rocking chair she had turned toward the window. She watched her for a moment and rehearsed the short conversation in her head. She thought about most of the patients in the hospital; most were well beyond cure and were left there to spend the rest of their days. Most patients were from wealthy families, although some were accepted as part of the Catholic Church's arrangement with the city of London. This, The Bethlem Royal Hospital, was the first of its kind. It was run by the Church in cooperation with the city of London and the King. As she watched Jillian rocking back and

< 433 >

forth, she hoped her William would come. *"William,"* she thought. *"I once had a William. I loved that boy. I wonder if God has been kind to him."* She questioned herself. She smiled, folded her arms, took a deep breath, and quietly said, "Oh, dear Father in Heaven, please bring her William to her." She turned, quietly closed the door, and returned to overseeing the hospital.

The Hoffman Home wasn't a desirable place to send a confused or deranged loved one. Unlike Bethlem Royal Hospital, it was not a treatment facility; it was more of a homeless shelter for the neglected and emotionally sick. Michael looked at the front of the building with its dilapidated exterior and missing brick-and-mortar sections. He walked to the door while the others waited in the carriage and cart. He banged the iron knocker against the door three times. A few moments passed with no answer. He repeated the knock again. This time, the door opened, and a small older hunched-back man stood in the doorway. His clothes were ragged, and his hair was disheveled. His face was dirty with traces of uneaten beats on either side of his mouth. He twisted to the right, lifted his head and shoulders as much as possible, looked at Michael, and then wiped his arm across his face and asked, "G'day, sir. What brings ya ta ur lovely ome t'day?"

He smiled and wiped his tongue over his toothless gums several times while waiting for a response. Michael felt his heart race. He hoped that his dear mother was not inside the building. He peaked his head into the door and noticed several people sitting and lying in a hallway. Most were sitting in their own filth. The repulsive smell passed through the doorway.

"Sir, did ya not hear me?" The man asked in an irritated voice.

Michael shook off his disgust and said, "Oh, yes, please forgive me. I am looking for my mother."

< 434 >

"And ya think she's here?" asked the man, who seemed amused by the question.

"Frankly, sir, I hope with all my heart that she is not here," Michael said.

"Can ya describe her to me?" the man asked.

"She is about this tall," he lifted his hand to his shoulder length, "and she has fair skin, long beautiful auburn hair, and bright green eyes."

"I am sorry, but I cannot say I have seen such a woman here."

Michael felt tremendous relief and sorrow at the same time. Suddenly a short boney naked man ran up to the door and attempted to push his way through as the old man held him back. Michael stepped back as the naked man yelled, "Where is she? Bring us the perty lady. We wants her!"

The old man pushed him back into the room and closed the door partway enough to keep his head revealed.

"I believe we do not have yer mother. But I will be sure to find ya if she arrives." He laughed and closed the door. Michael turned and faced the monks and Angelia. They stared at him, mouths open, eyes squinted, and faces in shock.

Brother Richard looked at the sky and said, "She is not here! Thank you, Lord!"

They spent the rest of the day traveling to each facility but not finding her. They asked people on the streets and local merchants if they had seen the red-haired woman; most shook their heads, and no one had seen her. Their last stop was the Bethlem Royal Hospital. The night was falling, and Michael decided to find rooms for the monks and Angelia, and the children. He found lodging in a hotel near the hospital. After settling everyone into the hotel, he walked to the building, where he found a sign on the door stating that it was closed for the night. He returned with the news and decided to wait until morning.

< 435 >

~*~*~

The monks excitedly greeted William and his friends. He introduced them to Earnest, Laurie, and his daughter Sarah. Tears of joy and gratitude were shared by all. William was happy to discover that Saxton, his wife, and his son had made it to the monastery. They exchanged their travel log over a large dinner. Afterward, William explained to Saxton that he believed his wife, son Michael, and others who survived the fire may have headed to London. They planned to search for William's family and retrieve William's belongings at 555 Copper Street. They agreed to leave after the morning meal.

"Will you be leaving today, sir?" asked the gentleman at the front desk.

"That depends on whether or not we find my mother. For now, let us arrange to stay another night."

Michael paid the man with coins from the large chest he had hidden on the carriage. He went back to the room where Angelia and the others were waiting.

"I have decided to walk to the hospital by myself. I need some time to think. I do not know what to do if I do not find my mother there. Please pray for her." Michael said as tears ran down his cheeks.

Angelia placed her hands on his cheeks and said, "Michael, my love. I know that God has kept your mother safe. And I know you will find her; we will wait here for you."

Michael kissed her, thanked her, and left for the hospital.

~*~*~

< 436 >

The others stayed at the monastery while William took the carriage with Saxton, Lucas, and Sarah. They could see the large buildings of the city ahead. Lucas felt a pit in his stomach as memories of living on the streets of London returned to him. William brushed his hand through Lucas' hair, and he felt Lucas' fear and uneasiness.

"This time is different, my son. We will find our loved ones this time and reunite our family." Lucas forced a half smile.

Saxton spoke, "Look, there is a man ahead on the side of the road, and it looks like he has lost a wheel on his wagon."

William stopped the carriage behind the wagon. He climbed off the carriage and walked to the man struggling to remove the broken wheel.

"May we be of help, sir?" William asked.

The man turned toward William and said, "Only if you have an extra wheel in your buggy."

"Actually, I do," William said with a smile. "Saxton, would you mind getting the wheel and bringing it here?" William asked.

"Of course!" said Saxton as he went to the back of the carriage and found the extra wheel.

"Thank you for your kindness, sir. My name is Beeves." He lifted his arm in a gesture to shake. William gripped the man's wrist and said, "It is a pleasure to meet you, Beeves. My name is William."

Beeves released the grip. With a surprised look, William asked, "Are you alright, my friend?"

Beeves eyes grew large. "Did you say your name was William?"

"Yes, I did." Said, William. Realizing the man was startled, William asked, "Is there a problem?"

"No! Of course, not. I just did not expect that I would be meeting a William. That is all."

< 437 >

"Well, William is a common name. However, you could call me John or Mark if that would make you more comfortable." William joked.

Saxton returned with the wheel and began replacing it as Beeves and William lifted the wagon.

"Forgive me, sir. It is just that yesterday I met a woman looking for a man named William." Said Beeves.

William felt an odd sensation. He said, "Really? Where did you meet her?"

"Actually, it was just outside of London about two leagues. She was just walking down the side of the road, alone and disoriented."

"Did she tell you her name?" William asked. His interest was piqued.

"Unfortunately, she could not remember her name?"

"Had she been attacked? Was she hurt?" William asked, concerned.

"No, but she was dressed in a nightgown and slippers. I thought it was odd for a woman to be so far from anyone dressed in such a way and walking alone on the road."

"Can you describe her to me?"

"Certainly, she was about this tall, thin, pale white skin, long auburn hair, and the most beautiful green eyes I have ever seen."

William felt shivers all over his body. His heart began to race. Saxton noticed the difference in William and asked, "William. Are you alright?"

"Her name is Jillian. Jillian Beorn. She is my wife." William said in a trembling voice. "Where did you take her?" William asked.

"Considering her confused state, I took her to Bethlem Royal Hospital. It is only a few blocks ahead."

William embraced the man and said, "Thank you, kind sir. You are a gift from God."

< 438 >

William pulled a gold coin from his tunic and gave it to Beeves.

"Please take this. It is all I have right now, but I want you to have it."

"Thank you, sir." Said Beeves. He looked at the gold coin and remembered the words of Sister Compati. *"God rewards all acts of kindness"* He smiled and put the coin in his tunic.

Saxton quickly finished attaching the wheel. He and William returned to the cart. William told the children that he had found their mother and that they would get her. He slapped the reins and headed for the hospital.

Michael opened the large door and entered the building. It was clean, organized, and very different than the other facilities he had been to.

Mabel was sitting at a large reception desk, and she saw Michael, and while fluffing her hair and batting her eyes, asked. "Is there something I can help you with, sir?" She looked him up and down, fixed her hair, and smiled at him flirtatiously. Michael didn't notice her obnoxious admiration.

"Um. Yes. I am looking for a woman named Jillian Beorn. She is about this tall," he raised his hand just below his shoulder, "with long red hair. Have you seen her? Is she here? " I am very sorry, sir, but I have not seen anyone who fits that description."

"I have looked everywhere; she must be here. Has anyone arrived recently?" He asked.

"No. But I will tell you this. You are welcome to look around and see if this woman, what did you say was her name?"

"Jillian. Her name is Jillian."

"Yes, Jilly Ann. You can look in the main breakfast area, just down the hall. All of the residents are eating now."

< 439 >

"Thank you!" Michael said. He walked past her and down the hall. He looked over his shoulder and saw Mabel, who smiled and then winked at him. It was at that point that he realized her insufferable advances toward him. He looked ahead and saw the room Mable had described. The room was large and filled with people. He slowly walked around, looking at each individual. Most residents were older, with a few in their mid to late thirties. He wondered how the place had faired during the plague. How did these people survive, and how many came here after the plague died?

There were approximately thirty tables, each seating four to five people, arranged in the middle of the room. Smaller two-person tables were lined against the walls on either side of the long rectangular room. The staff was all nuns. Some were holding the arms of elderly people as they walked to and from tables. The food was being brought to the tables by men and teenage boys. There were so many people in the room that the task of finding Jillian seemed overwhelming. Michael offered a silent prayer,

"Oh, dear God, please let my mother be here and let me find her. I have looked all over London and don't know where else to look. Please, God, let her be safe."

He ended his prayer, and he noticed a thin woman a few tables in front of him dressed in a nightgown and scarf, the last thing he remembered Jillian wearing. He felt his heart race as he got closer to her. Could it be her? He thought. When he was within reach, he stretched out his arm and gently touched the woman's right shoulder. He struggled to speak and forced out the word, "Mother?"

The others at the table didn't notice him. The woman placed her left hand on his hand over her shoulder. He moved around to see her face. She smiled and said, "My son, you have come for me."

Michael leaned in, looked into her large, sad, brown eyes, and realized that she was not Jillian. His heart skipped as

< 440 >

the excitement and relief quickly left him. She lifted her other hand and placed it on his cheek. He gently took her hand and put it back on her lap. He smiled and said, "Enjoy your food, and have a lovely day."

As he backed away, he noticed that her hands were clean and her nails were manicured. He looked at several other men and women and saw that each appeared to be from the nobility. Unlike the others he had visited, this facility seemed more particular about who they took in; there were no commoners. He walked around the room several times, noticing women who, at first glance, could have been Jillian. By the time he made it to the end of the hall, he had looked at every face, but none were Jillian. He felt despair and longed for God to answer his prayer. He spoke in his mind, *"Dear God, please don't let me lose my mother. Is it not enough, all that I have lost? Must I lose her too? I would give all that I possess to have her back. I would give my life to thee to have all my family back. Oh God, please hear my prayer. Please hear my prayer."* He felt tears run down his cheeks, and his breathing became heavy, like his heart.

William stood on the steps of the Bethlem Royal Hospital and looked at the large wooden door and the massive iron lion head knocker. His mind took him back to another time when he stood on the steps of a building like this. He was much smaller. He looked up at the door as he felt his mother's tight squeeze of his hand. He remembered her scent and her inviting smile. He looked up at her, wanting so much to embrace her. He squeezed her hand and suddenly heard a voice, "Father, are we going in?" asked Sarah, standing beside William, holding his hand.

He looked down at her and answered, "Yes, my dear. We are going in."

< 441 >

He felt a lump in his throat as he thought he would find his beautiful wife here after so long and so much. He opened the large door and walked into the room, with Lucas on one arm and Sarah on the other. He noticed a woman sitting at a desk further into the room. She looked up at him and said, "My, it is a busy morning. And what can I help you with today?"

"I, we, are looking for a woman, a beautiful woman, whom we believe may be here."

"Well, you are not the first man to ever say that to me." She smiled, revealing her missing teeth. She touched up her hair.

William did not react to her attempt at humor. Instead, he waited for her to respond to his statement.

She cleared her throat and said, "My name is Mable. Now, can you describe this woman you are looking for? Surely, you know that there are many women here."

"Of course," said William. "She is this high; she has large green eyes and thick, long, auburn hair. Her face is as white as an angel, and her voice as soft as a rose."

Mable shook her head and said, "I am sorry, sir, but I can assure you that the woman you described is not here. Now, if you will excuse me, I have other things to attend to."

William looked at the woman and said, "Pardon me, ma'am, but I believe she is here. I was told that she is here."

"Sir, I do not have time to argue with you! I have already told you that the woman you described is not here. Now, I am going to ask you to leave!" She demanded.

William stood back, surprised at her tone. He started to reply to her when another woman walked into the room.

"Mable!" She sternly stated. "There is no reason to be loud with this man." She looked at William and said, "Please forgive my associate. I am Sister Compati, the director of this facility; how can I help you?"

William looked at the woman. She seemed familiar to him. Although he did not know any Nuns, something about the

< 442 >

woman's mannerisms and tone intrigued him. He explained that he and his two children had been told by a man they helped on the side of the road that he had taken his wife, Jillian, to the hospital. Sister Compati smiled and said, "Oh my, you must be William."

William was surprised at her exclamation. Somewhat confused that she knew his name, he replied, "Yes, I am William. William Beorn, and I am looking for my wife, Jillian."

"Wonderful!" Said Sister Compati. "So, her name is Jillian. A beautiful name for a charming woman."

"Did she not tell you her name?" William asked.

"No. I am afraid that your wife is confused. She doesn't know her name or where she is from. But she knows you. You are all she has spoken of since she arrived." Sister Compati smiled. "I am so pleased that you are here. She is upstairs; I will take you to her."

William felt a warm spirit surround him. He pulled both Lucas and Sarah close to him. He kneeled and said to them, "My dearest children, you are a gift to me from God. While away from your mother, I lost so much and had forgotten almost everything. But God brought you back to me to help me remember her. Let us go and find her."

Sister Compati placed a hand on her lips to maintain her composure as she listened to his words that seemed so familiar. She felt tears well in her eyes. She pulled back on the side of her habit as she brushed the tears from her eyes. William looked at her and noticed a dark scar on the side of her face that had been covered by her habit. He felt a strange feeling overcome him. His memory again flashed back to an earlier time in his childhood. She stepped back a few feet and placed her hand into her pocket. Her hand wrapped around a small wooden cylinder. She pulled it from her pocket, opened the end, and carefully pulled a tarnished rolled-up piece of parchment from the tube. She unrolled it and read it to herself.

< 443 >

"My Dearest Lila, you are a gift from God. The older I get, the less I remember my mother. But God does not want me to forget her, so he gave me you. I think that she must have been just like you. I hope one day you can be a mother too. Your William"

She covered her mouth and could not hold back the tears. William looked at her; she was trembling and crying. Mable looked at the Nun and had no idea what was happening. William walked over to Sister Compati and asked, "Lila? Is it you?"

His large black eyes pierced her soul. She smiled; no one had called her by that name in years. Her last memory of hearing someone call her Lila came from a young boy in an orphanage too many years ago.

She nodded and said, "My William, God in his great love and mercy, has kept you safe all these years, and today he has brought you to me."

William quickly threw his arms around her and, holding her tightly, said, "Oh, the love of God. I am so happy that I do not know what to say."

They both laughed and cried, embracing each other for a moment. Mable and the children just stared, not knowing what to say or do. William released her and said, "You are still very beautiful, and I am sorry if that is inappropriate to say to a Nun."

They laughed quietly. William smiled and added, "And God did make you a mother after all, didn't he?"

She smiled and nodded.

"And you, a husband and a father," she added.

It was difficult for her to regain her composure. She gently placed her right hand on William's cheek, looked into his eyes, and said, "You were so strong. I knew you would make it." She withdrew her hand, regained her composure, and added, "My Dearest William, there will be time later to talk, but let us go and find your Jillian. Follow me."

< 444 >

She motioned for William and the children to follow her up the stairs. When they reached the doorway, they saw Jillian sitting across the room in the rocking chair, looking out the window.

"She is a lovely woman, William. However, she is lost in her own world, and I do not know the words to bring her back."

Sarah started to run for her; William grabbed her arm and said, "My sweet Sarah, please let me go to her first. I promise I will do so quickly."

She stepped back, and Lila reached down and held her hand. Lucas held her other hand. William slowly walked up behind Jillian. He kneeled and gently placed his hands on her shoulders. He breathed in deeply, held his breath for a moment, and then exhaled slowly. He was overcome by her presence. So much had happened. He had seen so many die, so many lose loved ones, so many give up hope and let go. And now, by the grace of God, he was kneeling behind the woman he loved above all others. It didn't seem real. It didn't seem fair.

Nevertheless, God allowed them to be separated under the most challenging conditions, and now He had brought them together again. With tears rolling down his cheeks, he looked up and quietly said, "Thank you, dear, Lord. Thank you!"

He felt the softness of her long auburn hair brush against his fingers; he felt the strength of her tender shoulders. Myriads of memories flashed through his mind. He closed his eyes and told his mind to stop. He knew there would be time for memories later. He opened his eyes and took another breath. He did not know what to say. He thought about what Lila had said, *"I do not know the words to bring her back."* A soft memory began to open in his mind. He saw himself lying on his back, near a tree, with his head in Jillian's lap. She leaned into him, draping his face with her long hair. She smiled and spoke. The memory vanished. William knew the words to bring her back.

< 445 >

He lowered his head until his lips gently caressed the back of her right ear. He felt her move slightly toward him.

He struggled to whisper, "Jillian, If I was lost, would you come find me." He breathed in, held his breath, and waited for her reply. Jillian's eyes filled with light. She remembered those words from many years ago. She remembered sitting against a large tree by the water in Bristol, with William lying on his back, his head in her lap, looking up at her as she spoke those words to him. The memory faded. Suddenly she was back in the present. She smiled, grabbed onto his hands, and said, "In a heartbeat, my love, in a heartbeat."

William walked around and kneeled in front of her. She smiled as tears filled her eyes and ran down her cheeks.

His voice cracked as he said, "My love, you are as beautiful as the first day I met you."

She smiled and placed her hands on his cheeks. He gently held each hand as he looked into her piercing green eyes.

"My William! Where have you been? Jillian asked as she sobbed. I have waited so long for you to come." William pulled her to him and wrapped his arms around her. He saw Sarah and Lucas standing next to the Nun in the doorway. He lifted his left hand and motioned for them to wait.

"I am here, my love. God has brought me to you, and we are together again."

It was hard to speak and control his emotion. Memories of his life over the past year flooded his head, and he could not stop them this time. Memories of being completely alone, not knowing who he was, where he was from, or how he had ended up on a ship with a dead crew. He remembered the friends he had made while in a rat and plague invested prison and the wonderful monks who took him in as one of their own. He remembered the day he found Lucas in the street in London and the hazy fog in his mind reminding him of a life he once lived. He remembered that his faith in God held him together and gave him hope. The scenes raced faster and faster through his mind,

< 446 >

finding Saxton, his precious little girl Sarah, and his friends after discovering the fiery devastation of the Chattingworth estate. And now, he was holding his beautiful wife Jillian, the love of his life.

Jillian continued to sob as she tried to speak. Between sobs, she said, "But William, we have lost so much." She cried while pressing her face into William's shoulder. "Please forgive me... Lucas and Sarah are gone. I tried to protect them, but God has taken them."

She buried her head in his chest and sobbed. William placed his hand under her chin and lifted her head up to his face. He said, "My dearest, the Lord giveth and the Lord taketh away."

"I know." Said Jillian as she looked at William.

William replied, "But today, my love, the Lord giveth." He motioned for the children to come. Lucas arrived first, and he walked around the chair and faced Jillian.

Jillian cried out, "Oh, dear Father in Heaven! My son! My son!" She raised her arms, and Lucas ran to her and threw his arms around her.

"Mother, isn't it wonderful what God has done? Isn't it wonderful?" Lucas cried.

Jillian was overcome with emotion and could not speak. She held Lucas and brushed her hand through his hair. William caressed her cheek and said, "My Jillian, he has done more, much more."

He waved for Sarah to come. She looked up at the Nun, who gently pushed her away. She rushed over and stood in front of Jillian. Jillian covered her mouth and shook her head in disbelief. Tears filled her eyes to the extent that she could not make out the features of the child who stood in front of her. She brushed away her tears and exclaimed, "Sarah! My Sarah! God has brought you back from heaven!"

She reached out and embraced Sarah. Sarah pulled back and said, "Mother, I have always been here."

< 447 >

Jillian shook her head and said, "But, I saw you in the house…" she hesitated, "as it burned to the ground."

"No, mother, Miss Laurie saved me. She opened the back door and took me from the fire. I lived with Miss Laurie and Mr. Earnest until father found us just days ago."

Jillian released Sarah and held her arms as she moved her in front of her. She looked into her eyes and said, "Michael was only doing what he thought was right. The plague had taken so many…he thought it had taken you…he thought…."

Sarah cut her off, "Mother, I know Michael was doing what he thought was right. Miss Laurie told me so, and she told me not to be angry with him, and she told me he loved me very much…" Sarah began to cry. "I don't blame Michael for doing what he thought was right. He protected us all for so long. I love him, and I hope God will bring him back to us too."

William pulled Jillian and the two children against him. They hugged and swam in tears of joy.

She looked up to Sister Compati and, between breaths and sobs, said, "My name is Jillian, and this is my William, my Lucas, and my Sarah. God has brought all of them back to me."

Lila wiped tears from her eyes. She walked toward them and placed her left hand on Jillian's left shoulder while covering her mouth with her right hand. It was a glorious and miraculous moment for each of them. Lila could not imagine anything more remarkable for this family. Jillian declared in a loud voice, "My name is Jillian!"

As Michael walked back into the main hall, he heard a familiar voice.

"It's Jillian!" He exclaimed.

He looked around and then up the stairway. Mabel was sitting at the desk when she noticed Michael. She quickly stood and asked, "Well, did you find her?"

Michael looked at her, pointed up the stairway, and then began to run up the stairway. He heard Jillian's voice again when he reached the top of the stairway. He turned down the

< 448 >

hallway and ran toward the voice. He saw an open door and quickly ran to the door. He stopped in the doorway and saw Jillian standing in a small crowd of people. He called out to her, "Mother! Oh, thank God, I have found you!"

Jillian turned, as did William, Lucas, and Sarah. At first, Michael thought he was seeing ghosts surrounding Jillian because she was the only person he knew was still alive.

He stood in the doorway, shocked at the scene. What was just a moment seemed like an eternity of mixed memories of happiness, anger, fear, frustration, and deep sorrow. Was God playing with his mind, he thought. Had he somehow gone to the same happy place as Jillian? Michael wondered. He could hardly breathe as his body stood frozen. He felt the blood rush to his head and dizziness overcome him. The emotion was too much to comprehend. Just as he began to lose consciousness and his eyes closed, he heard William's powerful voice call out to him, "Michael, my son!"

He opened his eyes, the blood had left his lower extremities, and he fell to his knees. He placed his hands on his head and cried, and William ran to him and wrapped his arms around him.

"Michael, it is a day of rejoicing, for God has reunited our family. We are all together again!" Exclaimed William.

Michael lifted his head and saw the watery figures of Lucas and Sarah standing next to Jillian through his tear-filled eyes. He struggled to speak, but all he could say was, "How?"

The children ran to him, each nestled into him, kissing his cheeks. Michael continued to cry, and he could no longer speak. Lila stood in the room next to the door, watching the scene unfold. She marveled at God's great love and mercy, who protected this family during the most terrible sickness the world had ever known. Then He brought them together again, something that most, at the time, only anticipated would happen to their families and loved ones after the pain and suffering of this life took them into the next.

< 449 >

After a few moments, William helped Michael stand. Jillian walked over to him and said, "Michael, I cannot tell you how much I love and appreciate you and all you have done for our family. I am sorry I was not there for you during the most difficult times. But, I remember everything, and I thank you, I love you and ask for your forgiveness." She smiled and kissed his cheek.

"Mother, I do not know how this moment can be real. I saw my father lying on the floor, lifeless. I dumped his body into a death cart. I burned the house to the ground while my precious little sister lay in her bed infected with the plague, and I didn't even notice when an evil man took my little brother, Lucas, from us a long time ago."

He cried and then continued, "And I was not aware when you wandered from us early in the morning. Do not thank me; you do not need my forgiveness; I failed all of you." He sobbed.

William placed his arms on Michael's shoulders and said, "Michael, we are all here together today because of you. You did not fail anyone. You stayed true to the last thing I asked of you the day I sent you all to Cardiff. I told you that I was entrusting you with all I loved. I told you that you were strong and capable of protecting our family. I told you to be careful and wise. You have done all of these things, Michael, my son."

William wrapped his arm around Michael's neck and pulled him against him. He kissed Michael's cheek and said, "Now, let us rejoice to know that God did not leave us without mercy, but that he protected each of us and has brought all of us together again." William raised his left arm and welcomed Jillian, Lucas, and Sarah into the embrace.

For Jillian, this was a long-anticipated reunion. For William, it was the fulfillment of his dreams. For Michael, it was unbelievable, confusing, and miraculous. It was just another of God's great miracles of love and mercy for Lila.

< 450 >

Considering the devastation caused by the Black Plague, it was improbable that such a reunion, a dream, and a miraculous event could occur, especially when, for most, at the time, life was ending all around them. But for this family, life had been preserved, protected, and reunited. What seemed like a lifetime was only a small moment in time, and God had left them Not Without Mercy. They were together again and ready for the passage home.

< 451 >

Chapter Twenty-Seven Notes

Bethlem Royal Hospital, also known as St Mary Bethlehem, Bethlehem Hospital, and most notoriously Bedlam, is an ancient hospital in London, the United Kingdom, for treating mental illness, part of the South London and Maudsley NHS Foundation Trust.

The word "bedlam," meaning uproar and confusion, is derived from the hospital's prior nickname. Although the hospital became a modern psychiatric facility, historically, it was representative of the worst excesses of asylums in the era of lunacy reform.

It is Europe's oldest extant psychiatric hospital and has operated continuously for over 600 years. It has also been the continent's most famous and infamous specialist institution for the care and treatment of the insane. Its popular designation – "Bedlam" – has long been synonymous with madness. Precisely dating its transition to this role is difficult. From 1330 it was routinely referred to as a "hospital," but that does not necessarily indicate a change in its primary function from alms collection – the word "hospital" could as likely have been used to denote a lodging for travelers, equivalent to a hostel, and could have described an institution acting as a center and providing accommodation for wandering beggars. It is unknown when it began to specialize in the care and control of the insane.

It was typical for a woman who became a Nun to also take on a new name, usually of her choosing. Lila, who understood how pain and suffering filled the world and how God had compassion for her and saved her from a life of misery and pain, believed that compassion, like charity, was one of the most significant traits a person could possess. For this reason, she chose the name Compati. It was a word that the modern word compassion derived from. It came from mid-14c., from Old French compassion "sympathy, pity" (12c.), from Late Latin compassionem (nominative compassio) "sympathy," noun of state from past participle stem of compati "to feel pity," from com- "together" (see com-) + pati "to suffer." Middle English: Old French, Latin patient- 'suffering,' from the verb pati.

< 452 >

Epilog

The struggles and hardships of the Beorn family were not unlike most families of their day. Avoiding the plague was not an easy task. For most, it was their greatest nightmare, and they lived it daily. Everyone knew someone who died of the plague. By Spring of 1349, the plague had killed six out of every ten people in London.

Life in England was dramatically different when the plague finally ended around 1350. It had taken the lives of over 1.5 million people out of approximately 4 million people who lived in England. Death toll estimates for Europe, Asia, and Africa topped 200 million people, over two-thirds of Europe's population.

After 1350, the plague returned six more times for short intervals before the end of the century. Due to the amount of death and the lack of peasant workers caused by the plague, England's social structure began to change. Peasants found themselves in a position of power as they negotiated for higher wages. This created turmoil for the Lords and nobles and eventually the Peasant revolt of 1381.

In book one, The Black Death, I discussed the importance of faith, family, love, courage, and hope. In book two, The Passage Home, I added the word redemption.

FAITH; the Apostle Paul calls it the "essence of things hoped for but not seen." Faith is a powerful thing that can guide one to success and happiness. A lack of it can cause tremendous heartache and despair. William was a man of great faith, and he never doubted God, regardless of his situation. Through his trials of this period, Michael also became a man of faith.

< 453 >

FAMILY; Most of those who survived clung to their family. As their world began crashing down around them, worldly treasure seemed on par with untended soil; it had no value on its own. But the family was the central unit of strength and faith in God. Family is what held the Beorn's and most others together at that time.

LOVE; Jesus said the second greatest commandment was to love thy neighbor as thyself. Many died as they tended loved ones who contracted the plague. Mothers and fathers cared for their sick children and stood helplessly as they each died within three to four days. That love usually extended to each other when that care only ended with the last breath of the surviving member of the family. Jillian never ceased loving, even when it meant she had to find a place in her mind to hold onto the memories of loved ones,' past and present.

COURAGE; this was the test for most who survived the plague and the changing social and economic circumstances it brought. It was also the ingredient that changed boys to men and husbands to fathers. William never wavered in his courage, and Michael discovered the power in courage, and he allowed it to change his life for the better.

HOPE; hope precedes faith. It is the beginning of every task, the foundation of every belief, and the fuel for every journey. Without hope, there is no success. Without hope, there is no joy.

Without hope, life cannot be lived. Hope is key to faith, family, love, and courage.

REDEMPTION; the adversary would have one believe that due to the magnitude of one's sins, God could never forgive them; therefore, repentance is futile. From the beginning, Satan, the great deceiver, has always played with the minds of men, showing them their weaknesses and highlighting their worldly lusts. His first success was convincing Cane that

< 454 >

he could never measure up to Able, and it was better for him to kill Able and surrender to the power of Satan. Too often, people get caught in the Devil's trap of despair, and forgiveness and redemption seem unattainable. Michael floundered in that trap until he finally realized that God had never left him alone. As this incredible and challenging journey ended, Michael realized God's great mercy saved him and his loved ones. And he understood that all men could be redeemed due to God's great Love and redeeming sacrifice of his son Jesus Christ. Michael understood that nothing worth anything came without a price. He knew the price his family and loved ones paid to survive the plague, which paled to the ultimate price paid by the son of God. The Pestilence of Great Mortality cleansed the Earth like a fire thinning the forest. It caused the survivors to appreciate life and the individual worth of mankind. It caused the faithless to become fearful and the faithful to become fearless. William was reunited with his family, and Michael will discover how God has prepared him for his next incredible journey as the story continues in book three, ***Redemption***.

< 455 >

Characters

(of Book One and Book Two)
Not Without Mercy—The Black Death
Not Without Mercy—The Passage Home

The author created many of over 100 Characters. Some were real people who lived during the time period of this book. The characters are listed in alphabetical order not the order of appearance.

	Alderman	City Council Member(Alderman) of Bristol
Flanagan		when Michael was 12
	Allard	One of the men who participated in the murder of Elizabeth, in book one. He is also the man who kidnaps Lucas.
	Andrew	Twelve-year-old son of the Stanley's who later
Stanley		becomes best friends with Michael Beorn
	Angelia Beorn	Wife of Lance Beorn and adopted mother of
		William Beorn
	Annabel	Annabel, a servant on the Beorn estate
	Anthony	Child of the street
	Anthony	Sailor on ship of Captain Russell
	Anthony	Prisoner in Newgate Prison in London
Olson		
	Agustus	Father of Ruth
Leavesly		
	Avery	A thief on the road to Bristol
	Beatrice	Wife of Terrance Edwards
Edwards		
	Bernarado	Benedictine Monk from Italy
Tolomei		
	Beth Belmond	Wife of Philip Belmond
	Big John	Foreman of Beorn shipping and good friend of
(Barrington)	William	
	Bishop	Dean of St Paul's in London
Richard Newport		
	Brother	Monk at Abby in London
Alexander		
	Brother John	Monk at Abby in London
	Brother	Monk at Abby in London
Johnson		
	Caldwell	A thief on the road to Bristol

< 456 >

Russell	Captain	Friend of William Beorn (Ship Captain)
	Chief Stenardi	Officer in Spain who discovers William on the shipwreck .
	Crotchet's	Couple who came to adopt at the orphanage
	Dalian	Sailor on ship of Captain Russell
	Dennis	Child of the street
Edwards	Derek	Sixteen-year-old son of the Edwards. (A twin)
	Dirk Edwards	Sixteen-year-old son of the Edwards. (A twin)
Friedman	Dom	Monk at Abby in London
	Dom Geoffrey	A Benedictine Monk who taught the children of William's estate.
	Ernest Collins	Worker at the Chattingworth Manor
Arbela	Edmund	Benedictine Monk who took over the orphanage in London where William lived as a boy
Belmond	Edward	Orphan boy who befriended William at the orphanage
	Elizabeth	A young woman who works in the horse stable with Ernest at the Chattingworth Manor. Becomes girlfriend and wife of Michael
	Erastus Gill	Former Priest and Headmaster of the Orphanage in London
Andrews	Father	Priest who marched with the Flagellants
Mueller	Father	The priest at the Monastery Monson found as a teenager.
Murdock	Father	Priest who marched with the Flagellants
Murphy	Father	Priest of William Beorn
Carmichael	Felix	The Warden at Newgate Prison in London
	Fillery	The Surname Michael used as a boy living on the streets
	Flagellants	A group of ultra-religious zealots who marched from town to town believing that through self-torture, God would end the plague
	Gentry	A guard in the palace of King Edward II
Murdock	Harold	Manager of the Beorn estate
	Hazlitt	A thief on the road to Bristol
Stanley	Heather	Youngest daughter of the Stanley's
France	Isabella of	(1295 – 22 August 1358), sometimes described as the She-wolf of France, was Queen consort of England as the wife of Edward II of England. She was the youngest

< 457 >

surviving child and only surviving daughter of Philip IV of France and Joan I of Navarre. Queen Isabella was notable at the time for her beauty, diplomatic skills, and intelligence.

Jared — Adult friend of Michael when he lived on the streets of Bristol

Jillian Beorn — Wife of William Beorn and the daughter of a Baron and wealthy family, she was from Cardiff a small town in Wales

John Wycliffe — First to translate the Vulgate (Latin Catholic Bible) into English

Kemp — A ten-year-old boy orphaned by the plague. He joins Michael and the others as they travel to a monastery

Kenneth — Sailor on ship of Captain Russell

King Edward I — King of England. Known as the warrior king

King Edward II — King of England. Known as the Artsy king. He was a terrible commander and accused of homosexuality and eventually deposed by his wife and other insiders. He died in exile.

Lance Beorn — Adopted father of William Beorn

Lance hackenshire — A very wealthy and successful merchant who owned one of the largest shipping fleets in England. He was the father of Mary Murdock

Laurie Collins — Wife of Ernest Collins, she was the chief cook at the Chattingworth Manor

Leann Stanley — LeAnn is the overseer of the livestock

Lila — Orphan girl who befriended William at the orphanage

Louise Stanley — Older daughter of the Stanley's

Lucas Beorn — First born son of William and Jillian Beorn

Lyle Codington — Prisoner in Newgate Prison in London

Madam Sanderson — Teacher at the orphanage when William was a boy

Maggie — Maggie one of the housemaids who lived on the Beorn estate.

Mark — A guard at Newgate Prison in London

Marcus — Son of Thebes, a plague victim who attempts to rob Michael and his family on the road to Cardiff

Margaret — A maid of Lady Chattingworth

Marie — Birth mother of William Beorn

Martha — Head maid of William and Jillian Beorn. A woman in her late 50's.

Mary Murdock — Wife of Harold Murdock and teacher of the children on the estate

< 458 >

Michael Beorn		Oldest child and adopted son of William and Jillian Beorn
Miles Stanley		Miles is the keeper of the stables
Miriam Chattingworth		Mother of Jillian Beorn
Monson		The Chief Butler of Lady Chattingworth, Jillian's mother in Cardiff
Mr. Darious		Store owner in Cardiff
Mr. Haley		Store owner in Cardiff
Mr. Rigby		Drinking buddy of Alderman Flanagan
Lady Chattingworth		Mother of Jillian Beorn (Miriam)
Mrs. Meeks		The cook at the orphanage
Nicholas Uvedale		Lord of the Manor of Wykeham and Governor of Winchester Castle
Officer Tenengo		Officer who reports to Chief Stenardi
Oliver		Prison guard at Newgate Prison in London
Philip Belmond		Friend of William Beorn (Ship Captain)
Pope Clement VI		Pope of the Catholic Church during the plague
Randolph		A worker at the orphanage
Reginald Worsted		Sheriff of Bristol
Richard Newport		Dean of St Paul's, London. (1317 and 1318)
Robert Winchelsey		The Archbishop of Canterbury
Samuel		Sailor on ship of Captain Russell
Sarah Beorn		Daughter of William and Jillian Beorn
Saxton Bentley		The assistant Warden at Newgate Prison in London
Scott Canter		Nephew of Timothy Canter
Simon Johnson		Son of Calvin and Andria, love interest of Ruth
Spanish Jailer		William encountered in Spain
Terrance Edwards		Terrance Edwards was a noble with German lineage. His father had become a noble due to his wealth while living in Germany.
Thaddeus		Son of Thebes, a plague victim who attempts to rob Michael and his family on the road to Cardiff
Thebes		Plague victim who attempts to rob Michael and his family on the road to Cardiff

< 459 >

Timothy	Merchant and friend of William Beorn
Canter	
Tommy	A boy at the orphanage who died of consumption
Vincent	First mate on ship of Captain Russell
Vincent	William's attorney in London
Carmichael	
William Beorn	The adopted son of Lance Beorn and birth son of William Wreghte
William	Birth Father of William Beorn
Wreghte	

< 460 >

Acknowledgments

Life is a series of dreams, some good, some bad, and some still in progress. I find it amazing how God has placed us here in our own time, to experience life. Although I envy the simple lives that most people lived in the middle ages, and at times long for a time when there weren't cell phones, computers, social media, or twenty-four-seven real-time connections, I can't honestly say that I would rather live in the middle-ages. However, I have great respect for those who did. I respect the way they valued honor, courage, and integrity. I appreciate how they rallied around each other and always put family first. Nothing was more important than family. We live in a world where we often get caught up in keeping up with our neighbors' latest gadgets, trinkets, and possessions. We tend to drift toward those things that have no lasting value, something that, in the end, fall apart and become dust, relics from a wasted life. The people in my story cherished each moment they lived. They longed to be together, grow together, live, laugh, and grow old together. They understood the fragility and sanctity of life. They held tight to one another because they didn't know if today would be the last day they would be together. As I completed book two in the NOT WITHOUT MERCY series, I realized how easy it is to get caught up in our modern day. I learned how often we take one another for granted and take life and all of God's gifts for granted. Although we live in a very different world in the 21st Century than my characters of the 14th Century, we still have many things in common, most importantly, our humanity. Whether we were placed on this earth to live at

< 461 >

the time of Eden, Kings, Monarchs, and Tyrants, or in the modern age, we all share in the human struggle of mortality.

I have been truly blessed, and many people have encouraged me to use my talents to tell this story. I appreciate those who read book one and kept asking me for book two. I apologize that it has taken four years for the sequel, but I couldn't rush the story and had to work around my regular life, waiting for those moments of inspiration to come.

There have been many who have helped and encouraged me along this journey. I thank my wife, Shaun, for her love, strength, and patience with me and my weaknesses. She has been my most extensive critique and fan. My daughter Samantha (Mercedes) gave me almost daily encouragement while writing book one, THE BLACK DEATH. She is an amazing young woman, wife, and mother. I am so blessed to be her father.

My daughter Ayrial is also on par with Sam. Unlike Sam, who had me read each chapter of book one after finishing it, Ayrial waited for the finished book and then devoured it.

I also thank my other children, Mickell, Angelia, Davis, Zackary, and Taylor, who remind me the greatest blessing in life is to be a father. I have been richly blessed with all my children, including my children's spouses, Brandon, Megan, Jesse, Jared, Leah, Kylie, and Nate. I thank them for their goodness and love. I thank them for making Shaun and me grandparents by giving us Amora, Lexi, Ambri, Bosley, Ari, Sabastian, Bella, Tiberius, Malachi, Sterling, Evie, Zariah, Sora, and Silas.

Thanks also to Rick and Susie Nelson, who played a big part in book one. They have been like family to us for over two decades.

Again, I thank my wonderful parents, Jim and Mary Wright, who raised my three brothers and me to believe in

< 462 >

and love God. I appreciate their example of staying together thru good times and bad. I have great love and respect for my late father-in-law Grant McKinney and my mother-in-law Loria McKinney who exemplify Christ-like love.

And thanks to you, the reader. I hope these books also remind you that regardless of the hardships and trials in your life, God will never leave you alone.

As I read and studied the life and times of medieval Europe during the Black Plague, I've marveled at the strength and endurance of those people who, amid tremendous heartache, pain, and loss of life, were strengthened when they looked toward God. Although I created over one hundred characters to tell this story, they represent real people who lived, loved, and died amid the world's most horrific killer. Those who put their trust and faith in God believed that he still loved them and that he left them *NOT WITHOUT MERCY*.

< 463 >

Here's a sneak peek at:
NOT WITHOUT MERCY- Redemption
Book Three in the NOT WITHOUT MERCY Series

Chapter One
555 Copper Street

William reached down to lift the lid on the trunk when he noticed folded parchment lying on top of it. He leaned down and blew the dust from the paper. He unfolded the parchment, which revealed a handwritten note. He surveyed it for a moment and quickly glanced to the bottom, where he saw the signature; Vincent. As he thought about Vincent, feelings of appreciation and thankfulness filled his heart. He wondered how and where his life ended. He began reading the letter,

"Dear William, I'm not sure when you will be in London again, so I thought I would write you a note about something interesting I came across the other day. It seems that my cold is persisting, and I have little strength. I do not want to forget to tell you about it, so I am writing this note and will send it to you as soon as my strength returns. I know your heritage's importance to you; we have spoken about it many times. Your father, Lance Beorn, kept several things in memory of your birth father, William Wreghte. Today, I came across a family crest belonging to your father, William. It is quite beautiful, with a silver shield, bright red leaves, two red stripes, a half moon, and a fierce-looking boar. The exciting thing is that I found it in a small metal box in a local merchant's shop, who

< 464 >

told me that he got it from a friend who worked as a servant of King Edward II. It seems that upon the banishment of the King, his wife, the queen, tossed many of his belongings in the street, and anyone who found them, kept them. The merchant kept the crest in a box with a few other trinkets. I just happened to be in his shop when he was cleaning a storage room and came across the box. It was odd that he looked at the crest and asked if I wanted it before throwing it out. At first, I hesitated because I did not need the crest of a family to which I had no tie. But then, I looked at the crest and read the family name, I remembered talking to you about your birth father, and I realized it was the same name. I put the stories together and realized that he was a knight of King Edward II, and indeed this was the crest that someone left behind when he went to his last great battle. However, as impressive as all of this sounds, the most intriguing part is that when I took the crest from the box, I also found a letter, I left it here for you as well, that was written by your father William to his friend Lance Beorn. Obviously, it was never given to Lance. In the letter, William mentions the pregnancy of your mother. There are several crossed-out words as if he was practicing what he wanted to say. I assume it was his first draft. He talked about his carelessness in falling in love with a peasant girl. And then he mentioned a younger brother, who was only eleven then. He spoke of the bad example he was to his younger brother and how he hoped that he did not also sow wild oats. The exciting part, you may be asking? The name of his younger brother was Fillery Michael Wreghte. I vaguely remember you telling me that your adopted son Michael once said to you that his father's surname was Fillery. Is it possible that Fillery was not his surname but his given name? If so, how interesting it would be if, many years later, William's younger brother did as William feared and impregnated a lady of the street, who gave birth to a son whom she named Michael, after his father? If so, your son Michael is your cousin and your blood relative. I apologize for all of this

< 465 >

supposition.   You know how much I love history, especially family history.

I look forward to discussing this and more the next time we meet.

Your dear friend, always, Vincent."

The story continues…

< 466 >

Made in the USA
Middletown, DE
28 October 2022

13664347R00283